Scourge of the Broken World

Book Four of the World of Ruin

Erik Scott de Bie

Scourge of the Broken World

Book Four of the World of Ruin

Erik Scott de Bie

DRAGON
MOON
PRESS

Scourge of the Broken World: Book Four of the World of Ruin
Copyright ©2021 Erik Scott de Bie
Map created by Cory Gelnett

ISBN 13 978-1-77400-031-1 paperback
ISBN 13 978-1-77400-032-8 epub
www.dragonmoonpress.com

DEDICATION

For all my readers—
Sorry about the wait!

ACKNOWLEDGMENTS

No creative project has only a single parent, and it often takes a whole village. This series has been over a decade in the writing and production, and would not have come to pass without the diligent work of my talented, long-suffering editor, coach, and friend, Gabrielle Harbowy. So many times we've dished and gossiped about these characters together, especially our favorite sweet summer child with a mean streak a mile wide. Also to be praised is Gwen Gades, the extremely patient publisher at Dragon Moon Press, for believing in me and in this project; she has always been great to work with, and her accomplishments in building up her catalog are worthy of acclaim. I will also acknowledge the inputs of friends and colleagues who've bounced ideas around, supported my concepts, and/or sat at gaming tables while I inflicted the World of Ruin upon them, including but hardly limited to Lyz Liddell, Landon Winkler, Robert Emerson, the legendary Jim Lowder, and the inestimable Robert Schwalb, whose Shadow of the Demon Lord © game provided such great grist for the idea mill.

Thank you all, and I look forward to many more nights of darkness to come.

PROLOGUE

Kuesh Guldur, lord of his blood and keeper of one of the most powerful merchant houses in Luether, ambled blissfully down the high thoroughfare amongst the workers struggling to repair the damage to Luether's high city with their cranes and lifters. All around him lay devastation, and smoke rose from fires still smoldering in the slums far, far below, but Kuesh kept his eyes only on the fair weather.

Thousands had starved and died in the two seasons that had passed since Alistra's ascension, but for Blood Guldur, the new order had proved a blessing. Following its words of "Working Strong" at the mines of Tuerine, the thinblood had long languished under the contempt and jeers of those higher born, and Guldur had ever been subservient to Vultara, despite how much coin they produced for the city. As a boy, Kuesh had grappled every day between the opposing indignities of supervising the dusty miners or scuffing his fingers on the stone, then lingering at the margins of noble revels by night, ignored or all but spat upon. Those Luetharr truly worthy, the highborn seemed to say, never had dirt-stained hands or wore the previous season's fashions.

That contempt, Kuesh swore, would never be directed his way again.

Kuesh paused when a whirring carriage rolled past ahead of him, and stepped back to clear the way. Warders in crimson surcoats escorted the armored transport, and Kuesh could see the pale-skinned faces of winterborn huddled inside. Prisoner transfer to the mines. More coin for his blood to earn.

He spat over the edge of the mage-glass that held up the few remaining structures of Luether's high city. The *Hecatomb*'s lift off and the *Avenger*'s fall had devastated much of the city, but the queen had made reconstruction a priority under her reign. The way a ruler should.

Alistra Ravalis.

Kuesh could smell the power on her. The ambition. Ruthless. That woman would lead Luether back to its state of grace and power. And Kuesh Guldur would be right there, standing beside her on the rising ship as it approached the clouds.

Not, of course, that he intended to share that ride. He would shove her over the side at the first available opportunity.

Winning the queen over had not proved too difficult. To consolidate her power in Luether, Alistra needed allies, and she was a terrible judge of character. Wolves surrounded her at all times, and she'd willingly bared her throat to them. Kuesh thought she was like all women: weak-willed and venal, prone to jealousy and easily moved to enforce her tenuous authority through violence. She seemed to like sex particularly, and she had proved an idiot for a pretty face and flattering manner. It had been simple for Kuesh to manipulate his rivals into offending her, and she had sent each of them to the mines. A compromising word here, a secret mistress there, and Alistra's would-be mate of the moment would vanish from her side. Some retired to their townhouses in disgrace, but many disappeared. Kuesh had no proof that Alistra had them slain, but the coincidence seemed too great.

It was a dangerous game he played, but Kuesh knew well how to make decisions based on logic rather than sentiment.

Not going to her bed was the first step. Denying Alistra his body whilst also suggesting that he might be available seemed to draw her attentions rather than repulse them, and she seemed fascinated with him. Not that he felt anything in return for her: she was lovely, aesthetically speaking, with her deep brown skin and close-cropped fringe of scarlet red hair that marked her as Ravalis. Those yellow wolf's eyes unsettled him, and sometimes when she looked at him, he thought she was a predator rather than a harmless woman. In those moments he felt uneasy, but he never wavered in his course.

This very day, he had finally allowed Alistra to touch him—to reach inside his tunic and his breeches. And while he could not deny that she had skillful fingers, he'd been careful not to show too much interest or allow her to win. Indeed, he'd left without allowing her to satisfy him, and he could sense the lust building within her. He took a certain delight in leaving her in that state. He would take care of his frustration at a brothel on the way back to his townhouse.

So complete was his victory that Kuesh Guldur had chosen to walk, rather than take a thaumaturgical carriage. He basked in the warmth of his beloved city—free, once more, and soon to be under his aegis. As well it should be.

He had her exactly where he wanted her. Soon enough, he would broach the subject of their marriage. And once that was done, and he was king, she would meet with some happy accident, and reign over the city would go to one who truly deserved it. One who had suffered all his life under supercilious nobles and barbarians but survived every challenge. He could defeat a foreign usurper made soft by her time in the pleasure palaces of Tar Vangr—or, at least, so he assumed had been her fate. Not that he particularly cared.

Gazing over the bay at the sunset, he never saw the man slip out of the alley just behind him. He was not aware of pursuit until something bright at the edge of his vision glinted in the last rays at dusk. "What—" he started, but never finished.

The knife sank into the side of his neck and his breath cut off. At first, it felt like something had slammed hard into him, like someone closed a door on his head. Kuesh reached up to feel at the source of the pain, only to find a foreign object there: a cold, hard, metallic object attached to someone's hand. A man stood just at his side and behind him, one blue eye burning, the other huge and white and dead.

Kuesh tried to speak—to cry out for help—but nothing came out but a strangled gasp.

"Touched her," the man said. "You touched her, you fool."

The man wrenched the blade free, and Kuesh's world exploded in pain and blood. He lurched dizzily to the side, his body abruptly trying and failing to stay upright, and the man caught him and knifed him again in the back. The threadbare silks parted like damp paper and the blade sank between two of his ribs. The point poked out his chest.

Belatedly, hot, sucking agony lit in his body and he contracted around the steel. His hands twitched toward the strike but his arms wouldn't reach it.

"I saved you." The man's voice was like a snake hissing. The dagger stabbed in and out, punctuating the curses. "You'll love *her*—she'll consume *you*— and you'll—be—*nothing*."

Kuesh could barely understand him. The knife fell over and over again, and he felt each stab less. The screaming, dancing pain in his body faded to a dull roar, like his ears burning in the distance.

He looked out at the graying world sideways, seeing the muck in the gutter running off over the slums. The stench of human filth filled his nostrils, and he thought he had just shat himself.

❧

Tithian Davargorn stabbed the lordling over a dozen times before he finally slowed. It was so easy: just grab hold and stab and stab and rip and tear and kill.

His first strike—the one to the neck—had been a lethal blow, but he hadn't stopped there. He pierced the man's heart, his lungs, his stomach. He wanted to tear him open and dance in the guts like ribbons at midsummer. The rage boiled hot and overpowering, and no matter how much he destroyed, it only seemed to grow worse. His arms shook and not just from fatigue. His breath wouldn't come under control. He couldn't even make himself drop the dagger stuck to his hands, tacky with blood.

He'd slaughtered half a dozen such lordlings in the course of the summer, venting his rage. The first of them was a perfumed courtier with pretty blue eyes Davargorn had taken pleasure in gouging out. He had fallen on the fool outside a brothel and stabbed him at least a hundred times before there was little untouched flesh left to pierce. He hadn't even known why at the time, but then he remembered seeing the waste of breath come out of *her* chambers, smiling, and he had known.

He had touched Alistra, and thus he had to die.

After he had worked the same gruesome death on this hapless fool, whose name Davargorn had never bothered to learn, he shoved the rest of the ruined body over the edge to plummet toward the smoky slums below. The haze of a hundred bellows and fires made Davargorn lose sight of the corpse in the smoke, but he did not care. Better that the lordling would never be found and have no proper ceremony: no one to mourn his passing. He was as much a fool as Davargorn himself, but he had made one grave mistake, and for that he would fade from memory.

Only after some time did Davargorn look up, and he realized that the alley into which he'd dragged the bloody mass at his feet was not as empty as he'd thought. Gone were the barbarians of Luether from before Alistra's rise, and what folk remained were, more often than not, cowards who would flee from any sign of blood. Two figures from the main thoroughfare moved toward Davargorn, rather than away, and he recognized the design stitched into the crimson cloaks the warders wore against the growing chill: the arms of Ravalis emblazoned upon the thorax of a spider. *Alistra.*

Davargorn hissed, presenting the blood-soaked dagger he'd used to commit the murder. "Back," he said. "Quarrel with me, and I slay you both."

They kept coming in silent discipline, like trained soldiers marching to war, and Davargorn lunged forward. He had warned them, after all.

A loud thud as of stone colliding with stone sounded, the air shimmered with a faint green light, and he slammed into an almost invisible shield hard enough to make his nose buckle and the dagger jar from his stinging fingers. He rebounded and stumbled to the ground, startled. Greasy smoke from the thaumaturgical discharge wafted into the air, and his face felt greasy where it had struck him.

The warders came on again, albeit slower this time.

Davargorn looked at the pooled blood and scraps of flesh on the mage-glass, which the curved shielding magic had pushed into a mound near his feet. The gore started to drain back toward the warders, and Davargorn took that as a sign to attack again. Surely the shield had fallen now—

He slammed again into the green magic, which sprang forth in twin cones of force from both warders, jostling him both toward and away from the mage-glass edge on his right, such that the combined shields pushed him back directly away from them. The sigils on their cloaks glowed with faint green light, and he realized the source of this shielding magic: thaumaturgy worked into their attire. Their faces hid behind steel helms, and he could only faintly see their eyes in the fading sunlight.

"Submit," one of them said—a woman with a strong, commanding voice.

That infuriated Davargorn, and he threw himself at the warders with a savage snarl that so startled one of them—the one on his left—that she fell back a step. Her shield fell aside, so he went around it. The foul stench missed him this time, and oil coated the wall.

"Silver Fire!" she shouted, her voice younger and weaker than the other's. Her eyes went wide.

He sensed an opening and took it. He would rip out her throat and steal that cloak and—

The other warder's shield manifested and Davargorn rebounded from its force. Without the other shield to redirect his stumble, he smashed into the wall. Something popped and his left arm went dead. Pain lanced up his side, and his ribs creaked as he tried to breathe. Smoke curled up into the air.

"Did you see that?" asked the younger warder. "More beast than man!"

"Ware," said the older, more experienced warder. "He's cornered. He—"

The shields activated when the warders were attacked, did they? Very well.

Davargorn sprang. A man who took a hit like that should have been down at least a moment or two, but his life magic soared within him and he shrugged off the injury. He had no weapon, but he needed only his hands. He grasped the younger warder around the throat and turned her shielding cloak toward her superior, whose eyes widened. "Wait—" she started.

He jammed his fist into the captive warder's side, a killing blow if he had a knife, and her shield obediently went off. The power smashed the other warder stumbling over the mage-glass edge, arms flailing. She fell abruptly and silently at first, giving voice to a startled cry only belatedly as she disappeared into the smoke below.

"What? No!" said the warder he held. "Master!"

Davargorn wrapped his arm around her throat, cutting off her words, while with his free hand he fumbled at her belt for a knife, a sword, any sort of weapon. He found none.

"Enough, Tithian," said a woman's voice that made his heart skip. "Enough."

He turned, still holding the warder—whose struggles grew less as she weakened in his hold—to face those approaching from the other direction. There were three, he saw: two warders in cloaks like this one wore, and the woman who strode before them, clad in gold-inlaid power armor that flattered her quite well. She'd filled out somewhat in the months since her long imprisonment, a short mess of crimson hair had appeared on her brown head, and he saw that her eyebrows had grown back, as had at least a stubble of hair under the arm she pointed at him. Primarily it was the wolf-yellow eyes that caught his attention, and he stood still, unable to flinch away under that intense scrutiny.

Alistra Ravalis, the Spider of Luether, treacherous and victorious Queen of all the Summerlands.

She who had driven the barbarians from Luether. She who had thrown down the invaders from the north. She who had ripped Davargorn's heart from his chest and eaten it in front of him.

None of those had actually occurred, but she may as well have done all three.

"Really, Tithian," she said. "Did you really think I would arm you?"

He took in his surroundings—her two warders, and the four more approaching from behind him, where the first two had come. These last ones had heavy double casters, he noted, which sizzled with unspent Thaumaturgical energy. If he made a false move, they could feather him faster than his magic could compensate. If they planned to herd him, at least he had forced Alistra to confront him at the mage-glass edge of certain death. He had but to lunge toward her, pull her over, and they could both meet a shattering death on the rocks below. Together.

Both knew he would do nothing of the sort.

"What will you?" Davargorn asked, his voice a broken rasp beyond his control. "What do you want of me, you treacherous, wretched, horrific thing?"

"Am I meant to take offense?"

Alistra smiled a thoroughly unlovely smile. Few would call her beautiful, and she cared not a whit for the distinction, but Davargorn had a hard time not looking at her face. Imagining what that mouth could do. *Had* done. Those lips. Those eyes...

"For a first," Alistra said. "Release my warder. She's quite blue in the face by now, I suspect."

12

Davargorn had forgotten about his captive entirely, and his arm automatically loosened to let the woman collapse gasping onto the glass. He obeyed without thinking and hated himself for doing it. And not just because the casters aligned better with his torso. They would have cast had not Alistra raised her hand. He stared at her, shoulders back, trying his best to light her aflame with his glare. If only he had Mask's gauntlet, he—

As though she heard his thoughts, Alistra raised her other hand from beneath her warm weather cloak, and Davargorn saw its sharp black talons seem to scratch the very air itself. Flames coursed around Mask's gauntlet, ready to lash out. Could he heal himself after a strike from that relic?

He watched her face and those yellow eyes. Davargorn could never tell what Alistra was thinking—whether she meant to kiss him or kill him, to spare him or devour him.

The warder at his feet coughed and groaned, coming back to awareness. At least he hadn't killed her. Shame, that. She stumbled up, wobbly on her feet, and glared back at Davargorn. "Let me slay him, Majesty," she said, her accent thick Free Islander. "He killed muh master."

"Shh," Alistra said. "Your pain will subside, child, I promise."

She didn't make the threat obvious, but Davargorn knew Alistra well enough to hear it. *Smell* it, and not just because of the faint stench of rot and decay rising from the war gauntlet. He wondered if Alistra's own power—her deadness to magic—would stop her from smiting him. He doubted that it would, and he didn't believe for a moment that she needed the magic to do so.

"Muh pain? Muh pain?" The warder looked to Davargorn with vicious eyes. "Muh pain'll fade when his blood's on muh hands."

Alistra's yellow eyes narrowed sharply. "Knight," she said to one of the armed warders at her side. "Give me your weapon."

Finally, the young warder seemed to understand. Her face paled. "Majesty. I—"

To her credit, the warder—knight, Alistra had called her—didn't hesitate but handed the caster over. The angry buzz of its thaumaturgical battery set his teeth on edge. The sound faded—muted somewhat—when Alistra took possession of the caster. She smiled at the insubordinate warder, then raised the caster to point at her face. The knight stiffened and took half a step back, toward the edge.

"We are both monsters, Tithian Davargorn," Alistra said, eyes only for him. "Where you wear yours like a cloak, I, on the other hand..."

Casually, she squeezed the caster's trigger, making the knight gasp, but nothing happened. Her curse must have spoiled the caster's magic, and it didn't function.

13

"I never forget myself," she said. "And nor should you."

Davargorn nodded once, slightly. He knew that well enough.

Alistra smiled. "I've already lost one knight today," she said. "I needn't kill a second, simply to make a point."

"Thank you, muh lady—Majesty," the knight said.

Alistra nodded absently to her.

The knight turned her attention to Davargorn and gave him a murderous glare. There was anger there. She would definitely avenge her master some other day.

Alistra saw it too.

With a sudden, furious movement, Alistra hurled the caster right at the knight, activating her warding cloak. The force slammed into Alistra herself, who stood neither touched nor moved, and the contrary force shoved the knight back just as it had her master. Davargorn flailed for her, startled by the sudden movement, but the hapless woman tumbled off the mage-glass. The woman screamed as she fell away, but Alistra was turning back to continue without a break in her words.

Even Davargorn, who had murdered over a hundred men and women in his brief but prolific slaying career, shivered slightly to see death so casually dispensed. No challenge. No defense. No reason. This woman was far deadlier than he.

Davargorn stood back up straight and met Alistra's eyes. "And you are to kill me too, is that it?" he asked. "Send me off into the smoke and be done with it?"

"Hardly." Alistra grasped the fringe of Davargorn's cloak, and he seized her hand. Every caster aimed at his face, and he could hear their Thaumaturgical batteries whining. All went still—except Alistra, who seemed perfectly at ease. She knew Davargorn would not harm her, and seeing her certainty, he recognized that fact himself, to his sorrow.

"I know all about your floating cloak," Alistra said. "I have been watching you for some time, you know. You've been serving my interests well."

"Piss and ashes, I have," Davargorn said. "I've been nothing but pain to you. A thorn in Luether's interests. Chopping off its heads of state and industry. Killing your would-be lovers."

"Yes," Alistra said, amusement in her huntress eyes. "My *lovers*—the rivals I marked with kisses and caresses and sent out into the world for my black wolf to slay for me. Keeping my own hands clean of their blood. What a shame."

Davargorn wanted to throw that back in her face, but he knew she spoke true. She'd cared nothing for these men and women he'd murdered, and he had aided her in removing them. Damn her, and damn him for allowing her to use him in such a coarse, simple manner.

"My dear lad," Alistra said. "You are trapped in the same pattern—a spiral in which you will be used over and over by love until you finally break it. But that will never happen, will it?"

Only now did he realize she had stepped close enough to touch his chin, and Davargorn recoiled.

"I won't kill for you," he said. "Not again. No more."

"Do not make promises you cannot keep." Alistra nodded to him, and her warders approached, casters trained on Davargorn. He offered no resistance as they bound him. She'd already defeated him.

"Kill me if you want," Davargorn said. "I don't care."

"Kill you?" Alistra uttered a short, cackling laugh. "Why would I kill you, when you're so useful?" She turned her head halfway and addressed her escorts. "Escort him to the docks. Give him clothes and a blade—whatever he needs. The *Man in Motley* sails on the morning tide. See that he sails on it. Out of my city." A faint smile crept across her face. "I'm sending you north."

To Tar Vangr, he realized. At first, he wondered what she would have of him there, then he shook his head. It didn't matter. He would do nothing.

"I won't kill for you," Davargorn said again.

"You say that now."

"And forever." His blades were in his hands, each pointed at one of the warders. Their eyes widened and their casters came back up to aim at his face. "I'll make you kill me first. I've nothing else."

"Really." Alistra stepped close, and he was awash in the smell of her. "Then I'll tell you a secret my brother told me, 'ere I tossed him in chains where no one would ever find him. Before I broke him, the way I have broken you."

"What." Davargorn raised his chin. "What do I care? Lan Ravalis is as much a monster as either of us. What care I for his secrets?"

"This one, alone." Alistra pressed her lips to Davargorn's ear. "Semana lives."

BOOK ONE: ORPHANS

Nine Years Ago—Winter, 973 Sorceris Annis—
Low-City Tar Vangr, City of Steel

THE CHILD HUDDLED AT the corner of Icy Furrow and Rhodovan's Way, one trembling hand outstretched with a little copper cup.

"Scarred," said a man, who spat at the child and averted his eyes as he passed.

"Warped," said a woman, scrunching up her upturned nose to look even more porcine.

"Ruined," said a third, whose boots scuffled on the cobbles.

This one actually put a coin in the cup, but the child bobbled it and the coin bounced out. The child had to scramble to collect it, and the moonlight caught one big white eye under the child's hood. The giver made a wet sound in their throat like pre-vomit, and hurried on muttering curses.

That was what they called the ugly little child of winter—those and fifty other names. "Ruinborn" was the most flattering, "ruinspawn" the most common, and sometimes just "monstrous."

And they were not wrong. One eye was small and dark, the other big and milky white—all but blind in the light, but capable of piercing the darkness. The child's nose was too big, the mouth crooked, the teeth too big. Other youths had smooth skin on their faces, while the child's was marked with deep furrows, like a grown Vangryur. These were not the result of an injury.

Nay—Ruin would not be so kind.

A dark-clad figure moved along the street, steel-lined boots crunching the slush on the forge-warmed stones underfoot. Every dozen paces or so, they paused to point a long metal rod at a post adorned with a lantern at the top. The air rippled hazily around the rod—the mark of magic—and flame sprang to life in the lantern atop the post. This job done, the lamplighter shuffled down the street, muttering curses softly under their breath.

The child slunk a little farther back into the darkness of the alley, unwilling to repeat the same mistake of asking the lamplighter for coin. They walked these same streets every night, a gradually simmering stew of rage and disappointment at the world, and anyone who crossed their path earned a string of invectives or a swift kick. Or worse, that rod might be turned upon a perceived threat, and the child already had enough deformities without adding horrendous burns to the list.

Folk born into the World of Ruin faced many perils, but few struck as deep or as cruelly as that of a child tainted by darkness at birth. Tales and speculation abounded as to the cause of such a curse: children born of hate rather than love, those touched by a terrible destiny, or perhaps those touched by dark magic in the womb. In Tar Vangyr, the most common legend claimed that ruinspawn were the result of a forbidden liaison—a union that should never have come to pass—and that the ugliness of its fruit is the undeniable evidence of such a sin. Many Tar Vangryur believed Ruinspawn were not of their kind at all, but a manifestation of the reckless hate that had doomed the old World of Wonder. An entirely new kind of being, one that wore its corruption on the outside as well as in.

The progenitors of such damaged offspring often hid them from their friends and loved ones, abandoning them to grow up neglected and unwanted in the steaming gutters of the worst streets of Low-City. Such was the fate of this particular ugly child, who had never known father or mother or sibling. By all rights, the child shuddering in the alley against the cold night should have died a lonely death of starvation years ago, but it seemed Ruin had another plan.

Despite the many names for what the child was, there was no name for *who* the child was. The child had not yet earned a name, and so—after the fashion of Tar Vangr and all of the north—when the need arose to refer to the child by a name, the name given was only Winter.

Ugly Winter, usually.

As darkness settled through Low-City, folk shut themselves in their hovels and halls, sealing windows and doors against the noxious fumes and searing snowdrifts of another Tar Vangr night. The forges deep beneath the city would keep the streets and houses warm, or else the burning magic would turn the entrapping snow to lung-scalding vapor. After inadvertently inhaling a cloud of the deadly stuff on one Hopedawn, the ugly Winter child had spent the following spring and summer getting over a wrenching cough that nearly took their life. If it had happened on Dark Solstice or Ruin's Night, such a misfortune would have done for the child for good and all.

For now, Winter needed to find shelter to escape the impending chill and toxic drifts, so the child shuffled back down the alley toward the likeliest, closest spot for such protection: the Burned Man.

The inn and tavern stood some two blocks distant, easily reached by scurrying through the back alley and up a fire escape ladder. Winter had struggled with such ladders up until a year ago, owing to their twisted club foot, but these days the child could move smoothly enough. That leg would always be weaker, but Winter had adapted. Survival in Tar Vangr demanded no less.

As the child went, they looked up through the swirling smoke and clouds to the glittering mage-glass plate that held up High-City far above. What wonders must lurk up there, so far out of Winter's reach? The child would never know—would never rise to see. This was Winter's lot: trawling the filthy gutter by day and struggling to find a hiding place by night, just to survive the magic-tainted weather.

The sound of laughter and revelry radiated through the fogged windows of the Burned Man, suggesting a full house of patrons. Winter shivered and glanced back down the alley. No sign of the scalding mist, so the child could steal a few moments. Winter looked in, nose pressed to glass, squeezing shut the bulbous white eye grown blind against the smoky light within.

Over a score of patrons huddled inside, drinking and carousing to keep the night and the tainted snow at bay. The roof bowed low, covered in pitch and grease accumulated over the years. Those with coin laughed and drank and hired sex for themselves and their companions, while those without clung on desperately in the orbit of their more fortunate friends. A dozen men and women, beautiful and sculpted and greased for the occasion, moved among the tables, passing out drink and food and offering themselves for the caressing. The smoke of pipeweed and a hundred candles lent the place a heady, close atmosphere, and Winter could smell the beer and sweat through the narrow cracks in the glass.

Winter could only dream of touching such a place.

There was one woman that Winter liked to watch in particular: little more than a girl, in fact, perhaps a few years older. She was just starting to look like a woman, but the master of the Burned Man had yet to employ her as a courtesan. She had no name either, or at least not one Winter had ever heard. She worked instead as a scullery maid and cleared tables. She leaned over a table near the window to wipe it clean, and Winter saw a soft hint of curves down the front of her shirt. The child's mouth went dry. Winter had heard once she was a slave: the barbarous Ravalis had brought that particular custom to Tar Vangr, whereby one man might own another.

One day, the child meant to rescue them both. They would flee into the darkness and make their way into the wilds outside the city, there to find a place to live, safe and warm. Lastly—and this was the most important part—she would never object to Winter's awful face. Not the first time she saw it, nor every morn after.

That, more than anything else, was the least believable part of the fantasy.

Winter dreamt sometimes of angels, and one in particular: a golden-haired woman, more beautiful than anyone Winter had ever seen in the waking world, her body and face perfect. Sometimes she had the slave's face, sometimes she looked like one of the statues Winter had seen at the disused temple of the Winter God Amanul, and sometimes she had a face the child dimly recognized but could not name. At times the angel caressed Winter, soothing bruises and aches with her soft touch, at times she held Winter to her breast and whispered gently while Winter nuzzled her neck and smelled the warm earth of her skin. When Winter was a little older, the woman would sometimes appear unclad, her skin gleaming by moonlight, and they would make love. In such moments, Winter's mangled, worthless body was washed clean of its imperfection, becoming strong and beautiful and attractive. It became a true reflection of the person Winter desperately wanted to be.

Until Winter awoke, of course, and remembered the awful truth: that all things must pass to Ruin, some sooner than others.

Winter realized the girl had looked up and their eyes met. The child flinched away, huddled in the tattered hood, suddenly terrified and ashamed. It seemed like a hundred eyes fell upon Winter, and the scrutiny burned. Tiny tendrils of mist crept into the alley, and Winter took the hint. It was time to go.

The door securing the Burned Man's stables was chained and locked securely, and Winter knew not to bother with it. The child went instead around the back, where a loose board allowed them to squeeze through. Winter was always careful to put the board back in place, to avoid discovery and keep the stables safe. This time, however, it seemed looser than normal and even slightly out of alignment. Perhaps a scavenging animal had pawed at it, or one of the horses kicked it. The horses seemed all right, though, so Winter saw no threat. The child made sure to secure it after entering.

Only by comparison to the increasingly frigid night did the stable seem warm, but it was the best Winter could hope for. The child glanced back and forth among the horses tied up in their stalls, quietly whickering against the murmuring breeze outside the thick, tarred wood. Sometimes one of the slaves of the Burned Man would sleep out here among the horses, and Winter knew there wasn't time to find a new hiding place tonight before the snows came. Fortunately, Winter saw no one—only the horses, which looked up idly and dismissed the child with equal indifference.

Finally a bit of luck.

Winter went to a favored corner, where the straw was deepest and mostly clean. The stablehands filled this stall last, and there was no horse in it this night. Winter burrowed into the straw like a mole into loose earth, taking comfortable, familiar shelter in—

A sound tore into the child's ears, so suddenly and near at hand that Winter didn't quite know what was happening. Something struck the child with several blows, making them fall backward more from surprise than the force. Winter yelped and staggered into the wall, almost tripping over their club foot. The child's attacker didn't follow, but instead partly hid in the pile of straw, shaking and trembling and trying to free itself.

Herself.

"Stay back!" The girl—perhaps Winter's own age—glared out with eyes that seemed orange in the moonlight through the cracks in the walls. "I—I have a knife!"

Winter didn't believe her—if she had a blade, she'd have used it—but he made no move toward her either. She crouched like a cat in the corner, her silver-blonde hair stuck with bits of straw. Her skin was darker than most winterborn, but it wasn't quite the coloration of the summerblood of Luether. A generation ago, her darker skin would have been quite rare in the City of Steel, but the child had never known a time when the summerblood did not dominate Tar Vangr in both culture and coin.

This girl's pale blonde hair looked clean and groomed, if a bit messy at the moment from her time in the straw pile. She had fine features—even better than those of the angel in the Burned Man—and straight teeth. A highborn girl—maybe even a noble—from up in High-City, perhaps.

"You," she said, and trailed away with that one word.

With anyone else, Winter's mind would go immediately to what she could do for them. Perhaps she carried useful equipments that the child could use, such as a warmer coat. Perhaps she carried some coin or could be ransomed to the Winter Rats, say, or the Circle of Tears. But the girl—just looking at her, Winter's mind emptied out of such selfish concerns. They just wanted to look at her.

She had asked a question, Winter realized. "What?"

The girl licked her lips. "Where are your parents?"

Winter shrugged. "No parents."

"Ruin smiles on you. I only have one parent, and I hate him." The girl flipped her hair back. "I'm Semana Denerre nô Ravalis, and I'm the crown princess of Tar Vangr. What's your name?"

"Haven't earned one." Winter shook his head. "I'm a child of Winter."

"Winter. That's no good." She got a cagey look, the way Ohlm the shopkeeper did when the child was trying to trick him out of an extra piece of bread. "Do I call you boy or girl or neither?"

Winter had never really thought about it. "Boy," he said, which seemed right. "Winter Boy."

"Winter boy," Semana said. "You're more than that. You need a name. It's right."

Winter became uncomfortably aware of his distorted face, and how she stared. She didn't look at him the way anyone else ever had—neither with fascination nor revulsion. The look she gave him was genuine.

"Tithian," she said. "That's the name I'll give you."

A name. *His* name.

And she had just given it to him—just like that. Without hesitation or pause, no matter how disgusting his visage. She was looking at him earnestly. Was this what it felt like to have a friend?

He was about to reply when a fist pounded on the door. "Semana!" came a woman's voice. "My lady, are you in there?"

The girl reached across and put her fingers to Tithian's lips. At his questioning look, she shook her head rapidly and mouthed the word "silence."

Tithian was no stranger to hiding from folk who wanted to hurt him, but whoever was outside the stable sounded concerned, not dangerous. He trusted Semana implicitly, however—the touch of her fingers both soothed and excited him. He didn't remember the last time someone had touched him without violence. Perhaps this was the first time in his life.

"This door," the woman said outside the stables. "Open it."

"I don't have the key, m'lady," a servant said. "Please come out of the fog—"

The fog.

Semana started toward the loose board, but Tithian took hold of her arm to restrain her. They both looked at his hand, then their eyes rose to meet. He felt presumptuous, but he also knew he had to protect her. In that moment, nothing seemed more important.

"No," he said. "The alley's full of fog. It's not safe."

Semana considered a breath, then nodded. She reached up to take his hand from her arm and grasped it tightly. Whatever befell, it would befall them both.

And Tithian agreed. If she would have him, he would stand with her for the rest of his life.

The princess rose with cultured grace, and Tithian stumbled to his feet beside her. If he was going to remain at her side, he'd had to learn to handle himself more smoothly.

"Open it!" the woman said again, and the servant dithered again in words Tithian could not make out. The woman cursed and Tithian heard the ring of steel, accompanied by a flash of crimson light that crept under the doors to the stable. A blade cut the air, and the chain securing the doors parted with a disconsolate thrumming sound. The doors burst inward under her boot, sending splinters of wood and a neatly severed link of chain scattering into the room. The bit of metal bounced end over end and landed about at Tithian's feet. The cut ends glowed faintly red with heat.

The woman who came through those doors was tall and broad of shoulder and chest. A warrior born and grown, who carried herself with a deadly sort of grace. Tithian made a habit of avoiding folk who moved like that, especially when they carried ensorcelled swords like hers: a wavy, flamed blade burnished with red energy from which smoke poured. It formed silhouettes and visages he barely recognized. The shadows looked almost like two small figures clutching each other in the corner.

She wore a thick leather mask with foggy goggles, but when she stepped inside the stables, she pulled it off to reveal vivid red hair, dark skin, and excellent features. Summerblooded, Tithian realized, and darker than Semana. They might have been related, but Semana had said she had only a father.

The woman saw them immediately, as though she had expected to find them. And he had covered his tracks so well, and neither of them had made a sound that would have given them away.

"Step away from her," she said, pointing her wavy sword at him like a spear. "Now."

Tithian swallowed, unsure how to respond. He couldn't possibly resist the warrior—not without dying in heartbeats—but neither could he abandon Semana. He squeezed her hand tighter, trying to reassure her without words that he would give himself to ward her.

Semana didn't seem frightened, though. Indeed, she pushed past Tithian and pulled her shoulders back, confronting the woman without fear. "Lady Ovelia," she said. "I am well. Your steel is not needed. Sheathe it, please."

"My lady." The woman—Ovelia—looked uncertain. Tithian could tell what she saw when she looked at him: the same thing everyone else saw. Everyone but Semana. "My lady, I think—"

"I told you to sheathe your steel," Semana said. "Or do you no longer obey me?"

23

Ovelia started to speak, then slid the sword into its scabbard. "Who is this child, my lady?"

"This is Tithian," Semana said, lacing her arm through his. "And he's coming back to High-City with us." She looked into his mismatched eyes. "To the palace."

Palace. Tithian blinked. *High-City.* Far, far above what he had ever imagined possible.

Ovelia frowned. "My lady," she said. "I don't think—"

"I've spoken." Semana squeezed Tithian's arm. "It's done."

At length, Ovelia nodded. "We need to take this before your greatfather. He will decide this."

"Oh, he'll choose me." Semana smirked, triumphant. "He always chooses me over you." She let go of Tithian's arm and instead clenched his hand in both of hers. "Come along, Tith."

And so it was done—for better or much, much worse.

ONE

Far north and east of Tar Vangr, the wind skirled the snow adrift across the split ridge, making the woman's silver-blonde hair float on the breeze. Two great chunks of stone rose above her, seemingly cut by a single massive force into rough arrowheads that lay one atop the other, both too heavy to lift. The Children of Ruin spoke of an ancient clash between mighty sorcerers in this place, one of whom slung a titanic spell that cleaved the stone in twain like the stump of a tree. Some legends claimed that a Druid had done the deed, animating the stone for a weapon and cracking it when she brought it down upon her foe. Another tale spoke of lightning, or else a mighty reaving spell that swept up from the lowlands and, jealous of the stone's strength, split it in two to diminish its potency.

At the base, however, the trickle of water *drip-drip-dripping* into Semana's hand told the truth.

No great event had carved this furrow, but the steady erosion of a stream over centuries—millennia, perhaps. While the barbarians would not be able to make sense of this explanation—they had little enough sense of time beyond the seasons, much less the sweep of natural history—she'd learned as a girl in Tar Vangr to recognize and respect the natural forces of the world. Oh, certainly, the World of Ruin was full of weather disasters, reaving spells, and unexplained earthquakes that spawned magical horrors. But it was in the slow, small, unrelenting forces that true power to shape the world lurked.

Patience.

She had waited patiently five years, teaching herself to kill—to become a weapon—while she bided her time and waited for her foes to reveal themselves. Her plan had been perfect. She had wielded Ovelia the Bloodbreaker and Regel the Frostburn like blades, and pushed Tithian in exactly the right direction at exactly the right time. She should have slain the Ravalis and seized her birthright. She *would* have, had it not been for the one thing she could not have predicted: her own heart.

Stepping into that room to save the Oathbreaker. Why had she done that?

Semana Denerre nô Ravalis would not make that mistake again.

Patience.

There were other worlds than these. Semana had seen them; still saw them, at times, in her dreams. She ascended through a column of mirrors, each of them a window into another world, from some distant corner of imagination or beyond. She could touch these other worlds. She could smell them. Taste them. Feel them on her skin and revel in their closeness. But she could not go to them. She could not break the mirrors and enter these other worlds.

Not *yet*.

Patience.

Raised voices drew her attention down the grassy hill, and she rose with a soft whisper of furs.

Patience was something her brother lacked.

Darak Ravalis nô Denerre—or Dar-Karsk, as the barbarians called him—came up the path, followed by a small honor guard and a handful of attendants, including two hulking Children of Ruin with numerous bones and blades thrust through their noses and cheeks. Rarely had Semana seen two barbarians who looked quite alike, and these two proved no exception, from their hair to their tattoos to their disparate builds and styles of walking. Only their piercings and pale skin seemed similar.

Semana occasionally pondered the origin of the Children of Ruin, most of whom seemed to share several key visual cues. They shared a pale skin tone with a pink base, yellow or brown or occasionally red hair, and their features were quite different from the brown faces of the Summerblooded or the yellow-based paleness of the Winterborn. Curious.

They came close enough for Semana to make out the harsh, guttural tongue of the barbarians. She'd grasped enough of it that she could make out one word in three, and between her dawning proficiency and Darak's wild gesticulation, she judged him to be relating dubious legends of this very rock formation. Claiming to have struck the cleft himself, no doubt.

The little group stopped short when they came upon Semana, and the two big barbarians looked her over, taking her measure. One of them gave her an openly interested look—one Semana had learned to recognize in her months with the Children—and she met his gaze with a burning glare of her own. The barbarians seemed to love staring at her comparatively fine features and her willowy body, so she tried to avoid showing her face. It kept things simpler.

She wished she could wear her black leathers at all times, but Darak had advised her not to do so. The more like an alien invader she looked, the less the Children would welcome or aid them. He wanted her to embrace the ways of the barbarians: their clothes, their manners, all of it. His expectations chafed almost as much as these stupid robes did.

Darak caught the look between the two of them, and his weathered face twisted into a scowl in the depths of his hood. "Back," he said in Ruinspeak. "*Mine.*"

Maybe she didn't understand properly. Maybe he was saying Semana was his sister or his ally or something of that nature. But she didn't like the possessiveness in his voice or stance.

Darak spoke at length. At one point, Semana recognized his name for her, "Marsk," and she inclined her head to them. They gave her the barbarian salute, which was to hold out their left hands to show they held no weapon. Semana did nothing of the sort, keeping her left hand under the cloak, starting to send up a faint lick of smoke through the folds. Her brother turned to her, and it was clear from his face that he saw it.

"Sister," Darak said. "These are Screeching Glaive and Cruelest Slice, sworn body warders to Chief Lathkgar of the Pounding Hooves."

"Charmed," Semana said without much enthusiasm. She'd met so many barbarians over her time as one of the Circle of Druids, she'd ceased to find their names grotesque or shocking. The last one that she remembered was Splintering Bone Spur, which sounded more uncomfortable than intimidating. No doubt the sight of hulking monsters such as these would make a smallborn shit their breeches.

The one Darak had noted as Screeching Glaive offered Semana an acknowledging grunt, which she understood as a snub. He was the one who had leered at her, and of course he didn't respect her.

Cruelest Slice had warmth in his eyes, and even something like ardor. "Blood Queen," he said.

Semana raised her chin and offered him a slight smile. That, she liked.

"Brother," she said. "I've been a High Druid but a season, so assuage my ignorance." She pointed at Glaive. "That one offers me disrespect, does he not? Should I brook such an insult?"

The barbarian didn't understand her words but he started to growl when she pointed at him.

"Sister," Darak said, his voice low and direct. Warning.

She hardly heard. She tasted the barbarians' blood in her mouth. Murky, flat, and toxic, but strong. Robust. Like a smoky wine that had gone mostly to vinegar but still possessed some bite. Their blood tasted similar enough she thought them brothers or cousins, perhaps lovers, or mayhap more than one of those. Who could say with barbarians? In any case, they were connected by shared blood, and it took her a breath to distinguish between them.

"Sister," Darak said. "What passes?"

Then Glaive reached up, his arm straining and his eyes bugging wide in sudden panic, and smashed a fist into his own face. Blood burst from his nose and mouth, and he staggered backward under the force. Slice uttered an interrogative and pulled the jagged axe from his belt. Glaive looked confused and afraid, and struck himself in the face with his other fist.

Semana smiled. Glaive's blood thundered through her mind. Both his arms were hers now, and she punched him a third time in the face with as much ease as she might strike herself. But *harder*.

"Sister!" Darak barked at her. "Stop."

She shot her eyes to him. Worldfire coursed around him—the power of the Druids of Ruin—and Semana felt the frozen turf under her feet tremble. It was an empty threat, she knew—he needed her as much as she needed him. She'd made her point, asserted her power, and offered him a little defiance.

"Well."

Semana eased her hold, and Screeching Glaive stumbled away, bloody and confused. Cruelest Slice offered her a bow of submission, then hurried after his fellow warder down the hill, both of them casting looks over their shoulders at her, full of fear and awe.

The rest of Darak's honor guard hardly reacted to her display of power, as though they expected it. One of them, a flame-haired barbarian lad called Crown of Fire, gave Semana a smile, but she looked away. Cold and aloof was her preferred presentation. It was the way her mother had always acted and thus, to Semana, it was the way a queen *should* act. Also, she remembered the last time she'd indulged Crown of Fire's obvious desire—just for a moment, just long enough to wrap him around her finger like a ribbon, but nothing she had enjoyed. At least he would be useful if Darak ever pushed her too far.

Case in point.

Face red with fury, Darak eased his Worldfire, stepped to her side, and seized her right arm in a fierce grip. "That," he said, "was not wise."

Semana shook off his hand. She meant to rebuke him, but tempered the harsh words. "Worried I'll outshine you in front of your honor guard?" They had mostly moved away, awkward, and Crown of Fire avoided her gaze. So much for his devotion.

Darak's scowl deepened. "Would you spoil our alliance with Lathkgar before it is struck?"

"I am a Druid now," she said instead, her tone level. "Should I not show my strength as one?"

"With blood magic?"

28

"As though those brutes know the difference." Semana shrugged. "They will speak of their experience, and we will have their respect. Or their fear. Either serves our cause, does it not?"

Darak loosed a low growl but couldn't very well argue. She was right, of course: the Children of Ruin respected strength and worshiped death. Perhaps Semana should have killed Screeching Glaive and let his companion tell the tale.

"I just wish you'd listen." Face sour, Darak leaned against the bisected boulder and picked at a black sore on the back of his hand. "Bringing Lathkgar into the fold will not be easy. We'll need him and his warriors."

Semana scoffed. If she hadn't listened to Ovelia Dracaris or Regel the Frostburn, then she definitely wouldn't listen to Darak the Rotpriest. Not that she needed to say that. She'd won all the available ground in their struggle for the moment.

"Agreed." Semana brushed pale hair out of her face that had come loose from the tail at the nape of her neck. Crown of Fire kept trying to catch her eye, but she ignored him. "I've not seen you so anxious since Hopedawn."

Darak grumbled, offering no intelligible words. Of course. He often shut her out when she offended him, intentionally or not. Semana sighed inwardly. If he heard, it would make it worse.

All defiance aside, Semana recognized her disadvantage. Darak had walked among the barbarians for a decade and knew their ways far better than she did. She could see in how he spoke with them—how he moved with them—that they acknowledged him as their own. In addition, his acumen for scheming and tactics had already proven indispensable. She wouldn't be a High Druid if not for him, and she suspected she would need his mind and position when it came to actual fighting.

If it ever did, of course.

She looked past him and his guard, at the hundreds of cookfires that dotted the valley below. Their army: a rag-tag band of screaming lunatics and vicious killers. They camped all in their separate circles, and wherever the territory met, fists were thrown and blood was shed. They hardly seemed like the cohesive force the two would need to storm Tar Vangr and take it back from the Ravalis. They'd spent months now beseeching the various tribes of the Children of Ruin to marshal support for their war on Tar Vangr, but it could be going better.

It began at Iseldra's Folly, when the Circle refused to back them, casting Semana and Darak on their own. The gathered hordes dispersed from that place, few of them even looking upon Darak as he spoke. Apparently, betraying Afferath and seizing her mantle was no quick path to claim the loyalty of her horde. Some had stayed: Mountain's Rage, for one, Afferath's chief enforcer, and Breaker of Frost and Ice and her twin bodyguards, Right and Left. Some hundred or so of her barbarians, who had seen Mask—the Angel of Ruin—flying above them that night before the moot. But otherwise, they'd had only Darak's own horde, who followed mostly him, less Semana.

Others had come. Barbarians from the wild lands, wanderers, and madmen who saw Semana's display of power or let Darak's silver tongue sway them. Their army had grown to perhaps a thousand strong, composed of clan-less rovers and wanderers and a few whose pre-existing loyalties Darak did not trust. Others would come. She had to believe that.

She had her own personal supporters as well. Crown of Fire was hers through and through, but that would last only as long as she kept him dancing on her leash. It was clear that he wanted her, as a man wants a woman, and so long as she kept herself just out of his reach, he would persist in following her. A few other barbarians cleaved more closely to her than to Darak: though they paid lip service to her brother, she saw their eyes upon what they perceived as the true power. How she could sway their loyalties openly, she was not quite certain.

Perhaps the magic she had been developing--the mixture of blood magic and Frostfire--but that was not yet ready. And Darak would be wroth with her if she moved too early.

Glancing into the shadows of the stone formation, she recalled also that she had allies who were not barbarians. She could not discount those.

Darak had apparently finished with his mumblings, because he looked to her, chin raised. "Be down at the camp at midday," he said. "We'd not want to offend Lathkgar once more by being late."

Semana offered no response but to stare at him until he flounced away. His reaction amused her, until Crown of Fire shared her faint smile and dampened her mood some. She sighed in their wake and looked up at the sun. Ruin's Eye was surprisingly yellow here in the comparatively clear air of the Winter Wilds. After so long under polluted Luether's sun, perpetually red or purple or green or blue because of the grotesque magic that fueled the city, Semana adored the vivid orange fire.

"You smile," the dark voice said, out of the shadow of the rock formation atop the hill. "Why?"

Smoothly, Semana looked to the shadows, where Gilt stood as though he'd been there all along. How exactly he moved—the dark ways that he traveled—still eluded her, and she found it a never-ending source of intrigue. That, and the dark power that beat inside his midnight-black body. Gilt was a Deathless Fae—neither living nor dead and no longer a man, if indeed he ever had been one.

"This is a smile of lamentation," Semana said. "I am lamenting the foolishness of it all."

"I did not know of such an expression." Gilt nodded. "Each day, I learn more from you."

And I, you, Semana thought but did not say.

When Semana dreamed, which had grown increasingly frequent over the past season, half the time she dreamed of having that power for herself. Always before, when she encountered a sorcerer or witch or druid or other practitioner of innate magic, she had learned how to wield it herself without too much difficulty. With Gilt, however, it had taken a season of scrutiny, and she still only barely grasped the fundamentals. She longed to know what made the Deathless move as he did—how he walked through shadows—and the secret of his apparent immortality.

The other half of her dreams were all of silver fire and her destiny. Her purpose that lay at the heart of Tar Vangr. Waiting.

"We've spent the summer and the autumn going to every chieftain Darak knows," Semana said. "I swear we've gone everywhere in the Winter Wilds, and this is what we've mustered. A few hundred, who will break under the first charge. There is no purpose in leading them against Tar Vangr—not in simply leading them to their deaths. And for what? So that I can fail?"

The wind swept past, stronger now. The sun hid behind darkening clouds.

"A storm approaches." Gilt stepped forward and offered Semana a cloak of black furs he had worn around his bare shoulders.

She didn't need the warmth—her Frostfire made the cold and heat much the same—but she accepted the furs. It was less about her actual needs and more about acknowledging his service. If she snubbed him too much, he would not come to help her in the future.

"This moot with Lathkgar is our best hope, and also our last." Semana adjusted the furs around her leathers. "If we convince him to aid us, that will double our forces, and perhaps make his allies reconsider. Our chances, though—" She shook her head. "Darak says Lathkgar is profoundly loyal to the Circle, and that's a problem."

"Should he not serve you?" Gilt asked. "He serves the Circle. You are a Druid of the Circle."

"*A* Druid." Semana set her jaw. "Newly elevated. An outsider. Barely more than a child. And the others of the Circle do not support us. What he thinks of that, we can only guess."

She ground her teeth. She knew what Darak thought of that: in his mind, *he* was the Druid, while she was only the face to help him gain audiences with chieftains. Meanwhile, her opinions he could ignore, dismiss, or—worst of all—pretend he had thought up himself. The longer this went on, the greater Semana's temptation grew to don her leather mask, forsake her brother, and fly off into the approaching storm. Leave him to his fate and leave all this behind her.

Darak sometimes said he would be prosecuting this war far better without her. Perhaps his armies would already camp in siege around Tar Vangr or perhaps he would already be king. He said this in his frustration when a chieftain refused to swear fealty to him, or a negotiation fell apart because he couldn't command the necessary respect. Sometimes she wondered if he was correct.

Sometimes.

Rarely.

Gilt didn't look much swayed by her doubts, and Semana envied his immovable self-assurance. "You walk your brother's path, in his shadow," he said. "Will it ever be thus?"

That was the crux of it. She watched Darak barking orders to their warriors and staring down barbarians and making deals and knew she could never do that. He insisted on being her superior—not a vow of fealty or something of the sort, but he never sacrificed a chance to put her in her "proper place." And when she spoke up or defied him, he lashed out and acted poorly and compromised everything.

"I need him," Semana said. "I can't afford to push him away."

The admission felt like a surrender.

To his credit, the Deathless didn't argue the point. Instead, he continued to watch her levelly, never wavering in his will or aim.

"You need him." Gilt shrugged. "But do you need his path?"

She opened her mouth to argue, then turned her frown into a smile. Mayhap he was right. Mayhap there was a way to keep her brother close but not have to suffer under his thumb.

Mayhap she'd gone about this all wrong from the beginning.

Blue flames started to spread down her arms and her fingers.

～

Despite the plentiful wine within reach, the lotus fumes that filled the tent, and the oiled flesh on display, Darak could barely restrain his displeasure. The tent stank thickly of horse and shit and sweaty bodies, and besides, his dream teetered on the edge of an abyss.

"Where is she, Dar-Karsk?" asked the big, muscular barbarian saddled on the beast before him in the tent. He had a thick, brutish voice that matched his huge body and made Darak feel small just hearing it. "You speak much of your pet Druid. But will you produce her? I wonder."

His apparent jest drew sniggers from around the tent.

Chief Lathkgar of the Pounding Hooves took his name from his army of Wind Reavers: a force two hundred or so strong of screaming barbarians mounted on horses, war goats, elk, and all manner of hooved creatures. Darak had heard stories of their deadly charges, against which no infantry foot could stand. They were folk of the saddle, and Lathkgar himself presented a perfect example. The chieftain had awaited Darak in the saddle of a great, serrate-horned elk when his warders inside his huge tent, and had made no move to climb down. Like as not, he did so to make himself more intimidating.

And it worked. Darak had a hard time meeting his eye.

"Soon." Darak ground his teeth. "She'll be along. *Soon.*"

Damn and burn his sister. What was she doing?

She knew how important this was—how their chances stood. He had dreamt of raising an army to take back Tar Vangr over a decade, and she'd proved a constant, chaotic disruption. Ungrateful, spoiled, uncooperative—arguing with his every suggestion and bit of advice. And now, even after he had specifically told her about the important of this audience, and cautioned her about the need to show the Lord of the Pounding Hooves every courtesy, she was nowhere to be found.

She did this to humiliate him, because she didn't understand her place. *He* was the proper ruler of the Children, not her. He was the High Druid, not her. He should rule Tar Vangr—not her.

One of Lathkgar's serving men offered him a bowl of wine, but Darak turned up his nose in a show of cool indifference he did not feel. "The lass is headstrong," he said. "She'll be here."

She had abandoned him. Darak started going over in his mind what to do next. What he would say to convince Lathkgar to let him leave this place peacefully, and what he would have to do if words failed. Worldfire tingled on his skin and churned in his guts, promising and demanding in equal measure. It would strengthen him and strike down his enemies. Lathkgar had laid his camp over a complex root system, and the plants practically yearned to be used as weapons. He could fight his way free, but his dream of reclaiming his birthright would die either way.

Lathkgar raised his chin, conveying without words that he didn't believe Darak for an instant. His honor guard had taken the hint as well. They were all smirking at him now, laughing behind their hands. Questioning his strength and cunning—his worthiness to lead this cause. And every moment that their stupid eyes watched him, it weakened his position.

Damn and *burn* Semana.

Under Lathkgar's scrutiny, Darak's heavy robes suddenly felt less stifling in the close interior. In fact, they barely concealed him at all, and he felt exposed: his city-born flesh made bare, and soon enough his secrets. More than once, Afferath had used his body as collateral to some interested chieftain, but Darak wouldn't stoop to such a thing as offering himself as tribute. Not after he'd gone to all the trouble to murder his former master. He could make himself wait.

The time fast approached that he'd have to act, though. He could see hands getting closer to blades, eyes hardening. Folk getting ready to fight. At least Lathkgar had no rotpriests to start drawing Worldfire. He might yet fight his way free...

"Just wait," Darak said, hating how desperate his voice sounded. He called upon the magic and it filled his body with cold pain. "She—"

A mighty sound like thunder split the air, making the tent dance as though struck by a small windstorm. Most of the horses panicked, rearing up against the reins of the barbarians striving to keep them under control. Lathkgar's own war elf gave a great hoot rather than a whinny, and the chieftain barely controlled the beast. The man's eyes were wild and his face painted in sudden terror.

Darak swore inwardly.

The gathering shoved free of the tent amongst the encampment of Lathkgar's forces. The camp had fallen to pandemonium, with horses and other steeds panicking as much as their riders. The folk pointed gnarled hands and weapons up into the sky in awe and fear.

Above them swooped a massive creature: a white-scaled serpentine monstrosity with at least five limbs and four great leathery wings. Its head resembled a three-sided blade that opened at the edges in a trisected mouth, leaking silver-blue flame. It spread wide its three jaws and loosed a resonant roar that shook the valley. A frostfire dragon, Darak recognized—the very creature that had come to Semana's aid on Iseldra's Folly. It had returned.

And flying right alongside it, gliding through the air with unnatural grace, came his sister.

The barbarians had seen the so-called Angel of Ruin before—flying high and wrapped in black leather like a man-sized raven. This day, however, she wore not the trappings of Mask but her earthen rotpriest robes and no face covering of any kind. Her silvery hair streamed behind her and her tan skin shone in the highsun light. There could be no doubt as to her identity, and he heard a cry go up among Lathkgar's warriors that turned his stomach.

"Vhas-rahn!" they called. "Vhas-rahn!"

Blood Queen.

The two figures swam through the misty highsun air, curling around each other. They engaged in a graceful dance, neither quite catching the other, both leading the movement. It looked beautiful and delicate, but the force of their passing dispersed clouds and revealed the hazy golden sun high overhead. A trail of greasy smoke marked Semana's wake—the power of her flying relics.

By Ruin, he'd *told* her. She could not show them a magic other than Worldfire. Any of Mask's relics or her blood magic or the Frostfire would be as anathema to the barbarians, securing them naught but quick, messy deaths.

Darak was suddenly alone and doomed.

Lathkgar let out a mighty bellowing roar, and Darak was ready for a blow. But instead the barbarian smiled broadly and then shouted the ruinspeak *Vhas-rahn*, titling his sister "Blood Queen."

With a glance at the dragon, Semana started to spiral downward, and the beast followed. Two score of Lathkgar's mounted screamers pulled out of its path, and the great beast crashed to earth with surprising dexterity but also enough force to send cracks through the icy ground in all directions. The great beast surveyed them all with a dozen eyes, and Darak could swear it was looking mostly at him.

His sister alighted in a cloud of smoke that dispersed in the wind of the dragon's wings. She gazed upon them, her face bare and her eyes bright with the magic raging within and around her. She strode toward Lathkgar, chin raised. "Chieftain of the Pounding Hooves," she said, in passable Ruinspeak. "I have come for your allegiance."

Heart thudding, Darak looked over to the chieftain's dark expression, which had solidified from awe to something belligerent. His stance resembled that of a cornered bear about to rise up. His hands moved casually to the hilts of the jagged single-bladed axes at his belt.

"And if I refuse?" Lathkgar asked. "If I do not kneel to you, what then, would-be Druid? Now that your beast is on the ground and our arrows trained upon it?"

Behind her, the dragon rumbled and silver smoke rose from the slits of its mouth.

"I come not to ask," Semana said. "I come to demand."

To his credit, Lathkgar didn't move. He stood strong, even as the barbarians around him shivered and looked about ready to turn their steeds and bolt. The stared at the chieftain, waiting.

He opened his mouth to speak, but Semana spoke right over him. "You are afraid," she said.

The chieftain's face went red and his offended pride put the axes in his hands. "No."

"Yes."

Semana stepped forward, into the air, seemingly indifferent to the axes, and floated right before the mounted chieftain so their faces almost touched. Her eyes flashed with crimson light, and Darak saw the veins on Lathkgar's neck pulsing hard. She raised her hand and touched her fingers to his neck.

"I can feel your fear," she said. "Taste it on my tongue. You have always lived in fear. Fear of Tar Vangr. Fear of the Circle. Fear of Ruin. Fear of looking weak."

She brushed a tail of hair out of his face with the power of the silver-chain glove on her left hand, not quite touching him.

"And so you fight a pointless, doomed crusade to destroy those who terrify you," she said. "Twice you have attacked Tar Vangr, and twice you've failed. But now—I offer you a power you have never had. The power to defeat your foes."

"What power?" Lathkgar glanced toward the frostfire dragon. "That?"

Semana shook her head. "Me."

Her clothes rustled and started to flake away, turning to ash without any obvious flame.

"This assault will not end as another wave crashing upon the rocks."

Smoke emerged from the belt at her waist—another of her relics activating—and darkness rippled across her.

"I will pull down their skyships and rip their high walls asunder."

It became black leather, and within heartbeats, she wore the mage-slayer's armor. Darkness spread across her face and resolved into a horrific mask that concealed her face entirely.

"I am Mask," she said, her voice ripped apart as though by fire.

Silence lingered on the snowy field, all eyes upon the chieftain.

Then, at length, Lathkgar bowed.

TWO

The Dusk Sea

A DARK STAIN SPREAD across the grey surface of the water in the wake of the *Thiakas*, sparkling with various colors caught in the fading daylight upon the restless waves. They'd made good time from Luether in the south, the mage-caravel clanking noisily and spouting an unending stream of greasy smoke. A dozen sailors worked onboard, constantly maintaining the rigging and mechanisms that kept the old tub afloat. One purple-faced passenger lingered near the aft rail, periodically and loudly gracing the sea with the contents of his stomach.

Few folk traveling the Dusk Sea by mage-caravel did so willingly. The *Thiakas* was a typical specimen of such a conveyance: old, rusty, continuously complaining and in need of vigilant attention. It boasted meager accommodations, forcing passengers to sleep in old, chafing hammocks strung between disused component machines in the hold with the crew. The *Thiakas* took on cheap labor: men and women of low character and even lower hygiene standards, who laughed uproariously, got into fights, and rutted loudly and frequently. Below-decks smelled of rot, vomit, sweat, and excrement, while above-decks added the unpleasant metallic tang of the sea air. It was quite enough to make most city-dwellers ill after less than an hour, and remain that way for the duration of the voyage.

This was only the third day.

"Haste, you foul oafs!" The captain, Lorath by name, had a boisterous voice and a crude manner. "Every day we waste on this afouled trek, our take dwindles. Don't you understand that? *Haste!*"

Even so, Davargorn preferred a mage-caravel to a skyship. The gentle rock of the caravel, the faint rumble of waves against the hull, and the persistent clank of the mage-engine... it all set him at ease, and he sometimes found himself nodding off in the midst of even the most active of situations. Also, ever since childhood, he'd disliked heights: on a mage-caravel, one had only to worry about plunging overboard and facing the tooth and fang of any of the horrendous creatures that prowled the Dusk Sea.

He realized the sea had lulled him into just such a restive state when a fresh bout of vomiting drew his attention to the hapless man at the rail. His curly red hair looked slick and greasy while sweat had soaked his clothes to the skin. His warm brown face had turned a rather unpleasant, dark purple color. Not that Davargorn much cared for his discomfort.

As he had at least been *paid* to care, Captain Lorath approached the man with a solicitous mien. "Pass well, syr? Do you require water? It helps the sick—"

"Fuck your water," the man said with a growl. "Your foul water gave me the shits yesterday. Bring me wine or nothing. Out of my sight."

Captain Lorath receded, his expression irritated. He wanted to get to Tar Vangr quickly, to take advantage of the political chaos of its king's absence to make a tidy profit on the goods the *Thiakas* carried. Davargorn wondered if he would appreciate the profound irony that his ship was itself carrying Lan Ravalis, the so-called Eunuch King. Not that Davargorn would call him by such a name to his face.

Lan caught his gaze and bid him approach. Davargorn did so with a sigh.

"I suppose you enjoy watching my misery," the man said.

"Yes." Davargorn shrugged. "Your sister gave me coin to ward you—not to make your path comfortable." He looked down at a few spatters of vomit on the deck. "You'll live through this."

With a grimace, Lan looked out over the endless gray of sea and sky, which grew so close they mingled in a hazy, indistinct horizon. "All knives on the table," he said at length. "Why do this for my sister? Surely she did not offer you enough coin to overcome your hatred of me."

Davargorn remembered Alistra coming to him while he hung, chained to the ceiling, and wrapping her lips around him. Another time, the feel of her ankles crossed at the small of his back, her wolf's eyes gleaming up at him. The exact sound of her gasps of pleasure and need.

"I thought as much." Lan wiped his mouth and grumbled disconsolately. "I didn't make the mistake of rutting her, but something much worse: I underestimated her. And now I will pay the price."

Davargorn leaned against the rail beside him, safely removed from the vomit. With the back of one gloved hand, he swept a white mound of seabird droppings overboard, leaving just a trace caked onto the metal. A knife slipped into his hand, and he picked at the mess. It reminded him of his life.

"You didn't answer my question," Lan said.

"You did it for yourself."

"But that isn't all of it." Lan's eyes narrowed and he smiled slyly. It was not a reassuring expression. "You're looking for something. Or someone."

He glanced around, found no eavesdroppers, and leaned in closer.

"The Winter Princess."

"No." Davargorn tried to keep his face clear of emotion. "She's nothing."

"You'd not have thrown yourself in the way of my caster if she were nothing," Lan said. "I think you love the icy little whelp. Yes?"

"As you love Ovelia Dracaris?"

The effect of Davargorn's words was as instantaneous as it was violent. Lan's body went taut and his expression screwed up in rage. His hand went into his cloak for the caster Davargorn knew he wore there. Two nights previous, he'd seen the king checking the weapon with its fire-ensorcelled thaumaturgical battery, and even if he hadn't, five years a slayer in Luether had taught Davargorn to recognize the body language of a man so armed. He stood unafraid in the face of Lan's anger.

"Cast." Davargorn wiped his small dagger clean. "Draw attention to yourself. Show them who you are." He jabbed the blade into the rail with a metallic whine, where it stood quivering. "Lorath will send you into the sea before the sun sets."

Lan hesitated, then eased his hand back out of his cloak. He didn't look at all pleased. "Let me guess," he said with a sour face. "You want to thrust yourself into Dracaris's sweet slit, too?"

Davargorn grimaced. "I'd see her blood on my hands. Her corpse at my feet."

That declaration made Lan relax slightly, and he even gave Davargorn a slight nod. Anger dug a deep well, but Lan "Lan always seemed to reserve its contents for his female enemies. Clearly Lan didn't much like looking at Davargorn's distorted face, but now there was a small measure of respect in his gaze. Unsettling.

"There's a lad." Lan grunted and cracked his knuckles with his other hand, the thick leather of his gloves creaking. "You and I, we've been ruined by women. The same women, in fact—Ovelia Dracaris, Semana Denerre, and my own sweet sister. That makes us allies, does it not?"

Davargorn sheathed his knife, then crossed his arms. "Does it," he said.

"Because I can cure you of your curse," Lan said. "Your love for your wayward princess."

"Oh?" Davargorn spat over the side. "And how's that?"

"Fuck her or kill her, of course." Lan smiled brilliantly. "Those are the only ways I know."

Davargorn opened his mouth to protest, then shut it again. That made as much sense as anything he had thought of. "Is that your plan for Ovelia Dracaris? If she yet lives?"

"If she yet lives," Lan said, his tone bitter. "I'd prefer to do both."

Davargorn started to reassure him that she did, in fact, yet live, but he thought better of it. He had begun to suspect that Lan wanted information out of him, and he wouldn't let anything else slip. At least not for free. With any luck, they would never see the rutting Ovelia Dracaris again.

Their words had trailed away, and the king looked out once more over the sea. Davargorn turned to go, but Lan spoke to arrest him.

"Lad," Lan said. "Tithian, is it?"

Davargorn shrugged. "If you want."

"Don't forget who your allies are," he said. "If we are to triumph, we need to fight together."

"Mayhap." Davargorn bowed slightly. "Your Majesty."

They parted, leaving Davargorn with plenty to consider.

Crack.

A man went flat on his back, blood streaming from his nose, and the gathered sailors erupted in shouts and jeers, coin changing hands. Davargorn spat on the deck and flexed his slightly misshapen shoulders. Enough muscle made his body look approximately right, and wearing his bone-set mask kept the worst of the looks away. Fighting and winning folks' coin did the rest.

The morning of the fourth day, as he had the previous two days, Davargorn spent brawling. The crew had little enough to do at sea while the captain's arcanist wrestled with the mage-engine after it had broken down yet again. They cast lots and laid wagers, and any who had bet early on the distorted lad with the club foot and the big milky-white eye had seen their winnings returned to them several fold. He had taken a few punches, but with his magic soothing his aches, it was hardly a concern.

It took only that first day of fighting to assess that Davargorn was the best warrior on the ship, but he found himself continually called upon to prove his proficiency against an apparently limitless stream of challengers. By highsun on the fourth day of the voyage, he'd beat down essentially every sailor at all inclined toward fighting on the *Thiakas*, and even some of those who were not. He had a reputation, and it amused him to maintain it at the ends of his fists.

Lan Ravalis, of course, had not participated in the fights, either as a contestant or as a spectator. And considering how regularly he had to run to the rail, Davargorn hardly minded.

The one who had come closest to defeating Davargorn was a young woman—a nameless hellion with jet black hair the others called Raven Summer. She hacked up a violent, long string of coughs before the fight, seemingly weakened. When Davargorn hesitated, she seized the opportunity to leap onto his back and fishhook her fingers into his mouth, practically immobilizing him. The pain had ultimately made him lash out, and he'd managed to throw her into a mast. The fight had ended in a draw, with both agreeing to a rematch the next day. Davargorn had noted her watching him periodically, her eyes angry and hungry, and he'd never been able to decide what to do about it. If anything.

He hardly feared a vengeful enemy among the crew, but exposing Lan's identity might endanger them both. Mayhap Davagorn should allow her to win the brawl on the fourth day, if she did not defeat him outright on her own merits. If she emerged the victor, then mayhap her interest would wane.

That fourth day, the mage-caravel was becalmed, and the fights lasted unto highsun. With his magic, Davargorn could have gone on fighting all day, but his heart was no longer in it. Fighting had begun to bore him, and the futility of it all weighed on his minds and fists.

On his way down to his bunk, Davargorn acknowledged that this indifference had grown for some time. It wasn't that his showdown with the Bloodbreaker still pained him—and it did, in his heart if not his body—but that he couldn't take as much pleasure in it anymore. What had he to fight for? Whom? Alistra? She'd killed one of her own people simply for threatening him, but was it out of love or as another trick? And wasn't merely pondering that question a sign of compromised judgment?

Mayhap Lan was right. Alistra still controlled him.

Rain threatened, and Davargorn went belowdecks to shelter from the inevitable burning. The sailors had to stay up on the deck to attend their duties. He slipped down the rust-speckled ladder, moving deftly despite his club foot. He'd long ago learned the art of manipulating the deformed body he'd had since birth, and more than once he'd used his handicaps to his advantage and tricked a foe into underestimating him. Not unlike the woman with her coughing.

He became aware of the intruder as he approached, and Davargorn slowed to a cautious roll between cover, as though stalking an animal in its own territory. He hid behind a pallet of metals from the mine in Luether, then kept out of sight behind a stacked roll of hemp rope. A figure moved near his hammock toward the back of the hold, where the metal clanked and shifted. It occurred to Davargorn only then that sleeping so close to the ship's cargo could prove dangerous. Particularly if the pallet happened to come unsecured…

Davargorn reached out and, with the knife he palmed earlier, sawed through the uppermost rope securing the long bars of metal. He might have cut the second and last lashing, but then he recognized a distinctive cough from the intruder. The knife went back into his sleeve, and he stepped out of the shadows to confront her.

The Summer woman from abovedecks whirled around from where she had been rummaging through Davargorn's things. Her hand twitched toward the inside of her half-cloak. "What?" she asked.

"That's for me to ask. Considering." Davargorn nodded toward the twisted wires of a lockpick protruding from the lock on Lan's chest of luggage.

"So you've caught me pilfering your master's things." She sat back on the chest, covering up the lock with her muscular leg, and leaned forward just enough to give him an excellent view. "What now?"

Davargorn's mouth went slightly dry. The way she was looking at him—

The unmistakable whine of a caster being charged behind Davargorn made him stand taut.

"Now you tell me why I shouldn't blow a hole in your head," Lan said. "Thief."

This wasn't the first time Davargorn had found himself standing between Lan's caster and the woman he menaced with it. And though he didn't know her beyond a single fight, he found himself determined to stop Lan from hurting her. He cursed himself for a fool. He didn't even know her. He—

On her feet in a flash, she stepped forward and smashed herself against his back, and he felt cold steel at his throat. "Back," she said to Lan, her words a hiss. "I'll kill him."

The disgraced king looked at them both with a bemused expression. He raised the caster.

"No, wait—" Davargorn started.

Then the caster sizzled and cracked, and pain in his arm ripped the world into a white-hot sea of light. The one they called Raven Summer staggered back, loosing Davargorn to stumble against the wall. They both clung to injuries—Davargorn to his shattered left arm, Raven to her winged shoulder.

"What," she said. "But—"

Then she froze, as Lan pointed the second quarrel of his double caster at her breast. She stood there, blood dripping down between her fingers, eyes wide and staring at her doom.

"You dare touch my things, woman?" Lan asked, his voice deadly.

Removed from the line of casting, Davargorn cursed and focused to push his magic into his broken arm. The bleeding slowed and stopped, and the bone started to pull itself together. Lan had dealt him a grievous wound, and it would take time to heal. "Could have aimed better," he said.

"I could try again." Lan's aim didn't waver, and Raven didn't move a finger. "You have to get over this fixation with wenches, boy. It's going to get you slain."

Davargorn's arm pulsed with pain, ripping up and down. "Lan—"

The king's hiss cut him off, and Davargorn shut his mouth. Damn and burn, he'd just used Lan's name. They were supposed to be traveling in secret. It was hard for him to think against all the pain. And he'd just got Raven killed. And by the way her face paled, she knew it, too.

"Listen," said the woman. "I don't know you. Never seen you. Never heard you. I'll go—"

"You'll go *nowhere*." Lan gestured to her shoulder. "That wound mortal?"

Raven shook her head. "Hardly."

"How unfortunate for you." Lan took a step forward and pressed the end of the caster to her chest. "In an hour, you'll wish I *had* aimed better with my cast, you foolish w—"

Shouts up on deck cut him off, and the ship shuddered powerfully by some sort of impact. Lan staggered aside, startled, and his caster fell off line. Raven and Davargorn both kept their wits about them, but his wounded arm slowed him. Unfortunately, Raven had no such hindrance. She reached to her coat and pulled a small handcaster. The movement was so fluid and subtle that Davargorn wouldn't have noticed if he hadn't been looking right at her. He could palm his knife but couldn't wind back and throw it quick enough. He could do nothing to save Lan from a cast right into his belly.

Then he remembered the other cord securing the metal, and before he had even finished the thought, his hand shot out and the blade split the binding.

The ship leaned to the side, and a long rectangular bar of metal slid across the top of the pallet and smashed, end-first, into the summerblooded woman's chest. Breath coughed out and blood spurted as the beam crushed her against the wall of the hold, and Davargorn heard the wet crunch of bones. Her eyes went wide in a face that leaked blood, and she gasped but could not breathe. One hand batted weakly at the bar for a heartbeat. Then the caster tumbled from nerveless fingers and she slumped to the side as much as she could, held in place by the beam.

Lan looked at Davargorn, who blinked back at him. The world stood still.

Then shouts of alarm from up on the deck snapped the world back into focus. There was a battle going on abovedecks, and another explosion ripped through the ship. Those weren't the strikes of some sea monster or a collision with a rock. Those were—

"Mortars," Lan said.

A slight nod passed between them, and they went in opposite directions. Davargorn rushed toward the ladder, while Lan ducked under the beam pinning the corpse to the wall and opened his trunk. Davargorn cast a single glance backward and frowned at the dead woman. He should have done something different, and this all might have ended differently. It seemed like a waste.

Davargorn climbed the ladder and poked his head out above the deck, careful to keep to the shadow of the aftcastle, to limit notice.

He needn't have bothered.

The mage-caravel was under attack from a skyship that hovered some fifty paces above, blotting out the sun with its sleek black bulk. Two dozen figures floated down from the ship, casters cracking and bows thrumming. Davargorn narrowly pulled himself belowdecks to avoid the fiery blast of a mortar. In the passing smoke, he scuttled out of the trapdoor and hid in the shadow of the steps to the aftcastle.

Lady Shard's pirates.

The battle was just about over, but Davargorn didn't much care. He came rolling through the smoke and dragged one falcat across the leg of a floating-cloaked pirate. The man's curse became a howl of pain, and as he descended, Davargorn shoved himself and his sword upward. He rose in a whirling arc and slashed the man's head from his shoulders as he came up. As the corpse fell, Davargorn locked blades with another pirate standing nearby. This one reacted quickly enough, knocking his sword away with a long straight sword of her own.

He expected his heart to thunder—his body to rage in enthusiasm—but somehow it didn't. The thrill of battle was gone. He just went through the motions.

Davargorn kept moving, whirling away when he couldn't get inside the pirate's defenses. She followed, thinking it an opening, and Davargorn lunged back in to slash his blade across her hand. Her weapon toppled to the deck and he stepped in, other falcat darting for the gap in her armor under her arm—

Something hard and fast smashed into Davargorn, sending him slipping and sliding across the deck. He slammed into the opposite railing, low enough to the deck that he went down, rather than over. He could feel the looseness in his chest—broken and dislocated ribs—and he suspected a hit like that would have proved fatal to someone without his magic. Still, his body lay broken and he couldn't bring himself to reach the falcata that lay on the deck half a pace from his hand, much less rise and fight on. The sun sparkled around the edge of the skyship above.

A shadow fell over him, and Davargorn looked up blearily at a large woman, as sturdy as an ox with the shoulders to match. She was short and built like a boar, and her deep brown eyes peered down at him through the steel faceplate of her helm. She held in her hands something that looked like a portable battering ram, which hung from her hands on two handles.

The pirate he'd struck cursed at the wound he'd dealt her. She held her sword awkwardly in her off hand and stalked toward Davargorn, but the stout wounded pirate stepped into her path. "Leave him," she said.

"What?" the woman with the handheld ram said. "You saw what he did to me—"

"Bah, you're fine," said the woman, her voice deep like shifting stone. "See that cloak? Boy's one of us, or else he stole that."

Davargorn realized he was still wearing the tattered remains of the floating cloak he'd taken from Ovelia in Luether. Its power was long-since gone, but its origin was clear.

"Take him with us," said the stout woman.

Pirates came forward and clapped shackles around Davargorn's wrists. He started to struggle, but then he saw the pirates leading Lan up from belowdecks. He gave Davargorn a faint shake of the head. And for some reason, Davargorn acceded to his wishes.

He bowed his head and went quietly.

THREE

Atropis, the Dusk Sea

WIND ROSE IN SWIRLING whips, snapping cables and chains against the jagged stone walls of the cracked fortress. At this height, thunder rolled overhead and all around while lightning crackled in the clouds. Seabirds hooted and cawed against the foul weather, sounding eerily like toddlers crying out for milk. Far, far below, the dark waters churned against the sharp stones at the city's base, where shards of its once magnificent construction corroded and deteriorated over the centuries.

Hundreds of years ago, the great mage-city of Atropis had been an edifice of impossible architecture: a castle suspended in the air on a pin-sized support halfway down its length. When it fell, it slid free from this pinnacle and crushed fully half itself into a mass of rubble strewn through the sea, making its environs extremely dangerous for Dusk Sea-bound craft. One day, the remaining leaning tower would finally collapse into the sea with a mighty roar that would slay all within. Perhaps it would be this day—or perhaps a hundred years hence.

All things must pass to ruin in their own time.

For the man who stood in the high cell of that castle, half of it scraped away by the elements so it was open to the rain and wind, that time was already past. His toes gripped the edge of the broken stone and his gnarled hands curled into claws at his sides as he gazed out into the void.

Death-dealer. Reaper of Men. Shadow of Ruin.

"No more," the man said. "I swore an oath: no more."

Yet another oath he had broken.

A man's face loomed before him, and the Oathbreaker hacked through it with the burning blue mage-glass of the fae sword Frostburn. Blood spurted into the air along with the steam of ice, and yet another body fell at his feet. Even then, he turned to strike down a second victim. And a third. And a fourth. And with each, their warmth flooded through the blade and up his arm, soothing his body.

"No," the man called Frostburn said. "I don't have it. I won't wield it again."

He woke again to the world and found himself leaning against the partial wall of his cell, his knuckles and the heel of his hand bloody where he'd

46

slammed it into the stone. He'd pounded his body against the stone more than once, and the markings of his blood and sweat and fury covered the room, only to be washed away in the rain.

How long had he been here? A year? A season? A day? An hour?

He could still feel it: the wicked, awful hunger in that blade, resonating through his whole body. He hadn't touched it in some time—not today, at least, and not the previous day—but it seemed as though it was in his hand now. He could feel it rippling up his arm. The power. The will. The darkness where nothing mattered but himself and his enemy.

He wanted nothing more.

He wanted nothing less.

"You are a weapon," said Mask's grotesque voice in his ear. "Embrace it, as I have."

Regel looked away, but the mage-slayer scuttled around him, moving like nothing human.

"This is your destiny, Oathbreaker," the creature said.

Lightning shot through the clouds and thunder almost drove him over the edge. He fell and smashed his chest into the lip of stone. He stared down, wet stringy hair hanging over the abyss. He stared Ruin in its ugly face while it raged around him. It promised his doom—begged for his death—and whispered of relief if he only took half a step forward. The hunger would end, as would his life.

The high cells of Atropis always offered a choice to their prisoners.

It would be so much easier to fall. To surrender the fight and let Ruin take him.

"Regel."

Ovelia wrapped her arms around him from behind, fingers trailing across his chest. He felt the warmth of her and the gentle comfort of her touch. She held him back.

"Regel, stop this," she said, pressing her cheek against his back. "Don't hurt yourself like this."

He knew she wasn't there. Sometimes he saw her standing in the cell, sometimes kneeling. Sometimes she had a belly heavy with child, sometimes not. Sometimes, in his more desperate moments, he'd used her for sex, then woken on the floor, weeping and shivering. That part of his life was over now—he knew that—but his body still wanted what it wanted. The shame almost drove him over the edge, but he managed to resist, and inevitably she appeared again to console him.

"Lia," said another, darker voice. Husky like a breeze through corn silk. "Step back."

Regel shivered. Ovelia was neither the only nor the worst specter who haunted him.

There she stood, in the center of the half-open cell, wrapped in darkness. Sometimes she looked as he remembered—tall and beautiful, her silvery-blonde hair shining, her face perfectly proportioned and her features sharp. Sometimes she looked as she did now: swathed in ratty black robes that flapped and flowed in the storm. She glared at him, beyond judgment and straight to condemnation.

"Stand away from him, Ovelia," she said. "That is a dead man."

She came to him often—Lenalin, Lady Shard, whatever name she wore. Sometimes she looked like she used to look—cold, beautiful, the perfect queen of all she surveyed. Sometimes she looked like a mass of scars and bandages, as though her body had suffered every wound he had ever dealt a foe.

But never before had she spoken. That was new. And terrible.

Regel reached out, but Ovelia wasn't there. She never was. He staggered, unsupported and woozy. He groped for the near wall and found it, but he could hold himself up. The raw emptiness in his core begged to be filled; it cried out for warmth that his own body could not generate. He reached for Lenalin and fell to his knees. His hand didn't quite reach her foot.

She stepped purposefully back as he reached for her.

"This oath you have broken, too," she said. "Just as you broke your oath to me all those years ago. As you have broken every oath." Her eyes burned down at him from deep behind her veil. He could feel her gaze despite the thin layer of black. "Just as you will break every oath you ever swear."

"No." Regel made another lunge. "Lena, I didn't—"

"Don't call me that." She snatched her foot back, then stamped hard on his hand. "Not ever."

"Princess—"

"No more, because of Paeter—and because of you." She ground the heel of her boot into his hand, sending pain shooting up his arm. "You knew what he was. And yet you did nothing."

Teeth gritted, Regel tried to reply. "You commanded me to do nothing."

"Does that matter?" Lenalin asked. "You told me you loved me."

Regel opened his mouth, then closed it. He had nothing to say.

He knew what he should have done. What he *had* done was nothing, and for that, he would always be an oathbreaker.

"You let him have his way with me." She stepped off his hand, then bent low to put her face to his. "You let him hurt me. You let him torture me. You let him *ruin* me."

He had. He had known the depths of Paeter's depravity even before witnessing his cruelty in the Echvar campaign. The Ravalis blood was tainted, driving some of its heirs aggressively mad, particularly against women. Regel had seen the bruises on Lenalin's body. He knew. And the weight of that—the shame and horror…

"I slew him," he said. "Paeter. I cut his throat like that of a cow. He had all but rotted away by then, ruined by drink and years of sloth, and—"

"I don't care." Lenalin grasped Regel's chin and wrenched his head up. "Do I look like I care?"

And with her other hand, she drew up her veil, revealing her face.

Every time she came to him, she looked different. Sometimes her face was a mess of boils, sometimes a swarm of leeches or locusts. Sometimes she was covered in blood and drooled it from her eyes and nose and lips. Sometimes she had no eyes or nose or lips but only yawning black holes full of blood and horror. Sometimes she looked like herself—the same beautiful icy statue she had always seemed to him—but even as he watched she began to melt, pieces of her face drooping and sloughing off to splat wetly onto the ground. Beneath lay a rotting mask, taut and shredded muscle laid bare before it, too, dissolved, leaving only bone behind. It never ceased to horrify Regel, no matter how many times he witnessed her face fall to ruin before his eyes.

"Look at me," she said when he hesitated to meet her gaze. "See my face."

This time, she looked almost human, but her face was scarred and twisted, her features out of alignment and distorted. The eyes he knew—those steely, determined eyes that he had loved so much—filled with rage and burning for vengeance.

"Look at me," she said again. "Do you see me? Not my face, but *me*?"

He saw only her eyes, not her ruined face. She was not the princess he had known, failed, and lost. Lenalin was something else now, as far beyond him as Ovelia was. He nodded.

"I can still serve you," he said. "Let me serve you."

Lenalin's eyes blazed with anger. "Why should I?" she asked. "When you have failed me again and again? Why do you deserve more than this?"

Regel trembled. He had no answer for her.

Slowly, Lenalin released him and rose to her full height. The black veil went back over her face, though Regel didn't see her hands move. Perhaps she had never revealed her face to him. Perhaps she had never bent down to speak to him. Perhaps she had never come to him at all.

"If you want to serve me, dead man," Lenalin said. "You have to live."

She couldn't have leveled a harder command upon him had she tried.

She gazed upon him for a time, then turned and vanished into the gloom.

He lay on the corroded stone for a time, letting the rain and wind lash him like a scourge. His muscles refused to move and he could only shudder under the onslaught.

You have to live, she had said.

Finally, he managed to move one arm, with which he pulled the rest of his body a little. He felt weak and empty. He had nothing to offer. The other arm he forced to move, and he scrabbled at the stone for a handhold. He found it finally and pulled himself an agonizingly short distance forward. It seemed to take hours, during which the storm only worsened until it seemed the World of Ruin itself was screaming at him, but finally he reached the ledge of the cell. On his belly, he stared once again into the black hollow of the broken world, which offered only pain and despair.

Live.

The Deathless had named him Frostburn, the Reaper of Men. He lived for no other purpose but to bring death. To ravage and destroy. To end life wherever he saw it. In that, he and Ruin served the same purpose. For this Necthana had trained him, had armed him, and sent him forth that first time, more than twenty years ago. When he was young and angry, seeking to make his mark upon the World of Ruin, they had granted him the gift of their death magic, a scourge for a broken world.

But ultimately, he had turned from that destiny, and now he clung to that last hope.

When he had returned as an old man, as they must have expected he would, he rejected their gift. He would not become one of them, no matter how the Deathless Rose had begged him. No matter how he had wanted to accept it. He had left Necthana by his own choice, and he would never return. Not least because the awful hunger of the sword of ice would kill him.

And what did Regel Winter—Regel the Frostburn, Regel the Oathbreaker—find waiting when he returned to this broken, mortal world? Nothing but pain. Regret. Sorrow.

This was what he deserved.

"No," he said, barely managing a whisper.

His fingers curled into fists.

Live.

If withering to nothing was to be his destiny, he rejected it.

The soul of rebellion rose within him, as it never truly had. All these years, all these false masters and impossible dreams, had left him nothing but himself. He would not lose that as well.

Regel had spent so long pushing thoughts of the sword away. It would not serve. He had no choice. It was part of him, and he could not rid himself of it.

So let it be part of him. Let it serve his purposes.

Purpose.

He could have one of those, once again. Or perhaps for the first time.

He shut his eyes against the torrent.

His princess still needed him.

His world still needed him.

Most of all, *he* still needed him.

He called out to himself across the dark expanse of the lashing, raging World of Ruin.

And he would answer.

FOUR

The Winter Wilds

AND LIKE THAT, IT all started coming together.

Over the remainder of the summer, Semana oversaw their swelling forces. More warriors appeared each day and night, tromping into camp and erecting their own unique standards and totems. The war camp bristled with thousands of animals, weapons, or corpses or some combination of the three wrought of sticks and twine, of blood and bone. Weapons thrust into the ground delineated the edges of camps, but spaces between provided neutral territory where Children of various backgrounds clashed and fought and rutted and gloried in the coming violence.

By the coming of autumn, their numbers had swollen from hundreds to thousands. Flying by cover of night, she counted roughly four thousand warriors, with more arriving every day.

As she did now, Semana passed among them sometimes, mask doffed to show her face, listening to their tales and working on her Ruinspeak. Assuming she understood them properly, they'd come for various reasons. Some had followed word of the youngest High Druid and her dragon—a beast out of legend with the power of a raging winter storm. Some sought to follow the Angel of Ruin, whose mere glance would bring the fiercest chieftains to their knees. Some spoke of the wind gathering to finally throw down the last mage-city of Tar Vangr, as was the destiny of the Children of Ruin. It made her smile—not because they spoke of her, but because these were the sorts of stories that spread.

And oh, they had.

She paused to listen for a time outside a camp with a totem constructed of a flayed rabbit stuck through with nails in its feet, ears drooping over its rotting body. The barbarians in that encampment made a point of wearing furs with bits of bloody flesh on the outside, letting it rot and stink to the tainted sky. They spoke animatedly of the powerful and awful Angel of Ruin, and they argued bitterly about who most deserved the chance to share her bed and become her champion.

"Best fortune with that," Semana said under her breath.

She smiled. Not because she was flattered—she wasn't—but because she was winning.

Which was precisely the moment an arrow thudded into the skinned rabbit half a pace from her head, making it bounce and squelch on the post. For a heartbeat, Semana could only blink at the dark shaft that had appeared so suddenly. Somehow, she wasn't surprised, as if her body had known the attack was coming. She flinched away as another arrow sank into the totem, some two fingers-breadth from the first shaft and an equal distance from her nose. The black fletchings tickled at her bare skin.

Another shape loomed out of the darkness, spear thrusting at her chest. It came too fast for Semana to dodge aside, and the weapon smashed hard into the protective blue shield that suddenly bloomed from her breastplate. Semana staggered back from the force, wisps of burnt magic rising around her, and tripped backward over a root or a stone. She fell heavily onto her backside and stared up at a leering barbarian face, spear raised over her for a killing blow.

Without thinking, Semana lashed out with her silver glove, knocking the feet out from under the barbarian. He toppled, spear stabbing wildly into the slushy mud beside her head, and fell bodily atop her. His weight blew the air from her lungs and his face smashed into her mask, so that Semana saw only dazzling stars for several heartbeats. When the world made sense again, his groaning bulk crushed her into the cold mud and breath came hard. She tried and failed to wriggle free.

Where was Darak? Or Gilt? They should have rushed to her aid. Her brother might not be able to get to her, but Gilt stalked her like her own shadow. Where was he? Had the assassins slain him?

Was she alone?

Another arrow whistled through the air and shattered off blue energy that flared from her armor, which also dislodged the barbarian weighing her down. Scuffs shone along the blue light from the force of the attack, and the arrow spun lazily off into the chilling dark. She managed to sit up.

The barbarian woke with a start and reached for his axe, giving Semana a chance. She drew power from her silver gauntlet, knocking him up and away with a startled grunt. The force put him back on his feet, and he wavered while Semana clawed her way to one knee. Alas, the barbarian's daze only lasted a heartbeat, because he chopped down with his axe and it narrowly bounced off a shield over Semana's head. Cracks ran through the blue protective nimbus and the force knocked her reeling.

"No!" Semana shouted at him. "Back off! Back—!"

The axe smashed into her again, and pieces of blue light fractured and splintered away like fragments of glass. They floated off and evaporated like snowflakes, and Semana coughed at the foul stench of the magic in operation. Her body shuddered as though the axe had struck her flesh, and her ears rang. The world shivered around her under the ongoing assault.

She saw Regel's face in her mind's eye, shouting at her from such a distance she couldn't make out his words. But she knew that expression. *Do something! Fight back!*

She did.

With a snarl, she summoned the magic in her silver chain-link glove and unleashed it full against the driving axe. The weapon ripped itself from the barbarian's hands so hard that it shattered and skittered back along the ground. The man looked momentarily startled before Semana lowered her hand toward his massive belly and opened her fingers wide to release another blast of force. The spell smashed into him and apart, and his midsection burst in a bloody eruption as Semana's magic literally tore him in half. Both pieces tumbled away while plumes of greasy smoke rose around Semana.

Two more barbarians were rushing toward her, weapons glittering.

How dare they strike her this way, like cowards in the night? Rage gave her power.

A pair of arrows came scything out of the gloom, but Semana caught them with her magic and sent them arcing instead toward her foes, where they buried themselves in a left shoulder and upper arm. The charging warrior wrenched the shafts apart with casual ease and roared out in challenge.

"Come then!" Semana shouted, wrenching her mask in place over her face. *"Come on!"*

Semana met the charging barbarian with a storm of reaving green tendrils from her mask that stabbed into him like seeking talons. Her magic lifted his suddenly taut body into the air and rotted away pieces of it at a touch. His arm and legs shriveled and started turning to pulp, and his breathless scream sounded more like choking than a cry. Semana's stomach lurched, but she was too angry to stop now.

Then something whistled through the air and smashed into the side of her head, laying her out flat as a board. The world went black and red, and she lay stunned on the ground, gasping and choking. Her mask lay about a pace away, along with a lock of her silver-blonde hair stuck to it with blood. The side of her head burned with fresh agony, and she vomited into the muddy slush.

What was this? It didn't make sense. She couldn't—

A cry from farther away drew Semana's attention, and she looked up to see a muscular woman with a shock of bright hair rushing toward her, jagged axe raised high.

Carr the Axe. One of the High Druids. They had come for her.

Another barbarian stood over Semana, this one with a sword decorated with blood—perhaps Semana's blood? The woman's horrid face resembled a child's puzzle of scars and fresh cuts that wept fresh blood and pus, and her triumphant smile made Semana shudder.

Blood pounded in Semana's head—her own and the scarred barbarian's blood. She couldn't focus. She couldn't draw on the power of her relics—it all seemed to be at a low ebb, after her flight.

She felt like a fool. A helpless, terrified fool.

The blade started to descend toward Semana's face, but even as it did, an axe swept across, streaming flame, and it cut clean through the blade and sheared it in two. The axe sank into the barbarian's midsection, making the woman's eyes bug wide. Carr ripped the axe free, splashing blood all over Semana's face—she barely managed to shut her eyes and mouth—then reversed the axe to cleave the woman's head from her shoulders in a fresh burst of gore.

"Nnh." Semana staggered away, scooping up her mask with fumbling fingers. She tried to put it back on, but it slipped and fell into the mud. She reached down and reclaimed it after two attempts.

No more arrows rained down upon her. No axe sank into her back.

Indeed, Carr was regarding her with a cool, patient expression.

The darkness moved around her, and suddenly Gilt was there, his sculpted frame like a pillar upon which Semana could lean and behind which she could take cover. She did both, panting and cursing. The Deathless said nothing, only stood at the ready. Finally, Semana managed to get the muddy mask back on, and it made the side of her head hurt as though grating her skin.

"Calm, lass." Carr had not stepped forward to attack. Perhaps she feared the Deathless's rebuke? But she didn't seem tense or even ready at arms. She looked relaxed. "Think."

"You—you attack me *here*?" Semana summoned forth plaguefire in her mask, and the world rippled with sickly green energies around her eyes. "Amongst my army?"

"*Your* army." Carr grinned and stretched with an easy, feline grace. "Ruin's army."

"Your army—our army." Fellis the Night Wolf stepped out from among the tents, bow trained upon Semana—and upon Gilt. "Whoever serves Ruin best."

The commotion had drawn a crowd of barbarians from the nearby camps, who stood ready, weapons drawn and glinting in the hazy moonlight. They bore witness to the confrontation between the High Druids. They told legends of these powerful women, many of which held no small amount of truth. And the chance to watch them battle Ruin's Angel? That would be a sight to behold.

Semana's shielding magic was weakened but not yet broken, and she still had most of a charge in her mask and her glove. She had the blood magic, but it would be too slow to be of much use against two High Druids determined to slay her. That meant the Worldfire, with which she was yet a novice. Her relics were her best bet for immediate, raw power, until the Druids drained it, the way Afferath had that first night they met. Perhaps she should strike the instant she felt her power start to waver.

Why had Carr chopped down her attacker, and not Semana herself? And why had Fellis stepped out from hiding, revealing herself and sacrificing her advantage? And why had her arrows missed?

Because they weren't here to kill her.

"Those arrows were to warn me," Semana said. "And you killed my attacker. Why?"

Fellis only had eyes for Gilt, however, who watched both druids placidly. His perfect body stood at ease, though Semana knew he could explode into sudden violence at any moment. The sheer volatile energy in the fae was almost unbearable.

"Send away your demon," said Carr, her words almost a growl. Her eyes flashed yellow and her face looked very vulpine in the haze. "And we'll talk."

What assurances do you offer, Semana almost asked, but held her tongue. These druids respected strength first, not bargaining.

She laid her hand on Gilt's arm, which might as well have been carved of black stone. He understood merely from her touch what she wished. Without a word or gesture, the darkness parted and swallowed him, as Gilt walked the unseen paths of the Deathless fae, leaving her alone. It was refreshing, how implicitly he trusted her judgment, and the effect it had upon the druids was noticeable.

"Talk then," Semana said in the ensuing silence. "Say what you wish."

Fellis's eyes flicked to Carr, who was always the more talkative of the two Druids.

"We would join the Blood Queen. Ruin's Angel. She who tamed the great Frostfire Dragon of the Winter Wilds. She who walks with the Deathless." She pointed her axe at Semana. "You, lass."

The barbarian Semana had wounded with the plaguefire made a sound that was half moan, half scream. Casually, Carr loped over to him and lopped off his head. The corpse bore her symbol: a cloven piece of steel wrapped in a bloody thong.

"Your warriors," Semana said. "These were your warriors."

"They were." With her boot, Carr nudged the dead barbarian.

Semana's frown deepened. "You tried to kill me."

Carr the Axe threw back her head and laughed. "Aye, but we didn't try particularly hard," she said. "We had to judge for ourselves. You slew Afferath, but that might have been luck."

"Judge for ourselves," Fellis said by way of agreement.

"Couldn't ally with a weakling, could we?" asked Carr.

That they could not, Semana realized. If they swore fealty or alliance to Semana and she later failed in her task, that would not end well for them. Unless this was a scheme of some sort.

"I thought the Circle stood against me," Semana said. "You told me as much at Iseldra's Folly."

"The *Circle*," Fellis said in her soft, dangerous voice. "Not all its points."

"The Circle of Druids int a monolith," Carr said. "Not all of us agree. But all of us look for how the fire flows, and in our eyes, it flows behind you. Lathkgar of the Thundering Hooves thinks so. And now, so do we." She shrugged. "We ally with victory in Ruin."

Semana believed them, but also knew Carr wouldn't hesitate to plunge that axe into the back of her head the instant she perceived the fire changing direction. "I care not for your games," Semana said. "You attack me here, with *my* army"—hers for the moment, at least—"and you expect to be friends?"

Fellis made a derisive sniffing sound. Carr chuckled. "Our army surrounds your army, camped within half a day's march," she said. "Call it an incentive to talk."

Semana could feel Carr's steady heartbeat. She spoke true. Damn and *burn*.

More and more barbarians had gathered around them—at least a hundred. So much scrutiny meant that whatever happened next took on additional significance. She had to say something—do something—to win them all over. Assert her position and consolidate her leadership.

If only she had the least idea what to say or do.

She had the urge to attack Fellis and Carr—perhaps slaying them would put an end to challenges to her authority—but she could not be sure of victory. The long delay had given her time to start tasting their blood, and perhaps she could overcome their wills to seize control of their bodies. Even if she could control one High Druid, could she control both at once? Not likely, and while she used one like a puppet, the other would cut her down easily enough. And what if they had come in earnest, and their promises of alliance were true? If she attacked, their armies would fall upon hers and her dream would end.

Semana realized she'd hesitated too long. Fellis stared at her, frown slowly deepening, while a smile spread at the same rate across Carr's face. They were mocking her. They saw an opportunity. They would win, because she didn't know how to fight back, and that filled her with unreasoning rage.

Semana started to draw energy into her relics, shrouding herself in a faint haze of air-distorting smoke. Fellis's frown turned into a feral snarl, and Carr cursed in Ruinspeak. They readied their weapons and Semana could feel their Worldfire surge. They'd spent much of their magic already, and now she would try them to the last measure of their strength. At least she could kill one of them.

A commotion among the barbarians drew Semana's anxious attention, and her breath caught as Darak pushed his way into the circle. Left and Right stood with him, and Crown of Fire followed none-too-far behind. Initially a wave of despair went through her, but she saw the confident look on her brother's face and read the swagger in his step. He bowed to the Druids, low and obsequious.

"Ladies," he said. "How honored we are that you grace us with your presence in this way."

"Pah." Carr spat. "You yet keep this traitor, Blood Queen? This snake what bit his own master?"

If Darak paid her any mind, he didn't show it. "Have you come to discuss the alliance I offered?"

Alliance that *he* offered? Semana blinked. What alliance?

Carr looked no less surprised, and she was not a woman who liked surprises. Her look of confusion screwed up into contempt. "Listen well, boy," she said, baring her teeth. "Int no—"

"Yes," said Fellis's soft voice, startling them all. She stepped forward, the feathers of the arrows in her quiver rustling faintly. "He offered us alliance, that day on Iseldra's Folly, without words."

Semana goggled at her brother, who grinned, completely in control. How did he do that?

"It would be to my honor and great pleasure, honored Druids," Darak said. "My warriors shall escort you to my tent, which I shall gladly cede to your use, and eat and drink. We shall talk."

With her rolling stride, Fellis followed the cadre of warriors Darak sent. The much shorter, more robust Carr followed her, grumbling and cursing. Darak was all smiles until they left the circle, and it was only when he turned back to Semana that she saw the fire in his eye.

"What?" she asked.

The other barbarians had started to disperse back to their camps, sharing any number of murmurs and speculations. Left and Right remained, flanking Darak, as did Crown of Fire.

Semana approached her smiling brother. "Let me guess," she said. "Poor fool Semana, nearly bringing us to disaster again. You going to berate me, brother?"

"Not remotely." Darak smirked. "I disagreed with you about Lathkgar, but you were right, and now he is our ally. I should have trusted you at Iseldra's Folly, as well, and that was *my* folly." He inclined his head to her. "For all of this, I apologize, and I will trust you. Your judgment. Your counsel." He made a sour face, as though he'd just bit into a lemon. "I'll try, anyway. It's not—it's not easy for me. I have gone without allies or friends for too long."

Whatever Semana had expected, that surprised her. "Truly?" she asked.

Behind Darak, Crown of Fire scowled in disbelief.

"Truly," Darak said. "We are the last heirs of the Blood of Winter. We are partners in this."

For a moment, Darak wore the charming look of his youth—the one Semana had always envied, for its ability to lure anyone into doing anything. That, and his wily tongue. He purred as much as spoke, and she felt herself relaxing around him. This was one of the primary reasons she needed him: this ability, far superior to her own. It occurred to her not to trust his words, but his eyes looked so honest.

She was no longer a child, however, and not so easily swayed.

"I shall believe it when your actions prove it," Semana said. "Stop struggling with me. Stop trying to embarrass me. We will lead this army together or not at all."

"Of course." Darak held out a hand. "This is our destiny—yours as well as mine."

This was no simple promise—no words of wind that lasted as long as a breeze. He meant this, or the brother she had known all those years ago was dead for true.

Semana reached up and took his proffered hand, wrapping her fingers around his wrist. His grip felt warm. Solid. Dependable. Mayhap. It reassured her.

"I should see to our guests," Darak said lightly. "If two of the Circle join our cause, perhaps more will follow. They'll want mead and food and to browbeat me a bit more. Leave it to me—they 'll aid us."

Semana nodded. "And me? What should I do?"

"You? Sister." Darak put his hands lightly on her shoulders. "You should carry on with what you have always done. Continue to terrify our warriors and inspire their loyalty. And—"

He touched his fingers to her breastplate—or, rather, the air a few fingers-breadth from it when her blue light sprang into being to push him away. Cracks shot through the protective magic, though it seemed marginally better than when Carr last attacked her.

"Perhaps a bit of training?" he suggested. "Maybe avoid taking so many strikes next time?"

Semana laughed in his face. "Speak for yourself, you rutter," she said. "I'd wager I could still pound your face into the mud given half a breath."

"Heh." Darak sneered. "Remind me not to upset you, then."

He walked away, his massive bodyguards Right and Left moving to flank him as he passed them. Crown of Fire took a few steps after Darak, then looked back to Semana. His expression made her rekindled sense of confidence dim and gutter.

"Barbarian," Semana said.

"Queen." Crown of Fire scowled deeply.

"Did you have something to say to me?" she asked. "If so, speak quickly. I have things to do, you know. Avenging my kingdom. Reclaiming my birthright. And the like."

With a slight hesitation, Crown of Fire finally came toward Semana in a rush and clasped her arm. "Stop being a fool. You—"

He trailed off when Semana stared down at his hand on her arm. She looked up, and she could see the dark visage of her mask reflected in his bright eyes. He let go of her, chastened without words.

She gave him some words anyway.

"Who are you to rebuke me?" Semana took a step forward, and he retreated half a step, his expression faltering. "I asked you a question."

Crown of Fire stood up straight. "Dar-Karsk is cunning. He means to deceive you. Trick you…"

Semana activated the slaying magic in her mask, and a forest of ropy tendrils of rotting green power reached out from her head to grasp for Crown. He backed away faster and tripped over a fresh stump where one of the barbarian cadres had chopped down a tree for lumber to build their camp.

"Do I look *weak* to you?" Semana asked. "Do I look like I need your guidance—your protection?"

Crown held up his hands. "I only wish to serve—"

Semana deactivated her plaguefire and leaned over the barbarian lad. "You want me. Yes?"

The barbarian opened his mouth, then closed it. He nodded once.

"You wish to win me." She pressed one booted foot on his chest, holding him in place, then leaned down over her knee. She stared him straight in the eyes. "You wish that I will be grateful to you and give you my body. Do not deny it."

The fire in Crown's eyes gave the answer. That, and the way his body reacted to hers. She could taste his blood in her mouth—feel it coursing through his body. "What else is there?" he asked.

"What indeed." Semana scowled. "My brother wants what I want. He wants our birthright. You, on the other hand—you would seize my body, as others would seize my destiny."

To his credit, Crown of Fire frowned. "I see an enemy, I tell my friend of that enemy," he said. "I want my friend—I will wait until she wants me. It will happen in time."

Semana felt sick. Her skin felt oily and her stomach roiled. She would have vomited all over him, though that would hardly make her look strong. The chance that Crown of Fire would help her was not worth dealing with this. Not for one more moment.

"That will never happen," she said. "You *disgust* me." She removed her foot from his chest and stepped away from him. "Begone, and do not return to me this day. Or any day soon."

The barbarian climbed to one knee and started to speak, but Semana closed her fingers and choked off his words. For a heartbeat, he seemed confused, then he started to gasp and wheeze, trying to make words come out of his closed throat. Semana felt as much as saw his body's growing panic. His eyes started to redden. Horribly, he was still ragingly aroused. Silver Fire.

It would be so easy to let him die. Just hold her concentration another dozen heartbeats and—

Semana released Crown of Fire, and he sagged to the ground, coughing.

"Thanks for your warning," she said. "But I will keep my own counsel regarding my brother. I have known him since we were children. I will pass quite well, thank you."

He blinked at her, barely comprehending. Somehow, he still wore that stupid, ingratiating smile of his. "Then you…" he said. "You don't know him at all. I can help—"

"Leave me." Semana glared. "Now."

Crown of Fire climbed up and staggered away, then disappeared into the gloom.

Semana loosed a sigh, both of relief and consternation. She looked through the camp to the distant western horizon, barely lit by the recently set sun.

If only they could march on Tar Vangr soon.

~

"Soon," Darak said, averting his eyes from the kneeling barbarian. "We march soon."

The curved blade scraped slowly and smoothly down Darak's thigh until it touched the edge of the furry black splotch that had started to grow just above and to the left of his knee. A twinge of pain made Darak want to pull his leg away from the razor, but over the years he'd grown more than used to the sharp treatment. Not that he would pass up the opportunity to rebuke the hand that pricked him.

"Ware as you work," he said. "This is a high honor, you know."

Down on one knee before Darak in the breezy tent, Crown of Fire bowed his head slightly in acknowledgement, though he did not meet Darak's eye. That was good—the lad could be trained after all. It had only taken him a year of punishment to learn his proper place: on his knees.

"I continue, Dar-Karsk?" Crown asked.

Darak looked down at his leg. A tiny bit of blood trickled around the blemish, meaning that this particular corruption wasn't yet ready to come free. Not cleanly, anyway. Crown could remove it, with some pain, and leave an angry red hollow where it had grown, or Darak could leave it in place and then suffer whenever the leg of his breeches or the fold of his robe touched it.

"Lathe it away," Darak said. "And be deft about it, lad."

"Yes." Crown went back to shaving Darak's leg, cutting around the sore.

He smiled crookedly. No doubt Crown of Fire had seen more winters than he had, but the barbarian was so far below him in station it seemed grotesque to acknowledge him as some sort of equal, let alone a superior. Crown owed Darak his life many times over, and he made an excellent servant. And Darak liked to look at him—his face, his body, his submission—and use him on occasion.

Such a useful boy.

62

"Tell me again my sister's words," Darak said. "Exactly. Word for word."

"She trusts you," Crown said. "She said you want what she wants, and that I disgust her."

Darak seized Crown's face, thumb and forefinger pressing his cheeks inward against his teeth. "Exactly," he said again, slower. "Word for word."

He would make his own assessment of what Semana's words meant.

The barbarian repeated it again, almost exactly. This time he said, "my brother wants what I want," but the meaning seemed the same. He had gone over it several times, and Darak had to admit it seemed telling. Semana trusted him, or at least she was his ally. For now.

The events of the High Moot at Iseldra's Folly had taught Darak something of great value, and again with Lathkgar of the Thundering Hooves. Semana had great power, and she had been fortunate enough in her use of it thus far. But she overplayed herself. She'd told him only a little of her time in hiding as Mask the mage-slayer, and she seemed to have completely reversed her course. Now that her secret was revealed, she reveled in the attention. Revealed all of her strength before she had to. And that was a vulnerability he could exploit. He could still control her.

"And I cannot put you in her bed," Darak said. "She has rejected you entirely?"

Crown made a disgusted face and shook his head.

"Pity."

The lathing sickle snagged and sharp pain surged up and down his leg. His foot went immediately numb and little shocks ripped through his hip and made him queasy.

"Stop," he said. "*Stop.*"

Crown of Fire's hands clenched tighter in his surprise, and that made the pain all the worse. Worldfire swelled within him, fueled by rage and terror, and Darak smashed a backhand into Crown's pretty face. He stumbled back and flopped to the floor. In doing so, Darak glimpsed a sliver of well-muscled flesh under the collar of his leathers, and a sudden thought stayed his sharp word. Crown looked up at him, confused—he expected the rebuke—but then he saw Darak's face. He licked his lips.

Yes. He knew what was coming.

Darak opened his mouth to issue the command, but another voice spoke up behind him first.

"Dar-Karsk," said Fellis the Night Wolf. "We will have words."

Darak looked around at her. She blended remarkably well into the shadows, between her almost purple skin and glittering eyes like pools of deeper black.

She was beautiful the way a storm on the evening horizon was beautiful, to be admired from a distance but feared as it approaches. Also, she had killed hundreds of men and women—a hundred times a hundred—and the instant she scented weakness, she would put an arrow through his eye before he even realized she'd drawn her bowstring.

"Your pet." She looked to Crown of Fire, her gaze suspicious and murderous.

"Do not concern yourself." Darak gestured to Crown, extending two fingers toward him. Obediently, the barbarian came forward on hands and knees until he knelt beside Darak. He ran his fingers over his forearm, then slid his lips around Darak's fingers. And sucked.

"Very well." Fellis cocked her head slightly to one side, intrigued.

"You did not bring Carr the Axe with you," Darak said. "I was surprised to see the two of you united in a single cause. I thought you hated one another."

"Your murder of Afferath changed many things," Fellis said. "Some among the Circle believe alliance more valuable than individual strength."

Interesting. "And so now you seek an alliance with me, but you are not yet convinced."

The Druid nodded once. "Convince me."

Darak pulled his fingers from Crown of Fire's mouth and ran them along his cheeks. "I suppose Carr has filled your ears with her own doubts," he said. "I have amassed a horde, yes, but the autumnal winds blow, dooming our cause. Even an Angel of Ruin cannot hold a horde through the winter. By spring, when we can march upon Tar Vangr, our armies will have dissolved to infighting and desertion."

Fellis nodded a second time. Indeed Carr had.

"I do not intend to wait until summer or even spring," Darak said. "We march upon Tar Vangr before the autumn is out, and we will throw down the mage-city before the year is done. Ruin's Night will be their undoing—Ruin's Night of this year."

"Bold, certainly." Fellis raised an eyebrow. "Foolish, perhaps."

Fellis's eyes were drawn to the Crown of Fire, who had moved from Darak's hand to kissing his belly. Darak liked the sensation, but liked the effect it had on Fellis more.

"Bold," Darak said. "The cold will claim many of us, but surprise will be our ally. I know the weaknesses of Tar Vangr's walls, and I know how to defeat them."

Crown of Fire worked on the laces of Darak's breeches.

"You worry about Semana," Darak said. "You worry that she rules, and not I."

Fellis nodded a third time.

"I defer to her when I have need," Darak said. "She has power and she has love. She inspires rage and fervor and passion. If my cause is to succeed, she must stand at my side. But such will not always be the case."

"No?" Fellis's hand had dipped to the mound between her legs. "You will turn upon her."

Crown of Fire slid Darak's breeches down around his ankles and worked upon him.

"When the time is right," Darak said. "You will know the moment. I will put her in her place and it is my destiny that will be fulfilled, not hers." He hissed a sharp intake of breath, little shivers passing all through him. "Until then, I will use her, as you will use me."

As he used Crown of Fire, who uttered a murmuring moan of pleasure. Whether it was true or not, Darak neither knew nor cared.

"We all use each other," said Fellis the Night Wolf. "Such is Ruin."

The Druid undid the laces of her leathers and let them fall to the ground.

FIVE

The Dusk Sea

H o!" called a woman's voice. "Ware!"

The ugly man up in the rigging looked, just in time to dodge a falling hunk of metal from above. Pirates scattered on the deck some ten paces below, and the slightly curved piece rebounded off the railing and spun out into the gray sky. Davargorn winced as it smashed into one of the rings with a hollow *bang*, sending a shower of sparks down among the greasy clouds. The rings continued their slow cycling, propelling the skyship through the air. They emitted a dull groaning sound, one he'd grown accustomed to over his time on the *Lancer*.

With a grunt, Davargorn swung back onto the rigging and climbed down toward the deck.

Life among Shard's pirates had not passed as Davargorn had expected. He'd thought they'd throw him in the brig immediately, if not right over the side of the *Lancer*, and by all rights, they should have. And yet, that second day, they'd had him out on the deck, learning the ropes and chains and mechanisms of the skyship. They hadn't armed him, of course—not at first, anyway—but taking a weapon and killing all of them wouldn't have offered much difficulty.

And yet, he'd done no such thing. Hadn't even been tempted.

Tanak—the squat, broad pirate captain who'd spared his life during the assault on the mage-caravel—looked up at him from the deck, wispy gray-and-purple hair wafting around her gray-skinned face. She'd spoken for him at every turn, though she had no reason to trust him. And the rest of the thirty or so crew had followed suit. They treated him like one of them.

Davargorn slipped down from the rigging and onto the deck, clapping his hands to rid them of the abrasive tingling. A powerfully built woman came up to him, scowling, and Davargorn braced for a confrontation. This one, at least, hated him, and why not? She still had bandages over the wounds Davargorn had given her.

"Chikar," he said.

"Ruined," she said in her Free Islands accent.

They faced each other over two paces, and Davargorn could feel her desire to cut him down with either the sword at her belt or the caster on her opposite hip. With that, she could kill him from any distance on the ship.

"Lieutenant," Tanak said in her gruff voice as she approached. "You have duties."

"Aye." The big woman spoke to Tanak but had eyes only for Davargorn. There was a promise in those eyes, one that he'd seen plenty often enough over his violent life. She went away, muttering.

"That one means to kill me," Davargorn said.

"Chikar is slow to forgive," she said, "and you did try to kill her."

"Fair." Davargorn shrugged. "The real question is, why don't you? Mean to kill me, I mean."

Tanak looked entirely unfazed. She was a solid block of muscle, more like a mountain than a woman, which made it especially odd when she stuck out her tongue and hissed, like a gutter child mocking someone for being a fool. "Come," she said.

"Where?" Davargorn glanced around. "Now?"

Tanak didn't answer—she just started walking away, toward the aftcastle and the stairs down to the bowels of the skyship. Davargorn followed her, dragging his club foot—which had pulsed with niggling pain every day since Luether. Small blue candles sparked to life as they went, though he didn't need them. His milky white eye could see perfectly well in the dim light. He'd never been in this part of the ship; his berth seemed to include access to the crew quarters, the deck, and the crow's nest. He had only once visited the hold, and the dirty looks he got there had chased him away. If Tanak was leading him somewhere dark to murder him, she had the advantage.

They climbed down a groaning metal staircase, the steps greasy and barely lit. The clank of a mage-engine running at fair efficiency resounded through the metal halls. Davargorn could feel the faint vibration through his feet and up his legs, but it wasn't as bad as any mage-caravel he'd ever ridden. Lady Shard insisted her fleet be kept in good working condition.

"Where are you taking me?" Davargorn asked, but Tanak offered no reply.

They crossed past the mage-engine—a riot of pistons, batteries, and wheels that spawned a churning maelstrom of blue and silver fire, burning without heat or fuel—and made their way along a rickety catwalk into a deeper chamber. Davargorn could feel the tingling energy of the engine on his skin. All the tiny aches and pains from his wounds and sore spots redoubled, tickling at him unsettlingly.

"Captain?"

Again, no answer.

Turning the crank, Tanak opened a hatch deeper into the ship, and they entered a small set of rooms connected by a short corridor. A small window of dusky glass allowed him to look into each of the cells, only one of which was lit inside with tiny blue candles. Davargorn looked to Tanak.

"Look," she said, gesturing toward the door.

Davargorn did as she suggested, closing his white eye, which got blurry in the light. Inside sat Lan Ravalis, looking sullen and a bit bruised, but otherwise unharmed. He slept on his side on the plain stone cot, head pillowed on his crossed arm. His chest rose and fell steadily. Seeing him surprised Davargorn, who would have expected the pirates to have thrown the man overboard. Lan wasn't the type to join them, after all, nor would he have begged for his life.

"You know him," Tanak said. Not a question.

Davargorn bit his lip. He wished he had Semana's inscrutability or even her will. He didn't even have a mask to hide his reactions. Denying all would only make her distrust him. A half-truth, then.

"I was to ward him," Davargorn said, which was true enough. "He's someone important."

"Does he have a name?" Tanak asked.

Davargorn shrugged.

Tanak scrutinized Davargorn closely but did not offer any clear sign she doubted him. Good.

"He has a noble bearing, fine features, a gentle living," she said. "In my profession, you learn to recognize these things. A potential ransom makes him a valuable prisoner."

"The others wanted to kill him, but you stopped them?" Davargorn asked.

"Not him." Tanak made a rough little sound in her throat like a chuckle. "All it took was one look to decide he was worth keeping alive. The whole crew agreed. That and the armor we found him scrambling to don when we took him prisoner. Gold-inlaid, you know." She scrunched her eyes and nose, and Davargorn realized the expression indicated wryness. "You, on the other hand."

"Me?" Davargorn scowled. "I'm nobody."

"I saw something in you," she said. "Do you have a name? Or do I call you Nobody?"

He opened his twisted mouth, then shut it again. He shook his head.

"Well then, Nobody," she said. "Come with me."

Without further preamble, she continued through the brig corridor. Davargorn frowned after her, unsure what to do. He glanced back into Lan's cell and found the man sitting on his cot, staring up at him. The king looked haggard and weary, his expression unreadable. Whether he had heard Tanak's words or not, Davargorn couldn't say, but the faint smile on Lan's lips made him uneasy.

After a moment, he turned from the viewport and followed the stocky captain through another oval door, deeper into the ship. The *Lancer* was built like the *Avenger*, upon which he had ridden more than once, but it was smaller and more efficient. He would learn its ways quickly enough.

Just on the other side of another oval door, Tanak waited for him to join her, then shuffled around him in the cramped corridor so she could get to the crank that sealed it. Davargorn saw no one nearby, and he couldn't help but feel the butt of her caster grinding into his hip as she moved past. Murdering her in the dark and tossing her body into the burning energies of the mage-engine occurred to him only as a passing fancy. Instead, he found himself primarily marveling at the thick, powerful muscles of her legs and hindquarters and how warm they felt up against him. She had to bend over slightly when the crank stuck, giving her better leverage and him a better feel.

Finally, Tanak ground the seal shut despite its protests, then blew out a brief exhalation. "Been meaning to get that scarred thing fixed." She looked up at him, cheeks slightly rosy. "What?"

Davargorn's throat had gone dry. He looked away.

"Heh." Tanak was not at all fooled. She intentionally thrust her way past him and continued on.

She took the corridor's turns with such sinuous efficiency that Davargorn had to fight to keep up. His foot ached by the time she finally stopped and spun open a porthole. Inside was a surprisingly comfortable chamber with pillows and furnishings and a rather spacious bed, considering the small space allotted. It took Davargorn a second to realize he was looking at Tanak's own quarters.

"Why bring me here?"

"I'm that hard to read, am I?" The captain turned to Davargorn and gave him a sympathetic look. "Tell me, boy—tell me about me."

Davargorn frowned at the odd question. She was short, broad of chest and shoulder, built more like a boulder than any woman he'd ever seen. A good fighter. A stern commander. And she was very, very short. "You're a dwarf?" he suggested.

"Angarran." Her face curled sourly. "Better than being a ruinscarred."

Davargorn bristled but kept his tongue. "I thought your people extinct," he said.

"No surprise." Tanak crossed her arms. "You don't strike me as well informed."

Her words nettled Davargorn. "I can strike you however I like."

Tanak didn't seem intimidated. In fact, she looked him up and down with an appraising eye. "That what you want? To strike me?"

"What?" Davargorn recoiled slightly at the odd suggestion. Then he realized, and it stunned him beyond words. "You want—you want to rut me?"

"Why not? I led you to my chamber. I opened my door to you." Tanak grinned wide. "Could be your last chance 'ere my lady sees you, and who knows what'll happen then?"

"What do you mean?"

Tanak leaned against the frame of her cabin's port door. "We put into Atropis in the morn," she said. "All new recruits gots to go before the lady— Lady Shard, Queen of the Dusk Skies—for her judgment. You're good enough to fly with me thus far, but if she don't like the look of you, over the side you go, and down into the depths. That's the kindest way to die, anyway." She reached out and touched his slightly pointed chin. "Besides, you're just ugly—not repulsive."

"My thanks," Davargorn said with a scowl.

"Could be your last chance," Tanak said again. "Lady Shard could be wearing your skin as a cloak tomorrow. You want a good rut, I'm offering. And best believe I'm good at it."

"I can't—" Davargorn frowned. "I can't. I've sworn off love."

"Love?" Tanak met his dramatic words with a raucous laugh and pounded her stomach. "*Love?* The fuck is that? I meant a good rutting. You don't want it, that's your burning loss."

She shoved him back against the wall, more playfully than in earnest. When he tried to speak up, she shoved him again, harder this time.

"Maybe it's better we don't, if you're gonna talk this way," Tanak said. "You get all weepy and moon over my nethers like some poet and I'll cut your blade off meself, and what good will that do anyone? Just a mess to clean up. Shard'll probably do you worse, unless you give her a reason not to."

Davargorn stared at her, entirely at a loss.

"So." Tanak cracked her knuckles one by one. "Is that a nay on the sex?"

"Of course it's a nay!" The reply had more heat than he intended and his voice wavered.

"Heh. Your ruin." Tanak clicked her tongue at his flustered reaction. "You ever change your mind, speak it. And remember—I'm looking for sex. Not your soul."

That concept boggled Davargorn's mind.

She turned away stiffly, without sway or grace as Alistra might have done. There was nothing suggestive about her movements or her body, but he couldn't stop watching her backside. Why did she fluster him so? Then she shut the cabin door and spun the crank to seal him out. It clicked firmly shut.

Ridiculous. There was no way she could allure him at all. Preposterous.

It was only then Davargorn realized he was hard as a rock and straining at his breeches.

There was something honest about the pirate's broad face and shoulders—the unaffected way she walked. The forthright way she had propositioned him had initially taken him off guard, but...

Well, standing here in the hall, he didn't much expect he could salvage any of this. Even if she would still be receptive—hadn't she suggested as much?—he felt like a fool. He looked both directions, but saw no observer of his shame. Good.

Davargorn slunk away, cursing under his breath. He thought about going by the brig to see Lan, but somehow he knew the king in exile would recognize his shame and laugh at him. And that, he could not stand. Instead, he took a detour to some isolated corner of the ship to relieve himself.

That accomplished, he slumped back to his hammock and watched the shadows lengthen through the small porthole near his head. Dusk fell, and the following morning, they would reach Atropis and the capricious Lady Shard. He knew only a little of her from his time in Luether, and suspected his excellent fighting skills might save his life. And then he would be one of her pirates for true.

And moreover, he *wanted* to be.

For the first time in what felt like years, Davargorn felt like he had a purpose.

He went to sleep thinking of that—of his new life—and tried not to dwell too long on Tanak's excellent backside or the strength in those muscles of hers.

~

The following morning dawned bleak and chill, and the dark clouds on the horizon blended so perfectly with the Dusk Sea that the world seemed to have no concrete directions. The *Lancer* seemed to drift, unhindered by sea or sky, and Davargorn thought if he did not keep his sharp eyes open, they would crash at any moment. It was a false confidence: he couldn't very well control the skyship, any more than he could control the direction of his own life.

Perhaps Lady Shard would approve of him and thus he could keep following this particular path, or perhaps she'd condemn him to execution. He could do little about that, either, though he mildly hoped she would not sentence him to die. The life of a sky-pirate seemed to agree with him.

It was the opposite for Lan, naturally. The fallen King of Tar Vangr lurked, sullen and brooding, in his cell in the *Lancer's* brig, and he'd had only sour looks for Davargorn when he visited before dawn.

"They'll kill us both," Lan had said. "You know that."

"Me, mayhap." Davargorn shrugged. "You're too valuable."

After that, Lan had tried to convince Davargorn to let him out—perhaps he could reclaim his armor and they could fight their way free—but to no avail. Davargorn hardly wanted to destroy his pact with Shard before he'd even attempted to strike it.

He'd seen Atropis before, of course—on the mage-caravel heading south the previous year, for example—but from an entirely different vantage point. From below, the broken mage-city towered above them, terrible and forbidding, a dire warning of the hubris of men and women long past. From above, however, level with the highest reaches of the city, Davargorn finally understood its scope. It rose a thousand paces above the sea, and at its zenith must have stood twice as tall. Below, Davargorn remembered a morass of great pillars tipped on their sides and edges, lashed by vicious waves. Up here, Davargorn saw a thriving port of a dozen skyships docked above the clouds, small ornithopters whirring among crumbling spires like tines of a crown. And when the sun finally burned through the storm clouds on the eastern horizon, its light sparkled off the bright stone and lent the place a majesty he hadn't seen since the fateful night he and Semana had stood at the prow of the *Avenger* as it approached Tar Vangr.

Why had he thought of that moment, just now? He shivered.

Davargorn counted fully thirteen skyships, including the *Lancer*. He hadn't imagined so many ships yet flew in the World of Ruin. Did Shard mean to sail to war? It seemed so, but against whom?

One of the skyships, a particularly large and sleek specimen, looked somehow familiar, but he had only half a heartbeat to squint into the sun before a woman's voice called his name from below. There stood Chikar on the deck, a loop of barbed chains in her hands. She was looking at him with an expression that would brook no nonsense, and he climbed down the rigging rapidly.

"Those for me?" He nodded to the chains.

Chikar offered a wicked smile. "If you want to lose your hands, 'haps." She slid out the loops so Davargorn could see the edges pounded to razor-fine edges. " 'Haps we try that."

"Go ahead," Davargorn said. "See what your captain has to say then."

Chikar's lips pulled back from jagged teeth. "Tanak won't always protect you, ruined boy."

Davargorn could say the same to her, but—as he didn't relish being thrown to his death before he even got to the hearing to decide whether he'd be thrown to his death—he restrained the urge.

Once, he'd have immediately stabbed her and watched her body topple into open air, but he restrained the urge. Of *course*, Chikar wouldn't trust him, and of course she'd want to upset him. He was a disruptive force who threatened her. He didn't hate her, nor did he blame her.

"I look forward to sailing with you," he said. "If that's the decision."

Chikar's eyes widened slightly in confusion, then her scowl returned, redoubled. "Mock me at your peril, ugly boy," she said. "I only hope I'm the one who gets to push you overboard."

Likewise. Silently, he nodded and let Chikar lead him over the plank and onto Atropis.

Other members of the crew pushed past them onto the dock, laughing and boasting and carrying on without a concern. All around them, skyships unloaded their cargo, rearmed their weapons, and discharged pirates of every shape and color, all of them lounging about listless.

Davargorn had only a moment to enjoy the sharp breeze before Tanak appeared, her expression sour. "No sense delaying this. We'll have the ugly boy straightened out before the sun rises high."

Along with four pirates came Lan, his hands bound with rusty manacles, his face a downcast glower of disapproval. At least he wasn't looking directly at Davargorn, so as not to give him away.

"What of him?" Chikar prodded Lan with her bladed chain, earning a scowl. "Your golden calf?"

"Oh, the Lady'll want to see this prisoner right away, I think," Tanak said. "Bring him."

With that, she turned on her heel and led them all down a set of steps into the towering city.

In contrast to the stocked skyport above, the halls and open rooms of the pirate haven were full to bursting with people at their ease, quite as though a war wasn't about to break out. They lounged, already lazy and growing fat on what Davargorn could only assume were ill-gotten coin and booty. The faces evinced various heritages: winterborn from the wilds of the north and summerblood from the hot lands of the south, boisterous folk from the Free Isles and a sort of folk he'd never seen before with sallow, yellow-green skin and hair the color of leaves in summer.

"The Lady does not sail to war," Chikar said as they walked. Davargorn couldn't say whether it was a question until Tanak replied with a shrug.

"You sound disappointed," Tanak said. "Ent her war. We'll do as we ever do—plunder the weak an' loot the corpses. Maybe even a mage-city will fall this time. Luether—even Tar Vangr."

"Didn't the Eunuch King sail south to redeem Luether from ruin?"

"Luether *again*, then," Tanak said. "Ent our business. We sail where the Lady says. As ever."

With a grunt, Chikar prodded Lan forward. He'd stiffened at the conversation, and Davargorn savored the irony. Chikar couldn't know the very man she spoke of was her prisoner. The Usurper King of Tar Vangr would be worth a mighty ransom indeed, if they could convince anyone to pay it.

Usurper King. The thought had come so smoothly Davargorn scowled. What did he care who sat on what gilded seat in Tar Vangr? He was long quit of all that, and he never meant to return.

At the end of the hall, Tanak wound a crank to summon a lift, and the little group huddled onto the small platform as it made its shaking, shuddering way down into the bowels of the city. Oddly enough, the outer, inverted triangle of the upper city of Atropis seemed to be partly hollow inside, like the interior of a bee's nest. Chambers connected by rusty catwalks studded the sides of the walls, leaving the space in the middle mostly empty except for tracks that lifts rode up and down, side to side, to service the whole of the suspended community. The lift they rode went down for a time, then turned at an intersection and rode toward what looked like the middle of the city: a tall spire like a blade sheathed in the larger casing of Atropis. That, it seemed, was the place from which Shard commanded.

The curious city might have seemed wondrous indeed had Davargorn bothered to document it all, but his mind churned over his forthcoming battle to convince the Pirate Queen of the Dusk Sea of his value and loyalty.

Davargorn took the opportunity to rehearse in his mind what he intended to say to Lady Shard to justify keeping him alive. He'd grown very accustomed to serving women of power. With any luck, the pirate queen would recognize the same thing in him that Semana and Alistra had—the thing that Lan had stabbed him with in their earlier conversation on the subject: that any woman could use him with a wink and a smile. Davargorn hated that about himself, but it didn't make it any less true.

He and Mask—*Semana*—had never actually met Lady Shard, and but he'd heard stories: that no one had ever seen her face and lived to speak of it, which was good, since Davargorn couldn't afford to fall in love with her as well. Also that Shard was notoriously duplicitous and wouldn't hesitate to betray a would-be ally for coin or advantage. Davargorn didn't much like working for such a mercenary master, but never in his life had he really had a choice of whom to serve: Semana, Alistra, and now Shard.

Unless she cast him over the side of her mountainous city and that was that.

Nay, this might be his best and last chance at living a good life, and he wouldn't let it slip through his fingers. So much rode upon this moment. He would swear any vow she demanded of him, and he would keep it. He was no oathbreaker—no longer, anyway.

All these things roiled in Davargorn's mind as the lift trembled and shuddered to a halt, and they filed off onto a platform fanning out from the internal spire. The partly open chamber into which they strode boasted a wide assortment of maps as large as tapestries that hung from the walls. They depicted the Dusk Sea and its environs, Tar Vangr and the winter wilds, the Luetharr archipelago and the nearby Free Isles. Other maps showed stretches so foreign to Davargorn they might have been utter gibberish.

Half a dozen sky pirates worked in this chamber—all women. Perhaps Lady Shard didn't much like the presence of menfolk. And when he came to think of it, he'd never met or heard of a male sky pirate captain. His perception of his chances dwindled somewhat.

There she was, in the center of the chamber, clad in a black robe and veil, every inch of her hidden from view. One had only to see and hear her for a moment to know Shard for the powerful woman she was. She turned as they entered, as though she had expected them.

"Tanak, well returned," she said. "And what have you brought me this time?"

Davargorn opened his mouth, but all that came out was a strangled moan.

Standing beside Lady Shard, her distinctive fire-red hair pulled up behind her head, stood Ovelia Dracaris the Bloodbreaker. She wore a crimson bandage over her eyes, just as she had when last Davargorn saw her, and she rested one hand on the ornate hilt of her flamed sword *Draca* at her belt, while the other she held lightly over her swollen belly.

She was with child, Davargorn realized, and that only drove him to new heights of rage.

"What is this?" Shard asked, even as Ovelia stepped in front of her, sword half-drawn.

A garbled shriek rang out, and Davargorn realized only belatedly that he had made the sound. Then he was leaping through the air, unarmed but uncaring. He had to kill her. Had to...

Two nearby sky pirates grabbed him and threw him to the ground. Hands were on his arms, legs, mouth, and he punched and bit and fought. There was no sense to his attack—no purpose to any of it.

He only knew that he had to kill Ovelia Dracaris, and if he managed that, he could die content.

Then a heavy boot smashed into his face, and he knew no more.

BOOK TWO: LONERS

Nineteen Years Ago—Spring, 962 Sorceris Annis—
the Palace of Winter, Tar Vangr, City of Steel

H IS MOUTH CLOSED AROUND the nipple of her left breast with a sharp
twinge of pain that gripped her, just as it did every time. Lenalin braced
herself for the inevitable discomfort, hoping that, this time, he wouldn't do it.
But of course, he did. When he sucked—rather strongly as he grew older—it
felt like he was pulling something out of her. Feeding on her. Taking her life.
Every day, she felt a bit weaker.

Perhaps that was simply the princess's foul mood—certainly it was no fault
of her child's. A child who looked more like his horrid, greedy father by the day.

Prince Darak offered her a gurgling little sound of contentment and sucked
deeper. Lenalin winced and looked away. Under her breath, she cursed the
wetnurse, who had taken sick and couldn't feed the prince that day or the
previous one. And with the same breath, she cursed herself for stubbornly
asserting she would feed her own child, rather than give him to one of the
Ravalis's slaves or hire some nursing woman from Low-City. Ovelia could
have at least *tried* to talk her out of it, but instead she'd simply accepted
Lenalin's word and left her alone.

Quite the friend, indeed.

The pain didn't pass—it never did—and each time, Lenalin had to grow
accustomed to it anew. Afterward, the soreness would pulse like its own
heartbeat in her breast. She could only imagine how awful the last year would
have been if she had to nurse him every day. The prince would see his first
Ruin's Night soon. Perhaps he could be weaned to eat food. Surely he was old
enough. Right?

When he was finally done, Lenalin set Darak aside with some relief. The
babe cuddled into his blankets, burped, and blessedly went to sleep. The
soreness in her breasts convinced Lenalin it was a mistake not to call for a
slave, but she hated to admit fault even more than she hated nursing.

Quiet so as not to wake the little beast, Lenalin wrapped her dress back in
place and rose. Her stomach growled, as it always did after feeding Darak, but
the concept of food passing her lips nauseated her. She really wanted to find

Ovelia, or perhaps her father. Not that she had something of import to convey, but she had so few friends, and she needed one of them. To feel less alone.

Walking made her backside twinge.

She thought about Paeter, and the bruises he'd given her the previous night ached. She wished she'd seen him for what he was when they first met—that she'd believed Ovelia's warnings—but what could she have done? The alliance between Denerre and Ravalis—crowns of the last two Mage-Cities of Calatan—was too important. In order for the race of man to survive, this marriage had to pass.

After two years in Paeter Ravalis's bed, Lenalin had little use for the race of man.

At least he rarely pushed himself on her these days. He already had his son and heir, after all, and he didn't much need her now. Often sex was part of his tortures, however, and his touch filled her with a dull, mute sort of horror. The previous night, after putting Darak down for the night, Paeter had bound Lenalin's wrists to the posts of her bed and alternated his pleasure with jolts of a thaumaturgical crop that made her body contort and buck. The prods left only small red marks on her skin that faded quickly but hurt for a long time. She'd long since stopped begging for mercy, as that only stoked his rage.

About halfway through, when he'd been paying particular attention to her backside—hence her pain in trying to walk—Lenalin had chanced to see his brother Lan watching from the shadows. Paeter did that sometimes: bid his brother to watch him torture his wife. She hadn't bothered calling out to Lan for comfort, but simply stared at him. She hadn't taken her eyes from his face, so that he had no choice but to feel her pain—force him to acknowledge her as a person. She wasn't sure it worked—wasn't sure he was a person at all, let alone that he had a conscience—but what else could she do?

As yet, Paeter had never given Lan leave to use Lenalin himself, but she wouldn't be surprised when he did. She expected all her defiance would only increase his fury, the way it did with Paeter.

The abuse had been going on for years. The first time it happened, Lenalin threatened a horrible vengeance, and Paeter hadn't reacted angrily. Instead, he'd sat calmly and explained the facts. As much as Ravalis needed the Denerre, so too did the Denerre need the Ravalis. Their Blood was reduced to almost nothing, and there were plenty of Ravalis heirs in the offing. If something befell Paeter, then the Blood Denerre would not long survive him. Demetrus was more than capable of taking her father's throne. They would make a show of mourning, of course, and bring several scapegoats to justice—Ovelia

Dracaris, for instance, and the Frostburn—and then the summerblood would rule Tar Vangr.

It was not *what* he said, exactly, but *how* he said it. Such confidence. Such assurance. As if he knew those facts as naturally as breathing. She believed him, and moreover, she could see the patterns he spoke of. Denerre had waned in power for years, becoming increasingly reliant upon the Ravalis. If she did not abase herself, her Blood—her people—her city would suffer.

In truth, it wasn't concern for others that stayed her hand. It was the utter certainty that whatever she said, whoever she said it to, it would make no difference. The abuse would continue, and only her silence kept it from growing worse. She had no escape. No hope.

Silence was her only defiance these days. Lenalin had schooled herself not to react to the terror—learned to ignore the pain. At first, Paeter simply hurt her more, but that only increased her resolve. That first night she'd tried the technique, she'd outlasted him, and he'd finally given up. He came less frequently after that. She absorbed this hate, holding fast to that bright shining moment when he would walk away, exhausted and angry that she had denied him satisfaction. It had become her only recourse.

Relief was coming, she knew. The war in Echvar would take Paeter far from this place, and Lenalin would finally have some peace. Perhaps she'd even have some good fortune for once, and a fortunate barbarian would part his head or at least his little blade from his body. It seemed too much to wish for, particularly with her father's Shadow watching over him. The Frostburn would not let any harm come to Tar Vangr's crown prince, of course. He would never neglect his duty. His fate.

Fate had never been Lenalin's ally.

Darak woke with a hiccup and started squalling, and she cursed.

This time Lenalin didn't hesitate to ring the bell to summon a servant, who arrived within a ten count or so. A young, dark-skinned Ravalis woman with big breasts full of milk for the greedy prince. Probably a slave. Disgusting practice, slavery, much like being Paeter's "wife." No one should have to bow and scrape to anyone's will—not unless they chose to, anyway.

"Highness," she said with a low bow. "How may I serve you?"

It wasn't her fault Lenalin hated her. She hated everyone—except Ovelia and her father.

"Take care of that." Lenalin gestured vaguely in the direction of the whining Darak, and the servant woman immediately crossed toward the small bed. "I'm going."

"Going where, Highness?"

By the time she looked back, Lenalin was gone.

～

The dusty air of the passages surrounded her in warm darkness, heated from the rising Narfire pulsing through the mountain at the heart of Tar Vangr. The life of the world coursed beneath her feet, and it always made her vaguely sick at such close proximity. It felt like her guts came untethered and started to drift, and her thoughts unspooled in unnatural ways. She became unmoored—out of control.

As a little girl, exploring the tunnels with Ovelia, she'd liked the buoyant freedom—loved disconnecting from the world. The Narfire made her giddy and relaxed, but she was past the time when she could ease her grasp on anything. These days, holding tight was the only way she could survive.

Tiny blue candles flickered to life at her approach, their relatively simple magic drawing a flicker of her body's warmth to power themselves. The candles in the passages between the walls were placed in such a way as to proffer the bare minimum of light without reflecting any illumination near any of the dozens of spyholes where it might be noted. Whoever had designed the corridors had done so with a masterful plan for espionage in mind, and though Lenalin was no expert at such things, she had often admired the foresight of the builders of the Winter Palace.

Along her course, she looked into the chambers of the palace, noted the secret negotiations and veiled threats exchanged between nobles, servants, and spies. Few knew these corridors even existed, much less the location of all the peep holes and listening spaces where the acoustics enhanced even the slightest whispers. When she was young, Lenalin loved spying this way, secrets she barely understood, but as a woman grown, it lost much of its luster. These folk and their small conflicts; all about coin and trade and sex and other equally petty concerns. She'd moved beyond such things, as a matter of fate and necessity. She looked in each chamber, saw folk she didn't recognize or care about, and passed each by. She moved cautiously enough that anyone in those rooms would think any sound but the quiet scamper of rats. She only cared for Orbrin and Ovelia; either would make her feel better.

She found them both, and not at all how she expected.

It came to pass near the top of the palace, in one of the guest rooms. She almost passed by as easily and quickly as the others, but the sparkling candlelight caught her attention.

She saw Ovelia's hair first, the way such fire always attracted attention. Lenalin loved and envied her friend's wild flow of scarlet locks, the shock of red clashing with her rich brown skin. Her red dress was halfway open, pulled down from her chest and up over her waist while she half-sat, half-lay on the bed, back arched, body taut in pleasure. One hand grasped one of her big breasts, while the other clutched the silver-haired head between her thighs as she rocked forward and back.

Powerful moans escaped Ovelia's lips, and Lenalin felt a sudden rush of envious desire. She just had to stay and watch. Her lord and husband never pleased her in that way—Paeter had never even *tried*—and seeing Ovelia in the grip of such shuddering pleasure lit a spark in Lenalin's core. She reached down and pulled her skirt up over the lacy stocking of one long leg.

Then Ovelia said a single word that froze Lenalin and blew a cold wind over her rising heat.

"Orbrin."

It was only then that Lenalin recognized her father. She'd rarely seen him at this angle, since he was much taller than she. The closest analogy she could draw was watching him at table, eating—gah, she didn't even want to *think* about that. Now that he rose, hooking his elbows under Ovelia's knees, Lenalin saw is his powerful stature and she shivered again. She didn't want to see this.

"My queen," Orbrin said. "Matir—"

Ovelia gasped in pleasure and nodded vigorously. "My king…"

Lenalin hardly knew what was going on, but hearing her father call her best friend by her mother's name while he rutted her… That was simply too much. She didn't know what to think.

And she was still on fire.

Lenalin hurried away, faster and much less carefully than when she made her way up through the passages. She didn't care if anyone heard—couldn't even think about it. She just had to get away. Had to keep moving. Had to escape the heat growing inside her. This terrible, terrifying desire—

And it was at that moment that she came across the Frostburn.

He loomed out of the darkness ahead of her like a ghost, like a shadow detaching itself from the larger darkness. Only his face had a touch of color, and if the blue light hadn't reflected off his pale chin, she wouldn't have seen him at all. His dark eyes were like daggers in the darkness.

"Princess?" he asked.

Lenalin staggered back, startled but not afraid, and pressed herself up against the wall. She put one hand over her heart, which was pounding hard enough to burst her chest. And her core was on fire, as though her whole body would melt around her shameful desire.

She knew him, as much as anyone could. He was Orbrin's devoted servant—his squire—and he had served the Blood of Winter for Lenalin's entire life. He had been a constant companion—her shadow, who watched from beyond her sight. She could trust him implicitly and knew that he cared only for her safety. And yet, she could not recall a single full conversation she had shared with the man.

"Do—do you pass well, princess?" the Frostburn asked after a long pause. "Are you hurt?"

"No," Lenalin said. "I—I pass well. I'm well."

The Frostburn nodded. "Good."

They stood looking at one another for a long moment, the blue candles flickering to either side. The corridors were not built for ease of passage, and less than an arm's length separated them. Lenalin breathed heavily, trembling. She saw the muscles working in his jaw, the blood pumping in his neck. Lenalin tried to catch her breath but couldn't. Not with the hungry way he was looking at her now—

"Well," the Frostburn said. "Take care."

He started to go, but Lenalin caught his wrist. "Wait."

The Frostburn looked down at her hand on his arm, eyes wide in utter surprise. She had not, to her memory, ever touched him at all, let alone like this. But something had risen up inside her: something angry that refused to let him abandon her as well. Something warm and desperate.

"Princess," the Frostburn said. "What passes—?"

She pressed her fingers to his lips to silence him, then traced them along his cheek until she could take tentative hold of his head. He made no objection. She twisted her fingers in the faintly sweat-damp curls at the back of his neck and she moved her face close to his. Their shared gaze never wavered, and she could read all she needed in those deep dark eyes of his.

She knew he loved her. Always had, from the moment they had met. He loved her almost as much as Ovelia did. She'd used them both, in different ways. Used their love and their loyalty and their need. She knew it hurt them both, and while that didn't bother her, at least she hadn't done it for that reason. She wasn't like Paeter. She was cruel but not sadistic. And what she would do now...

It didn't matter. It wouldn't stop her.

Lenalin reached down and pulled her skirts aside. She drew the Frostburn's hand down and guided his fingers. She showed him what to do, and soon enough she was inhaling sharply as he touched her. His rough hands were unexpectedly dexterous, but perhaps she shouldn't have been surprised. He was a man who lived by grace and skill, and he mastered every task set before him. He would master pleasing her, even if he would not master her. No man ever would.

His face moved toward hers, but she pulled away, freeing herself a little from his embrace. Before he could ask the question, she leaned back in, pressed her cheek against his chest, and reached down to unlace his breeches. That headed off any words he might say, and instead he stood, trembling.

It was no simple task, those laces, because she was shaking a bit as well. His touch left her wet and ready, but she fought to keep her reactions under control. Finally, she pulled his breeches open and reached inside. The Frostburn murmured a small, wordless sound like a groan at her cold fingers upon him. He didn't need her mouth, and that was good. She hated doing that.

"I need you," she said, backing up against the wall. "Now."

The Frostburn put his hands on her arms tentatively, unsure what to do, and she moved them to her hips. She pulled him in and he pushed inside. He felt different from Paeter—colder, perhaps, but the cold rarely bothered her. His hard body pressed against hers and he moved inside her and she moved around him. She could sense his anxiety and his urgency, but she didn't care. She gasped and let herself float. She kept seeing Paeter's stupid, arrogant face, and she reveled in hurting him this way. She saw Ovelia's face full of love and adoration and wondered what it would be like to feel that.

Maybe that was part of it. She saw that same ardor and love in the Frostburn's eyes. What would it feel like to love someone that much?

Lenalin pressed her lips to the Frostburn's ear. She spoke in a breathless whisper.

"I love you."

She did not love him. She barely knew him and barely *cared* to know him. She didn't even find him all that attractive, in truth: all hard, winter-scoured flesh with glinting eyes like flint and a hard, merciless mouth. This wasn't about that. It wasn't about Paeter or his cruelty. It wasn't about the City of Steel or the Winter King's tenuous power. It wasn't even really about punishing her father and her best friend and what they were doing.

This was about her.

They never kissed, not during all of their rutting. If the Frostburn ever told anyone of this, he would no doubt call it making love, and Lenalin would not care to correct him. It was sex—the first and, she suspected, the last time they would do this.

It was not beautiful.

It was not special.

But it was hers.

"Princess." The Frostburn pushed harder, his breathing quickened, and Lenalin knew he had drawn close. She liked it more than she had expected to, and she was grateful for that.

"Not yet," she whispered. "Not—"

It was too late, of course. Once past that point, few men can return. The Frostburn struggled but could not restrain himself. She felt him spend himself inside her, warming and filling her. She knew little about his sexual habits, but the time it took, she wondered if he had ever known a woman, much less rutted one any time recently. She'd not be surprised if he had been holding it in his whole life.

She was pleased enough.

When it was over, Lenalin adjusted her clothing and slipped away, and Regel did not try to stop her. She could feel his longing eyes. She knew he wanted to speak but didn't have the words.

Idly, Lenalin wondered if she should ask him to kill Paeter for her, or perhaps simply let him die in battle. It would be a kindness. It would prove his love for her.

But no. And not just because the Ravalis would kill them all.

Lenalin did not need the Frostburn to save her. She would not give him that chance. The Frostburn did not deserve redemption, any more than Paeter himself. Any more than Lenalin did.

Snow owed no favors to anyone. Ice had no allies or friends.

With casual, practiced grace, Lenalin forced herself to smile. She touched his arm. "What is your name?" she asked. "Not Frostburn—but the name my father gave you. Your secret name."

The Frostburn's eyes gleamed at her. "Regel," he said. "I—please call me Regel, highness."

"Go," she said. "Ward yourself. Win this war. Come back to me."

She did not remind him to ward Paeter as well. She could offer just that little defiance.

Silence was all she had.

For now.

SIX

Now—Autumn 982—Atropis, the Dusk Sea

A T THE HEIGHT OF Atropis, the high wind tore at clothes and unsecured hair like a living thing, grasping and clawing desperately for companionship, if only for the moment or two it would take to plummet to the dark water far, far below. The sudden gusts had carried many an unwary visitor to this doom, and the wind only grew harder as the sun slid beneath the horizon and darkness reigned. The chill set in, enough to freeze even the hardiest dock worker, and the pirates under Shard's command often spent their mornings chipping ice from their skyships in preparation for the day's raids.

Lady Shard stood in one of the open sky cells, scrutinizing the turbulent night all around her. She liked the threat—bracing herself against the dangers of the world. When she was younger, Shard the Pirate Queen had always found the darkness frightening but strangely compelling. Now, after so many years, it felt like her only friend. Perhaps "friend" was the wrong word, and she should instead call Ruin her "ally" or "rival." Regardless, the bleak world and its hollow offerings had been her constant companion for years. It had shattered her brittle, perfect icy visage, then rebuilt her from the shards.

Partly, at least. She still felt the constant pain, every day. It'd been worse, of course, but her once shattered knee still ached in the rain or the cold or whenever it felt like bothering her. The two first fingers of her left hand didn't close to her palm, and she was missing half her right small finger. Her legs weren't quite the same length as one another, and though she'd got used to it years ago, it made her shuffle oddly, and stairs made her hips ache. To say nothing of the havoc wreaked upon her face...

Oh, how she hated Ruin, and yet it had made her what she was. What she had to be.

"Princess," the prisoner said. "Princess... forgive me."

No. Shard ground her teeth. *Never.*

She looked down at the man sitting at her feet. For the past season, he'd spent most of the time talking to himself while she stood there, or else he rocked back and forth, moaning. Sometimes he seemed aware of her presence, other times he couldn't see her at all. She kept expecting him to throw himself to his death in the rocky waters far below, or perhaps bash his brains out against the wall.

Regel Winter, the Frostburn, the Shadow of the Winter King—reduced to a gibbering wreck.

He was better today. When she had first brought him up here, he'd wept and screamed and pleaded to have his mage-glass sword back. That awful weapon she kept wrapped in half a dozen furs in her vault, where none could see it, much less touch it. And even so, she still felt a chill whenever she drew near the outer door to the room. It was a vile, awful thing, built only for killing and extremely efficient at doing so. Shard knew and cared little for magic, but even she recognized that, were there any justice in this world, no one would ever wield that sword again.

Alas, the World of Ruin had little in the way of justice, which she knew better than most.

Now he sat silent and peaceful. Perhaps he had made some sort of breakthrough.

She had little to say to him. Too many years had passed. Too much pain. Too much loss, his and hers both. That he yet lived impressed but did not surprise her. Perhaps he had some part to play yet.

"Lena?" asked a voice, barely audible over the howling winds. "What passes?"

Ovelia, of course. She stood behind Shard, on the threshold of the cell, her blindfolded eyes elevated a little over Shard's shoulder. She couldn't see her, but she never failed to find Shard, no matter where she went in the complex. The pirate queen found it ironic: after she'd spent so many years in hiding, she could no longer conceal her presence, especially from Ovelia.

"Princess," Regel murmured.

"She's not here," Shard said, her tone sharp and corrective. "Shard will suffice."

That other name wasn't hers anymore. She'd fled from it as much as anything else.

"You shouldn't be out here." Ovelia came forward, her boots splashing in the small puddles in the stone. She hadn't yet reached the stage in her pregnancy when it would significantly hinder her mobility, but she kept one hand on her belly anyway. "It's dangerous."

And yet there you are, with that precious cargo, Shard thought but did not say. Instead, she shrugged. "I trained my legs for a ship fifteen years ago— once they started working again, anyway." She looked down to Regel. "Or did you mean him? He's no threat. No longer, at least."

Ovelia looked at Regel as though she could see him, and Lenalin was again given pause. Perhaps it was merely habit, but if so, how did Ovelia even know where to look?

"I think he is awake." Ovelia knelt down and touched Regel on the forehead. "He passes well." Her face was full of such compassion it made Shard's stomach slightly queasy.

"Well," Shard said. "He hasn't killed himself yet, so I suppose we can still use him."

Ovelia started to object, but Shard was already sweeping out of the sky cell. Rain slicked off her oiled silk, though the cold and wet still made her hips ache and her skin burn. She would need another warm bath before the night was out, but no matter.

At first, when the worst of the pain subsided, she'd lamented the loss of her beauty and the frustrating state of her body. The sorrow persisted until she realized the truth: the Winter Princess had been a prisoner as well, if not more so.

She caught the arm of Aeldad, who stood waiting just inside the corridor out of the rain.

"Clean the prisoner up and see him to one of the finer chambers," she said. "The Alavar suite should suffice. See that a warm bath is prepared." She glanced back at Regel. "Perhaps a cold one."

Ovelia rose from beside Regel. "Le—" She paused, probably because Aeldad was listening. "My queen," she said. "What passes?"

Shard bit her lip. Ovelia had spoken her dead name before, which not all her pirates knew—or else one would surely have betrayed her for coin by now. Aeldad, on the other hand, Shard could trust implicitly. Her first mate was the one who had found a broken princess and helped her become a queen, and they had shared many things. Aeldad loved her more than anything, and Shard could rely upon her.

Use her, Shard thought. *Just as everyone uses everyone else.*

"Clean him up," she said again. "I'll call upon him anon."

Then she strode past Aeldad and down the corridor toward another set of cells, these not open to the elements. Her hip ached as she walked, but she embraced the familiar pain. It had become a constant companion after so many years. Ovelia followed, of course, silently dogging Shard's steps like a loyal hound long past her prime. Perhaps she sensed torture had replaced her as Shard's oldest, most reliable friend? The thought almost made the pirate queen smile.

Almost.

Shard paused at another door and fumbled with the ring of keys she carried. Her clumsy fingers didn't want to cooperate. She was accustomed to the frustration, but now she experienced the extra embarrassment of failing such a simple task in front of Ovelia. At least the woman was blind and didn't have to see how foolish she looked.

"My Queen," Ovelia said, her voice quiet. "You are releasing him?"

"We'll see if he's useful." Shard dismissed the question. "And even if he isn't, I need the space."

At that moment, down the hall, Aeldad led Regel out of his prison, even as two of Shard's pirates hauled someone into the sky cell he had just vacated: the weakly-struggling ruinscarred whom Tanak had brought earlier that day. Ovelia stiffened despite the five paces that separated them. The man cursed and spat until he fixed eyes on Regel, and Shard could see the hate drooling from his face.

Interesting. She wasn't the only one with secrets, it seemed.

Regel himself hardly seemed to notice, though he looked forlornly in Ovelia and Shard's direction. Perhaps he even recognized them.

"If you care so much for him, Lia, why not go to his chambers yourself?" Shard smiled mirthlessly behind her veil. "I'm sure he'd appreciate your hands on his shoulders, your lips on his, or perhaps your legs wrapped 'round his waist?"

Ovelia flushed slightly. "Shard—"

"An idle jest. Pay it no mind." The Pirate Queen shrugged. Finally, a key stuck in the lock and she sighed in relief. "I'm going to need you to talk to this one, I think."

"Who—?" Ovelia cut off the question, realizing. "You mean—"

"Yes." Shard turned the key to the interior cell across from the sky cell. This one was furnished with soft if threadbare pillows, a feather-stuffed mattress, and even a blanket. There was a copper chamberpot, fortunately unused and empty. A tray of food—a triangle of white cheese, a crust of rich black bread, a chunk of lime, all of it half-eaten—lay strewn about the foot of the crude bed.

And there, in the center of the room, stood Lan Ravalis, his hands folded at the small of his back. He'd looked better, that could not be denied. Tanak's pirates hadn't picked him up in a particularly gentle way. Both of his eyes showed signs of damage—one black and the other swollen nearly shut.

"Your Majesty," she said. "You'll forgive me if I don't bow. I am old and worn."

"Your Highness." He bowed. Then his lip curled when he looked at Ovelia. "Lady Dracaris."

Shard didn't miss the barely restrained hate in those two words.

"You certainly seem to make enemies, Lia," Shard said. "The Oathbreaker, the ruinscarred, and now the king of Tar Vangr? And I thought beauty counted for something."

She expected Lan to chuckle or add a barb of his own—the man couldn't resist the opportunity to mock or belittle a woman—but instead he narrowed his eyes. "Tithian Davargorn is here?"

"Who?" Shard asked.

"Pay it no mind." Lan smiled faintly. "I can see by the Bloodbreaker's face. He'll prove a threat to you. You should have killed him immediately."

"I still might," Shard said. "Maybe you can hold hands on your way down to the sea."

That got his attention. Lan grimaced at her. "You'd not dare," he said. "Alive, I can secure you a mighty ransom. My corpse is worth nothing."

"Ransom, is it?" Shard folded her arms. "Is that your play? Rely upon my greed for coin?"

"Not—" Lan glanced sharply at Ovelia, then back to Shard. "Can we speak alone?"

Ovelia sucked in a breath to object, but Shard raised her mangled left hand. "Anything you say to me, Lan Dracaris, you can say to my protector. She and I have no secrets from one another."

Not *anymore*, at least.

Ovelia had regained her inscrutable composure and gave nothing away by her muted reaction to Shard's assertion. By contrast, Lan's scowling contempt and obvious loathing made him an unfurled scroll. He hated Ovelia with a passion that could light metal on fire, and now some of that enmity had begun to diffuse to Shard as well. She realized belatedly that she'd called her "Lia" and committed herself to avoiding such a show of intimacy around Lan Ravalis and his whole infernal clan.

"Very well." Lan raised his chin, scraping together whatever pride he had left. "I would have your aid in reclaiming Luether from my sister, Alistra the Spider."

Shard drew in a breath. She hadn't expected that.

"Surely a capable woman of your intellect can imagine the value of an alliance with the king of Tar Vangr," Lan said. "And if we are successful, I shall rule Luether as well."

"You would have my aid," Shard said in her quiet, cold voice. "Leaving aside the question of the coin you don't have, or the fact that you're my prisoner and in no place to make such demands." She folded her arms. "Why am I to believe you'll not turn upon me at the first opportunity? Your Blood—"

Unexpectedly, she choked on the words. She remembered hands around her throat. A shove. Lancing, burning pain all over. And then the screaming. A scream rose up in the depths of her throat, and her hands veritably shook with her rising desire to leap across the room and strangle him. He was much larger than she, and would surely defend himself. But Ovelia would leap to her aid, and then the World of Ruin would be rid of this monster…

Ovelia's hand touched hers, down at her side, and Shard abruptly reclaimed hold of herself. She pulled pointedly away from Ovelia's touch.

"Your Blood is not known for its forgiveness." Shard hoped she sounded as mild as ever.

Lan smirked. He couldn't have failed to notice the slip, but he seemed to interpret it as fear, rather than a spark of rage. "Worry not. As far as the Blood Ravalis is concerned, you rescued me from vicious, foul treatment by wayward subordinates who did not recognize me. I failed to identify myself, and their ignorance is not their fault. You'll have to punish them, of course. Perhaps an ear from each?"

"Perhaps." He looked so like Paeter that Shard clutched her left hand as painfully tight as it would close. "And me? I've hardly treated you in a manner befitting your station. Quite the tragedy, that is. I suppose you'll want more comfortable arrangements?"

"I'd not object, of course." Lan relaxed, obviously put at ease by her manner. "Some proper food—not this refuse you feed dogs. Some wine. New clothes." He tapped the edge of the splintery bedframe, then gave her a charming smile. "You are a woman. Surely you can appreciate how such comforts can stimulate friendship and trust?"

At her side, Ovelia stiffened. "Highness—"

Shard held up a hand once more, but continued to address Lan alone. "I suppose you'll want some pleasurable company, as well?" she asked.

The question hit Lan like a punch to the gut, and Shard could see him shrink away a bit, his eyes flashing with renewed heat. The confident façade he'd been building since they put him in this room crumbled, and for an instant she saw the angry boy that she remembered, desperate to prove himself.

There he is, she thought. *The spiteful boy, grown up to be a king.* A *Eunuch King*, if reports were to be believed, and by his face, Shard suspected it was true.

"No," Lan said at length. "That's not necessary. Though—" He grinned evilly. "Should you leave me the Bloodbreaker, I would consider it a personal favor. No doubt we could find some… diversions."

"No doubt. But I've my own uses for her." Shard clutched Ovelia's arm as hard as her left hand would allow, making the woman gasp slightly in surprise. "I shall consider your offer."

"Consider it?" Lan blinked. "What do you mean?"

"Surely you can appreciate that I think before I act," said Shard. "As you said, I am a woman."

Anger rose up in Lan, written in the tension in his jaw and the fire in his eyes. Anger that she had not immediately complied. Anger at her defiance. Her insolence. Shard felt like laughing.

"Pass well, Your Majesty." Shard inclined her head. "I'll arrange better accommodations for you in the interim. No reason you have to await my decision in squalor like this."

"Well." Lan bit off the word sharply. "I shall await your audience again then. Tomorrow?"

"If I've made up my mind by then," Shard said. "Confound this feminine body and its indecisiveness. If only I were a man. Could be several days. Could be Dark Solstice."

Lan's brown face grew increasingly purple.

Shard turned and swept from the room, dragging Ovelia behind her. Lan almost followed, but Aeldad was there, arms crossed over her mighty chest. The fire-haired man didn't try her, but backed down like the cowardly cur he was.

"Bath," Aeldad said. "Come now."

Lan only sputtered in argument. For a man who once wore the mantle of the Bear of Luether, he looked very small and weak indeed beside Shard's first mate. Finally, he nodded and slunk after her, his face dejected and his demeanor slumped.

"What does he look like?" Ovelia asked as they walked away, her voice soft.

"Like a lad deprived of his favorite sweets," Shard said. "Which is all he is. A spoiled lad."

Ovelia wore a blank expression. "Did you just send both Lan and Regel to the baths together?"

Lady Shard grinned beneath her veil.

~

They ascended from the brig wing onto one of the spiraling catwalks that connected to the central pillar. The metal steps rattled under their feet and Ovelia needed Lenalin's help to find the rusted railing. The world was a mess of swirling shadows to her, but Lenalin strode purposefully along these paths with the confidence born of decades of practice.

Lenalin had grown cold indeed, but her hand felt warm and reassuring. It was the Pirate Queen's right hand, the smallest finger of which was far shorter than it should have been. Ovelia wanted to run her fingers over the stump—to kiss it—but of course that was madness. Shadows leaked from Draca, sheathed at her belt, but Ovelia was too distracted by Lenalin to pay attention to them.

That, and the baby, who took the opportunity to kick her sharply. Her child-to-be—prince or princess or otherwise—was her constant companion. Somehow, the presence of such a defenseless growing life should have made her more worried for her own safety, but the opposite was true. Ovelia felt stronger. Empowered. This child was a steadying presence.

She had only two people to trust in the World of Ruin: her child and Lenalin.

It occurred to her how powerfully she had to trust in Lenalin in this unfamiliar place. She couldn't *see* her, after all. She could only see those who meant her harm, and even when she'd thought Lady Shard her enemy, the woman hadn't meant her harm. It had been this blindness in part that led Ovelia to trust her enough to let her get close. And now—well, here they were.

After Luether, she'd been able to perceive her foes and chart the path of her victory and survival with remarkable clarity, but over the intervening months spent on the *Hecatomb* and here at Atropis, her vision had faded once more. In all that time, they'd rarely spoken. Lenalin had avoided her—always found some excuse to dismiss her, to be escorted back to her room like a kept animal. Was it the child she carried—Garin's child, a child of the Blood Ravalis that had so ruined Lenalin's life—that drove this wedge between them? Or was it some deeper hatred, pain, or loathing?

Such would not have surprised Ovelia, considering the curse under which she had labored for so many years. The hated breaker of the Blood she had loved more than her own—liar, traitor, assassin, and thief. Twice over the last year, she had completed an impossible task that should have seen her dead, and she had survived while those who deserved to live had not. The World of Ruin was saving her for something, but it would not let her see it.

And if she lost hold of Lenalin's hand, what would she do then? Fall into darkness, her purpose unfulfilled? What else did she deserve?

"What." The Pirate Queen's word was short and blunt. Accusatory.

Such an echo Ovelia's own questions startled her. She couldn't speak of her doubts, so she settled upon something else. "Mayhap—" Ovelia reminded herself to calm her breathing. "Mayhap you shouldn't have antagonized Lan Ravalis. He is a dangerous man."

"Is he."

The platform groaned under their weight, and something popped free and flicked away into the darkness below. Lenalin's hand was suddenly gone. Off-balance, Ovelia swayed, uncertain which direction to fall for safety. Then strong hands caught her and steadied her against the rail.

"Lena," Ovelia said, wishing she could see her face, even with the veil. "I—"

Shard pressed one finger to her lips, silencing her. Her glove tasted of salt and something flowery. A skin cream, perhaps, under the silk. Ovelia's heart quickened.

"I'll allow you to call me that," Lenalin said, her voice a cool whisper. "But only when we are alone. Do you understand?"

Ovelia opened her mouth but Shard covered it with the silk-wrapped fingers of her right hand. Her diminished little finger traced the edge of her lower lip. Muscles taut, Ovelia hardly dared breathe.

"Nod if you understand," Shard said.

After a breath, Ovelia nodded. It had become hard to think. Her heart thudded against her ribs. She wanted to take the tips of Lenalin's fingers into her mouth...

"No, Lia." Lenalin drew her hand away sharply, and Ovelia gasped. She was lost again in the darkness, but—there. The faint outline of Lenalin's robed form appeared before her benighted eyes, faintly limned in silvery light. She had turned to survey the cavernous honeycomb of chambers and walkways that made up Atropis's interior. Ovelia could perceive it only dimly, because of the magic-burning torches that loomed out of the darkness above and below them.

"I've always felt an affinity for this burned ruin," Lenalin said. "When I first came here, broken and all but worthless, the place wasn't fit for habitation. It wasn't much to look at either: as if one mountain had fallen atop another. The lower levels were the worst of all. Down there, amongst the grinding boulders and shards of metal, no life could subsist. Dead. Worthless."

Lenalin's silks scratched against the corroded metal, surprisingly loud in the stillness.

"You remember the stories we used to read? About the amazing Atropis, City of Life, shifting and rippling in the sunlight, a diamond mage-city resting on the tiny point of a pyramid?" She kicked a spare bolt free of the catwalk, and it spiraled down to land with a faint ring on the stone walls far, far below. "A hulking wreck—a standing corpse with only some function left. That way ever to remain."

She closed her fingers tight around the rail, and Ovelia fancied she could hear it creaking. Lenalin was angry, Ovelia realized, but she exercised tight control over it.

"My ship ran aground below, amongst the haunted ruin, marked with the greasy shadows of long-dead folk burned upon the stones. A falling hunk of twisted metal almost killed me. It crushed our captain, and I was the only one left who even spoke Calatite. Which we needed to convince the pirates in this place not to kill us all. It took two years, but then I was their master. They did my will."

Lenalin drew in a deep breath.

"I brought small teams of engineers from Luether and laborers from the Free Isles—whoever we could hire or steal away—to batter and kick it into functional shape, but not to restore it."

Lenalin turned to her, and Ovelia felt the power radiating from her. The terrible strength.

"I could not fix it," she said. "And once I came to accept that—long after the pain faded, and some of the scars—only then was Lady Shard born. So you see, Lia."

She stepped closer to Ovelia, pushing her up against the rail with her hips. Ovelia's swollen belly held some space between them—a barrier that kept them apart. Leaning in, Lenalin pressed her face against Ovelia's cheek, the veil whispering between them, and placed one hand flat against Ovelia's chest, right over her thundering heart. Belatedly, Ovelia realized the danger: just a gentle push, and she would topple right over into the darkness, vanishing without a fuss. She probably wouldn't even scream.

A tiny spark of worry flared for her child, but equally, her deep and abiding trust for Lenalin welled up within her. She lost herself in the uncertain euphoria. The edge of life and death.

"Lan Ravalis may be a dangerous man," Lenalin said. "But I have become a dangerous woman."

Ovelia's body stiffened and trembled under her touch. Surely Lenalin could feel her heart racing.

They stood there, poised on the edge of a precipitous drop, their bodies stretched to the utmost tension and beyond. Ovelia shook, and she could sense a slight tremble in Lenalin as well. And something more: Power. Control. Authority. It spoke to the darkness deep within Ovelia—summoned it—demanded it come forth. Lenalin was her captor, her master, and her destroyer. She always had been, and always would be. Unless she pushed Ovelia over the edge, just at that moment.

Ovelia could not say whether she would, nor whether she would blame her.

That ambiguity filled her and would not allow her to think. She only knew Lenalin. The scent of her lotions. The warm sweat under her silks. The steel in her voice and eyes.

Her vision cleared a little, and she thought she could see flames burning inside her lost princess, now finally returned. But the flames were black, and Ovelia could not say if her beloved Lenalin were miraculously restored or long dead.

"Lia," Shard said, the whisper like fire in Ovelia's ear. "Come with me."

It was not a request.

Ovelia, trembling, did exactly that.

SEVEN

The Winter Wilds

W"HAT."

The horde was already on the march before Darak made his plans known, and that only fueled Carr's disapproval. She shattered her earthen tankard on the table, cutting through the thick calluses of her hand. Dark blood welled in the gash and dripped down, but Carr the Axe hardly seemed to notice it. She glared at the rotpriest with such fire and hate in her eyes as promised his swift death were it not for the score of honor guard waiting just outside the tent. Perhaps even then.

The smoky darkness felt cold despite how many had crowded into the tent—Semana herself, Darak, Fellis the Night Wolf, Carr the Axe, and Lathkgar of the Thundering Hooves, their field general to the horde. Crown was there as well, shivering as he stood somewhat removed from the congress, in case one of them desired something. The chill never bothered Semana—she recognized temperature only distantly—but Carr's burning rage and Lathkgar's cold fury were immediate and could not be ignored.

They stood around a wide, flat stump in the middle of the tent, from which Darak's Worldfire grew bits of wood forth into mountains and tiny sprouts into trees to form a map of the Winter Wilds. It was around this topography that they gathered and grumbled. A flower sprouted from the tree, blooming twice, to represent two-tiered Tar Vangr, and Darak drove a blade into the stump to represent the horde. Much, much closer than any of them had expected, and it could only mean one thing.

"Ridiculous," Carr the Axe said. "You cannot keep the horde together over the winter, let alone mount an offensive." She snorted. "When I pushed you to move, I didn't mean to throw yourself over the cliff, stupid boy."

The Druid had made no secret of her impatience to get moving—to do something—rather than sit in place and wait while more barbarians joined their cause. As she saw it, once winter grew too close, that spelled the end of their efforts, and that moment had already passed. She'd been about to command her barbarians to leave when she saw the horde mustering to march.

96

"Who are you to command this horde, Dar-Karsk?" she asked. "You are no Druid, but a treacherous apprentice to a member of the Circle. You have no standing here. Certainly not to command thousands to their deaths in the cold to no end. No victory."

"Aye." Lathkgar, nodded his shaggy head. Off his horse, he walked with a pronounced sway from his bow-curved legs. "You've guts, give you that. But you're mad or stupid."

"Neither," Darak said. "I act with the agreement and blessing of a member of the Circle. This march is the will of the Worldfire. The will of Ruin."

All eyes turned to Semana, and she chewed at her lip. What could her brother be playing at? He hadn't consulted her before he gave the orders, and now he laid political pressure on her to approve his decisions after the fact. Damn and burn the man! She thought they were past this. That—

Fortunately, Semana didn't have to respond. Apparently, he hadn't meant her at all.

"Dar-Karsk speaks with my voice in this matter," Fellis said in her soft voice. "His means and aims are as sound as any well loosed shaft."

Semana stared. Lathkgar started to chuckle. Carr looked stricken and furious.

"Explain it then." Carr sunk her axe into the table. She sharpened her thumbnail against it in short little twitches, then moved to her forefinger. "Before I finish all ten."

"Nine," Fellis said. "You lost your third finger twenty years ago—"

Carr gave her fellow druid a withering glance that cut her off in a little satisfied smile. Semana could tell any alliance between those two walked a treacherous path, and why not? If Fellis had just betrayed her interests—made her look the fool in front of the council—then of course Carr would not take that well. She idly touched at the edge of her mask, scratching at an itch on her neck.

"I traveled south for this?" Carr asked no one.

Frustratingly, Darak seemed completely at ease—not taking the serious threat of a murderous woman at all seriously. "Tar Vangr has stood for centuries, unbroken and inviolate, because none have ever exploited its vulnerability," he said. "It is a city of ice, and it is brittle. It barely survives the winter on its own. If we strike when the snows are deepest, the defenders will be at their weakest."

Lathkgar scowled. "Rutting idiot boy."

"Fine words, and the tactics of a child," Carr said. "The winter will fall ten times as heavy upon us. They have their homes and their beds and their fires, and we must camp out in the snow and wind. And how will the horde survive the winter, eh? The Children of Ruin are hardy, never doubt, but as the chill sets in, morale will vanish and folk will desert by the day. Your thousands will be hundreds and then tens and then nothing within ten days at the most. Count yourself lucky if you have even a fraction of the horde left when you arrive—and if one of the deserters doesn't take your head."

Darak shook his head. "You're wrong, honored one."

"Insolent pustule." Carr bared her teeth at him. "Tell us *why*. Prove to us your idiocy is more valid than centuries of experience. Because—"

"Very well."

Darak drew a knife from under the table, and the council suddenly grew very quiet indeed. Semana held her breath, ready to draw upon her relics. Carr made no obvious movement, other than to smile dangerously, her hand already poised on the haft of her axe. Lathkgar's face went deeper red and he made ready to draw his weapons. Only Fellis seemed unaffected and calm.

"Sister." Darak passed the knife to Semana. "Be so good as to assuage Carr's curiosity."

Semana blinked at him. *What?*

They were all looking at her now. Lathkgar leered at her, as he often did, and Fellis wore a self-conceited smirk. Even Carr looked genuinely intrigued. Darak had the expression of a fox who had just eaten a hen and blamed the inn's hound for it. Damn and burn him thrice over. And after she had defended him to Regel, Gilt, and Crown of Fire.

From behind Darak, Crown met Semana's eye, and he made a sweeping gesture with one finger up the side of his throat, the way Children of Ruin often indicated a threat. Unless he was offering to slay all of them for her, she didn't much see the point of that, but perhaps he meant *bloodletting*.

Silver Fire. Did Darak mean her to use her blood magic?

She looked at him, grateful for the mask that hid her expression. "Right here, brother?" she asked. "I thought we meant it to be a surprise."

Darak's face slipped, but only a touch. "Now's a day for surprises."

Semana cursed inwardly, her mind racing. She had privately been experimenting with combining her Frostfire and blood magic for a season now, but how did Darak know that? He'd warned her never to let on that she had this power around the barbarians, and particularly in front of druids of the Circle. But now he was asking her to use that self-same power?

Semana accepted the knife with some hesitation. Damn him for forcing her into this position.

"Does something pass?" Lathkgar asked. "Some magic?"

Carr shushed him with a sharp hiss. Fellis hid a sly chuckle behind her hand.

Semana felt Darak's intense eyes burning into her. Expectant. Demanding.

She fell into a state of stillness, listening to the blood coursing in the bodies around her. Feeling it. Tasting it. There was power in Darak's blood—the faint, quiescent stirring of his Frostfire—and his blood tasted faintly sour. Corrupt. Other barbarians tasted the same, especially Lathkgar and old warriors like him, but surprisingly the High Druids had blood that seemed clean, if bitter. Considering how much Worldfire they channeled, Semana wondered how they kept themselves uncorrupted.

"Any time, lass," Carr said under her breath.

With the blood roaring in her ears, Semana reached for her Frostfire. It proved elusive, as it always did when she tried to call upon it, especially when her attention was divided. But it was there, and in her desperation she caught hold of it. Despite Darak's warnings, she forced it to rise within her.

Eyes closed, she could tell from the reactions of those around her in the tent that flame had begun to leak from her. Fellis gasped faintly in her surprise, while Carr loosed a low growl. Lathkgar didn't make a sound, but Semana could hear his heavy breathing pick up its pace. And she could feel their blood as though it were her own, and all of it in the tent started coursing faster and harder. All of it except Darak's. His heart maintained its slow, confident beat, and that gave Semana a calm center to which she could cling. She held both the Frostfire and the vile magic that seized the blood and brought them together with force of will...

And by some miracle, it worked.

She soaked the Frostfire in her blood, and it turned the silvery blue of the magic. She combined her magics, distilling liquid Frostfire in her arteries and veins. She stripped off her right glove and gripped the knife in the dull, half-numb fingers of her left hand. She didn't have the necessary dexterity.

"I will aid my queen?" asked Crown of Fire at her side.

Semana hadn't noted his approach and his sudden proximity unnerved her. Still, better him than Lathkgar or her brother. Like as not, Darak expected to be the one to aid her. She nodded to Crown.

"Tankard." When everyone looked at her with confusion, she amended to "kup," the Ruinspeak for "bowl." Another servant produced a rough wood vessel, and she put her bare hand over it.

More gently than she might have credited him, Crown of Fire cut a tiny slit in her wrist, and blood immediately welled forth. The blood dripped and drizzled into the bowl, so blue as to seem almost black, and it did not turn red in the air. It remained fresh black lifeblood, full of tingling magic.

"What's this supposed to be?" Carr scowled. "A bleeding game? Should I prick my finger next?"

"Drink," Darak said.

The stout druid bared her teeth. Fellis's eyes gleamed.

"You," Darak said to Lathkgar. "Unless you fear."

The barbarian puffed up in response, but he had nothing to say—not with the two High Druids glaring at him. He took the bowl with a contemptuous flair of his hand and put it to his lips. He drank with a sucking, guzzling sound, yellowed eyes fixed upon Semana. She thought he was considering how best to wear her guts as an adornment over his armor.

Then he paused, and the bowl fell from his hands to clatter and roll to a stop on the stump map. He looked about in wonder, and Semana saw the faint blue flames at the edges of his eyes.

"What is it?" Fellis asked in her soft, patient voice.

"It's warm." Lathkgar's face split in a yellow-toothed smile, and he stormed out of the tent, ripping his shirt of furs and bones off as he went. He started by smearing snow on his hairy chest, then threw himself into the snow outside and barked with laughter as he rolled around like a child.

Semana did not share this joy. She had developed this power in secret for over a season, and Darak has claimed her victory for his own by forcing her to show them all.

Semana remembered seeing such simple joy only when she wrestled her brother in their mother's garden, as the snow fell around them and they crammed it into each other's faces and clothes. They'd both taken a chill and spent the following ten days alternating between hot baths and beds heaped with furs, but it had been worth it. She realized Darak was staring at her, smiling slightly.

How did you know, you dastard? she wanted to ask. *How do you always steal my triumphs?*

"Impressive," Fellis the Night Wolf said.

Carr the Axe took one look at the upset bowl, dribbling a tiny bit of blood onto the table, and wrenched her axe out of the stump. She glared first at Semana, then Darak, then turned on her heel and stormed out. She gave Lathkgar a kick on his naked backside as she went, and he sprawled in the snow.

Finally, Darak had the good grace to look a bit surprised. He started forward, then stopped and looked away from them. Just slightly—craning his head toward something Semana did not perceive. Perhaps he heard something she did not? Regardless, he shrugged and turned back to the stump.

"Carr the Axe is a proud woman," Fellis said softly. "I think you insulted her."

"Really," Semana said. "What insight."

The Night Wolf gave her a mild look full of the promise of a quiet death one night. Semana hardly cared. Darak looked entirely too pleased with himself, and her body kept tensing up. Soon enough she would have to scream at him or throttle him. Instead, she snatched the scrap of cloth Crown of Fire offered her, pressed it against her wrist, and put her glove on over it.

Then she strode out of the tent without another word.

⌇

Finding Carr the Axe wasn't difficult. Semana had only to follow the cries of steel and pain.

The High Druid had carved herself a circle of bloodied men and women: barbarians of various tribes and states of injury and agony, who appeared to have been interrupted during their belated preparations to march. That she'd managed to cut down, maim, or otherwise render senseless some six warriors before Semana got up with her, despite only having perhaps a thirty-count head start, was testament not only to her skill but also her ferocity. Carr fought like a wild dog or a wolf.

As Semana approached, Carr chopped her axe into a hastily-raised shield, plunging right through to leave a deep gouge in the barbarian's arm. Blood welled and traced swaths across the fresh snow. Her voice like a throaty growl, Carr shouted something in Ruinspeak—something full of curses about fools and impending death. Despite the onslaught of words and steel, the barbarians arrayed against her seemed eager to attack her. They probably thought it a great honor.

"Mayhap you should stop wounding my warriors," Semana said. "We're on the same side, no?"

"Are we?" Carr fixed her with a hot glare. Her eyes gleamed yellow. "If you think Dar-Karsk is your ally or mine, you are more a fool than I thought."

"I'm not the fool here." Semana bit her tongue. She'd said that without meaning to do so.

"Speak that again." Carr raised the axe in challenge. "With your hands, not your tongue."

Semana drew in a deep breath, then let it slowly escape her lips. Too many folk were watching, which meant she couldn't back down from the challenge. Surely only a madwoman would try to kill her so brazenly, but that didn't mean Carr wouldn't cut her down in an instant, given the opportunity. She hadn't met a single barbarian in all her time in the Winter Wilds who deserved the descriptor of "sane."

Semana extended her smoking left hand toward one of the nearby barbarians Carr had already vanquished. Her sword rose up into the air, then flashed end over end into Semana's right hand.

"A sword," Carr said. "You."

"Me."

The heavy, serrated blade almost felt like a living thing that longed to cut and maim. Semana tested its weight and balance, as Regel had shown her. The vicious weapon was crude but it would serve. She took a defensive posture, eyes set on Carr. The woman returned a bemused smile.

"I expected an argument, not an amusement," Carr said.

"Arrogance ill becomes you," Semana said.

The Druid's face darkened. "If I must hack your head open to put understanding into it, I will."

"You—"

Semana started to speak when Carr suddenly flowed through the air toward her, moving faster than anyone she had ever seen. Neither Regel nor even one of the Deathless Fae could match that grace, and Semana knew it was magically driven. The axe crashed through her hasty parry, cutting the sword in half with an ugly screech, and plunged right into her chest.

Or would have, had not the protective magic of her hauberk activated and saved her. The axe ground into the blue-glowing shield with an almost leonine roar, and the force of the strike sent her tumbling end over end. Semana ended up crunching heavily into the snow, the thigh she landed on barking in pain, and she lay there, stunned. She looked up at the cloudy sky, her thoughts rattling around in her skull, and wondered if it would snow again soon.

An axe descended over her face, only to sink into the ground a hair from the edge of her mask.

"Just one stroke?" Carr's face leered into Semana's vision. "I'm insulted *and* disappointed."

Panic rose in Semana, turning to sudden anger, and it pushed magic through her glove in an unseen ram of force that knocked Carr up and away. The woman hit the snow, rolled, and came back to her feet in one fluid motion. The axe was in her hands, and she was laughing.

"Tragic," Carr said. "You fight me to defend your master leading you around like a dog."

"No." Semana climbed awkwardly up, shrouded in magic. "This is our birthright. His and mine."

The High Druid gave her a look reserved for disapproving mothers and bored kings. She raised the axe. "Try again? I'll wait."

Semana caught her breath, then extended her hand. Her magic claimed another sword from a different barbarian, who scrambled back, startled. Semana ignored the little aches as best she could. Her breath steamed in the cold air, mingling with the rising smoke of her silver-chain glove.

This time, when Carr attacked—just as fast, just as sudden—Semana was ready for it. She met the Druid's charge with her borrowed sword raised and backed by her glove's power. Carr drove the blade back half a span, but Semana thrust forward with her glove's unseen force and pushed her back.

They exchanged blows that way for a time, Semana matching Carr's hideous strength with the aid of her own magic. The battle could have ended at any moment, if Semana simply discharged a slaying bolt of Plaguefire from her mask, but she couldn't very well do that. If she slew Carr in front of so many of the axe wielder's own warriors, the horde would shatter into half a dozen warring splinters.

When Carr spoke up again, it was after she smashed Semana's borrowed sword out of her hand and drove her back and to the ground. The Druid stood over her, one foot on Semana's chest.

"So you'll feed a swallow of your blood to every man or woman in the horde? You're hardly fat enough to have that much blood." Carr scowled, drawing the skin of her face together in a network of angry lines. "Are you to be his bloodmare?"

"No." When she thought about it, Semana suspected that with enough effort, she could instill the magic into anyone's blood. The limiting factor was her Frostfire, not her blood. Not that she could explain something like that to Carr, even if she wanted to do so. She wrapped her arm around Carr's ankle, though she could not wrest her off.

"You are clever." Carr leaned down to whisper in her ear. "You play the role of dutiful apprentice—you play him to your advantage by allowing him to believe himself lord over you."

No, Semana wanted to say, but Carr didn't seem to like that answer. Instead, she said the best thing she could say, which was nothing.

"We can be allies," Carr said. "You saw how Dar-Karsk asserted his power over you. A man must not stand over a woman. It is anathema."

Semana gritted her teeth against the pressure. "Fellis didn't seem to mind."

That brought a grimace out of Carr. "You will leave Fellis to me," she said. "A man must not be a High Druid. It is not done."

"It is a challenge to your power. Your unquestioned rule over generations of the Children."

Carr looked frustrated but mostly perplexed. "Are you not a woman?" she asked, anger creeping into her voice. "You would suffer a man to stand above you in this way?"

"I will suffer one to stand *beside* me, so long as he is useful."

Carr's eyes gleamed. "And what of a woman, if she be useful?"

"Why not," Semana said. "Is not one woman like another? You—"

She would have said more, but Carr abruptly locked her lips with Semana's, kissing her hard and soundly. Every muscle in her body jerked taut, and Semana could hardly move—hardly even think.

"No!" Semana discharged a blast from her silver glove suddenly, knocking Carr tumbling off her, and rolled quickly to her feet. She was still shivering from the unwanted kiss.

They came up facing one another, and Semana saw tendrils of green magic swaying in front of her eyes. The Plaguefire veritably boiled from her mask.

"How dare you," Semana said. "I did not give you leave—"

"Leave?" Carr laughed. "We are the Twelve Most High. We are greater than any other woman in this world. I am greater. You are greater. What you want, take it. What you desire, take it." She touched her lips and smiled, becoming surprisingly appealing in that moment. A lesser will might have shivered to see such a thing. "Do you want me to kiss you again?"

Semana bit back a scathing retort and considered. Not another kiss—she had no desire for such a thing—but the alliance Carr offered…

Dimly, Semana remembered the many barbarians watching the confrontation. Perhaps that was why Carr had not struck her again. If she attacked and failed, she would lose face and prestige in front of the Children. She would have to kill Semana, and that she hadn't struck yet meant she had chosen not to do so. Semana had already won, even if Carr hadn't realized it yet.

"What armies do you offer?" she asked.

Carr frowned. "You have seen my warriors."

"I see warriors that serve the Circle, not you personally," Semana said. "What chieftains answer your call? Which ones kneel in obedience to Carr the Axe alone?"

Carr glared at Semana. Gone was any sense of sensuality or desire, wilted to disapproval. "What does that matter, sister?" she asked. "When Dar-Karsk is dead, his rabble will be yours."

"How is that?" Semana pressed. "You think they are foolish enough to pledge loyalty to she who killed their master? Some of these men and women have served my brother for ten years. They are his blood. His kin. Do you know their tribes? Their clans? Any of their names?"

Carr laughed mirthlessly. "And you do?"

"No, and that is my point. It takes time to win these men and women—to earn their trust. Their undying loyalty. It cannot simply be demanded or traded on a whim. My brother owns them. And even if he did not, he knows strategy. Warfare. Neither you nor I can claim the same."

Carr's expression soured. "So you will tolerate his lecherous glances and his contempt?"

By the Nar, she was just like Crown of Fire—she attempted to allure Semana, to win her over, but not out of any love for Semana herself. The woman simply could not stand to see a man so elevated.

She was a reverse Ravalis.

That comparison cast Semana's resolve in stone.

She clenched her fists. "If that is the only price I will pay for my kingdom, then I shall pay it."

"That is all you want, a kingdom?" Carr raised her axe high. "I can offer you a world, lovely girl."

"A world shared with the Circle."

Carr spat on the ground and kicked grimy snow over it. "Think on my offer. I'll not ward you when the time comes, but neither will I aid you—not until you agree to our pact."

When what time comes? Semana wanted to ask, but knew she'd get no answer. She nodded.

Carr drew herself up to her full height. "Despite all, we are your sisters."

"And he is my brother," Semana said. "And he asks for no such pact."

Carr's eyes were dubious. Semana could feel her hard, wind-bitten lips lingering on hers. She hadn't wanted the kiss—hadn't invited it. That violation meant she could not side with Carr. Unless...

Unless she was right.

Then she felt the familiar tugging sensation of Carr's Worldfire, draining the power out of her artifacts. Sure enough, the Druid meant to kill her, but now Semana was ready for it. She pulled Worldfire of her own, lacing it around Carr's magic, redirecting her channeling.

The ground around them darkened, and the spindly trees choked in snow abruptly withered as though burning without flame. Carr sucked the life right out of them, through Semana, and into herself. The Druid's eyes widened, and Semana felt the connection abruptly snap free. Semana poised herself, ready to strike with the raging Plaguefire in her mask. She might have smiled, if her heart weren't thudding fit to burst her chest.

Carr stared at her, startled and unnerved, then spat into the snow and stormed away.

Damn and burn, Semana hadn't wanted that. If she could have parted from Carr without offending her, she would have done so. But at least she knew she could defeat the Druids' trick of draining her relics. That could prove a needed edge. Though now Carr knew it too. Damn and burn.

"Sister?"

Darak stood there, wind tugging at his long, auburn hair. How much he had witnessed, Semana could not say. "You saw that, did you?" she asked.

"Your swordplay could use some work," he said.

She scowled at him. "As if you even know how to hold a sword."

Darak shrugged. "Who needs a sword when you have magic?"

Magic. Of course.

Here she tried not to rely so heavily on magic, and his scheme required her to explore her own powers more heavily. Even if the strain didn't tire her out worse than a thousand of Carr's bone-splintering hits, she would almost certainly go mad before she managed to ward the whole horde.

"Folly," she said under her breath.

"What's that?" Darak asked.

"A chieftain here, a druid there, but I don't have enough Frostfire to enchant thousands of warriors. I can't deliver on the promise you made—on my behalf, of course." Semana crossed her arms.

"Calm yourself," Darak said. "I have a plan."

"A plan, is it." Semana set her jaw. "Let's hear it."

Darak sighed. "Witness," he says. "The horde doesn't need any protection yet. With luck, we'll breach the walls of Tar Vangr before the worst of the cold sets in."

"Luck."

"Luck," he said again, grinding his teeth. "You have to compromise a bit—"

"Me?" Semana shrugged off his placating hand. "I've done nothing *but* compromise. I've tolerated your rutting secrets and lies for half a year now. Time for truth."

"Truth." Darak blew out a sigh. "Very well. I have a plan for the Frostfire."

Semana raised an eyebrow. "I'm waiting to hear it."

As if on cue, a roar rippled across the icy wasteland, and Semana looked into the sky. The three-mawed dragon thrust itself into the air, massive wings spreading around its bulk. When she looked back down, Darak was grinning.

"Silver Fire," Semana said. "That—"

"That enough Frostfire for you?" Darak asked. "With that beast, you can enchant ten armies."

Semana blinked. "I'll—I'll have to think on it," she said.

"Perfect."

Darak put his arm around her shoulders. Semana wanted to object, but just at the moment she couldn't turn away his physical support. The confrontation with Carr had left her exhausted.

"I need you to do something else for me," Darak said. "Something that will take you away from the horde for a few days. While you consider how to make the protection serve."

Semana nodded. She didn't much relish spending time anywhere near a murderous Carr the Axe, and an absence would give her time to ponder the magic, and to reason out how Darak knew so much about it. "Speak," she said. "If it is worthy, I'll indulge you."

"Oh," Darak said. "Only if you want to win this war."

Semana took to the sky, and the dragon rose from its perch on the nearby bluff to meet her. They traced graceful patterns through the air, communicating with one another without words. The great beast naturally echoed her movements, twisting as she twisted, circling over itself as she spun. They danced adeptly and beautifully, drawing the eyes and admiration of thousands.

Perhaps it was their magic, perhaps it was their nature, but the two of them had a sort of connection that transcended anything Darak had ever seen, let alone experienced. He watched from under the shadow of a spindly tree, thoughts stirring around his mind, as the wind of their flight rustled his hair and clothes. He smiled slightly.

A hand slipped around his stomach and teased dexterous fingers over the laces of his breeches.

"Why do you smile, Dar-Karsk?" Fellis the Night Wolf asked in his ear. "Is this love?"

"Aesthetics," he said.

She hissed softly in his ear, more like an animal than a human woman, and Darak stiffened in mingled alarm and interest. Not fear—there was none of that and never had been—but he knew caution. And this was a moment to be cautious.

Finally, the two broke apart—the dragon swooping back toward its favored bluff, while Semana took off, borne on the power of her relics toward the south. Despite the High Druid reaching inside his clothes, he kept watching his sister until her tiny profile vanished against the horizon.

"Is this the moment?" Fellis asked. "You said I would know."

"Not yet," Darak said. "But soon." He turned his head back toward her. "Do you desire—?"

But Fellis the Night Wolf was gone, leaving him shivering and alone. At first he frowned, then he had to chuckle. All was going according to his plan.

"Crown of Fire."

The man appeared dutifully, bowing his head low.

"Spread the word," Darak said. "We strike Tar Vangr two days hence."

EIGHT

Atropis, the Dusk Sea

*I*N HER DREAM, THERE *is fire. It flows before her, a coursing sea of flame so hot it defies color. Perhaps it is white, perhaps gray, perhaps silver. Yes—silver.*

It pulses like a living thing, breathing in the same air and expelling smoke. It stops just short of her outstretched fingers, held in place by an invisible barrier as cold as rimefrost and as thin as paper. The silver fire burns with no perceivable fuel, no limit, and no end.

There is a sword in her hand: a blade sculpted like a flowing wave, burning with a fire of its own and expelling smoke to warn of an impending ending. When its steel would part the veil of the world and reveal what lies beneath. She longs for it and fears it in equal measure.

Someone screams at her in the darkness. Calls her name.

She starts to turn, and that is when the fire overtakes her. It rushes around her, filling her and consuming her and—

~

Ovelia woke, slick with sweat and momentarily confused as to her surroundings. The world flowed around her in shades of gray and black flame, painting indistinct outlines of faintly visible objects all around her. Her sight faded in and out, and she could almost perceive, but not quite. She closed her eyes and let the threatening panic subside. She was safe, or at least as safe as she could be, here in Atropis—with a warm body pressed against hers, sitting up while she lay half asleep.

A loud noise intruded into her world—the sound of knuckles on wood—and she could see the shadows vibrating. A door, she realized, somewhere in the middle distance. She started to turn in that direction, but a sharp, authoritative voice stayed her.

"Begone," the voice said, the word chipping away even as it left the speaker's throat. "Trouble me some other time." A hand touched Ovelia's cheek. "I am occupied."

Lady Shard. Princess Lenalin Denerre. Her master and her goddess.

"You're awake." Lenalin's fingers teased through Ovelia's hair, trailing lightly along the edge of her face. "Did you dream?"

Gently, Ovelia shook her head back and forth. A lie, but an easy one.

And by the slight pause in the unseen caresses, Lenalin knew it. "It will pass," she said. "In time, you will forget those terrors you carry with you. You will be with me, and that will be enough."

How much Ovelia wanted that life. The simplicity of it. To move forward. To forget. To escape.

Ovelia shifted, but Lenalin's warm hand on the back of her neck stopped her. "I'm not finished."

A shudder passed through Ovelia at the instruction, but she complied without hesitation. The tension in her shoulders and neck seemed to excite Lenalin, who offered her a soft purr of approval. Lenalin ran her fingers along Ovelia's spine: soft flesh in one direction, then nails in the other, always just on the edge of pain. Heat rippled out in waves from the touch. She lay shivering, forcing her limbs not to move, willing herself not to gasp and cry out. Instead, she hissed with a series of sharp breaths, torn from her by Lenalin's delicate touch, and finally a moan when she could stand it no longer. Sweat beaded on her brow and she lay panting and shuddering in the wake of her unspooling pleasure.

No one had ever touched her like that. Pleased her in that way. And she didn't want it to stop.

Ovelia heard the murmur of voices, and the rap on the door sounded again, louder and more insistent this time. Abruptly the touch was gone. Lenalin made a harsh growling noise and sent something sailing through the room—one of her pillows—to crash into the door with a dull thump.

"Ruin rot these interruptions," Lenalin said. "And just when I thought of a use for you."

"I know." Ovelia kissed the inside of Lenalin's thigh. "I was there."

The skin there was rough. She had a scar—one of dozens, all over her body, that Ovelia could not see but could feel. The pirate queen stiffened slightly when Ovelia touched one of these marks, and that made her heart ache. There was pain there, and Ovelia wanted nothing more than to soothe it.

"Hmm." Lenalin ran her fingers through Ovelia's hair and caught hold. "Another use, then."

Another knock at the door, however, and she growled anew.

"I shall throw someone from Atropis this day," she said. "You can dress yourself, yes?"

Ovelia nodded. "I'm blind, not helpless."

Lenalin must have nodded in return, for she left it at that. She moved away, toward a standing wardrobe, and Ovelia heard her putting on her silks and veil. Ovelia found her own attire—still where it lay discarded from the night before—at the foot of the pirate queen's bed. It felt cool and rumpled and not quite clean—a sensation she rather enjoyed.

"What was it you wanted of me?" Ovelia asked as they dressed. "This use you spoke of?"

"I need your insights. Your tactical knowledge. Your vision."

"My—" Ovelia unconsciously touched at her unseeing eyes. "What do you mean?"

"In time, you'll know." Lenalin came close, which Ovelia only knew because a hand touched her shoulder. "When the time comes, you'll answer my plea, when I make it? Say you will."

"Of course." It hardly seemed possible that Ovelia could decline. She nodded gently but firmly.

"Good." Lenalin's lips touched the brow over her left eye, then her right. "You're so beautiful."

Ovelia's breath caught. Lenalin had always been the jewel of winter: the most beautiful of women in the World of Ruin, as far as Ovelia had ever known or seen. Her perfection rivaled that of heroines of legend, and the angels themselves who first rose from the cold earth to fulfill the Prophecy of Return. As a girl, Ovelia could sit and gaze upon Lenalin for hours and know no passage of time. She needed nothing else. The very concept of beauty and Lenalin were one and the same to her.

But Ovelia could say none of these things. The one time she had even remotely inquired about Lenalin's scars or the years since her injuries, the woman had locked herself away for days on end and refused to speak to her. Ovelia's heart quickened at the delicate subject, as though she trod upon the fine edge of a vast, fathomless abyss she could not see but only feel.

Gently, she reached out and touched Lenalin's cheek. The pirate queen sat absolutely still, the muscles in her face as taut as iron bars. Ovelia could not see her expression, but she could feel the heat of her eyes. Was it anger? Sorrow? Hope?

Ovelia's child prodded her from the inside. She could feel Lenalin tense, then chuckle.

"And there's this." Lenalin spread her fingers on Ovelia's belly through the silks she'd put on. "Is this a Summer you carry, or perhaps a Winter? You've never told me the truth."

Ovelia was ready for this question, which Lenalin had asked more than once before. "I have to keep some secrets," she said, "or the chase loses its savor."

"Hmm." Lenalin sounded amused. "Very well then." Her fingers trailed up Ovelia's chest to her collar, her neck, and her chin. "But I'll have your secrets in time."

Ovelia suppressed a shiver. Every time Lenalin asked this question, Ovelia deflected or misled or bought a little delay in answering, ostensibly as part of a game. More than half a year hadn't pried loose her tongue. In truth, she hadn't told Lenalin the truth, because she couldn't predict how she would react. Lenalin had every reason to hate the Ravalis, and Lady Shard had betrayed Garin Ravalis to his death. How would she treat his child? And what would she think of Ovelia herself?

And.

And she was not ready to talk about Garin.

This time, when the loud bang came at the door, the seal swiveled and the door swung open to admit the hulking Aeldad, Shard's second in command, sword at her belt. She provided a solid bulwark of a physical presence, like a small mountain in whatever room she entered. The big Free Islander had never much liked Ovelia, which no one needed to see her face to realize. The way she warmed near Lenalin, Ovelia well understood why. At least she'd given them enough time to dress.

"Mistress," Aeldad said.

"Squire," Lady Shard said. "This is a surprise."

Lenalin had her veil on, Ovelia realized, and her voice evolved to match. It touched Ovelia's heart that Lenalin used her old voice only for her, but Ovelia couldn't for certain call it her *true* voice. She'd spent enough time with Mask to know the difference.

"We've a guest," Aeldad said. "A Druid of the Circle. Clad all in black and reeking of death."

A sudden realization both terrible and wonderful struck Ovelia. It cut through the haze of her time with Lenalin like a bolt of sunlight through a hazy day. Silver Fire—

"A barbarian," Lady Shard said, voice level but intrigued. "She's come alone?"

"Yes," Ovelia said, touching her belly as it shivered. "She has."

They both stared at Ovelia, and she could feel the question neither asked.

Aeldad uttered a curse in one of the many tongues of her homeland. "You be silent, Bloodbreaker," she said. "There's no way you can know—"

"She knows," Lenalin said. "Inform our guest we'll receive her on the overlook."

With a dubious grunt, Aeldad turned on her heel and swept out of the room. Ovelia breathed out a breath she didn't realize she'd been holding.

"How *do* you know, exactly?" Lenalin asked. "Do your powers extend so far?"

Ovelia trembled. She knew because she had dreamed it. Because destiny could not be denied.

She held out her hand, and after a moment, Lenalin took it. Her touch let Ovelia breathe freely.

"What passes?" Lenalin asked. "Lia, you're crying."

Ovelia took her hand back and wiped her face. Tucked into the folds of her doublet, she found the crimson cloth she used to bind her eyes and tied it around her head. It made no difference to the world of shadows and darkness that she saw in every moment, but it absorbed the tears.

"Nothing," she said. "My eyes are... sensitive."

The time she'd spent with Lenalin had been the happiest, warmest of her adult life. Then they had found Regel. Then Lan Ravalis and Davargorn. And now, after this, it would never be the same.

Flanked by six of her best warriors, including Aeldad and Tanak, Lady Shard climbed the steps to the overlook. Her hip ached with the climb, but once she hit that rushing, cool air, her pains eased into a sense of power and purpose. This was her place, these her swords. This barbarian came to her at the height of her strength—she would not be afraid, regardless of Ovelia's own reaction.

Something troubled Ovelia, for certain. The knight lingered behind, remaining down in the catwalks and shadows of Atropis, and Shard had managed not to question her in doing so. Ovelia had complained of aches, but Shard knew that for a lie. Had she seen something, mayhap? If her magic had grown so great that she could see things far beyond herself—and perhaps things that had yet to pass...

Shard would have appreciated having her magic just at the moment: with the burning sun of the late day, she could barely see anything up here. With a growl, Shard held her arm up against the glare.

Mayhap she should have met with the barbarian in the darker recesses of the city, but she rather liked standing here, surrounded by the glittering array of her power. Her fleet numbered thirteen skyships: most small battle craft, but two capital ships—the *Fury* and her former flagship, the *Talon*—that could carry a small ornithopter fleet of their own. Her pirates had worked hard to make some forty of the smaller craft operational and battle-worthy, to be deployed from the larger ships. And, of course, the gleaming *Hecatomb* hovering above Atropis, its great golden rings rotating slowly. In its shining, almost new state, it resembled some impossible work of art more than a weapon that had destroyed half a city. Shard might as well be meeting this barbarian emissary in an armory.

The emissary, on the other hand, had an entrance of her own to make.

At first, Shard took the rapidly moving black object against the sun-burned sky for a bird. One of the World of Ruin's misshapen gulls flying high above the turbulent sea or perhaps an albatross to foretell doom. But it moved too quickly—turned with too much agility. And as it drew closer, Shard could see a trail of greasy gray smoke streaming behind it. The barbarian made a rapid and jagged approach, like a hurled axe, and landed in a stagger that became a strange, disjointed walk toward them. The druid hardly resembled a woman or even a human being: all angles and hard lines, like a collection of spears lashed together and encased in black leather. Her leathern mask resembled a skull.

"Lady Shard," the barbarian said with a slight bow, her voice rasping and harsh. "I am Mask the Blood Queen, High Druid of the Circle. And I bring you greetings."

If she even noticed the casters pointed at her, the druid hardly seemed to care.

Shard had seen and dealt with many a Child of Ruin in her time, but none who arrayed themselves or behaved quite like this. Mask's demeanor seemed calm, her words cordial and shaped in etiquette. It clashed so sharply with every other interaction Shard had ever had with the brutish, violent, volatile folk that she fell instantly on her guard. And when on guard, she turned to an offensive posture.

"Indeed, Your Highness," Shard said, in her own dark and deep-pitched voice. "Though I'm unfamiliar with the land of Blood. Where does it lie? Somewhere over yon horizon?"

She gestured around to her armada of skyships, which should intimidate even the most hardened general of a powerful army, but Mask hardly spared them a second glance. Even the *Hecatomb* barely warranted more than a heartbeat's consideration. Mask's indifference to the threat was either laughable in its arrogance or terrifying in its certainty.

At her side, Aeldad uttered a low growl of warning and challenge. Shard laid a hand on her arm.

"I've come to bargain with you, Lady Shard, Queen of the Skies," Mask said. "Will you hear me?"

Not rattled. Fine.

"Speak," Shard said. "I will listen. Can't promise I'll hear."

The Druid spread her hands, which steamed with the black smoke of her power. "You and I have something in common, sky queen," she said. "We are both survivors. No matter how many bodies we must crawl over to see that next dawn."

Aeldad tensed, the way she always did when she heard a threat. Shard nodded slightly.

"Even now," Mask said, "the forces of the High Circle march upon the last bastion of civilization. Tar Vangr will fall within the season, and Ruin shall hold sway over all."

That was not entirely news to Shard, though she hadn't entirely trusted the ravings of a half-mad old man in the snow. It seemed Regel had spoken true after all.

"Tar Vangr is hardly the last bastion, or have you not heard?" Shard asked. "The Spider of Luether has driven your Ruin King from his throne and now there are two mage-cities in your broken world. What do you think of that, Blood Queen?"

"Irrelevant," Mask said, seeming bored. "I have been to Luether, and know the quality of its people. No doubt they'll fall by their own hand before we're even finished with Tar Vangr."

"You sound thoroughly invested."

Mask waved a hand as though brushing away a stinging fly.

Interesting. Perhaps this High Druid wasn't so fanatical about destruction as she pretended. She had a different agenda, but what? And *why?*

"You said you came to bargain, not threaten," Shard said. "Surely 'twas not your thought you could persuade me to join your screaming barbarians."

"Mayhap." Mask shrugged. "I thought you a woman of sense."

"Likewise," Shard said, hardly bothering to keep the surprise out of her voice. "You're here to persuade me *not* to sail north to aid my brethren—that is, all civilized people—against the threat of madness and death you so kindly offer them. Unless I am much mistaken?"

After a hesitation, Mask nodded warily. The Druid must not have expected such a casual reaction, but why would she? They were discussing the lives of thousands.

"What do you offer me?" Shard asked. "Can you promise me non-interference? That your perverse band of scum will not seize the skyships of Tar Vangr and wage war upon Atropis? That future generations of insane vermin will not sail to my threshold?"

The barbs didn't seem to bother Mask. Did she hold so little regard for Shard's opinion, or perhaps she thought herself above mere Children of Ruin? Both?

"I can make no such promises," Mask said. "But know that *I* will not strike against you, nor will any under my power. And you will have a far more trustworthy bargaining partner in the Winter King."

Shard blinked. "What?" she asked.

Radiating smugness, Mask drew herself to her full height. "He that leads those you so blithely dismiss as savages and vermin is Darak Ravalis nô Denerre," she said. "I had understood you to be a woman who aided those whose birthrights were stolen from them, so perhaps you will do the same for the Winter King? I've no doubt he will treat well with those who assist in his ascension."

Shard couldn't hear any more. Her mind roiled. Darak. Alive. Among the barbarians...

Mask wasn't here to ward her off the impending war. Mask was here to gain her support for Darak's bit for the throne of Tar Vangr. Her *son*.

"My lady," Aeldad said at her elbow. "What ails? Are you under attack?"

"No," Shard tried to say. "No, I—"

That was the moment. She couldn't say exactly what happened— whether Mask saw an opportunity and took it, or whether in the tension of the moment, one of her warders misinterpreted the Blood Queen's slight movement as an attack. But Mask reached forward and a caster cracked in the high winds of the height of Atropis, steel flashed like an arrow through the air, and protective blue power flared. Mask reeled back, the jagged metal shaft of a casterbolt transfixed in her right hand.

"Who cast that?" Shard demanded. "Who struck? Lady Mask—"

Smoke boiling from her body, the druid lowered her masked head and uttered a curse.

Now that—*that* was pure Child of Ruin.

Green power swirled around the skull face, and Mask threw back her shoulders and let the magic erupt out of her in a rush. It painted the world around them in clashing shades of green and gray, and ropy tendrils of disgusting magic sailed toward Shard's group. The power stabbed into one of her warders, closer to Mask than the others, and the tendrils lifted her screaming into the air. As Shard watched, the woman's flesh rotted away, and her face drew thin and aged in a mere heartbeat. Mask slashed her hand to the side, hurling the hapless warder from Atropis, then turned to Shard.

"If it is to be war," Mask said, "then so be it."

Aeldad cried out a warning and tried to grab Shard, perhaps to shield her, but she succeeded only in knocking her over. The Pirate Queen took half a step backward, and her left hip exploded in sudden pain. When it stopped supporting her weight, she fell to one knee with a hiss, and looked up just in time to see the cruel green magic rushing toward her.

Then the slaying spell exploded into a red-hot churning storm of power, stopping just short.

There stood Ovelia, her robe flapping around her muscular body, Draca interposed between Shard and Mask. The vines of rotting green magic flowed into the sword, sucked into it like water into a thirsty sponge that never seemed to grow saturated. Mask roared in frustration and sent even more power rushing forward, fully two dozen tendrils of destructive power, but it sank harmlessly into the sword, which vibrated in Ovelia's hands like an overactive mage engine.

Finally the assault slackened, then tore messily free, green tendrils raking across the iron plating of Atropis's roof. Where it touched, the magic left corroded grooves in the metal. The forest of tentacles dissipated, dissolving in the air like evaporating rain clouds, leaving only Mask herself standing before them, her thin body trembling in rage and frustration.

Ovelia fell back half a step, holding the white-hot Draca steaming in the air. Shard's heart leaped in her chest, and she had a mad urge to rush toward her savior and embrace her.

Seething, Mask leaned toward Ovelia look like a looming insect or a snake about to lunge for its prey. Then a shudder passed through her seemingly frail body and she righted herself, back under control. A degree of self-discipline Shard could well respect.

"Bloodbreaker." Mask pointed her spitted hand toward Ovelia and Shard. "You yet live."

"Semana, wait," Ovelia said, and Shard was certain she'd heard wrong. "We can—"

More casters cracked and Shard saw the blue magic flash around Mask, knocking the bolts away like a shield. One particularly well-aimed bolt got through, though, and smashed fully into the Druid's mask, ripping it half off her head. She curled away from them, covering her face with her arms.

"Hold!" Shard shoved Aeldad's caster out of line. "Hold your casts, burn you!"

Silence gripped the rooftop, but for the howl of wind, the distant whir of mage-engines, and the thundering of Shard's heart in her chest. What was going on? What had happened?

Then the Druid rose slowly, pulling her mask the rest of the way free as she did so. Tiny red lines cut along her skin like veins, and a bruise spread around a cut on her cheek, but it was definitely her. There was no mistaking the golden skin and silver-white hair, the elegant cast of her features, and the fire in her burning, blood-shot eyes.

Semana Denerre nô Ravalis.

They stared at one another, Semana and Ovelia, and there was so much between them in that moment that Shard couldn't say what either thought or would have said. Semana looked at Ovelia's blindfold, her sword, then at her swollen belly, and her grimace deepened. Ovelia put out a hand, as though just by reaching toward her, she could make it better.

Then Mask turned, tattered cloak flowing in the wind behind her, and something came barreling out of her shadow, right toward Ovelia. The woman cried out in surprise and raised her sword, narrowly catching a blade of shimmering black that smashed into it with a rain of sparks. Her attacker moved like a whirlwind, twisting around to launch a powerful kick at her midsection. Ovelia must have sensed it, for she twisted to catch the kick on her side, rather than on her belly, and she came staggering back toward Shard and the others. Between them and the Blood Queen stood a man of surpassing physical perfection and impossible musculature, his skin gray like that of a corpse and his eyes of ineffable black.

"I gave you a chance, Pirate Queen, but you rejected my kindness." Semana's boots smoked with magic, and she lifted off the metal. She pulled her mask back into place, and her voice changed to its former, sinister aspect. "Now you pay the price."

So speaking, Mask rose into the sky, arms outstretched. Green magic flowed from her mask, wrapping around her arms and dancing among her fingers. Aeldad stepped in front of Shard as though to shield her, but the Pirate Queen realized they were not Mask's targets.

Indeed, Mask threw out her hand and sent a churning ball of rotting magic not toward them, but toward the nearest skyship—a lancer-class, sized for a crew of twenty, with room for a hundred soldiers—and smashed into the core of the ship with a sickly wet sound. Corroded veins spread along the decks and down the hull of the ship. The hapless folk who'd been working on the ship scurried off like rats, crying out in terror. Within heartbeats, the motivator rings dulled and fell away, and the ship listed to the left in dock. Metal squealed and the ship cracked through the middle and fell in two pieces away from the skydock atop Atropis.

"No!" Ovelia took a step forward, but Mask's demon warder was there, driving her back with a threatening obsidian sword. His face bore no malice, only purpose.

It seemed Mask intended them to do nothing but watch. The sorcerer was already flying past the next docked ship, scoring its length with green bolts of rotting magic. A handful of Shard's pirates ran to intercept her, but she threw out a hand and sent them sprawling off Atropis with a wave of force. She flew on like a hunting hawk and spiraled up around another skyship, ripping holes in its hull and motivator rings with her burning green magic.

Mask. Princess Semana Denerre. The Blood Queen.

Shard shivered.

"My lady?" Aeldad asked. "What do we do?"

Shard hesitated, her mind whirring, as foul smoke rose around them, obscuring the warm day.

"What are you?" Ovelia asked the man with the obsidian sword. She didn't look directly at him, the way she usually didn't with anyone. She didn't see him with her eyes.

"I am the Deathless Gilt," he said. "I do not wish to slay you, but do not think I will not."

"No," said another voice. "You will not."

Regel the Frostburn stepped through the smoke—a wiry, nearly skeletal form in black breeches and nothing else, neither cloak nor shoes. His torso was a mass of scars and bruises and cuts, and his graying black hair spilled long down his back. His icy eyes cut just as sharp as ever, however, as did the curved sword of burnished blue mage-glass he held pointed toward the Deathless: the Frostburn.

At the words, Shard stirred from her hesitation. Mask destroyed another of the skyships and flew toward a fourth. She looked to Aeldad and rasped out two words. "Battle stations."

Then she looked to the *Hecatomb*, floating above the rest, and nodded.

She knew just what to do.

The three of them stood on the windswept height of Atropis, shrouded in foul-smelling smoke.

"Begone, turncoat," Regel said, his words as cold as Frostburn blazing in his hand. He swept the blade up, letting it hang forward and down like a stalactite. "Or we will cut you down."

Ovelia raised Draca, holding it about level with her belly, both hands on the handle. Her crimson hair flowed out behind her. She felt Shard and the others retreating, rushing toward the other skyships, and it was only Regel and herself that kept this Deathless from pursuing them. They had to hold him.

She had never faced a Deathless—never even seen one—but if Regel's stories held any truth...

"I cannot abandon my Blood Queen," Gilt said. "I love her, as you do."

"Exactly why we cannot allow this," Regel said.

"Then this duel shall be to my honor and yours." Bending low, Gilt split his obsidian sword into two smaller blades and swept them up behind himself like the wings of a perched bird of prey.

What Ovelia perceived could not be real. She saw him not as the man whose voice he bore but a nightmare beast of indistinct black lines and talons. He was not living nor dead—he was death, and he had come for them. Shadows boiled from Draca, warning her of the duel, and she steeled herself.

"Throw away eternity at your peril," Regel said. "I am an exile too, and so have no honor left."

"Then I shall take what honor I may in dying upon the edge of the Frostburn."

Then he struck, and if Ovelia had not seen his rush in the shadows, he'd have surprised them both. He moved with lightning speed, his blades cutting for throats and armpits and faces—all strikes that might have been lethal. Ovelia smashed his attacks away, and he took the opportunity to kick off her and propel himself like a thrown spear toward Regel. The way he moved— the sheer speed and grace—was like that of no mortal being Ovelia had ever seen, except for when Regel had returned to Tar Vangr trained in the ways of the Deathless. As a young man, he'd been able to emulate such mastery of movement, but he was no longer a young man.

But Regel bore Frostburn, and its power protected him.

Had Ovelia mundane sight, she could not have tracked the flashing weapons. Gilt crashed into Regel's slashing defense like his body had no physical limits, increasing in speed where fatigue should have slowed him, striking Regel's defense half a dozen times within a single breath. Every clash of stone on mage-glass sent flecks of ice showering around them. His movements put her horribly in mind of the street thresher she had narrowly avoided in Luether: as vicious and uncaring and destructive.

And somehow, despite his obvious weakness of body, Regel kept defending. He moved in tight, minimalist patterns, stepping only as he had to in order to protect himself. Gilt fought to overwhelm him, and if Ovelia did not come to his aid...

Move.

Ovelia charged in, blade low and leading, heedless of Regel's cry of warning. Of a sudden, her world filled with shadows of a dozen strikes in a dozen different directions, and she could hardly tell which to block in which order. Draca came to her aid, leaping across and around in flashing red arcs, and she could hear and feel but not see Gilt's blade rebound from her defense. At least he tried to keep from striking her defense hard—that sword must be brittle in comparison to her own relic. His obisidan swords scraped across Draca, then one abruptly shot past her head, close enough to slit open her cheek.

She slapped the sword away, ducked the second swing, and countered with a rising slash that hit only air. The Deathless evaded with a grace and speed far beyond her, and she couldn't even begin to catch him. What good was foresight if she lacked the speed to exploit it?

An explosion rocked Atropis as pieces of another skyship plummeted from dock and smashed into the roof some hundred paces away. Ovelia fell to one knee and steadied herself on the roof, Draca still raised protectively over herself. She put her free hand to her belly, which had taken the opportunity to thrash about, as though it fought a battle of its own. An entirely new dread ripped through her, and her body refused to get up and rejoin the fight.

Regel had engaged Gilt again, and they fenced in a half-circle away from her. Ovelia managed to stagger that way, until a green blast of power slashed through the deck some twenty paces away, between her and Lenalin. The Pirate Queen's little party was headed toward the lift in the middle of Atropis's roof, but could they reach it unaided? Her heart shuddered.

"Can you hold him?" she asked over the clash of blades and scream of steel.

She moved before Regel grunted in the affirmative, stumbling across the rocking, shuddering deck after her princess.

"Your seer abandons you." Gilt's dark voice cut through the smoke to Ovelia's ears.

Regel fought on silently, but Ovelia could hear his joints crackling as he forced himself to move. Rimefrost sheathed his arms and legs, flowing from his blue sword, but he fought on.

And that was all Ovelia could perceive before a listing, half-rotted skyship slammed into the deck before her with nerve-shattering force. Ovelia lost her footing and rolled, closing herself around her belly, and crashed painfully back against some sort of bulkhead. The impact jarred Draca from her hand, and the sword went skittering across the iron roof to vanish amongst the smoke and heat.

"Up," Ovelia told herself. "*Move.*"

After two ragged breaths, she pulled herself up to one knee, only to perceive a glowing white angel of wrath descending toward her. In all likelihood, the black leather would have hid her from anyone else, but Ovelia could see those who meant her harm very brightly indeed, and the sorcerer looked like the sun by comparison to any other threat she had ever known. She glowed such that Ovelia could almost make out her specific facial features through the mask that swirled with horrible death.

Semana.

And Ovelia had no sword to shield her.

"You live, Bloodbreaker," Semana said, declaiming the words like a thunderclap. "And what's more, you are with child. Is that Regel's, I wonder? My bastard sibling growing inside you?"

She knows. Ovelia shivered.

Power roared from Semana, rotting holes in skyships and Atropis itself. The sheer amount of power she was channeling should have killed a mortal woman. Ovelia had never seen anyone use that much magic. How mighty was that relic, and did Semana know what she was doing?

"Stop this madness," Ovelia said. "The Children of Ruin? Wanton destruction? This isn't you."

"That woman is dead," Semana said. "Only Mask remains."

Ovelia set her stance firmly. "I don't believe that."

Even as the destructive plaguefire rent the world around them asunder, Semana raised her left hand in a strangely delicate motion. Ovelia felt unseen force surround her, crushing like a steel vice. She fought for breath, but her chest would only expand so far. Her thoughts immediately went to the growing child inside her, but she couldn't even move her hand to touch.

"I made a mistake in thinking you dead before," Semana said. "This time, I'll make sure. *Slowly.*"

She spread the fingers of her left hand, and the magic stretched Ovelia's arms and legs out wide. She expelled the last breath in her lungs in a gurgle of pain, and then she had nothing left. The shadows she could see started to quiver, and her body fought for breath.

Tell her. If Ovelia had the breath, that's what she would do. If only she had the breath.

They heard it at the same time: a sizzling roar of growing strength. The shadows moved, and Ovelia saw it coming before it arrived. Her heart raced.

Put me down, she thought. *Fly. Fly away—*

A massive blast of swirling crimson magic shot toward Semana, and she vanished in a cloud of fire and smoke. Abruptly, her glove's magic fell apart, and Ovelia collapsed onto her back on the roof with a strangled protest. Above her, the sleek, crackling visage of the *Hecatomb* loomed like a dragon out of legend above her. And flying that beautiful monstrosity had to be Lenalin.

Lenalin had fired the skyship's main weapon on Semana.

Ovelia rolled to her side and stared, trying to make out the shadows through the surging mass of destructive power. Surely she would see Semana, who hated her so much she blazed like a star. Surely—

"No," she said, barely able to make a sound. "No—"

Then Semana swooped out of the storm of power, her full attention turned to the *Hecatomb*. Power swirled around her, but before she could unleash it, the deadly skyship opened fire with its secondary weapons. Spears of fire and bolts of lightning arced through the air, and Semana weaved and danced through the air around some of the shots, while others sparked off the blue shielding magic that flared around her. She loosed a cry of frustration, but that reassured Ovelia. Semana yet lived, and she—

Another mighty blast slammed into Semana, and she sailed senseless off the edge of Atropis, like a bird whose wings had suddenly broken. Watching her fall, Ovelia's heart all but stopped.

She heard, faintly, a cry from across the roof, and she dimly saw the roaring threat of Gilt, the Deathless fae. She couldn't see his face, but she could feel his sudden shock, much like her own. The blazing blue blade of Frostburn showed up clear against the shadows, even if Ovelia could not see Regel himself, and it slashed across Gilt's torso in his distraction. The Deathless tumbled back and vanished as abruptly as he had appeared.

"Ovelia?" Regel called. "Do you live?"

She tried to speak but couldn't. Her heart pounded in her head.

She sank to her knees at the edge of the roof, clutched her arms around her stomach, and sobbed without tears.

NINE

The Winter Wilds

THE CITY OF STEEL sparkled in the near distance, built into and around the tallest peak in a fringe of mountains on the southern shore of the northernmost lands. Tar Vangr stood tall and indomitable, a bastion of civilization that pinned the edge of the Winter Wilds, and held sway over all it surveyed. Its towering height and the sweeping valleys that extended around it offered an excellent view of an approaching threat, and the great black walls offered a seemingly impenetrable defense.

"Seeming," Darak said under his breath. He closed his cowl tighter against the snow and a slow smile spread across his face.

A warm hand touched his waist, and Darak sucked in a sharp breath. Fellis bore the name Night Wolf for good reason. "There it stands," she said, her voice a whisper in his ear. "Your destiny."

"*No.*" He pulled away from her as though from an open flame. "Not where others can see."

Irritation flickered across her face before she once again smiled blithely. "Why, Dar-Karsk?"

"Why."

Darak looked around the hill upon which they stood. The bulk of the horde remained camped under the rise, hidden from Tar Vangr, but a number of honor guard had accompanied them onto the overlook. Though they stood at a respectful distance, surely they would see Fellis touching him in the way of lovers, and rumors would spread faster than fire or sickness. That was the last thing he needed.

Fellis must have sensed his unease, for she waved her hand dismissively. "Do you doubt yourself, Dar-Karsk?" she asked. "Do you doubt all things you see belong to you?" Her body moved subtly, drawing his eyes and sparking his imagination. "*All* things."

He opened his mouth, then closed it again, words left unspoken.

He did not doubt himself, but he had begun to doubt *her.* Fellis had taken to him rather quickly, above and beyond the alliance they'd formed, and he saw through her fawning and flirtation. She meant to bend him to her will, and fair enough: he might have done the same, were their positions reversed. He *had* done the same with Afferath, and the feelings he'd planted in her had proved her undoing. Darak could not afford to underestimate or ignore Fellis the Night Wolf, nor could he tolerate her attempts to undermine him in front of the horde. *He* commanded them, not her—it was *his* destiny to smash Tar Vangr, not hers—and he would find a suitable way to make that clear.

But he needed her. He had seen the way the horde looked upon him and heard the whispers. *Where is the Blood Queen?* they asked, as though Semana had some greater claim on Tar Vangr or their swords. It was unjust—it was an *insult*—but it was true. Darak was a man and only a rotpriest, not a member of the Circle, so he needed a Druid. Carr had made no secret of her contempt for him and Semana had not yet returned from her mission to the south, so he needed Fellis's loyalty and support.

For now.

Darak heard Carr before he saw her, strings of bones rattling on her boiled leather hauberk. Her deep brown skin seemed oddly pale in the cold and her breath steamed. The perpetual scowl on her face was nothing new, but at least she didn't seem to have seen Fellis pawing at Darak.

"Well, we've come this far," Carr said. "And now, we'll have to turn back."

"What." Darak clenched his shoulders in irritation. He looked to Fellis, who looked as indifferent as ever. "I think I misheard you, Lady Druid."

Carr sneered, the scars on her face making the expression particularly horrific. "I told you, boy," she said. "No one can hold together a horde through the winter. The winds have come, and even if the warriors can survive, their morale will not. We'll come back together in the spring." Her contempt deepened and she directed a glare at Fellis. "Some of us, anyway."

No doubt she thought this her moment of victory, when Darak's power would fracture just on the eve of his victory. She'd marched this far not to support him but to make a point. He could see it in the cold-pale faces of the honor guards who'd accompanied them onto the rise and the cold damp soaking their armor and boots. He himself never felt the cold, not with his Frostfire, but the Children of Ruin were not so fortunate.

"Too bad the Blood Queen never came back," Carr said. "She could have protected us from the cold. But you? What can you do? Hey—"

Darak marched down the hill without a word, right past the stunned Carr and her bemused honor guard. She said something angry, but he had a point of his own to make.

Darak walked among the gathered barbarians, who had marched this far and begun to make camp for the swiftly approaching night. Boots and furs gritty with frost made them look more like snow-covered trees and boulders than men and women, and Darak knew the prohibition against setting fires so close to Tar Vangr had not won him much love. Scarred faces stared accusingly at him from beneath rime-encrusted cowls and helms. He saw their weariness in their slumped shoulders and felt their discontent in their glares, and with good reason: they were freezing. Slowly but surely, the abominable cold of the Winter Wilds would sap their strength and then their lives. He did not care a single jot.

What *did* trouble him, however, was the toll it had taken on his efforts. Hundreds of barbarians had already left, melted away in the night, and those who remained had begun to waver. Now, they looked more like shambling corpses than warriors. He had hoped drawing within sight of their goal would spur them, but as the momentum of their march ground to a halt, so had their fire had gone out.

Time to reignite it.

He strode out into a natural opening amongst the horde, a rocky patch of ground where broken rocks had sunk into a pit. No one wanted to make camp there, on the chance that deeper disturbances might prompt it to sink further, and the barbarians had given it a wide berth. The snow made his footing treacherous, and Darak paused at the edge of the natural bowl. He cast his gaze around to the many eyes that had tracked him, then efficiently and purposefully unbuttoned his own cloak.

"What passes?" Carr scoffed. "Offering us all a show?"

He ignored the two High Druids, who had followed him down the slope. Crown of Fire had materialized from somewhere, his eyes downcast, but Darak held up a hand to keep him at bay.

This he would do alone.

"Heritors of Ruin," he said, his voice loud enough to sweep through the small valley where the vanguard of the army camped. He poured a little Worldfire into the words, setting them dancing on the wind. Not all in the horde would hear him, but stories of this moment would spread.

"I have led you this far. I, Dar-Karsk, who learned the ways of the Worldfire under Afferath of the Burning Rain. I, Dar-Karsk, consort to the Blood Queen Mask."

Heads nodded in acknowledgement. It galled Darak to have to name these women—one of them dead at his own hand, the other missing and perhaps dead—to anchor his own authority, but so be it. If all went as he hoped, he'd no longer need any woman to prop him up after long.

"You have followed me this far upon faith," he said. "I asked you to follow, and you did, longing to fulfill your destiny as destroyers. As bringers of Ruin. And now—now that destiny draws nigh!"

He finished unbuttoning his cloak and unfurled it in a flourish, casting it into the snow. The light sparkled off his pale brown body covered with scars and patches of raw pink flesh. He'd had Crown of Fire scrape away his Worldfire sores the night before, which had taken quite some time after all the exertions of the march. Not using the magic to strengthen his body the last few hours had left him sore and weak, but having no blemishes made it worth it.

Having no marks of Woldfire showed the Children an illusion of strength: that he did not need the power of a rotpriest to make the long, hard trek. They did not know of his Frostfire, let alone understand it, so they would not know he needed no magic to repel the chill.

Darak felt their ambivalence and struck at the right moment. Just as he had planned.

"I know you are cold," he said. "I know what Ruin asks of you is a mighty challenge, that it pushes you beyond the limits of the flesh, but your courage— your *conviction*—will be rewarded."

He caught Carr's face in the corner of his eye, scowling in self-satisfaction. No doubt she expected him to falter and make a fool of himself. Fellis wore an easy smile.

Does she know? He wondered.

"For generations, unto the unremembered time before, we have hurled ourselves screaming against the walls of the abominable mage-cities," Darak said. "It has taken a thousand years, but all lie in ruins but for the strongest. Tar Vangr, the City of Steel, has repelled all our assaults with its weapons and its skyships. It has never fallen—until today." He raised his arms toward the sky. "Because Ruin herself rides on the winds of our crusade. She blesses our efforts, and she will crush our foes. Have faith!"

The barbarians murmured, stirred by his speech but not yet inflamed. Darak had always had a fine tongue and a sense for the dramatic.

"You mean the dragon?" Carr loosed a guffaw. "The Blood Queen could control that beast, but she is gone, perhaps never to return. You think you can stand where she has abandoned us?"

Darak smiled slightly.

Then he called upon his Frostfire.

Cries of shock and disbelief rose from among the watchers as silver-white flames leaked from Darak's flesh like sweat. Flames touched the falling snowflakes, converting them instantly to steam that rose around Darak, stirring his hair. In response to his push, the power flared outward and up until he became the center of a Frostfire bonfire. It felt unexpectedly good to loose his control in this way, despite his carefully cultivated restraint. Giddiness rose in him, and he did his best to strangle it.

He'd spent years hiding this potentially mortal secret about himself. He could see it now, in the faces of the wiser barbarians—particularly Carr and Fellis, and surprisingly Crown of Fire. They saw his exotic magic and made the lethal connection. This was anathema he practiced: profane, vile arts not worthy of the Children of Ruin, let alone the Circle of High Druids. Carr's hand closed tightly around the haft of her axe, and Fellis's look of surprise shifted into suspicion. Even Crown of Fire, Darak's most trusted and loyal servant, stared at him with mingled horror and awe. At least in his case, he had seen Semana's powers, and his irritating desire for Darak's sister colored his impressions.

Darak realized Carr had started moving toward him, axe in hand and a violent glint in her eye. He felt no fear, but instead registered her threat with mounting irritation. Of *course* she sought to undo his efforts. The powerful were also jealous—so it would always be.

A roar sounded above and around Darak, and the massive silver-white dragon landed just over the natural pit at his feet. Its wings swept out behind its huge body, dispersing a hurricane wave of air that sent scores of nearby barbarians staggering back. The creature spread its three jaws and oozed silver-white fire around its head, much like Darak's own power. The Frostfire was in its blood, and it responded in kind to another wielder.

The Children of Ruin stood at a wary distance as Darak turned to the beast. Its six eyes stared down at him, two of them cloudy and murky with disease and one scarred from long-ago violence. Its body was a mass of scars and malformed flesh, where it had healed improperly from countless wounds both incidental and purposeful. The Children had told legends of attempts to slay this very creature for centuries, and Darak realized that the dragon must have slain hundreds, perhaps even thousands of Children of Ruin. His brethren. His brothers and sisters.

Darak, however, stood above any mere Child of Ruin. A fact he would demonstrate this day.

He stretched forth his hand to the dragon, which to any onlooker must have resembled reaching out to a raging inferno. He knew the beast would not strike, though, and indeed, fate rewarded his confidence. The creature turned its head so it could scrutinize him from all angles, displaying an unsettling range of motion. It could nearly rotate its head all the way around.

Deciding if I'm my sister, Darak thought but did not say.

"I am not the Blood Queen," he said to the dragon, loud enough for Carr and Fellis to hear him. "But I am your master. You will serve me in her stead."

Whether the dragon understood him or not, it bowed its head until its snout came to his level. Tentatively, Darak took half a step forward and laid his hand on its nose. He could feel the heat and power within the creature, rippling under its flesh like blood. It seemed to vibrate slightly, making his hand tingle as they touched. Was this what Semana felt when she touched the beast? What did it mean?

Its huge, luminous eyes blinked at him in sequence. Waiting. Trusting.

He turned his head slightly toward Fellis. "Your blade," he said.

All eyes turned toward the Druid, and she did not hesitate as Darak himself had. Face carefully blank, she stepped forward and drew a sharp, curved dagger from her belt. The beast did not react—it hardly seemed to notice her—and did not so much as flinch when she carefully slid the blade into the scales of its neck. Bright blue blood leaked out from the tiny wound, running down her knife and over her wrist. The dragon's eyes remained on those of Darak, their connection unwavering.

"Taste it," Darak said to Fellis.

The Druid gave him a dubious look, then raised the blade to her bright red tongue. Slowly, she licked the steel clean, and power sparked within her. Abruptly, her eyes lightened, turning a kind of blue gray and becoming luminous. She blinked and a broad smile spread across her face.

"The cold," she said. "It bites no longer."

Behind him, Darak heard Carr's sharp intake of breath, followed by a quiet oath, and he knew he had won the day. He continued to fix the dragon with his gaze, however: keep it calm and focused upon him. Its blue blood dripped steadily from its neck into the hollow in the snowy ground, like sap oozing from a wound in a tree. The blood did not melt through the snow but instead collected in a viscous pool.

"Drink, all of you," Darak said. "Take this power into yourselves, and let us find our destiny."

They came, one or two at first, then by the dozen and score. They spooned blood into their hands and drank or pressed their mouths to the dragon's wound. Fellis cut several more slits with her sharp little blade until half a dozen barbarians could feed at once like leeches. Each went away with a tiny spark of Frostfire that repelled the winter's chill. Some blinked, disbelieving, while some danced and capered through the snow. Every display of joy brought yet more Children seeking the dragon's blessing.

Through it all, Darak held the dragon's focus, and other than a rumble here and there, it hardly seemed to notice what was happening. Maintaining the flow of Frostfire demanded an effort, and soon his body started to feel sore all over. Sweat dripped from his brow, but he didn't dare wipe it away.

Half a hundred barbarians now clustered around the dragon, and those near the front scrabbled desperately at the tiny pools of blue blood melting into the snow of the pit. Their tramping boots corrupted and polluted the blood, smearing dozens with a mixture of blood, mud, and wet. The happy cheers when the cold vanished turned into arguments and bickering about who got to drink first, and Darak realized he should have thought this through a little further. The logistics of feeding an entire army from one source, no matter how large, made matters difficult.

Dimly, Darak realized someone had organized the barbarians to carry skins of blue Frostfire blood back to their camps. No doubt it was Crown of Fire, who had a head for such things. He'd have to remember to reward his slave later.

Finally, Carr forced her way through the crowd, and Darak looked over at her, blinking through sweat. The axe was in her hand, and he had a brief thought that perhaps she would try to strike him down after all. Wouldn't that be amusing? At the height of his power and influence, as he stood among his army, she could still kill him, and perhaps she should. Perhaps this was her moment.

Instead, she stepped past him, axe raised. "This is taking too long," she said.

She smashed the axe into the dragon's neck, and blood welled around the blade. A tremor spread through the creature, and its head twisted to the side. Darak almost fell to his knees at the effort to hold the dragon, and he fought to pull power from deep in his core. His arms trembled and his legs started to go numb. Sweat coated him and he gritted his teeth, his whole body shaking.

"Pass well, Dar-Karsk?" Carr asked, her voice pitched in mock concern.

He grimaced at her. Then nodded.

With a twist of her powerful arms, Carr wrenched the blade free and a torrent of blood so dark blue it seemed black poured from the creature. When it hit the air, it blossomed into bright blue in a spreading sheen. Barbarians fell into the stream, the blood spurting into their faces—their mouths and eyes. They licked it off each other. They reveled in it.

Darak felt the dragon struggling to break free. Some part of its mind and soul wanted to pull away, but he refused to let go. It took every ounce of his

Frostfire, but he kept the creature under control. Semana was not here to guide, so he would compel. This was his day, and he would not falter.

The dragon uttered a series of mewling groans as its wound gushed, and he could feel the fierce vitality in the creature ebbing somewhat, but it was strong. It would survive. It would recover. And in the meantime, all of them would have the blessings of the Frostfire.

In time, his misgivings gave way to irritation. He resented having to work so hard to hold the dragon, and he should never have had to take such a risk as this. He had won the day, but he shouldn't have had to try so hard.

"Burn you, Semana," he said under his breath. "Where are you?"

TEN

Atropis, the Dusk Sea

THE RAINS CAME AND went, filling the cell with puddles and the constant stink of rot. It had become his world—that, and the periodic roar of skyships in the gray sky. The coming and going craft produced a near constant hum that, without a wall against the noise, he could feel in his bones. How many days had passed? It could have been years for all he knew.

Once again in prison, once again adrift in time.

It occurred to Davargorn that he'd spent a good part of his life in one prison or another. Perhaps all of it. When he was a child, he was a prisoner to his own poverty. Then he was a prisoner as Semana's companion, then as a slayer in service to Mask. He'd spent countless days in the moldering darkness beneath Tar Vangr and Luether, so why wouldn't he also grace the skycells in Atropis, legendary lost mage-city at the heart of Old Calatan?

It was such a bizarre thought, Davargorn wondered if he had lost his mind.

His senses warped in the cell. His hearing grew either muted, constantly battered by the shrieking winds, or painfully acute when those winds faded. The world beyond looked gray and hazy, until he looked down at his own hands, where he could see every tiny scratch and speck of dirt. His mind came unspooled as he sat staring, counting his fingers for the hundredth time and trying not to go mad.

Only belatedly did he realize he had started to slide slowly, temptingly, toward the edge.

Davargorn corrected his slide, tucking himself against the wall where he could cling, muscles taut, until Atropis rocked back the other way.

One of the worst aspects of the sky cells, Davargorn thought, was how Atropis moved. Like a ship at sea, buffeted by wind or tide or both, the towering mage-city rocked from side to side. Some of these shifts were precipitous: once Davargorn made the mistake of falling asleep for too long, and he woke up with his cell angled steeply toward the sea, his legs dangling over the long drop. He'd considered the possibility it was a dream, but a spray of rain in his face convinced him otherwise, and he scrambled back up into the cell. He didn't sleep much after that.

Only one thing kept him grounded, and that was his neighbor, Lan Ravalis.

Or more accurately, Lan's voice, which he confessed might have been in his head. The once-prince, then-king, now-prisoner alternated between ranting about the injustice of his situation, condemnation of the many traitors and conspirators who surrounded him, and musings about the proper place of menfolk and womenfolk—with emphasis on how his sister had stolen his rightful throne. Most of what he said was about himself, and Davargorn could just listen and say nothing.

"Hateful, awful creature, Alistra," he said. "She killed my mother, you know. The queen never did recover after giving birth to that wretch. Just wasted away, as though all the life went out of her."

Davargorn must have heard the story ten times now. Or fifty.

Occasionally Lan would speak of Davargorn, when he could see past himself, and those were the moments he had to reply, or Lan would simply keep repeating his questions even as it grew dark.

"I wonder why Lady Shard is keeping us alive," Lan said once or ten times. "I've heard she's hideous under that veil. Maybe she likes her men hideous as well? You have an advantage, Tithian."

For certain Davargorn had lost his mind, for he started to think that sounded reasonable.

He blinked out at the gray sky. The edge looked inviting.

"Ay." Lan smashed his hand on the wall. "Ay—listen to me. Listen."

With a sigh, Davargorn tapped on the wall in acknowledgement.

"This isn't your doing, Tithian," Lan said. "You did not drive yourself to this place. Choices not yours have shaped this destiny for you."

"Choices." Davargorn considered the edge once more. He shied a little closer against the wall.

"You lived with Semana for years, and yet you never?" Lan asked.

Of course, Lan eventually asked this. He seemed to think of little else.

Davargorn shook his head, and only belatedly realized Lan could not see him, so the gesture held no purpose. "No," he said. "Never."

The prince's laughter rang out, reverberating through the wall and around the open space outside their adjoining cells. "Oh, my friend, my friend," Lan said. "She used you, Tithian, just as my sister used me. We are alike—both of our lives seized and warped by women."

He'd said such things before, but Davargorn had never quite heard them so clearly. He wanted to argue, but the more days passed, with only these accusations for company, and they became hard to deny. He put his head against the stone wall and listened.

Lan always used the name Semana had given him: Tithian. Did he understand the significance?

"You are a good man, Tithian," Lan said. "You give and you aid and you suffer, and what do you have to show for it? What kindness did she ever show you? What reward for your devotion? Does she even see you, Tithian?" He tapped on the wall. "Does she see you?"

He thought of Semana—Mask—rising up above him, rebuking him, tearing his own mask off his face with her magic. Casting him aside like so much detritus.

Had she seen him?

Had she bothered to look?

He wasn't sure she ever had.

～

He must have drifted off at some point, because Davargorn awoke to a fury of sound and trembling. Atropis shook under some manner of assault, and he saw flaming chunks of steel and wood tumbling down past his cell. Pieces of skyships, he realized, rent asunder by powerful magic.

In the adjoining cell, Lan Ravalis cackled madly and cheered louder for each destroyed ship that appeared—at least until the shattered propulsion ring of one of the ships crashed into his cell, and Davargorn heard him curse and scramble away. His ears, unbearably keen, made his head explode as the ships rained around them. He could pick out the sounds of heavy casters firing above, and the unmistakable roar of the *Hecatomb's* main weapon.

Then a particularly massive explosion rocked Atropis, not far off his cell, and Davargorn staggered back against the wall near the door. He struck with a jarring impact that made his bones shudder. He sank to one knee, sucking in smoke. There was a wet slapping sound from somewhere in the haze, and he saw dying spirals of green magic that he recognized with a heart-turning certainty.

He heard his name through ringing ears, and realized Lan was shouting to him. "Tithian!" the man cried. "Pass well? Do you live?"

"Yes." Davargorn ducked low to crawl under the dispersing smoke. He reached forward, groping blindly, and—yes. He touched something. *Someone.*

"What is it?" Lan asked. "What passes?"

The smoke cleared, and Davargorn looked down on the black-wrapped body of Semana Denerre nô Ravalis, his beloved tormentor. She lay senseless, her black leathers burned and scored from multiple strikes. She wheezed and her chest heaved erratically, as her body struggled to breathe despite significant injuries. A collapsed lung, certainly. Davargorn touched her side—broken ribs—and hard belly—internal bleeding. His attention made her shiver and groan. Her mask had come loose and hung half over her face. Davargorn reached out and, with trembling fingers, pulled it fully free of her head. She murmured something as he did, and her eyes fluttered, but she did not wake. Her face was bruised, her eyes sunken and hollow, and he'd never seen her brown skin so pale.

Outside Atropis, the battle had faded, and now he could hear the cries and shouts of others up above. Their words vanished on the winds.

"What passes?" Lan asked again, his voice increasingly demanding. "Speak to me!"

"It's her." Davargorn wondered if he was dreaming. But no, the mask was real, and he cast it flopping against the wall. "Semana."

Why hadn't he called her Mask? He was so accustomed to thinking of her by that name.

Carefully, Davargorn knelt on Semana's left hand, pinning her chain-glove helplessly to the floor. Semana moaned in her swoon. One of her legs hung listless over the edge. Sweat plastered her nearly white hair to her brow, and Davargorn saw now the trickle of blood that stuck to it. Without aid...

Lan was silent for a moment, then suddenly erupted in a peal of laughter loud as any thunder. "Fate kisses you, Tithian," he said. "Go on. Avenge yourself."

A shudder passed through Davargorn's body. How often had he dreamed of this moment? How often had he cursed she who had so destroyed his life?

Avenge yourself.

It would be so easy. After so long helpless, he had all the power. He could simply push her over the edge and let her near-lifeless body plummet to the rocks far below. He could seize her relics—the smoldering flying boots, the white-hot chain glove, the protective breastplate and even the mask itself— and leave her here to her fate. She provided the means of revenge and also his salvation.

Or.

Before he knew himself, Davargorn had slipped his hands around Semana's throat and begun to squeeze. She uttered a faint rattling sound, and her eyes shot open. Bloodshot and weak, her red-brown eyes blinked up at him. There was confusion but also understanding—a kind of acceptance. *Hurk* sounds emerged from her choking throat.

"Yes," Lan said in the adjoining cell. "Kill her, Tithian. Take your life back. *Kill her!*"

Semana didn't fight. She managed to raise her right hand, past his murderous arms, and brushed her fingers against his twisted cheek. Her touch might as well have turned him to a statue.

Davargorn shivered and they stared at one another for a moment that seemed to stretch on.

Then something appeared on her cheek—a drop of moisture, spreading in a little dark circle through the grime—and another drop. Had it begun to rain?

Then Davargorn realized he was weeping.

"What passes?" Lan asked. "Tithian!"

Davargorn eased his grip, and let healing power flow through his hands. For a moment, he and Semana were one, their bodies and hearts conjoined. He found so much pain and injury within her, and he sent waves of soothing warmth into her hurts. He felt them in his own body and let them dissipate. She cried out in pain and he placed a soothing hand on her cheek, mirroring her own on his face. His magic started to slacken, its strength ebbing, and he gritted his teeth and redoubled his efforts.

Then he was done, and they gazed into one another's eyes. A faint smile touched her lips, and Davargorn smiled in return despite himself. Her hand groped for her mask, near the wall, and he retrieved it for her. When she took it, they both clung to the mask, and it hovered between them like a talisman of the life they had chosen together.

"What passes!" Lan was screaming now. "Kill her! Tithian!"

"Farewell," Davargorn said.

Semana nodded faintly.

A strangled cry came from the adjoining cell. "Warders!" Lan cried. "Warders! To me! Alarm!"

Too late.

Davargorn helped Mask shakily to her feet, and helped her replace the mask. He wrapped his arms around her as she embraced him, and he thought she felt so warm and so strong.

Together they stepped out into the open air out of the skycell. The magic of her boots propelled them into the smoke-filled sky.

BOOK THREE: SERVANTS

Four years ago—Summer, 978 Sorceris Annis—Luether Bay

THE SPLASH MASK MADE when she hit the water in Luether Bay was intense. At that speed, from that height, she might as well have fallen onto stone. Bits of burning caravel rained around her, and the surface of the water resembled a charnel heap upon which the folk of Luether cast their refuse.

A second splash followed the first, as Davargorn dived down into the water after her. He had run for the edge, stripping off his shirt, and leaped as she fell. Her larger waves absorbed his without effort.

He pulled himself down into the churning, chaotic dark, as chunks of burning wood and searing metal plunged into the water around him. A casterbolt zipped past, losing momentum as it plunged until it stopped entirely and floated listlessly, hissing like an angry insect until its magic burned out. He brushed it aside with one outstretched hand and felt the momentary sting of its heat on his palm.

Davargorn shut his normal eye and let his huge, milky white one survey the deeps. It helped somewhat, but the sinking morass of junk blocked most of his view. He had to find his master, and fast. There were things in this water that would kill and consume him if he stayed too long.

As if drawn by his thoughts, something slimy slithered past his right arm, disturbed by his progress. His arm felt numb where the creature had touched it. Sudden fear made him shiver, and he hesitated long enough for it to slip away. He hoped it would not return.

He looked... *there!*

Sickly green tendrils of magic reached up from just below him, faintly illumining Mask's face. The blasted armor dragged her inexorably down, overcoming her body's buoyancy, like a curse wrought through so many years of murder. Only a few bubbles trailed from her nose and mouthslit, and her body hung limp and lifeless. She had lost consciousness or worse, Davargorn knew, but seeing her gave him a swell of hope. He dragged his arms through the murk and shot down toward her.

He reached for her trailing hand and caught her wrist.

Mask did not react as Davargorn put his arm under her shoulders, nor did she protest when he reversed his course and projected himself upward. His head started to ache, and he blew water out of his lungs to equalize the pressure within and without. Above them, he could see the fires of the battle in Luether Bay, and beyond the muddy radiance of the daylight.

And so he might have swum them to safety, had not a tendril wrapped itself around one of his legs, making it go numb, and he realized the creature he'd disturbed *had* returned.

It unspooled below him like a yawning cacophony of tendrils and fanged mouths, each containing a milky crimson eye that gleamed up at him. It looked more like a flower than any sort of fish he had ever seen, only the petals were teeth. Its body was a mass of scars and rippling pustules. It bloomed in the dark, gnashing at him and dragging him with impossible strength toward its maws. Yellowish fluid leaked from those mouths, like the creature was drooling in anticipation.

Fighting the shock and the horror, for he could see it all too clearly in the dark, Davargorn reached for the caster at his waist, only to discover it had gone dark and cold, its magic smothered in the bay. He tried to cast anyway, but it would not discharge. This gave the creature time to slap at him with a second tendril, and he managed to ward it off from his face only by sacrificing his left forearm. He felt tiny barbs cutting into his unprotected flesh, which went instantly numb from the toxin.

He had no weapon he could use and no free hand to use it. The creature pulled them slowly and inexorably toward its mouths. Another tentacle scrabbled at his arm around Mask, and he could feel the paralysis setting in there as well. It would pull them apart, devour him first, then eat her after.

Davargorn shut his eyes, blocking out the fear, and fell into his power. He reached into Mask's cold, seemingly lifeless body, and found a tiny spark. Her body might be all but dead, but he latched onto that spark and fanned it. He poured his life essence into it, demanding it spring back to a flame.

His gift surged in him, consuming every bit of his strength. He'd never tried to heal her or anyone when they were so badly hurt, but he had no choice. He had to try.

The grasping mouths came within a hand's breadth of his ensnared foot. It was hauling him down and there was nothing he could do against it. They would both die.

Suddenly, Mask's eyes opened, and she stared dully into the darkness.

Then the murky water churned around them in great billowing plumes. Mask's boots were loosing their energy, propelling them upward. The creature pulled harder for a three-count, until Davargorn thought the opposing forces would wrench him asunder.

Then abruptly it let go, and they surged upward toward the surface.

They broke into the smoke-filled air with a triumphant burst, only to fly madly toward the shore. Davargorn realized Mask was not awake—indeed, her eyes had rolled up in their sockets and polluted water streamed from her mouth—and she could not control their flight. They spun through the air, end over end, and smashed into—

The world vanished for a heartbeat, only to rush back in with a gasp.

Trembling, Davargorn sat halfway up and inspected his body, which seemed intact. Both arms were numb and useless, and he could only faintly feel the leg the creature had grabbed. They had landed on the soft sand of the nearest beach, from whence Davargorn had dived. It was a small miracle, but he had no time to consider his luck just now.

Mask lay face-down on her belly in the sand, unmoving.

As explosions went off in the bay, Davargorn crawled and pulled himself toward her, dragging his half-numb body by his shoulders. Neither arm worked, and one of his legs felt like a dead log. He didn't even think of healing himself, but reserved what power he had left for Mask.

It took an agonizingly long time, but finally he pulled himself up to her. It took three tries, but ultimately he shoved her over onto her back. Water trickled from Mask's lips and nose, and a stray wisp of silvery blonde hair escaped from one of the eyeholes of her mask. She appeared, to any casual observation, quite dead.

Davargorn tried to get his hands to cooperate and touch Mask, but they refused to move. With a series of grunts, he levered himself over her, putting their faces together.

In that moment, he didn't hesitate.

He kissed her.

Her lips were cold as ice through the mouth-slit, but he managed to touch his skin to hers. He fell into her body, which felt cold and empty. A spike of pure terror ran through his heart. Had he moved too slowly? Should he have healed himself first, so he could have got to her in time? Had he lost her?

Then he found it as he had before: a tiny little blue spark, deep in the core of her being. It burned not in her heart or in her head, as he might have expected, but deep in her guts. The last flame flickered at the precise balancing point of her body, where the tiniest pressure in any direction would send her careening away. Into this last light he poured all of his strength and vitality, coaxing it to life.

The flame grew, feasting hungrily upon his power, and finally Mask choked and coughed, expelling water from her lungs. Davargorn sat back, dazed, as she lay panting and retching in the sand.

"That," she said at length. "Let's never… *never* do that again."

Of course she meant their botched quest, wherein they'd slain Lord Shapior on his iron-clad caravel fortress—though fighting through a horde of Children and demolishing the craft hadn't been the plan. Of *course* she didn't mean the kiss, which she probably didn't even realize had happened. She wasn't rejecting him so sharply—she wouldn't do that. Probably.

But he still felt it, like a knife to the guts.

"What?" she asked.

He shook his head. "Nothing."

She managed to climb to her feet in the time it took him to heal his paralyzed limbs. "Come," she said. "We should get back before our contact abandons us for dead." She looked at him sidelong, eyes slitted. "You're *sure* you pass well?"

He nodded and took her proffered hand, then embraced her tightly. She smiled faintly, and smoke rose around her boots. In a moment, they were flying.

She would never love him. He knew that for a certainty.

But he knew that he wouldn't stop serving her.

Not now.

Not ever.

ELEVEN

THE FIRST SNOWS OF the season swirled across a stretch of snowy plain painted blue and purple as the sun set over the blasted waste far to the west. Adjusting himself in the little nook blown in the walls in some long-ago struggle, Dain Duldur tamped his pipe, lit it with a sparker, and set it in his lips. His left foot ached after so much standing that day, and he adjusted it to be more comfortable, even as he cradled the warm power core of his unused caster against his belly. A storm was brewing, he felt and saw, but he could watch the last rays of the sun before the clouds descended.

Twilight was his favorite time of day, toward the end of his ward shift, with the pipe warming him against the chill of dusk and the vibrant colors of the west painting the frozen, wind-swept Winter Wilds. Rarely did he see the same colors two days in a row, and though he'd seen hundreds of sunsets from this very spot, he couldn't recall two quite the same. How glorious must they be in the destroyed land that spawned them?

Dain barely remembered the Sunset Lands himself, of course, but Berric had described them to him once, as they lay against each other in this very spot on the walls of Low-City. In retrospect, the bleak gray and orange desert he described was quite inhospitable, but the warm romance in his voice when he spoke of the wind kissing his cheeks and neck, even as he did the same to Dain... Well. He could make the starkest ruin sound rather appealing. Turn doom into glory.

The sunset, Berric had said, held hope: that such ruin could be turned to something beautiful.

That summer, Berric had sailed south with King Lan and the bulk of Tar Vangr's army, their mission to seize Luether from the Children of Ruin after their twenty years of despotic rule. Leaving Dain the much less glorious task of guarding the wall—especially this stretch, which had seen damage in some long-ago war, and no one had ever bothered patching it or trying to fix the cracks. That was how likely the kings and queens of winter thought an assault.

The irony of the circumstances had made them both laugh: that Berric, a pale-skinned winterborn Tar Vangruyr, would go to fight for Dain's homeland, while dark-skinned, summerblooded Dain would remain behind and guard his adoptive City of Steel. Berric had spun some poesy before he left, saying that this, much like their love, symbolized the union of opposites and something about peace at long last, and Dain had stifled his words with a kiss. Dain never had the ear for such artful ramblings, even if he enjoyed the sound of his lover's voice, but he knew when action was needed.

He felt that stirring now, and it turned his reverie to darker thoughts.

The bulk of the assault force had not returned from Luether as planned. Only a few ships, limping back from the battle with tales of disaster. The *Avenger* had led the charge that smashed the defenses of the Children of Ruin, and those defenses had fallen quickly to the unexpected attack. The day seemed won until, like a harbinger of Ruin itself, a massive skyship had risen through the city itself, unleashing a torrent of destruction and death that dashed the *Avenger* to the earth like an annoying insect. The loss of their flagship had shattered Tar Vangryur morale: some ships had fallen, many fled, and thousands of soldiers were presumed captured or slain.

The sun was just a dim line on the horizon now, and thick gray clouds choked the snowy landscape. Dain could feel the winds rising, and knew a storm approached. He should get back inside—take shelter from the elements and perhaps warm himself with a mulled wine. He pitied poor Elegma, who would relieve him for the night watch. That storm did not look pleasant.

Still, he lingered a bit, casting his thoughts far, far southward once more.

Hope was what drove Dain now: hope that Berric had survived the rout at Luether and would return, someday, when it was safe to do so. Somehow, Dain knew his lover yet lived, but not knowing the particulars gnawed at his sanity. Berric was the imaginative one, but Dain couldn't stop himself obsessing over the wildest scenarios. He languished in a dungeon, perhaps, seeking freedom to return north; or perhaps he lay alone, possibly wounded, in the summerlands, eluding the pursuit of horrid barbarians; or he even now worked with Summer Lives to take back the city. Even if he had deserted and become a pirate, Dain would not care. He just wanted him back.

Moisture welled in his eyes, and Dain wiped it away mournfully. He was a child of Luether, and his father had not allowed him to weep since the day they fled the city to escape the ravaging barbarians. Half his family had died in the fall, and a stray casterbolt had smashed his left foot so badly most thought he would never walk again, but his father had refused to tolerate tears. At the time, he'd thought this made his father strong, but in time he'd come to realize it was a protective measure: that if Dain had wept, then his father would have lost his mind. Berric had taught him how to cry, after much resistance to the "soft" ways of the Tar Vangruyr, but Dain had succumbed in time. The child of a land far different, where the heart did not have to hide behind layers of posturing for show, Berric had taught him truths Dain himself had known but not understood, much less accepted.

Berric had taught him *many* things.

So caught up was Dain in the remembrance of his love, that it took him several moments before he realized he was seeing something strange out on the plain beyond the city. The storm had started to drop heaps of snow onto the plains and mountains, but there was something moving down on the ground. Snow blew away from Tar Vangr and over some sort of barrier that slowly approached them, like a ripple in the earth. A moving hill? He stared, trying to understand it.

So preoccupied was Dain that when a hand fell on his arm, he just about jumped out of his armor. He flinched and nearly fell from his perch in the broken part of the wall, and his left foot ground painfully against the rough stone. "Silver Fire, Leg!" he said. "Scared me."

"What passes?" asked Elegma, her mask and goggles all but hiding her pale winterborn face. "Your service ended an hour ago. I've been trying to find—"

"Look." Dain pointed out onto the field. "What is that?"

The disturbance on the plain had come closer to the walls, and Dain could see the snow sweeping over it and billowing past it, as off the top of a hill. As he watched, it swept over a few tents of hunters and traders camping outside the wall, and it subsumed them with only the slightest hesitation. There was something darker than the snowy ground behind the wave, and—

"No," he said, realizing.

"What is it?" Elegma asked. "Dain—"

Whatever else she might have said vanished in a massive rush of sound, like exploding thunder with no lightning, so loud that it drove them back half a step. Dain looked up, his forgotten pipe tumbling from his mouth to clatter off the broken wall and fall out into the swirling mist.

It came out of the clouds level with High-City, a shape so massive he took it at first for a skyship, somehow flying with no motivator rings. Its massive frame shone silver in the dusk light and blue flame rippled in its passing. Only when it spread its wings and rose up, roaring again, did he realize it was a living creature and not a vessel. Its massive snout parted in three different directions to reveal row upon row of teeth like swords, and blue and white flame erupted from its jaws.

"That's a *dragon*," he said.

"Wh-what?" Elegma's voice trembled. "There's no such things as dragons!"

Another cry went up, not as devastating but taken up by thousands of throats. Dain looked down in time to see the moving ridge abruptly tear apart as warriors cast aside snow-choked tree branches that had disguised them and charged forward. Over a thousand screaming barbarians, weapons raised, rushing toward the wall of Low-City.

"Children!" Elegma raised her voice to the alarm. "Children of Ru—"

A spear hurtled through the darkness and slammed so hard into her middle it drove clean through and nailed her to the wall behind. Dain uttered a strangled cry and reached for her. Elegma blinked in confusion and batted at the spear with limp hands, blood streaming from her mouth.

"Stay." Dain tried vainly to pull the spear free. "Leg! Stay—"

Her eyes rolled and she slumped over the fatal weapon.

More spears hurtled out of the snowy darkness, one nicking his shoulder to stab deep into Elegma's chest behind him. He staggered in sudden pain and so avoided a spear that would have taken him in the throat. It skipped off his iron helmet, knocking the frosty thing clattering away. Dain fell as much as ducked behind the wall crenellations, and the rest of the volley of spears sailed harmlessly past. Up and down the wall, a cry of alarm went up as the barbarians left stealth for a sudden assault.

Move, he thought. *Get up. Fight back.*

He thought these things, and only slowly did his body obey his commands. He found his caster where he'd left it in his little alcove and pressed himself against the crenellation. After a breath to steady himself, he rolled over and looked down into the horde. The barbarians were still raising a storm of shouts and curses and screams, and casting down into that churning mass of bodies would surely hit someone. He didn't even have to aim, just point the weapon and squeeze—

He realized the barbarians had raised numerous bodies that they held spread-eagled atop their churning mass. The folk screamed and thrashed but couldn't escape, because—Silver Fire, those were spears thrust through their limbs, holding them aloft. At first, Dain thought they were meant as shields, and true enough, he couldn't get a clear cast around one of them. Then he realized the barbarians were continually cutting and stabbing and ripping at the wailing captives, and blood rained down onto them. The sight shook the defenders of Tar Vangr to their bones.

Paralyzed with horror, Dain fought to remember what he had meant to do. The caster.

He loosed a bolt with a loud *crack*, and it took one barbarian square in the chest, knocking him flying back and to the ground. Dain had never killed a man before, but he found it remarkably easy. Immediately, his extensive training took over: he ducked back behind cover and his hands started winding the caster for another shot without being commanded to do so.

Dain could stomach this. They were on foot. They could not pierce the walls of Tar Vangr. Even here, at the weakest point, what could their spears do? They didn't even have casters.

Dain and the others were safe. They could kill barbarians at their leisure.

Then the dragon reappeared, swooping out of the gloom just over the massed army, and smashed into the cracked wall with enough force to shatter the stones inward, and the resulting explosion threw Dain against something hard—

Awareness crept in slowly, and it took a moment before Dain remembered where or who he was. He lay slumped on the ruined edge of a splintered stone wall, one leg dangling uselessly over the void. Darkness churned a few paces below him, and at first he thought it the lapping waves of the Dusk Sea—that Berric had come back and they sat down at the docks in summer in each other's arms. Then the intense cold set in, and Dain coughed in the freezing air. His whole body screamed at him in pain, particularly his long-ago broken foot. That, and his face, which felt like it was burning.

Below him, barbarians swarmed into Low-City, and already fires erupted in the buildings nearest the wall. He heard screamed filtering in and amongst their shouts. It seemed like something out of a dream, and Dain could hardly comprehend it. A powerfully built woman appeared amongst them, screaming for blood and death, and the massive axe she hoisted over her head burned with green flame. It made him shiver and pray to whatever gods remained in the World of Ruin that he would wake from this nightmare.

He touched at his face, and his hand came away bloody. He had some sort of wound that itched and burned. How…? He hadn't even fought an invader yet.

Then a hand appeared over the edge only two paces from him, and his heart all but leaped out of his chest. He could do nothing but watch, horrified, as a barbarian climbed up onto the ledge, metal shards clicking against the stone.

He hadn't seen a Child of Ruin in the flesh since their flight from Luether, twenty years gone, but he'd never shaken the nightmares. This warrior clad in a set of scintillating metal shards like a hauberk of knives, their face leering at Dain like a sun with rays of daggers thrust into the cheeks and brow, could have sprung from one of those very dreams. The barbarian saw him staring wide-eyed, murmured something in the guttural language of Ruin, and reached up to pluck one of the knives from their face. As though the scar tissue of the barbarian's cheek was a sheath, the blade came free with a slick sound of rent flesh, and blood welled. Throughout, the barbarian stared at Dain with huge blood-shot eyes.

Dain remembered his caster and groped at his belt—to no avail. Nor did he see it anywhere. He must have dropped it somewhere, perhaps into the invading horde. "Wait," he said. "Wait—"

Then the barbarian was on him with a roar, tackling him back against the wall. The blades on the armor cut into Dain, lighting dozens of points of pain across his body. His head smashed into something soft and cold: Elegma's stomach. Her corpse stared down at him from where it sat propped against the wall, bloody tongue lolling down, and his hand slapped into the sludgy black pool of blood underneath.

Silver Fire. Dain trembled all over, all but frozen in terror.

The barbarian loomed over him, the distorted mouth spreading in a hideous leer. The knife that had come from the barbarian's face rose and fell, stabbing into Dain's shoulder. He screamed at the sudden sucking pain and his arm went all but dead. He managed to raise his hand in a vain attempt to catch the barbarian's hand or deflect the knife, and instead the second thrust skipped under his vambrace and plunged through the meat of his forearm. Dain could feel the weapon rattling against the bones in his arm, sending electric flashes of agony up to his brain. He screamed in surprise and horror.

"*Gath ka vaas,*" the barbarian said in a clearly female voice. It hadn't even occurred to Dain that his attacker might be a woman: she was so distorted and scarred she barely resembled a human at all.

The barbarian tried to rip the blade free, redoubling the pain, but apparently it was well and truly wedged. With a high-pitched cackle, she simply reached up to pull another knife from her face with a fresh little burst of blood, like a popped blemish. His stomach fought its way toward his mouth, and he looked desperately aside. Even if he could crawl away—his body barely functioned and his foot was a white hot mass of pain—the barbarian's weight pinned him down. There was no escape.

Then he saw it—a faint glint of steel covered in snowflakes, peeking up from Elegma's belt. Her caster, with its power core crackling with electric thaumaturgy. He reached for it, desperately, but fell short. His fingers flicked across the handle, knocking it just a little further away.

An explosion ripped through the night, followed by a chorus of screams—some of pain and terror, some of rage and lust. The wall shook under Dain, and while the blade-faced barbarian swayed, she locked her knees around his middle and clung on. He realized that knives sticking out of her legs held them together.

"*Vaas tak tat.*" The barbarian made a show of flicking her own blood and pus off her dagger into the air, then licked the blade with a knobby purple tongue.

Soon, that disgusting blade would sink into his throat.

He reached as far as he could and felt the cool wood of the caster's grip in his hand. The blast must have shifted everything just slightly—just enough. The caster stuck in Elegma's holster and he pulled as hard as he could, panic rising. The blade swept down toward his face.

An explosive *crack* split the night, and the barbarian tumbled back from Dain in a sizzling rictus of lightning. Her upper body heaved back, blasted almost in half by the close cast, then sagged forward and smashed down atop Dain anew. Knives drove back into him, and he yelped in pain and horror as her bloody flesh slapped against his face. Elegma's caster smoked in his hand, and he lay panting beneath the dead barbarian, who oozed blood all over him like a ruptured sieve.

He must have lay there for some time, because when sense returned to him, it was to the sound of the dragon roaring in the storm. Sizzles of fire and lightning burst from High-City, a thousand feet above, and Dain could see the discharge of Tar Vangr's thaumaturgical arsenal at the beast. It evaded the blasts well enough, twisting through the sky like a bird. Why wasn't it attacking the city? The sound it made sounded hollow, almost hesitant. And that, oddly, gave him a flicker of hope.

Berric.

Dain shoved the corpse off—an effort that left him panting and wheezing in the cold air. His face was torn open and he bled from dozens of shallow wounds, the deeper puncture in his shoulder, and the knife still wedged in his arm. He set the caster on his belly and gingerly took hold of the knife's hilt, but even that caused too much pain. If he tried to pull it out, he would lose his senses for sure. No good.

He had to survive. To see Berric again.

Gritting his teeth, Dain forced himself to his feet in a panting, sweating, heaving exercise that took ten breaths. Finally he stood, his left foot screaming in pain, and laid his hand on Elegma's forehead. She was cold as the stone walls of Tar Vangr. At least her suffering was over.

His, he realized as he looked out over the burning city, was just beginning.

A massive groan of metal on metal sounded, and Dain looked to the north, his heart sinking. There stretched one of the massive chain-operated lifts that connected Low-City and High-City Tar Vangr. As he watched, one of the great chains snapped and started to fall, dislodging a number of barbarians climbing along its length. The lift platform shuddered, tilting wildly to one side and disgorging—Silver Fire, those were Tar Vangryur up there!

"No," Dain said. "No—"

He watched in horror as a dozen flailing forms tumbled free from the lift, weathercloaks flapping out behind them as they tumbled. An iron-clad slid to the side, its mounted casters unleashing bolts of fire and lightning as barbarians swarmed it like murderflies on a faltering raven. Finally it went over, taking its attackers with it, and crashed against a burning building in its descent. Shortly thereafter, the second chain snapped off and the lift came away entirely to crash with a thundering report into Low-City, smashing a residential hall.

The barbarians had taken Low-City, Dain realized. Why else would High-City sever the lifts? They would be cut off and left to their fate.

This was no longer a battle. This was a race to survive.

Dain looked to Elegma and almost started weeping, but there was no time for tears. He tried to pull the spear free, but his foot went out from under him and he couldn't get leverage. Finally, Dain closed Elegma's staring eyes, collected her spare power core with shaking fingers, then headed down into the city as quickly as he could with his aching foot.

～

Upside down, Thelisa snapped back into awareness, panting and heaving in the stuffy confines of her Lancer. The mage-glass viewport on the front of the war machine was blasted and shadowed with smoke. All had gone dark inside, but for the occasional crackle of red lightning and a persistent whine her training recognized immediately as a cracked power core mounted behind the metal against her back. She could feel the intense heat growing more powerful as she tried to get her body to work.

"Out," she said through clenched teeth. "Out!"

Her arms and legs moved, and she shoved at the shell that protected and also trapped her inside the war machine. The release wouldn't obey her vocal commands, let alone her mental ones. She touched the release rune, but the red energy crackled and didn't fill the whole rune. Damn and burn!

The heat grew, humming loud enough to set her teeth on edge.

"Aid!" she called as she smashed her hand against the mage-glass. "In here!"

Something was moving outside the iron-clad. More attackers? Allies? It didn't matter. Thelisa had to get out before that core went up. She pounded her elbows against the shell, filling her arms with shuddering jolts of agony. Her blood flecked the smeared mage-glass, but she gritted her teeth and kept hitting. Finally a crack spread through the mage-glass, which must have already been weakened by the impact. Some small shred of hope sparked in Thelisa, and she redoubled her efforts.

The heat coated her back, making her tunic smolder, and the mage-glass grew hot as well. It felt like repeatedly striking a heating stove, and she started screaming with every touch. Sweat poured down her face and into her eyes, and her strikes slipped off the blood and sweat and grime.

Finally the shell gave way in a sudden burst of shattering glass and a rush of freezing air. Thelisa peeled her way free of the scalding metal of her seat, which clutched at her. She tore loose the clasps on her harness and lurched up, and her back lit with ripping pain. Her skin had fused to the metal in patches and it tore free. Tears welled in Thelisa's eyes but she had to move. She could be hurt later.

She climbed out of the Lancer into the shattered square, staggered over the edge, and stumbled onto a pile of bodies. A wild man with a sword appeared in front of her, howling a threat, and Thelisa discharged her handcaster into its chest. The barbarian—she hoped it was a barbarian—collapsed with a choking, sputtering sound. Shapes moved in the darkness—figures with weapons—but Thelisa had no time. She tried to shout a warning, but all that emerged was a scream of pain. She stumbled amongst the corpses on the ground, and came face to face with the broken corpse of a Tar Vangryur soldier.

Then a shattering clap of thunder burst behind her as the Lancer exploded, sending bodies tumbling in pieces all around her. Her ears rang, blocking out any other sound, and she stared up at swirling smoke. She wondered if she had survived.

What had happened? She remembered fighting on the lift to protect the evacuating citizens from the barbarians who had climbed aboard, and... she was falling...

Silver Fire, they cut the chains. High-City had sacrificed everyone on the lift.

She lay in a hollow of a mound of bodies and broken stone. All around her, buildings burned and the scream of steel and of folk in pain rose into the darkness. Her eyes ached from the smoke and her skin stung all over. She should be dead, she knew, but her heart kept thudding low and deep.

A face loomed into her vision, and Thelisa brought the caster in line without thinking. A hand knocked the weapon wide, and she held her cast when she recognized the man's weathercloak. He was a warder, even if he had the dark skin and reddish hair common to the summerblood of the south. His face was a mangled, bloody mess, but he seemed somehow familiar.

He mouthed something she couldn't understand.

"What?" Her voice sounded like an echo under water in her ears.

"Can you stand?" he asked.

That, Thelisa could do. With his help, she managed to get to her feet. Her back was a burning ruin of pain, but she couldn't focus on that. He was limping, and she could see that he bled from a dozen wounds of his own. A lightning-charged caster burned in his other hand, and she could tell at a glance that its charge had run low. Her own handcaster was good for three or four more casts before its power core ran down, and any additional dust cores had gone up with the Lancer.

"I'm Thelisa," she said. "Second Lancers group. Last—Silver Fire, I'm the last survivor."

"Dain Duldur—West Vigil," he said. "They're cutting the Northsky lift, and I saw invaders heading for the Sunrise lift. Our best chance is the Harborside. Can you walk?"

She nodded. "We save anyone we can," she said.

He nodded.

~

True night had not yet fallen, and the Children of Ruin had all but destroyed Low-City in such a short time. Everywhere she looked as they made their way toward the Harborside lift, Thelisa saw only devastation and ruin. Buildings had become burned out husks, streaming smoke into the sky and oozing blood and ash. They saw hundreds of bodies, at least ten Tar Vangruyr for every single barbarian corpse, as well as crashed and ruined vehicles and even a few iron-clad war machines.

"You're from Luether and of age," Thelisa said after a time. "Did you see the Fall?"

Dain nodded, wincing as he tried to tread on his injured foot. "It looked a little like this," he said.

"That make any of this easier to see?"

"It does not."

It surprised her how quickly they'd become the best of friends, despite meeting less than an hour before, but perhaps it shouldn't have. Common cause and necessity were powerful factors. Thelisa had to lean on him and he on her, but they kept moving. They were certainly in no shape to fight any barbarians, so they avoided the main roads, and kept to alleys, and worked around the backs of buildings. Foreigner he might have been, but Dain knew Low-City well enough.

As they moved, they took what supplies and weapons they could. Thelisa managed to salvage a working thaumaturgical core from a downed Lancer, while Dain excused himself to expel the contents of his stomach into the alley. She herself had to fight against the urge to vomit, because there wasn't time. She tried to sling the dust magic core over her back, but just touching the burned flesh made her gasp in pain. Dain took it instead, securing it in a rucksack he had found somewhere along the way.

Yowls and laughter grasped their attention, and they ducked into an alley to hide from a passing band of twelve barbarians, dragging two bruised and bloodied citizens behind them through the street. Thelisa and Dain pressed themselves into hiding and tried to stay silent. Thelisa trembled with rage and frustration that she could do nothing against so many. Dain sounded on the verge of weeping.

"How could this happen?" Dain asked when they had passed by. "How could they attack in winter? And a *dragon*? How?"

Thelisa grimaced and shook her head. She didn't know how the barbarians had survived the long march across the wintry plains around Tar Vangr, and until this night, she hadn't believed in dragons outside of bards' tales, nor did she believe in chance. She *did* believe in tactics and in strategy. The barbarians had known of the weakness in the wall, which was not obvious from outside the city, and once inside, they must have gone straight for the lifts. Such a comprehensive, devastating strike added up to inside knowledge. Someone had betrayed Tar Vangr, and if they survived this night, Thelisa resolved to find out who. They moved on, just as careful and quiet as before.

Fortunately, for all their knowledge of the city's defenses, the labyrinthine streets slowed the invaders' advance to a crawl past the immediate environs of the west wall. The Children of Ruin hadn't yet penetrated as far as the harbor, so when they entered the south side of the city, they found it heavily embattled as the citizens had more time to prepare the defense met them. Not that it served: the vanguard of the barbarians still swept over them like a wave of howling death.

Thelisa saw a bulky woman hurl a mighty axe into a makeshift barricade, which exploded in fire and sent citizens scattering. The woman flew through the air, drawn to the axe by some sort of magical force, and landed atop the devastation. She raised her weapon to the sky and cackled a warcry.

"That's her," Dain said. "The general. I saw her at the wall."

Thelisa thought about drawing a bead with her caster and taking down the woman, but that was foolish. The weapon could manage only a few casts, and even if her attack succeeded, the swarm of barbarians would slay both Thelisa and Dain in heartbeats. Horribly. Again, she had to fight down a wave of desperate helplessness.

"Come." She pulled Dain through a tight squeeze between two buildings that led directly south.

"A shortcut?" Dain asked.

Thelisa nodded. "Children won't know it," she said. "I only know it because I grew up here."

"In Low-City?" Dain made a face. "Apologies, I didn't—nrr." His foot turned under him and they leaned heavily against the wall of a building for support. "I didn't mean to sound priggish."

"Pass well." Thelisa shivered. They'd found a new fur coat for her, but her scorched back was a continuing source of niggling pain that made it hard to think, let alone walk. "Keep—keep moving."

Shortly beyond the alley, they found the square around the Harborside lift. Had Thelisa any breath to catch in relief, she would have done so: the lift still operated, and as they watched, a teeming crowd of Tar Vangryur rose up into the swirling snow and smoke toward the safety of High-City. Two or three score folk clustered around the base of the lift, waiting for it to descend once more.

"You there!"

The shout startled them both, and Thelisa would have raised her caster if not for Dain's hand on her wrist. A ring of half a dozen dark weathercloaked figures stood at the edge of the teeming group, pointing light and heavy casters in their direction. One warder even had a bow with an arrow set to the string. If she'd reacted to attack, they might have bolted and feathered them to the nearest wall.

"Down arms," said a dark-haired winterborn woman, her scarred face bare to the snow and clearly accustomed to command. She was definitely in charge here. The hilt of a sword rose over her shoulder, and she had a bundle strapped to her chest. "They're allies."

Thelisa knew her, she realized, and it shocked her to see the woman in this context. Many a Low-City night after training, Thelisa had spent the dark hours drinking in the Burning Man, enjoying the songs and dances. Of the folk who worked in that establishment, the one who had consistently caught her eye was the fiery Nacacia: a few seasons her elder, possessed of the windswept sort of beauty that came with a lifetime of hard choices and action.

Thelisa had always wanted to talk to Nacacia but always fell silent around her despite herself. Their eyes conveyed all the words they would ever share.

"Goodwoman," Dain said. "We—"

"You're Dain of Blood Duldur, warder on the west wall," Nacacia said. "And that's Thelisa of no Blood, who captains a Lancer with the Thunderbolt Cadre."

He blinked, taken completely aback by her recitation, but Thelisa only smiled. Of course Nacacia knew her. The Circle of Tears knew everyone in Tar Vangr, or near about.

"What passes here?" Dain asked.

"Everyone who can be saved." Nacacia glanced up at the lift, which had reached High-City in the interim. "Not sure it'll come back down. The cowardly Ravalis prefer to hide from the Children, rather than face them. One of my agents is up there, keeping them from cutting the lift." She turned her sharp eyes again toward them. "Speak. Details. Everything you remember."

Dain made a confused face at her answer, but Thelisa prodded him. He detailed what they had seen on their trek here, and Nacacia's expression turned darker as he spoke. She nodded at each terrible revelation, then looked to Thelisa, her eyes sparkling. Thelisa found herself rather enjoying Nacacia's face and wondered why she might be looking at her so hard. Then, abruptly, all the strength went out of Thelisa, the world blurred, and she found herself in Nacacia's strong arms.

"What—what passes?" Thelisa asked, her voice far away even in her own ears.

Her cheeks immediately felt warm, as those were the first words she had ever spoken to the woman. Including that silent moment between the two of them in the private room of the Burning Man, where Nacacia had put her finger to Thelisa's lips to stay her voice. And then other things.

The chains quivered and reversed their course. The lift had started to descend anew.

Nacacia gave Dain a nod, and the man limped away to join the other defenders ringing the lift. "You collapsed, Little Lance," she said, her voice surprisingly gentle for her hard visage. Nacacia had opened Thelisa's weathercloak, and shockingly cold fingers made her seared back crackle with pain. "Your injuries are severe. Surprising you're still on your feet."

Thelisa might have made some reply, had she words, but a small hand reached out from the bundle on Nacacia's chest and touched her on the cheek. The soft round face of a toddler looked out from among a furred hood, bright eyes sparkling in the moonlight.

"Is that a *child*?" Thelisa asked. "Your child?"

"Sarelle, the child of my bond." The woman smiled despite the grim circumstances. "Rest, Thelisa, Burned Angel. Your fight has ended this night, but there will be other nights."

A second name. Thelisa trembled with honor and love.

With that permission, Thelisa let the combined weight of her injuries, her weariness, and her horror at the night's events slide over her in a wave. She shivered and coughed as Nacacia held her, fighting and failing to stay awake. The world started to fade.

Then a cry went up from the sentries, and Thelisa saw a man fall with a spear thrust through his chest. A wave of barbarians came howling into the square, weapons high. The defenders leveled shaking casters, and might have fired but for a loud cry that split the square. Everyone froze, Tar Vangryur and Children of Ruin alike, and all eyes went to Nacacia in the wake of her shout. None could ignore the fire in her eyes, and even the barbarians deferred to her.

A loud, guttural question came from behind the barbarians, and the muscular axe-woman Thelisa had seen before shoved her way through their ranks. Close up, she grew more terrible: she looked more like a bull than a woman, her body wide and tough as any war machine. Rage and disgust gnarled her broad face, but she grinned when she saw Nacacia. The two recognized the strength in one another, and as if in respect, the axe-wielder gave Nacacia a moment to rally her forces.

Nacacia laid Thelisa near the lift controls and closed her fingers tight around the light caster she had carried through the city. Thelisa wanted to say something, but Nacacia touched her lips to silence her, just as she had once before, not so long ago. It wouldn't have kept her silent, but for Sarelle giggling and pawing at Thelisa's nose as well. Emotion welled up within her, stealing words.

Then she saw a flash of red light out of the corner of her eye and started to suck in air for a cry.

Nacacia reacted. The sword sang from the sheath on her back, and she interposed it. The hurled axe smashed off the sword hard enough to drive Nacacia down to one knee, then skipped off into the dark night. The barbarian who had thrown it extended her hand, and the axe reversed its course and shot back to her grasp as though pulled by a coil.

"Turn your back on Carr the Axe at your peril," the woman said in the trade tongue, surprisingly understandable despite her thick accent.

Nacacia climbed back to her feet, her body obviously sore, and raised the sword in both hands. Sarelle still hung strapped to her chest, but Nacacia seemed to have no fear for the child. If anything, her bond gave her strength and presence, and all fear bled away from her. Thelisa's breath caught.

"You think you will defeat me, child?" asked Carr the Axe. "I will cut you down, and you'll watch while I crush that babe to death before your eyes. I—"

Whatever words she might have intended to share vanished in a loud *crack*. A casterbolt smashed into the axe in her hands like a bolt of lightning and shattered it into pieces, driving Carr staggering back. Nacacia turned to the source of the attack, and Thelisa looked down at the caster in her hand, its last power spent on that blow. She smiled sheepishly and tried to salute the woman.

Nacacia grinned as though she'd never smiled in her life.

A howl broke the stillness. Carr, shards of her axe buried in her arms and face, threw back her head to the swirling storm and bellowed a cry of challenge. Thelisa felt power ripple out from her like a tide, and in just that way, it pulled back toward her as well, draining warmth and life from the ground and the folk around them. Cold gripped Thelisa, and she drifted, not sure of her perceptions.

Somehow, Carr's body stretched and blurred and became a bear—no, a *wolf* in the shape of a woman—and then she lunged toward Nacacia, jaws slavering. Thelisa wouldn't have believed it possible but for the reactions of the other warriors, who shouted and fell back in terror.

Then the tide of barbarians rushed toward them, and the night was full of cracking casters, singing blades, and screams. Thelisa couldn't track it—couldn't see beyond Nacacia, who lay beneath the black-furred wolf creature, the flat of her sword wedged in the beast's jaws. This close, Thelisa could smell the horrific stench of the beast and see viscid yellow pus dripping from its eyes.

The wolf creature wrenched the sword from Nacacia and hurled it aside, giving her just enough to time to get her arm up and into its mouth. Thelisa gasped, but the jaws only closed so far. Nacacia must have worn armor under her sleeve. Not that it would stop Carr the Wolf, who had only to wrench Nacacia's arm away with her superior strength, then wrap those massive jaws around her throat—

Thelisa watched, unable to breathe, as a small hand extended up from the bundle on Nacacia's chest, curled into a tiny fist, and jabbed into the wolf's luminous yellow eye.

The effect upon the beast was instantaneous. Carr the Wolf loosed Nacacia and roared in agony, turning her head aside, and almost in the same moment, Nacacia seized the initiative to palm a dagger from her sleeve and sink it into the same eye. With a yowl of pain, Carr sprang back off her, and Nacacia sat panting, her hand and arm covered in blood and pus.

"Nacacia?" Thelisa asked, but the woman hardly seemed to hear.

All around them, the defenders of Tar Vangr cast into the horde and engaged with sword and spear and fist. Barbarians had fallen by the score, but so too had citizens of Tar Vangr perished in the press. They faced insurmountable numbers, but when Carr fled the field, that gave the warders hope.

Nacacia semed deaf to it all. She beamed down at Sarelle, and the child giggled mischievously.

"Sarelle Wolfsbane." Nacacia smiled fiercely, blood spattered across her face, some of it her own. The bloodlust on her face was unsettling. "I give two names this night."

Sarelle mumbled something that sounded like agreement.

Thelisa choked on a cry as a barbarian burst through the ring of warders, lunging right for her, but Nacacia was there. The woman surged to her feet, sword reclaimed, and slashed the barbarian's head from his shoulders. Blood spattered Thelisa's face and the lift controls.

"Fight on!" Nacacia raised her sword high and roared. "Those who fight, *fight on!*"

The surge when Carr quit the field seemed to have died away, and the barbarians once against pressed the defenders hard. Thelisa managed to crawl over to a fallen warder, two spears in his chest, and claimed his caster. She fired into the horde, slaying a barbarian with each cast, but they came on. She saw Dain's distinctive red hair among the warders to her left, engaging the barbarians with axe and shield. He favored his lame foot, of course, but moved with the fervor and rage of a hardened warrior.

The lift was still coming down, and half a hundred Tar Vangryur non-combatants crowded around. Many had taken up arms to fight back against the Children, and as Thelisa watched, half a dozen fell screaming on the rotted, tarnished weapons of the invaders. If only the lift would descend faster.

The last of Thelisa's caster core was expended, and she tried to get up but failed. Her back was constant agony now, and she could barely feel the rest of her body. A gentle warmth swept over her.

Nacacia stood over her, blood-soaked sword held over her head in a two-handed grip, dark eyes shining through a gore-painted face. Somehow, none of the attackers had touched her—she was a devil with that blade, or perhaps Sarelle was a talisman after all. She glared defiance at the barbarians, ready to sell her life for the rest of the folk gathered by the lift.

A shuddering lurch made Thelisa's world swim, and she looked up, heart in her throat. *No*, she thought. *Not yet. We need more time.*

But she'd been wrong. The chains were intact, and the lift arrived on the ground level with a heavy crunch on the bodies that had fallen into the hollow where it rested. Thelisa saw, through a gap in the fighting, what had come down from High-City on the lift. Her breath came raggedly and she could barely see by straining. She coughed and blood dripped down her chin.

The twelve iron-clads—seven Lancers, four Chargers, and, towering above them, the watch's one Juggernaut—loosed a storm of lightning and fire on the invaders, filling the square with billowing ash and flying bone. It was beautiful and terrible and Thelisa tried to smile.

"Come," Nacacia was saying, her hand on Thelisa's cheek. "Come—"

But Thelisa was beyond reply. She continued to smile weakly at the avenging iron-clad angels, even after Nacacia gently closed her eyes.

TWELVE

REGEL STOOD PATIENTLY OUTSIDE Lady Shard's chambers, subtly flexing his sore leg as he waited. He could hear the raised voices within, and he tracked them only absently. He had no talisman to focus his senses, but he did not need it. The words exchanged behind Shard's thick door were not his to hear.

Two pirates stood in the corridor with him, ostensibly there to escort him, but in truth they wanted to stay as far from the madman as possible. The last hours had not been easy for Shard's pirates, and some of their frustration had naturally turned toward him. Before his arrival, days had passed smoothly in Atropis, but—as had proved the case many times over his life—he had come only to bear witness to profoundly life-altering events. At best, they considered him the harbinger of misfortune, and quite possibly they suspected him of alliance with their newfound enemies.

Ultimately, Regel found the situation acceptable. Indeed, he rather preferred matters pass this way. At his belt, Frostburn yearned for hot blood to sate its hunger, but Regel allowed the impulse to wash over and past him. The sword's lust diminished, and he patted the hilt as if in approval. If someone stood nearer, it might not have been so easy.

Finally. the door opened, and Ovelia's voice cut off in a strangled gasp. He could see her in there, standing near Shard's massive bed piled high with the banners of dozens of ships she had waylaid over her career. Ovelia's brown cheeks glistened with tears, and she stared at him without seeing. Lady Shard stood just inside the door, having pulled it inward. The veil hid her face, but her aggressive stance told Regel everything her face might have. The Pirate Queen was not pleased.

"Come." She gave Regel a curt nod, turned away, and stepped deeper into the room.

He joined them inside and the pirates on guard closed the door behind him.

The three of them stood silent for a moment, refusing to speak or meet one another's eye.

The rap of knuckles on wood finally broke the silence as Lady Shard put her fist down on a narrow table set with the remnants of a meal. Two plates, one mostly consumed, the other hardly touched. Regel had but to consider a moment before he knew Ovelia had not eaten. Her grief was almost as palpable as Shard's wrath.

"But for the *Hecatomb*, every ship in my fleet, damaged or destroyed." Shard tapped on the table again, then accentuated each word: "Every. Single. Ship."

"Lena—" Ovelia started.

Lady Shard uttered a roar, cutting her off, and slammed her fists on the table. "Every ship!"

With another cry, she swept the plates, candelabra, and remains of the meal off the table to shatter against the wall. She threw the table aside and kicked one of the chairs skittering across the floor. She rounded on Regel, who had taken half a step forward, and her veiled gaze froze him in place.

"You bring Ruin everywhere you go, Winter's Shadow!" She nodded toward Ovelia, who had hurried to put out the candles before they lit the blankets afire. "You and the Bloodbreaker *both*."

With an effort of will, Regel did not draw Frostburn but instead put his hands out in a peaceful gesture. "The Blood Queen meant to strike you regardless, Lady Shard," he said. "With Lan defeated in Luether, you pose the last threat to the Children's crusade. Because Ovelia was here, you live."

"Yes—I live, my power crippled." Shard spat the words, then laughed mirthlessly. "Ruin has a sense of irony, it seems. Constantly repeating itself." She pressed her gloved hands to the sides of her veiled face. "I suppose you think I should thank her, yes? Is that how you will rebuke me... *Frostburn?*"

He heard the icy knives in the words and he could not say if she meant Semana or Ruin herself.

He bowed his head. "I would not speak so to a queen."

That earned him a sound like a guttural scoff. "Well, she has her wish," Shard said. "I could not sail to Tar Vangr even if I wanted to. Not now, with my fleet in ruins. It will take my finest builders a year to repair all our ships, and your precious City of Steel will not last that long."

She pointed an accusing finger toward Ovelia, who had put out the flames with a blanket.

"And you," she said, which made Ovelia flinch in surprise. "You could not have warned me of that... *thing* before it tore my fleet apart and nearly killed me?"

Ovelia shook her head. "It doesn't pass that way."

"Don't lie to me, by the Fire." Shard took a menacing step toward her. "We all know your vision has expanded. You can see farther and more than ever before, and not just with your eyes. When she arrived, you *knew* it was her. You knew to come to my aid. Do not deny it."

Ovelia had opened her mouth to object, but instead she hung her head. "I did not know she would strike as she did," she said. "I could not have predicted that."

"You could have told me that she was burning *Semana Denerre.*"

The three fell silent for a long moment. Again, while Regel could not see through Shard's veil, he could perceive the anger flowing from her, and Ovelia's sorrow all but pulled her apart. The Bloodbreaker's every muscle trembled, to restrain sobs or screams, Regel could not say. This he understood also, in a way that Shard apparently did not comprehend. Or chose not to see.

Shard sighed. "It matters little, now," she said. "My fleet is in ruins, and even had I wanted to save Tar Vangr, I could not. And the Blood Queen—Semana—that masked thing is dead. Shame, really." She picked up a rotund bottle of wine and shook it next to her ear. She shrugged and popped the cork off with her thumb. "If she hadn't attacked, I might still have my fleet and she might still live."

Ovelia stiffened as though Shard had punched her in the gut.

"And so the last mage-city falls to Ruin," said Regel.

Shard sniffed. "You say that like I should care."

She pulled her veil slightly up to accommodate the mouth of the bottle. Regel caught sight of a stretch of pale skin, marred by a red-pink mark. He looked away. She drank greedily from the bottle, draining its contents at one go. Wine dribbled down her scarred neck and onto her black silks.

"You've come to convince me to sail," Shard said. "You want me to muster what ships I can repair quickly and make for the northland. To fight this war. Is that not true?"

Regel shrugged. "I do not command or compel," he said.

"But you advise." Shard cast the bottle carelessly aside, and it bounced and rolled onto her bed. "You'll tell me that we civilized folk—that we've a duty to resist the march of Ruin. Yes?"

Regel only looked at the floor.

"Really?" Shard seemed surprised, and perhaps a touch disappointed. She looked to Ovelia, who was also gazing mutely at the floor. "Neither of you?"

When Regel and Ovelia made no reply, Shard barked out another short laugh. "How wonderful," she said. "I cannot say which of us three is the most wretched, but it's certainly not me."

She might have said more, but at that moment a fist rapped on the door. Instantly, the jesting died away and Shard drew herself up straight. "Enter," she said. "I trust you interrupt me to a purpose?"

Aeldad stood in the doorway, stooping to maneuver her massive body inside. She and Regel exchanged a slight nod, and she moved to confer with Shard in soft voices. Regel noted Ovelia standing near at hand, so fragile and weak on her feet a stout breeze or harsh word might knock her to the floor. It occurred to him he should say something, but he hadn't the first idea what to say.

"She nodded to you, not to me," Ovelia said.

Regel frowned, then nodded. "She fears me."

"Respects you," Ovelia said. "She hates me."

"She should fear you." Regel looked away. "I do."

Ovelia glanced up at him—her blindfolded eyes not quite finding his face—and almost smiled.

Shard waved a hand. "Fine, show him in," she said. "I'll either listen or I'll kill him."

Aeldad hadn't even returned to the door before Lan Ravalis swept in, shrugging off the attempts of the guards to restrain him. He looked a bit worse for his time in the skycells—his clothes worn and soiled with sweat and rain, his hair grown long and his beard grown out—but he still looked robust. He hadn't yet broken.

"Your Highness, Queen of the Dusk Sea, I must—" He saw Regel standing there, Frostburn at his belt, and the words died on his lips. Now his bravado seemed to shrink. "You've freed him and given him the sword?" He looked to Ovelia and his grimace redoubled. "Oh good. The Bloodbreaker remains, and some fool has got her with child. Is that the Frostburn's child, you traitor, or something even worse?"

Ovelia's face darkened. Distantly, Regel was aware of rising indignation. It burned behind an icy wall, and he could see the flames but feel no heat.

"My advisors are not yet your concern," Shard said. "Until I order the Frostburn to take your head, that is." She waved. "Speak your business or begone. I've little patience left today."

Lan drew himself up to his full height despite his obvious weariness and uncertainty. He carried himself with the composure of his high birth. Since he was a Ravalis, it took the form of an arrogant sneer and cocksure manner, but at least he seemed uncowed.

"I've come to demand your aid in protecting Tar Vangr and defeating the Children of Ruin."

They all stared at him, startled by his abrupt words.

At first, Shard made a coughing sound, then it became a chuckle, then a full throated laugh. "Either I've gone mad, or the world has," she said. "Now a fallen prince is here to beg me—"

"King," Lan said, the word a distant peal of thunder. "And I come not to beg, but to *demand.*"

Ovelia visibly bristled, and Regel touched her arm lightly with his hand. He realized the irony immediately: in days not so long gone, he might have reacted in much the same way, and she the one to soothe. Even now, Frostburn scalded his fingers in its hunger for Lan's blood.

Shard, for her part, stared at Lan for a full ten-count, then burst into wild, unrestrained laughter.

Ovelia and Regel looked at one another, startled. Lan looked first confused, then irritated.

"I am serious," he said.

"Oh, I *know* you're serious." Shard turned her gaze entirely upon Lan, her mirth become contempt. "You call yourself a king, but I see no crown. No throne. No army. What—do you think your birth or your blood entitles you to make demands of me, your position be burned?"

"It's not my position that matters, but yours." Lan spread his chapped hands. "You have suffered a potent wound, but you are not defeated. You must gather your forces and strike while you might still take your enemy by surprise. Repel the threat to Tar Vangr, give me back my throne, and you shall have a potent ally in the days to come. My gratitude will be great, as will my generosity."

"The generosity of a Ravalis with empty pockets." Shard made a dismissive sound in her throat. "You'll have to do better than that."

"Very well." Lan cleared his throat and crossed his arms. "I would have you redeem my city, but what if it were also your city?"

Regel heard the faint suggestion in the words, but dismissed their import. At his side, Ovelia tensed. "No," she said under her breath.

Stiffly, as though the movements pained his sore body, Lan sank to one knee and bowed his head. He raised his hands in supplication toward Shard. "Join your cause to mine," Lan said. "Be my wife, and together, we shall liberate Tar Vangr and rule it side-by-side."

Ovelia made a strangled sound in her throat. She started to object, but Shard raised a hand, cutting off her words. "That's quite an offer," she said. "I had understood that you had a wife. Surely she would have some say in this."

"Hardly a hindrance." Lan waved. "Laegra Vargaen has never given me, and thus Tar Vangr, an heir. Setting her aside would be for the good of the mage-city, for me, and, of course, for you."

"How generous." Shard touched her fingers to her veiled mouth. "I'm sure you've heard stories of my hideousness. Is it your hope that your deformity will match my own?" She glanced down at his crotch. "If an heir is what you seek, I mean."

Hot little flames burned high on Lan's heavy cheeks for a moment as anger rose in him. He opened his mouth to deny it, then fell silent. He cast an accusatory look toward Ovelia.

"My offer stands," Lan said, turning to Shard only belatedly. "Power, riches, and the gratitude of a king. Focus your efforts on repairing a few skyships and sail north with me, now, while you've the initiative. I've no need of anything else from you but your fleet and your hand."

"No doubt." Shard clicked her tongue and glanced to Aeldad, who stepped within reach of Lan. Shard crossed to her sideboard and claimed a fresh decanter of wine. "I'll consider your offer."

"That—" Lan shut his mouth and raised his chin. "You'll return me to my cell?"

"I think that's best."

Aeldad put her hand on Lan, and he flinched away. "Wait," he said. "I've one more thing to say."

"Oh." Shard poured wine into a silver goblet. "Something that will impress me?"

"Only that the one who destroyed your fleet yet lives," he said. "How's that?"

"She—" Ovelia started forward, reaching vaguely toward Shard.

"Aye." The reaction was slight, but Lan saw it. His brows furrowed and he kept staring at Ovelia, his expression considering. "Semana, the Princess of Tar Vangr. I doubt she'll make you a better offer."

"Hrm." Shard waved, and Aeldad closed her hands around Lan's arms. He objected with a growl, and she released him to walk on his own.

He left silence in the room. Shard put the decanter back down, lifted her veil, and put the cup to her lips. The sound of gulping vied with the faint hum of vibrating metal all around them.

Ovelia spoke first. "Your Highness—"

Shard raised a hand. "No doubt you've changed your mind," she said. "I wonder why."

Ovelia looked away. "We will come with you," she said. "If we sail to Tar Vangr, we must all fight. I know that. We—" She winced and clutched her swollen belly.

"Hrn." Shard waved dismissively. "Looks like you won't be fighting for much longer."

Ovelia made a face at Shard. "I can fight," she said.

"And you." Shard turned on Regel. "What of you?"

Regel forced himself to take his hand away from Frostburn. It had frozen his world, and he could only dimly sense what had come to pass. Now that Shard turned her attention to him, her gaze seemed to melt the wall of ice. Regel tried to speak, but he couldn't manage to produce any words.

"Leave us," Shard said.

Regel almost moved before he realized she meant Ovelia, not him. It surprised Ovelia as well, and she nodded at length. She started to move past, but Shard caught her by the arm and stayed her in place. Ovelia started to speak, but Shard seized her throat in her other hand, stopping her words. They gazed at one another, their faces close, and Shard pressed her veiled lips against Ovelia's own. A shiver passed through Ovelia's body, and her face slid away. She moved past and left the chamber.

Regel and Lady Shard stood in the chamber together, silence hanging between them. He wanted to speak, but nothing occurred to him to say. Perhaps too much time had passed—too many events in their lives. He stood, waiting for the moment she would dismiss him.

"I still need you," she said finally, her voice soft and weak. "That is why you are free. Why you wield that sword. And because of Ovelia. Is any of this unclear to you?"

Regel shook his head.

Shard crossed to the sideboard to pour yet another goblet. He could hear the slur in her words, and also see the limp in her left hip. She usually tried to hide it, but the liquor must have got to her.

"Are—" Shard paused, and took a deep drink of her wine. So fast and so much that she choked and sputtered. Regel stepped forward, but Shard waved him off and slapped the goblet onto the table. It took a moment for her coughing to pass, then she walked toward him and laid a hand on his chest.

Their gazes met, and though he could not see her eyes, he could feel her vehemence. Her fingers tapped his sternum. "Are you still my knight?" she asked. "Still Winter's Shadow?"

"Yes, Highness." Regel nodded. "Until my life passes this broken world."

"Good." She loosed a soft sigh of breath and raised her hands—one at his shoulder, the other at his waist. It was an unmistakeable invitation. "Dance with me."

Regel frowned. "Why?"

"Have you not always wanted to?" she asked. "I saw you watching from the shadows all those times. Do not think I have forgotten." She put one hand on his shoulder and the other on his hip.

"There is no music," he said, even as he mirrored her gesture.

"Good."

They danced. They moved slowly—awkwardly at first, but with growing confidence and purpose—around the small chamber. They turned and stepped to a song that existed only in their minds. His leg protested, but she supported that side of his body. The same thing happened on his other side, as her left hip plagued her as well. They were reversed mirrors of one another, neither of them young and strong for years now. They had missed that chance.

Missed so many things, and now they would never seek them again.

It reminded him of dancing with Mask what seemed so long ago on Ruin's Night in the palace of Tar Vangr, only he knew Shard did not feign her weakness or clumsiness. There was strength there: an unyielding endurance he had never felt in Shard when she was the ice princess of Tar Vangr. When she rested her head against his chest and sighed, he understood. They danced because they had no words.

Lenalin Denerre was gone, and he had only just begun to realize that Regel no longer existed either. He was burning away as they danced, leaving only ice and steel in his place.

At length, she drew away, and their hands parted. "Are you still my knight?" she asked again.

The Frostburn nodded.

In that moment, he did not need Ovelia's foresight to know their future.

THIRTEEN

Low-City Tar Vangr, City of Steel

"M ASTER?"

The flame-haired servant asked a question with his eyes, but it went unanswered. This moment must not be broken in such a way.

Drawing in a breath, Darak Ravalis nô Denerre strode over the shattered walls and into Tar Vangr. He didn't feel different in any meaningful way, though he hadn't set foot in the city in over a decade. The air tasted foul with smoke of buildings reduced to blackened husks after days of burning, and the reek of bodily waste and sour blood turned his stomach. Somehow, even in the midst of war, Darak had expected to experience something other than the same corruption he'd lived, day by day, for years.

Now that he had finally returned, Darak found Low-City Tar Vangr no longer a mage-city—a bastion of civilization—but just one more ruin the Children had left in their wake.

Ultimately, he decided he could accept that.

"Speak," he said to Crown of Fire at his side.

"Master." Crown's forehead beaded with sweat. "We should go. Standing in the open…"

"Well." Darak raised a hand to cut him off. "In a moment."

Crown was not wrong. Standing in the opening, Darak may as well have been inviting a Tar Vangryur sniper from on-high to put a casterbolt through his torso. But he reveled in the moment.

He had done this. He was the warlord who had accomplished what Ruin's Children had never managed in nearly a thousand years of striving: bring down the great Tar Vangr. He had smashed Low-City, and soon he would bring High-City low. There would be no hero of Winter to rise up to redeem the city—nay, for he *was* that hero. The turn of thought amused him, and he smiled slightly.

"Give me your report."

Crown swallowed. "A single lift yet functions," he said. "In the southeast quarter, by the—"

"By the docks," Darak said. "Harborside, that quarter is called. And the fighting there?"

"Fierce, Master."

"No doubt." Darak waved, and they passed over the ruined wall and into the city proper.

As they walked through the filthy streets, Darak looked up at High-City, towering hundreds of paces overhead atop a vast, semi-translucent ceiling covered in snow and ice. Today was clear, and he could see buzzing activity through the mage-glass. He wondered how many had escaped into High-City, and what sort of defense they could mount against a concerted attack. He would find out.

"They are still ferrying supplies?" he asked.

"Aye, Master," said Crown. "Rarely, and always well-defended."

"And Carr has been unable to cut off their supply," said Darak.

"She—" Crown of Fire wet his lips, hesitant to speak ill of a High Druid. "So it seems, Master."

"We'll see about that."

They passed through the maze of streets, and Darak noted the hollow, haunted faces of folk. Over the previous few days, the Children had taken near complete control of Low-City, seizing both its industrial plants and its urban farms. Of course the barbarians had eaten or despoiled almost everything green in the city, but the grain stores in Low-City's bowels would keep them fed throughout the winter. At Darak's direction, they'd bound most of the survivors of Low-City as slaves and forced them to work the forges and supply posts, which he had turned to support the invaders.

Darak stopped while a pack of five or six passed them, huddled in a circle and prodded by barbarian escorts. For a foolish second, he wondered if any of them would know him for their exiled prince and rightful king, but of course his cowl would prevent anyone from recognizing him. When the slaves went past, they kept their eyes down and only muttered to themselves.

Crown of Fire sweated in the unseasonable warmth of the city. The winter persisted in Low-City Tar Vangr, but gone was the bone-chilling cold of the world outside. This, he had expected, and so he had prioritized breaching the walls and occupying Low-City as soon as possible. Inside, they strode with confidence, flesh bared to the elements, and praised the name of Dar-Karsk, who offered paradise.

"Comfortable, my slave?" he asked, though he knew the answer.

Crown of Fire stammered something in reply. "Master?"

Darak smiled at the man's unease, then furthered it by putting a hand on his neck. "Did you ever wonder why the mage-cities stand where they do? Why civilization can flourish in this place?"

Wordlessly, the slave shook his head of vibrant red hair.

"The Narfire flows beneath these streets, like lifeblood of this broken world. And its heat, it makes this city... viable."

The warlords had wanted to bring the full horde into the city—to dominate by force of numbers and enjoy the comforting warmth—but Darak had spoken against the idea. Clustering their forces too tightly would make it easier for the defenders to strike back. If reinforcements did arrive, as unlikely as that seemed, he did not want to be trapped in Tar Vangr and besieged from above and without. And secretly, some part of him yet wanted to take his rightful place as king, not as a foreign conqueror. If he derived all his power from a horde of barbarians, how could he make such a claim?

No. The time was not yet right. He hoped the dragon's blood lasted a bit longer. But even if it did not—well, that would take care of the horde, wouldn't it?

"It is more than comfort." Darak ran his fingers over Crown's neck. "The Silver Fire fuels the mage-cities. They use it. Refine it. It gives them their power, and powers their weapons."

He wrapped his hand around Crown's throat and squeezed with a grip that belied his slender fingers. Worldfire gave him the strength of a man many times his size. His slave went taut, his eyes wide and terrified as those of a deer. Darak pressed his body against Crown, reveling in his trembling terror.

"And now we possess it," he said. "Their food. Their heat. And soon—" He leaned close to Crown's face. "All their power."

The barbarian's watery eyes locked upon Darak now, and he could see the terror there. He savored it a second more, then released his hand. Crown of Fire sucked in air but dared not move away. He had eyes only for Darak, and seemed certain that movement would bring worse punishment.

"Imagine." Darak traced his fingers up Crown of Fire's cheek and across his brow. "What I could do with that power. Power over Tar Vangr and all of Winter. Over the Children. The Circle. All of Ruin."

"You—you will rule over all," Crown of Fire said, his voice scratchy.

"In time." Darak leaned in close, and their lips nearly touched. "Does that excite you?"

With their bodies pressed together, Darak could feel that it did. It both excited and terrified.

"Boy," came a harsh voice from behind them.

Darak regarded one-eyed Carr the Axe over his shoulder with a contemptuous sneer. He drew away from Crown of Fire and joined the Druid on her way toward the shouts and jeers.

"Why, High Lady," Darak said. "You look positively a fright."

Carr's face and neck were a mass of purple bruises, her clothing scuffed and torn, but it'd been worse that first night. After the failure at the Harborside lift, she'd returned to camp in far worse shape: limping badly, her body a mass of bruises and cuts, her hair gnarled and half torn away. She'd somewhat repaired the mighty axe from which she took her name, but it had lost some of its luster. He'd never seen a battle damage her so badly, and the rage inside only built as her body healed, sped by magic.

"Picked a fine time to join the fight, boy," Carr said. "Almost all over and done with."

She scowled at him, and when he didn't reply, her contempt deepened.

Darak could well understand her displeasure. His gambit to take Low-City succeeded and the Frostfire protection had won him the love and loyalty of the horde, while she seemed to be losing in every way that mattered. Semana hadn't yet returned, so the horde had turned to Darak instead, leaving Carr increasingly isolated. She no longer spoke with Fellis, her once close companion. Her expression, simmering just this side of rage, said she had backed the wrong power, and she knew it.

They entered the outskirts of Harborside, surrounded on all sides by barbarians cheering and offering Darak salutes. Every single show of appreciation made Carr's glower darken.

"Come to see my work, have ya?" she asked. "You—"

"Come to finish it," Darak said over her. "If you haven't rutted it all up by now."

Her face went redder than usual and he left her sputtering. Turning his back on Carr the Axe was a daring gesture—some might say foolish—but he felt completely safe there amongst the horde. He'd even managed to leave Fellis behind, though no doubt she followed unobtrusively at a distance. The woman was a snake, and he meant to deal with her as soon as he could afford to lose her support.

The horde had closed a rough perimeter outside effective caster range around the Harborside lift, which fairly bristled with casters gleaming in the morning light. The Tar Vangryur had managed to fend off the invasion so far, clustered here, ready to cast and charge at the least provocation. They maintained this small foothold in all of Low-City, where the lift had worked almost constantly to ferry desperate folk and salvaged supplies to High-City. The highborn seemed unable or—Darak thought it more likely, *unwilling*—to take everyone, however, and Darak counted a hundred souls lurking around the lift, their faces haggard and their eyes lifeless, hoping that the next lift would whisk them to safety.

The Children had made multiple attempts to take the lift, and each time, the defenders had repelled them. The square itself bore the marks of those battles: the place lay littered with corpses three-high and stank of rot and corruption. The Narfire below prevented the chill from preserving the dead, and the whole place was a festering cesspool of rancid gray and black flesh. The defenders at the center of the heap looked nearly dead themselves: profoundly exhausted, battered, and barely standing. Darak picked one out particularly: a dark-eyed woman, her body and face smeared with dried blood, her stance an active threat. She almost looked like a Child of Ruin herself.

As he had always known, there was little distance between these folk and the barbarians.

Spontaneously, Darak stepped from the barricade that besieged the lift, his stained gray cloak slipping over the corpses underfoot. Crown of Fire took in a sharp breath, but Carr restrained him, looking pleased at Darak's sudden departure from safety. He stepped forward, bare hands raised.

Casters came up to point at Darak, but the woman he had picked out raised her hand to stay their casts. "I am Nacacia of the Circle of Tears," she said. "Do you lead this horde?"

"I do." Darak felt a tiny spark of tension at the base of his neck. Excitement. "I am called Dar-Karsk among the Children of Ruin, and I would speak with he who has voice over Tar Vangr. The Summer King, or his proxy—someone with authority."

Her brow furrowed, and Darak expected his eloquent tone and the sophisticated words "proxy" and "authority" had surprised her. Few barbarians spoke so.

"The king, is it," Nacacia said. "Why. You come to surrender?"

Darak almost wanted to laugh, but Nacacia's face held not a spark of mirth. Good.

The power in this place—the Narfire beating beneath the ground—begged to fuel his Worldfire. He longed to devour it, to turn it upon these fools who stood against them and destroy them all. But that would not serve his cause—not this day, anyway.

"I come not to offer terms, but to demand your submission," he said. "You will bow to me."

She raised her chin. "Nacacia does not bow."

"Before this is done," he said, "you will."

He summoned his Frostfire, and it built around him in a column of blue-white flame. He could have lashed out with the power and struck her down—could have slain any of them—but he had another purpose, and so he restrained the urge. Instead he spread his arms, letting the flames rise.

"Because I am Darak Ravalis nô Denerre," he said. "And I am your rightful king."

He expected shock, and he got it. Few gathered here had probably seen the Winter King in the flesh, and would not necessarily recognize any resemblance between Orbrin and Darak, but they would know the distinctive power of Frostfire. It had made its way into the tales and dreams of Tar Vangr, and every child raised in the City of Steel dreamed of one day wielding the beautiful blue-white flames. Just as potent as the fantasy was the knowledge of its rarity, and everyone knew that only those of the Blood of Winter could harness such power. The Frostfire proved Darak's identity and claim far better than any signet ring.

He was their prince—their king—and all of them knew it.

Nacacia stepped forward, mouth opening to speak, when abruptly a distant sound caught everyone's attention. It resembled an alarm horn, such as one might sound on a ship approaching an unfamiliar port on a fog-filled night. The character of the horn was so loud, so clear, and so powerful, however, that it shook the bones and demanded attention. Darak felt the confusion and dread rippling through the barbarians at his back, and he understood why when he looked up and to the south. There, out of the dark clouds some ways beyond Tar Vangr's bay, a crimson craft cut its way out of the storm, gray wisps escaping around it like mighty waves crashing upon rocks. Lightning crackled along the length of three scything propulsion rings as the skyship revealed itself in its shimmering glory and menace.

Darak knew two things in that instant: that Semana had failed to keep Shard's pirates away, and that his bid to claim the hearts and imagination of the Tar Vangryur had also failed.

"No," he said under his breath.

It wasn't fair. This city had spat on him—abandoned him—sent him out into the cold to die. But he had fought and scraped to survive and return to take his rightful place and collect what they owed him. The revelation of his identity alone should have put them all on their knees before him. And yet...

Rage roiled in his gut, escaping from a hot ember simmering deep in the core of his being. It had always been there, warming him in the coldest nights, granting him the drive to keep pushing even when it seemed impossible. And now—*now* it would not rest. He could not stand and do nothing in the face of ridiculous fate.

"*No.*"

Power pulsed there, just beneath the surface of the stone. The Narfire was the life of the world of Ruin, and never before had it been so close—so accessible to his Worldfire. He had but to reach out and seize it. And even as he had the thought, he recognized the danger. The sheer power and force of the Silver Fire. It could so easily overwhelm him, turn him to ash, and yet...

And yet, if any had the strength of will to wield the Narfire, it was he.

"No!" Darak shouted it this time, raising his hands and wrenching forth power.

A mighty tremor swept through the plaza, and the heavy bricks split apart and burst. Silver flames flowed into the air, like water from a geyser, as a fissure pulled itself open between Darak and the lift. The force of the Worldfire sent the defenders staggering back and to the ground, and Nacacia herself went flying off her feet and back.

Belatedly, Darak realized he was the one screaming, but he did not care. He sucked on the power under the ground like a child at his mother's milk, and ripped another tremor of rage through the square. The lift bent and warped under the sheer power of his anger. Fire sprang up from these new rents in the ground, but it slowed to a trickle, seeping like blood from torn flesh.

He hadn't lost control like this in so long, not in the decade he'd walked among the barbarians. He understood anger, but always told himself that it would make him vulnerable. But the strength of it—the power of his rage—intoxicated him. Now that he'd given himself to it, he could not stop.

Only when he heard a thunderous *crack* and pain bloomed in his upper arm did he realize his error. The force of the near-miss knocked him to the ground, and he saw blood welling from a gash in his robed shoulder. One of the Tar Vangryur had cast at him, narrowly missing his neck. The rest of the defenders rallied and aimed a small forest of casters.

Darak knew he should run, but in the depths of his rage, he couldn't make himself flee. He wanted nothing more than to roll to his knees, drink all the power the world had to offer, and throw it at the defenders until they were all dead.

How dare they stand against him. How *dare* they not fall prostrate and *worship* him.

Rough hands fell on Darak's shoulders, making pain radiate from his wound. He flinched and shoved up and away with Worldfire-enhanced muscles. A barbarian flew a pace into the air off him, just in time to catch two casterbolts in a defensive volley. He tumbled to the cracked stone two paces from Darak.

That—seeing a man broken and killed within arm's reach—shook Darak from his hesitation. He saw the Tar Vangryur recharging and readying another volley, so he scrambled toward the near buildings before they could take aim. Thunder tore through the square again, and a bolt exploded off the bricks near his head, making him duck lower.

He could hear the cries of alarm and rage from the square. The barbarians must have charged when Darak attacked, and now he could hear the sounds of a rout. It had all fallen apart.

He cast his gaze to the skies, and watched the massive skyship pass over the city. Tar Vangr's weapons hadn't fired upon it, and why would they? It was their shining savior. It was, perhaps, the most beautiful construct he'd ever seen: a shining vessel, gleaming with condensation and roaring with power. He'd watched the *Avenger* at the head of his mother's funerary parade, polished as bright as it could be, and still it was not a match for such a wonder. He could not recall the last time he had seen such a thing newly made, rather than recycled after centuries of use.

Hecatomb, he had heard it called. Shard's flagship after the fall of the Ruin King.

And now it bore down upon the bulk of his horde, still camped outside Tar Vangr.

Darak tried to focus. Power surged even as he tried to release it. He needed it. Needed—

A figure stumbled into the alley, and he recognized her with a shock through his whole body.

Carr the Axe reacted in much the same way, brandishing her bloody axe right in his face. They stared at one another, her weapon raised against his hands swirling with tingling power. Darak was not summoning a slaying spell, though, and Carr could surely cut him down before he could respond.

"I must call the dragon," he said through gritted teeth.

Carr stared at him, remaining eye wide. At length, she nodded and turned her two-bearded axe toward the entrance to the alley. Protecting Darak, rather than threatening him. For now.

The last thing her presence did was reassure him, but the sudden sharp lance of fear had diminished Darak's rage. With that little bit of clarity, he could finally put the Worldfire aside and instead reach for the Frostfire. It came to him, as quickly and gently as an old friend—one who had comforted him so many years ago, when he first began his exile. His oldest and only friend. Silver-blue flames rose up around him and reached up into the sky.

At first, Darak didn't know if it would work. Perhaps all was lost.

Then he felt it—a resonant *thrum* deep inside him, like the beating of his heart but far bigger. Impossibly powerful. Ancient and impossible for mortal minds to understand.

Across the field, a mighty roar rolled like thunder, making the city tremble. The dragon swept its massive wings around the gathered camp like icy curtains, then leaped from the frozen plain and surged into the sky. It rose to meet the approaching skyship as it loosed a torrential rain of fire and death.

And in that way, Darak bore witness to the clash over the snowy fields of Tar Vangr.

~

Thereafter, the battle between the winter dragon and the *Hecatomb* would be described in many ways. Thunder and lightning met without a storm, and titans danced such that the earth quaked fit to burst apart. Blue flame and bursts of slashing red lightning lanced around one another, and blood poured into the air alongside black smoke.

The dragon whipped and darted around the skyship, casters and the main cannon raining volleys of destruction upon it. The creature's agility and speed kept it harrying the skyship, pouring on gouts of silver and blue flame. The Frostfire breath scored the skyship's armored hull, cooking ablative plates to withered, pitted crisps of metal. The beast painted burn scars across the *Hecatomb*'s polished surface, making it appear just as old and weathered as any other skyship in the World of Ruin.

Smoke and fire flared through the air, obscuring the combatants but for flashes of light and trumpeting cries of pain and shrieks of metal. Ash, flecks of skyship armor, and dragon scales—the detritus of the battle in the skies—rained down on the hapless folk below, killing and wounding. The leavings painted great black and crimson swaths across the snow, like a chronicle of the battle. Come the spring, these scars in the earth would remain, and perhaps they would last for years to come.

Then of a sudden, a fearful roar spread through the hollow, sweeping over the snowy plains like a windstorm. A shape fell from the smoke, trailing blue flame and blood into the air. The dragon crashed down into the snow, broken and groaning and crying out in agony. The *Hecatomb* limped free of the cloud of crackling fire and lightning, smoke pouring from its hull and its propulsion rings clanking. It listed to the left slightly, but at least it remained aloft. It floated toward Tar Vangr, leaving a raining mist of destruction in its wake. Finally, the threatening clouds began to snow.

FOURTEEN

THE ARRIVAL OF THE *Hecatomb* to Tar Vangr was the brightest moment in the city's darkest season in years. Over the past days, the Vangryur had seen a dragon out of legend swoop out of the gathering darkness against their city, smashing a wall that had stood for nearly a millennium to hold them safe against the wilds. Then, when that self-same madness poured through the breach, thousands of their fellows had died in the initial push, and more still in a vain attempt to flee the invasion. The wealthy and powerful of the city had cut three of four High-City lifts, abandoning much of Low-City to the barbarians, and the fourth lift was heavily embattled and under constant siege.

And so it was that the thousand or so folk awaiting the arrival of the skyship that had struck back at their foes looked worn, thin, and ragged. Hollow-eyed and disheveled, they gathered to welcome their saviors with a distinctive aura of distrust. Banners streamed in the cold wind, and they shivered. Some wore the fine warm clothes of the wealthy, but hundreds wore the colorless leathers and furs of Low-City poor. These folk likely had nowhere else to go, and the *Hecatomb* was their only ray of hope. Hundreds of soldiers stood waiting, hands on the hilts of their blades or casters leaning against their shoulders. They displayed a certain mixture of hope and wariness.

First down the ramp from the mighty skyship's deck was King Lan Ravalis himself, and the sight of his gleaming golden power armor sent a thrill through the crowd. They'd never expected to see him again, much less off the ramp of the skyship that had just saved them. They stared, breathless, and the hum of a drawn blade could be heard in that space. They waited, dumbfounded.

Then Lan raised his hands, and as though that sudden movement made it all real—made him physical and not just an illusion—the crowd erupted into sound. Cheers, shouts, and weeping filled the square: an explosion of joy that sounded like thunder. Many of those assembled surely hated the Blood of Ravalis, but hope had just reappeared despite Ruin all around.

Shadowing Lan down the ramp, full cloak obscuring the hand on his sword hilt, Regel could hardly begrudge them this. Even if he knew the truth of the matter.

The cheers and applause began to wane, replaced on many faces with expressions of confusion and growing alarm. Behind Regel on the ramp approached Lady Shard in her black cloak and veil, as well as Ovelia Dracaris wrapped all in crimson leather and white linen, her infamous sword slung across her back. The folk might not have known Shard, but they recognized the Bloodbreaker well enough, marked by her distinctive brown skin and especially her fiery red mane. Celebration faded, and they quavered to see their king side-by-side with one of the greatest traitors in Tar Vangr's history.

"Well." Lan spread his hands wide, smiling fatuously with pride. His resonant voice carried over the assembled people, audible mostly because of their shocked silence. "I see the flower of chivalry spread out before me. I see hope and determination. " He indicated Ovelia and Shard—not Regel, who stood unassumingly beside the other pirates who had descended the ramp. "In this darkest of times, when Ruin threatens, we shall forge what alliances we may…"

Regel stopped hearing the words themselves, but listened mostly to the tone and read the reactions of the crowd. Lan spoke off the cuff, though perhaps he'd rehearsed this particular speech for the duration of their journey, appealing to nationalism and valor. Looking up at Shard now, he thought she might be making a similar consideration. She stood up on the deck of the *Hecatomb*, hands clenched around the rail, and though he could not see her face, he could imagine her teeth grinding.

"Watch him," he said under his breath to Aeldad, who stood near at his side.

"The fool int flying anywhere soon." The towering pirate sneered at Regel and clapped one big hand on his upper arm. Her fingers squeezed hard. "And you don't order me, little man."

"A request, then," Regel said.

"Aye," she said. "If he tries to fly, cut him down. Got it."

Regel couldn't say if she was jesting, but ultimately decided it didn't matter. He touched her hand on his arm, and a shiver went through her. Respect, fear, or Frostburn's power? He could not say, and that did not matter either. They nodded to one another and he slipped back up to the deck.

"You'd think he single-handedly cast that monster down himself," Shard said as Regel slid into place beside her, a note of wryness in her voice. "Rather than spent the whole battle in the brig."

Ovelia stood silently, her sightless gaze cast over the crowd toward the palace. Its pinnacle was still a crushed, splintered blemish where Mask had destroyed the massive window. The Ravalis had apparently not rebuilt it over the intervening year, leaving it instead a wind-swept ruin.

Shard must have noticed his scrutiny, for she made a little scoffing sound in her throat. "A fitting symbol of a dying Blood." She turned and leaned back against the rail, arms crossed. "Mayhap we should sail away and leave this city to Ruin."

"You don't mean that," Ovelia said without turning.

"Don't I?" Shard adjusted her posture with a soft grunt. "I left for a reason, you know."

They stood silent for a long moment, while the miraculously returned king continued to mop up the adulation of the masses. Some had come forward to paw at him, as though they might touch divinity, and others kissed his boots. Regel knew this was the plan—that Lan and Shard had discussed this arrival and entrance in great detail—but seeing it now, he found himself agreeing with Shard. Perhaps they should retract the ramp from the *Hecatomb* and sail away, leaving Tar Vangr—and Lan Ravalis—to whatever fate Ruin had for them.

"We stand together," Regel said at length. "Or we fall."

The unexpected words prompted Ovelia to glance over at him. At first, it seemed she might speak, but finally she merely nodded her head.

Shard proved less agreeable.

"What need have we of this cursed city," she said, "if the *Hecatomb* can throw down a dragon?"

The logic was compelling. Did the Children pose any threat to Lady Shard? Surely the horde could not come against Atropis in sufficient numbers on the sea, and the barbarians lacked the resources to pilot enough skyships to challenge Shard's fleet. And finally, if Shard's flagship could defeat their only real weapon against her, even damaged as the battle had left it…

But Regel knew, at the back of his mind, that it was folly. He'd seen the dragon at its full strength, and the battle with *Hecatomb* should not have gone so smoothly. There was only one conclusion he could reach.

"It was weakened," Regel said.

"What do you mean?" Shard asked.

"He speaks true," Ovelia said. "When the *Hecatomb* clashed with the dragon, it had recently undergone a terrible ordeal, and not yet recovered. We defeated it, barely, at less than half strength."

"And you know this, how?" Shard asked. "Familiar with beasts of legend, are you?"

Ovelia lowered her sightless eyes, not rising to that question.

"Well." Shard stretched her arms with audible clicks. "We should get repairs under way immediately. Unless you can tell me when the dragon will be back on the field?" Ovelia shook her head and Shard looked away. "Frostburn. When Lord Shining Knight is done with the mob's adulation, bring him to me. I've need of him."

Regel asked a question with a glance, but Shard was already moving away, a slightly limp in her otherwise confident stride. With a slight nod to bid him farewell, Ovelia followed behind the pirate queen. Regel considered calling after them, then dropped his hand to his side. The tone of command in Shard's voice compelled his obedience, and he would not fail her.

They returned to the *Hecatomb* while he descended the ramp to join King Lan amongst his worshiping people. Aeldad and the other pirates looked conspicuously uncomfortable being so near the object of such adoration. When Regel approached, Aeldad nodded and gestured her soldiers to give up their flanking positions. Regel became Lan's singular shadow, just as he had at times followed the Winter King on his walks through the city, so many years ago, albeit with a slightly different purpose. Then, he had followed to protect—now, he followed to protect and slay if need be.

They made it halfway to the palace before Lan noticed Regel lurked there amongst the cheering people. The returned king flared his nostrils, then beckoned Regel over with a crooked finger.

"She sent you after me, did she? My keeper." Lan scoffed. "You'll at least allow me to see my kin, yes? They'll want to welcome me as a hero, no doubt, and I must accept." He smiled for the crowd, but Regel saw the tension in it. "One must keep up appearances."

"Appearances." Regel nodded slightly.

They both knew the score: Lan was too valuable—and too dangerous— for Shard to let out of her sight for long. Lan's skin oozed a sheen of sweat whenever he laid eyes on Regel; he knew who held the power here. Perhaps Lan would break and run into the crowd, try to fight back, or something of that nature. Would he strain on his leash, testing its limits, or would he try to break it?

One hand on Frostburn's frigid hilt, Regel rather hoped for the latter.

A delegation of folk came toward them through the adulant crowd: three people in the crimson cloaks of Blood Ravalis, two men and a woman, as well as four warders in the gold-inlaid steel armor favored by their Blood. Of the party, Regel recognized only the woman, whose deep frown drew her face downward. The youngest of the Ravalis—a boy who'd seen perhaps seven winters—smiled broadly as they approached. He was the only one who looked even remotely pleased to see them.

"Uncle!" said the lad, rushing forward when they came within a dozen paces.

He caught Lan's hands in his own and raised them in greeting. He gave the fallen king what was perhaps the first genuine smile Regel had seen in some time, and Lan looked just as startled. After a heartbeat's hesitation, he jerked his hands away from the boy and scowled.

"Has Tar Vangr gone so soft in my absence?" Lan said. "I've been gone only half a year."

The youngest Ravalis went pale, and his jubilant expression fell apart into something considerably less glad. He backed away, chastened, and took shelter under the woman's arm. The action was so child-like, Regel thought perhaps he'd overestimated his age based on his size. The woman gave Lan a sharp look, but it lasted only a heartbeat before her eyes fell.

"Laegra." He dismissed his wife with a slight grimace, then looked to the other Ravalis man. "You're the cousin they chose to warm my throne, is it? I know your face, but not—"

"Laud," the man said, his voice tight. "Laud Ravalis, cousin."

"Truly?" Lan cocked an eyebrow, and his expression turned intrigued. "Little cousin Laud?"

Despite the man's obvious youth—perhaps he'd seen eighteen or nineteen winters—he stood straight and strong beneath Lan's scrutiny. A well-built lad with obvious strength and the bloom of health, he had the coloration of the Ravalis blood, though his brown skin was lighter and his hair a ruddy crimson rather than fierce scarlet. It took Regel a moment, but he realized Laud Ravalis was not a pure summerblood, which surprised him. Of all the Bloods who had come north after the fall of Luether, the Ravalis most stringently kept to their own people.

Apparently, Lan thought the same. He spoke softly and directly, but Regel could hear him with his senses attuned. "Little Laud Ravalis, the pale heir," Lan said. "Who'd have thought the little bastard spawn of a winterborn harlot would grow to sit as regent of the city?"

Despite the insult, Laud bared his teeth and stood firm. "It was thought my mingled heritage would earn me the trust of the people." He gestured around at the clamoring crowd, who were pressing in on the party's warders, desperate for a look at the returned king. "It seems to have served."

"Indeed." Lan grinned. "You were just a boy when I left, little cousin. I see you are a man now." He looked to the younger of the two. "Is that little fop your brother then?"

The boy retreated behind Laegra, his aunt, and avoided Lan's eye.

"Caetus," said Laud. "And yes. Forgive his enthusiasm. You're something of a hero to him."

"Really." Lan scoffed. "Perhaps he might express it in less girlish ways."

The king had spoken loudly enough that the boy could hear, and Regel saw tears welling in his eyes. Laegra gave Lan a long-suffering, poisonous look, then turned to escort the boy away. She hadn't said anything and seemed to have no intention of doing so, and neither did Lan had any interest in her. Regel had seen them together before, of course, but never quite so strained. What Lan had promised Lady Shard about the ease of setting her aside rang true.

Silver Fire, she wasn't really going to accept his proposal, was she? This horrid waste of a man?

Laud Ravalis was looking hard at Regel, who bore the scrutiny without unease. There was something noble about the young man; in his bearing Regel saw a refusal to bow to Lan's bullying. He reminded Regel a bit of Garin Ravalis, and the comparison brought a pang to his gut. He'd never liked the man—never had much of a chance to befriend him—but Regel had come to respect Garin and he was glad of the choices the Fox of Luether had made. For without Garin, would any of them be standing here?

"Cousin," Laud said. "Who is that?"

Lan stiffened slightly, as though reminded for the first time that Regel had followed him. "No one," he said. "My shadow. I need protection, after all—even in my own city. Can't have me dying and miraculously returning more than once. No one would believe it."

"I see," said Laud, his tone cautious. "I take it you've come to reclaim your throne."

Lan laughed. "Soon enough, lad, soon enough," he said. "We've a war to win first, aye? Let's see to that." He clapped his hand on Laud's shoulder. "And see how well you've been sitting my throne."

They headed away toward the palace of Tar Vangr, the tension obvious between them. Lan had seemingly brushed it aside, but the threat he posed was about as subtle as a drawn blade. Regel paused and looked back at the *Hecatomb* in the middle distance, where he could dimly see Ovelia's vivid red hair through a hazy window. Somehow, he knew she was looking at him as well, as though she could see him at all, much less from so far away

So much had passed between them, and he could not say how he felt, but he knew he cared about Ovelia. Indeed, she—more than Semana, more than Shard, more than anything—was what warmed him against Frostburn's cold. They were all of them fighting for the world, but he was fighting especially for her.

Regel turned and followed the Ravalis.

⌯

Through the bleary window streaked with drizzle, Ovelia watched the shadowy shapes move outside the *Hecatomb* as tools sparked and dust mages fretted over the repairs to the mighty craft.

The weather over Tar Vangr mirrored Lenalin's own inner storm. Ovelia could hardly breathe in the stifling atmosphere of the captain's quarters on the *Hecatomb*, but she remained firstly out of duty, and secondly because it had grown uncomfortable to carry her belly far these last days. She touched it now, and her babe kicked irritably. The child was in as foul a mood as her mistress.

"I hear that bastard Laud Ravalis sits the throne." Lenalin made a derisive sound. "I thought the city mad when I left. I see the boys who've inherited it are no better or wiser than the last crop."

"That is not fair." Ovelia pushed away from the window and crossed her arms as she regarded Lenalin. Her clear view of the woman had faded of late, but she could still make out the dim outlines of her shadowy form. "Laud is not a bad man, and his blood could have chosen far worse."

Lenalin made a disgusted sound in her throat. "He is a Ravalis."

"Yes. A Ravalis who seeks to save our city. Who does what he must to protect our folk."

"Our folk. Tsch." Lenalin poured a bowl of wine, with which she toasted in mock solemnity. "Best of luck to him. As soon as the *Hecatomb* is skyworthy once more, I plan to point her prow southward and quit this awful place." She pulled her veil up over her face and set the bowl to her lips.

"No, you don't."

"Oh?"

"You—" She turned, but Lenalin had gone.

Ovelia searched the cabin carefully and found the door open, a gust of cold air billowing through. Lenalin must have left. Thus, Ovelia reclaimed her cloak, buttoned it tight over her swollen middle, pulled her cowl low, and went out into the growing rain.

Dimly, she could make out the sleek lines of *Hecatomb*, somewhat worse for wear after the battle with the dragon. Dust magic batteries powered a number of casters in the hands of Lenalin's pirates, and Aeldad herself carried at least three of the destructive weapons. She could perceive them clearly enough, suggesting a significant threat to her.

When Ovelia finally found Lenalin, she seemed indistinct but present— an uncertain shadow that Ovelia found both threatening and impossibly magnetic. She stood at the rail of the *Hecatomb*, no doubt looking out at the setting sun over the burned lands far to the west. Ovelia slid into place next to her, hands anxiously gripping and relaxing on the rail.

"I never thought I'd see this sunset again," the princess said. "Isn't it beautiful and terrible?" Ovelia held her tongue, and at length Lenalin cleared her throat. "Ah, of course. I forget sometimes."

"Of course." Ovelia shook her head. "Highness."

Lenalin paused a moment, chewing the edge of her lip. Ovelia could feel her irritation, and for a moment, it seemed Lenalin might admonish her for titling her thus. Ultimately, she let it pass.

"I doubt the King of Tar Vangr will gladly accommodate another ruler in his city."

"Yes, Your Highness." Ovelia wanted very much to touch Lenalin's hand, but she restrained herself. She took a deep breath, then let it out in a long sigh. "You know he is right."

"The Frostburn, you mean." Lenalin's fingers clicked against the railing.

"This is a war all of us must fight," Ovelia said. "You know that."

"If Tar Vangr is to triumph," she said. "If that is what we all want."

"If that isn't what you wanted, why did you come?" Ovelia asked.

"True."

For a quiet moment, Ovelia thought she might leave it at that, but instead Lenalin put a hand on her wrist and clutched hard. It startled her, and she realized Lenalin's face hovered close to hers.

"Come with me."

Ovelia didn't resist as Lenalin hauled her away. They climbed the short flight of steps back to the captain's suite, where mage-glass windows allowed a broad-spectrum view of the world around the skyship. Lenalin immediately activated the windows, and Ovelia felt the faint vibration as they dimmed to an opaque hue. She couldn't have seen through them anyway, but now they had privacy.

Lenalin shut the door behind them and locked it. Ovelia could feel the immediate tension, and when Lenalin stepped forward, seizing her about the shoulders, she stood straight as an arrow. The room's closeness and stuffiness didn't intrude now. Now, Ovelia felt entirely too comfortable.

"Your power has grown," she said. "Why aren't you using it for me?"

"I—" Ovelia hesitated. "I do not understand."

"You do," Lenalin said. "When I told you we were to sail for Tar Vangr, you did not warn me about any burning Frostfire dragon. Why did you not warn me?"

"I can't—"

"You *can*." Suddenly clearer in her vision, Lenalin squeezed Ovelia's wrist with bruising strength. "I know what you can see. I need you to see it." Her grip eased, and her hand brushed Ovelia's face. "I need you to tell me about the Blood Queen."

The words hung between them.

"She is dangerous," Ovelia said at length.

Lenalin uttered a mirthless sound. "I need no seer to tell me that," she said. "And I know you want to see her again. Don't think I didn't see your face when Lan claimed she lived." She crossed her arms. "What I need to know is when she will return, and what she will do. The threat she poses."

Ovelia wasn't sure what to say. She remembered fire. She remembered seeing Semana in her dreams, and knew things were not ended between them.

And, as though thinking of it opened a window in her mind, she saw something else: fire in the sky, a flitting bird soaring around a burning hulk. Lances of green fire connected the two, and as she watched, the skyship—the *Hecatomb*—began to fall...

"Do not—" She caught her breath and spoke again, softly enough that none could hear beyond Lenalin. "Do not take the field against Semana. She will triumph."

Lenalin regarded Ovelia levelly. "You'd have me believe," she said, "that the *Hecatomb*, the finest skyship made by mortal hands, which slew a *dragon*, cannot match a child in black leathers?"

"Do you trust my visions or not?" Ovelia asked.

Lenalin sighed. "What else."

"She—" Ovelia shook her head. "It is not too late for her."

"Is this something you've seen," Lenalin said. "Or something you hope?"

The question made Ovelia shiver. She couldn't answer it. Her child abruptly kicked, and she touched at her belly despite herself.

"It's moving," Lenalin said. "Your child."

Ovelia nodded. "It shouldn't slow my sword," she said. "I am yours, Highness. Now and—"

"Enough." Lenalin held up a hand. "Your purpose now is to advise, not to swing a blade."

Heart rose in Ovelia's belly. "I can fight," she said. "Even this way, I'm still worth more than a hundred Swords of Winter, and all those of Summer."

"That's not—" Lenalin sighed. "You've talents I can't waste in battle. And." She laid her hand gently on Ovelia's belly, making her shiver. "This child you're carrying... they're more important than your sword. More important than any battle. More important than winning the war."

Ovelia hadn't expected her to say something like that. "What do you mean?"

"I know you, Lia." Lenalin laid her fingers alongside Ovelia's cheeks. "I know what you value."

"You're deflecting." Ovelia realized. "Speak plainly."

"Bold. I like that." Lenalin chuckled. "It's no secret—not between you and I, at least. Garin's child is heir to two thrones. Would you endanger that legacy?"

For a heartbeat, Ovelia had the mad idea to challenge her—to demand "how did you know?" of Lenalin—but she held her tongue. There was cold command there, yes, but also concern.

"We will need every sword to win this war," Ovelia said. "If I do not fight, and that makes the difference between Tar Vangr's survival and its fall, what throne will remain?"

Lenalin considered that for a moment and nodded. "Then you've my permission to fight, if the stakes are victory or defeat. But only"—she squeezed Ovelia's hand—"only in that case."

"Only in that case."

"Good." Lenalin loosed Ovelia's hands and expelled a breath. "And right now, I have other orders for you."

"You—?"

Ovelia started to speak, but Lenalin lashed a hand across her face, knocking the words out. She turned back, shocked, and Lenalin caught her face in her hands. She pressed her lips to Ovelia's, with no veil of cloth between them. Ovelia shivered at the cool touch of her skin and the warmth of her breath.

They came together soon enough, using the captain's chair to best effect. Eventually, they retired to Lenalin's chambers, where they held each other through the night, listening to the rain.

FIFTEEN

WHEN DARAK RETURNED TO the horde after the *Hecatomb*'s arrival, it was to angry glares and dark growls. It was not the way of the Children of Ruin to whisper their discontent: instead, they made it very clear with tongues and eyes that Darak had failed them, and their faith wavered.

The dragon's fall was bad enough, but the Frostfire protection had begun to wane, requiring more doses to maintain. Even now, as the great creature lay groaning and shivering in a hollow in the snowy landscape, dozens of barbarians swarmed it like flies on a rotting pile of offal, digging into its scales. They pressed their mouths to the tiny rents, obscene tongues licking at traces of blue blood. The mewling beast could not even stir in its own defense. At the sight, Darak curled his lip in disgust.

It was not fair. None of it was remotely fair.

A figure emerged out of the darkness. At first he thought it Fellis, come to reassure him, but it was only Crown of Fire. The man looked haggard and there was a bruise on his right cheek. Someone had laid a hand on him, and that in itself was an attack on Darak. The insult of it.

"Master?" Crown flinched from Darak's expression. "You are wroth."

"No." Darak sighed. "Not wroth. Only… disappointed."

Would Fellis's return truly have made him feel better? Perhaps. Not that he needed her pity, but at least it would indicate she'd not abandoned him entirely. She hadn't shared his bed since that first attack on the walls, and since the *Hecatomb* came upon them, he hadn't even seen her. And without her presence and its tacit support, he could feel it all turning against him.

Burning Semana and her failure. It was all *her* fault.

The horde's scrutiny made Darak itch all over, and he was painfully aware of the many lesions so much use of the Worldfire had left on his flesh. He needed a bath, and for Crown to lathe and scrape him clean. And then a rest, perhaps: he hadn't slept since the setback in Low-City Tar Vangr. His campaign hung by a thread, and here came Carr to cut it with one swipe of her notched axe.

He saw her parting the sea of barbarians like a cutting ship, sending up ripples in her wake. When she strode forth, she wore a self-satisfied smile that made Darak want to throttle her.

"Dar-Karsk." Her axe gleamed, lowered but an obvious threat. "The Goddess turns from you."

The simmering rage in Darak's gut boiled up, but he managed to avoid spitting at her. There was no Goddess of Ruin, and they both knew it. Power belonged to the triumphant, and now that the course upon which he had set them had ceased to yield success, his power was slipping away.

Instead of addressing her directly, Darak raised his arms and addressed the gathered barbarians. "The cold presses in upon us all," he said to the gathered horde. "Follow me into the city. The skyship cannot strike there without destroying their own foundations. We will wait there, in warmth and comfort, until they starve in their city in the sky. We've dug their grave, and they flew right into it." He pumped his fist in the air. "We march immediately, under cover of darkness. Gather your things."

Not a single barbarian moved. They stared at him in angry silence.

There was no doubt now. Carr had bided her time, waiting for an opportunity to turn against him, and this was it. He had overstepped and she meant to exact the payment from his corpse.

"Fools!" Darak cursed. "Will you stay out here and freeze? Follow me to refuge—"

"None will follow you any longer." Carr's voice cut through Darak's like a blade. "Your course has led us into disaster after disaster: broken promises and now a broken spear." She gestured to the dragon, heaving in the snow, and murmurs and cries broke out around her.

Darak saw Fellis the Night Wolf standing among them, a black cloak mostly hiding her distinctive visage. She gazed upon him, and her expression held disappointment. She had abandoned him too.

"This is *war*." Darak's raised voice sounded strangled and furious. "War sees casualties and broken blades. We stride over the corpses of our allies and enemies both, but we keep moving. We do not retreat in the face of difficulty. Have you no stomach for what must be done?"

"What must be *done*." Carr sneered. "What we must do is choose better leaders."

"Better—" Sweat broke out on his face as he addressed the horde. "Don't be foolish. I have led you so far. I shall lead you to safety. Will you follow her, and die in the snow? I am your only hope."

"We can find warmth after you are gone." Carr gestured toward him with her axe.

No, Darak thought. *No.*

He saw barbarians moving toward him out of the corners of his vision. They'd formed a circle around him, and the ring gradually tightened. They carried naked swords and tapped the ground with spears, and he could hear them hiss as they approached, like angry serpents thirsty for his blood.

"Master." At Darak's side, Crown of Fire tensed and his hands went to his daggers. "Master!"

The point of a spear sank into Crown of Fire's side, and he gave a cry of pain. He cast a terrified look at Darak before the threatening points pushed him back into the mass of barbarians and he disappeared. It should have reassured Darak, even a little, to see Crown's loyalty, but just at the moment, Darak could have happily burned the man along with all these disloyal savages.

"We should never have followed you." Carr strode forward. "Who will make that m—"

Abruptly her words cut off and she shot up straight as though stabbed with a blade. The barbarians around her stiffened, surprised, then backed away, making warding signs with their fingers as they went. There Carr stood like a scarecrow, her stout, strong body stretched to the edge of breaking. Her mouth worked, but no words came forth, and her face grew increasingly red as Darak watched.

"*I* will," said a harsh voice.

Sweat cold on the back of his neck, Darak turned to a patch of deeper darkness that had formed in the night air, out of which appeared a man seemingly made of ebony, a shambling man in leathers and a mask made of bones, and—

Darak smiled. His sister had returned.

"I will," Semana said again. With a wave of her hand, she forced Carr's ensorcelled body to its knees, and the woman glared up at her through bloodshot, murderous eyes. "Will you?"

Carr managed to force open her jaws, from which the lips peeled back to reveal her chipped, yellowed teeth. "No more," she said. "Kill me if you will, sister, but no more."

Hope leapt inside Darak, but Semana shook her head. "Exile," she said. "Go back to the rest of the cowards of the Circle and inform them of your failure."

"Fool girl," Carr said. "I shall return, with a horde of my own—"

"You are welcome," Semana said. "When you return, it shall be to a fallen mage-city—an edifice to destruction and death. One you did not have the courage to help tear down."

Abruptly Semana's magic vanished, like a taut cord cut by a knife. Carr all but collapsed to the ground, heaving and growling like an animal. As he watched, Darak thought he saw thick black hair bristling on her body, and her eyes looked like those of a predator. But perhaps he only imagined it.

"Go," Semana said. "Tell them."

Carr forced herself to her feet, her body trembling with the effort. He couldn't stop himself from giving Carr a self-satisfied smile, and he delighted in the look of pure fury she returned. Then she shoved her way through the gathered barbarians, grunting and seething as she went. She kept her head down as she passed Fellis, who continued to gaze at Darak, her face as impassive as ever.

Darak would not forget that she had not stepped forward to defend him. No, he would not.

Green slaying magic dancing around her head and hands, Semana surveyed the horde, and everywhere her gaze fell, barbarians dropped to one knee. They all knew her visage, and those farther back could easily see the swell of her deadly magic. They looked at her in a way they would never look at Darak, and that discontented him. She was their queen, by force and by power.

"Make ready to march." Her ragged voice drifted over the horde. "Leave your fires burning and take what you need. We move immediately, under cover of darkness."

The sea of warriors and weapons shifted away from them, back to their camps to acquire their weapons. It was a dark, overcast night, and High-City was partly obscured in those same clouds. Leaving the fires was a good idea: a sentry would surely grow suspicious if all their cookfires winked out in the middle of the night. This way, none would suspect they had moved until they were upon Tar Vangr. A good move, and necessary for the horde's survival.

It was his own command, but rather than take pleasure at its execution, Darak knew only resentment that the horde snapped so quickly to obey his sister. He turned to confront Semana, but found the man in black leathers and the bone mask blocking his path. Darak shrank back, though he could not have said why, precisely. The man was not large or imposing, but he had a weight of violence about him that brooked no challenge. One of the eyes gazing out through the bone mask was milky-white and seemed to glow in the moonlight.

"Stand away," he said, his voice guttural and nearly as ragged as Mask's own.

Darak sneered. "My queen," he said over the man's shoulder.

But Semana was looking away, down the snowy hill and away from the bulk of the horde. Darak furrowed his brow and started toward her, but the bone-masked man shifted with surprising dexterity into his path. He had an odd, unbalanced gait, dragging one twisted foot in the snow.

"I am Dar-Karsk, advisor and general to the Blood Queen," he said. "Let me pass."

"And I am Tithian Davargorn, her shadow," he said. "And burn you."

"Let him pass." Gilt's voice rumbled like distant thunder. "He is harmless."

Darak made himself smile at Davargorn, even as anger twisted in his gut. *Harmless.* He wanted to snap back but he knew there was no purpose. Threats did not work upon the Deathless Fae. When Darak looked into Gilt's glassy black eyes, he saw nothing but his own reflection. It unsettled him.

Davargorn sniffed and stepped back, scuffing through the snow. His club foot and mismatched eyes marked the man as ruinscarred. Darak could almost feel the man's rage as he strode past. Just what he needed: yet another utterly loyal, murderous companion who would cut him down in a heartbeat, if given enough leash to work with. His sister seemed to collect such men.

Abruptly, Gilt bowed to Semana, and she nodded slightly to him. Darak hardly knew the Deathless well enough to predict or interpret his actions, but this exchange seemed both formal and, in some way, final. There was something on the Deathless's perfect black face—something like hesitation. Without another word, Gilt turned away and vanished into darkness.

"Where's he gone?" Darak asked. "We could make use of his powers—"

"Gone," Semana said. "Never to return."

Darak had to fight to keep from smiling. Perhaps he'd despaired too soon. If the Deathless would not return, that was good for him. And the Frostburn was gone—perhaps even dead, though in Darak's experience, the World of Ruin rarely rewarded hope. Now it was just this twisted freak of a man who hardly seemed much of a threat by comparison. Semana would be his to wield.

"Blood Queen," he said, raising his voice to be heard over the chill night wind. "We must—"

Without even seeming to notice his presence, Semana turned down the slope to the hollow where the Frostfire dragon lay groaning, barbarians clinging to it like leeches. Many had given up by now, but a handful still clung to it, shivering, and one had even taken to hacking at its exposed flesh with a small axe, trying to gouge out some blood. The chain lace on Semana's left hand burned with sudden power, and she swept them away with invisible force as though dismissing flies. They skittered and tumbled into the snow. One of the barbarians rolled to a crouch, blade raised and face gnarled with rage, but one look at the Blood Queen in her forbidding leather mask and he fled for his life.

Semana crossed to the dragon's bruised and battered head, which gurgled labored breaths. Several of its multifarious eyes had darkened or popped, and those that remained drifted lazily across her. She laid a hand on the dragon, and its breathing eased.

"What," she asked, seemingly far away, "has passed?"

"Lady Shard's *Hecatomb*," Darak said. "They attacked—"

"Not you."

It took Darak one terrible heartbeat to realize what she meant. She hadn't even spoken to him, but to the dragon. He swallowed his reaction—fear, which he'd never felt of his sister—and straightened his back. He gripped his forearms in his opposite hands and squeezed. His body itched.

"You were weakened before. I felt it." Semana ran her hand along the icy carapace, blue-white flames sparking between her fingers and the dragon's scales. "Easy. Your part in this is done."

"Done?" Darak goggled. "What passes, sister? Surely you—?"

The itch in his head built into blinding pain of a sudden, and he staggered, hands pressed to his temples to hold in the pressure. His heart thundered in his head. Blood magic? She'd used it so easily and without warning. And even as he thought this, the magic filled him, seizing his body and putting it entirely at her command. His words choked off and he could not make his mouth move.

As Darak watched through tear-filled eyes, Semana sent a flicker of her Frostfire into the creature, and the power swept through the massvie body like a wave. The dragon loosed a mighty groan and rolled over onto its belly. It stared down at Darak with hungry, angry eyes. Semana glanced at it sidelong, acknowledging him for the first time.

"You did this," she said. "Weakened them. Called them into battle they could not win."

Darak felt it then: weakness washing over him, as though his life drained from him as he knelt. He'd experienced this before, when Afferath was displeased with him, and felt her soaking up his strength. Now all Darak's power flowed into Semana.

The dragon uttered a resonant growl from down inside its thrice slit maw, revealing row upon row of jagged teeth the length of small swords. Frostfire flared deep in its gullet. The stench of corruption and burning washed over Darak, and he nearly lost his senses right then.

"Sis-ter…" He could barely make sounds through his clenched teeth. "Please—"

He could barely breathe. Could barely think…

"No." Semana held up a hand. "He is my brother, and I still need him."

The dragon gave a soft, disappointed sigh. It pushed itself up, unfurled its tattered wings, and, with a quiver of snow-covered earth, propelled itself into the sky. They watched as the dragon flapped away, vanishing into the darkness. Darak experienced both relief and trepidation: the creature had not eaten him, true, but perhaps it had left him with a deadlier foe.

Finally Semana waved and the blood magic gripping Darak faded. He fell to his knees, panting and gagging. She watched impassively, waiting for him to rise.

"You," he said. "You return. Finally."

"I return." Semana's voice was cold. "But it will not be the same as before. Understood?"

Darak nodded up at her. He even managed a smile, despite the howling fury inside.

The World of Ruin rarely rewarded hope.

"Good," Semana said. "This is how it will pass. Listen carefully."

SIXTEEN

THE WARM FLUSH HAD mostly drained away by the time Lan Ravalis returned from his triumphant parade through the city. Ovelia sensed his approach, of course, before he trod upon the *Hecatomb's* deck. Through the window of the aftcastle, she saw the burning aura of his power armor standing at the plank, as well as the cold blue power of Frostburn, which Regel carried not too far behind him.

She well understood Lan's hesitation. The Bear of Luether and the King of Tar Vangr was not a man to relinquish power voluntarily, least of all to a woman. She half expected Regel to report back alone, having slain the man when he tried to flee. And somehow, Ovelia had not hoped for Lan's death. He was an awful, violent, abusive man who deserved far worse than he had suffered, but she did not hate him. He was as broken as all of them—more so than some. She did not forgive, but she understood.

"What is it?" Lenalin asked languidly from the bed just behind her. She'd hesitated to rise, seemingly preferring to let their time together linger as long as possible.

"Nothing," Ovelia said. "They've returned."

"Pity." Lenalin laid her fingers on the base of Ovelia's spine, and even through her clothes the warmth of her touch made her tingle. "To business, then."

"Business." Ovelia tried not to think about Lenalin's lips on her neck.

Ultimately, Lan's hesitation broke and he stepped forward onto the skyship, and Ovelia relaxed. "You didn't think he would return." She reached for her undergarments. "But he does his duty."

"Or he doesn't want the Frostburn to stab him in the back." Lenalin huffed and tried to straighten her scarred arms to put on her underslip. Without being asked, Ovelia stepped to help her, and Lenalin tensed under her hands. Then the princess relaxed and let Ovelia assist her.

"He's not just a sword," Ovelia said. "He's a man."

"Is that so." Idly, Lenalin put her hands lightly on Ovelia's neck, thumbs caressing her throat. It made Ovelia tingle. "And how would you know."

Ovelia grimaced and continued dressing Lenalin. "The usual way."

"I see." Lenalin slipped one hand up to Ovelia's cheek and slid her thumb around the edge of Ovelia's mouth. "And I should treat him as a man then? In the usual way?"

193

That wasn't what Ovelia had meant, of course, but she didn't need to say so. Lenalin slipped her thumb into her mouth, and Ovelia closed her lips around it. It tasted bittersweet. She sucked lightly.

"Mmm," Lenalin said, the sound approving. "Later."

A knock at the door announced Aeldad, and Lan and Regel arrived shortly thereafter. She could see them both with equal clarity—almost well enough to make out their features. She knew Lan would love nothing so well as to strangle her where she stood, so it made sense she could see the threat he posed. Regel, on the other hand... Ovelia had come to believe she could see him more because of the threat he presented to *anyone*, not to her specifically. With Frostburn in hand, he could slaughter them all within heartbeats, and probably conquer Tar Vangr by himself within an hour. Of course, everyone would be dead at the end of his conquest.

For the first time, Ovelia felt glad of Lenalin's grip on his leash.

The King of Tar Vangr took one look at the haphazard captain's chamber cluttered with discarded blankets and clothes and cleared his throat with a sound of distaste. "Enjoying your stay in my city, I see?" He sniffed loudly. "And smell?"

Ovelia bristled at that, but she knew Lenalin's strategy for setting him off balance. Not that she liked it. By contrast, the princess seemed completely at ease, arrayed in her black gown and veil.

"Your city," Lenalin said in her low, cool voice. "Your Blood still acknowledges your crown then."

"As I assured you they would, my Lady." Lan waved dismissively. "These lesser Ravalis could not abdicate their responsibilities fast enough." He stretched, muscles rippling. "Though I suppose I should say a kind word for my cousin Laud. The dithering cretins on the merchant council had called for the destruction of the fourth lift, but Laud managed to delay them. Not bad, for an inbred fop."

Ovelia recoiled from the cruelty in his dismissal. She knew Laud Ravalis only dimly from her time as Tar Vangr's spymaster. He'd always struck her as a kindly boy, if steeped in the toxic contempt of the Ravalis. She found herself hoping he hadn't lost that spark of decency in the year or so since she'd left for that fateful journey south that had brought them to this point.

Had it really only been a year? It seemed so much longer.

Lan was looking at her, Ovelia realized, so she straightened slightly, assuming an aspect of inscrutability. Across the room, Regel leaned against the doorframe, arms crossed, Frostburn loose in its scabbard. He reminded her of a great cat, ready to spring on any apparent foe or danger. And while

ERIK SCOTT DE BIE

she didn't have her eyes to know for certain, he seemed… younger. More vital
than he had in years.

"Apparently," Lan continued, seemingly unfazed by Lenalin's indifference.
"The *Hecatomb* has raised morale in the city, and many are pushing to descend
to Low-City in force. A massive offensive to drive the Children out and into
the cold. Now, within the hour, while they are scattered and weak. So long as
they don't swell their numbers, we should purge them with our charge." He
raised his chin. "A charge I will lead. I go to gird myself immediately."

Ovelia's breath caught. That, she had not expected. "You would risk
yourself?" she asked.

"For my city?" Lan asked. "Yes."

"For glory and your own self-promotion, you mean," Lenalin said. "I
suppose the adoration of your loyal subjects was not enough when we landed."

She sounded spiteful—jealous—but Ovelia knew it for a deception.
Lenalin, as Lady Shard, was a bastion of icy control, not prone to such
reactions. Especially not when it came to Lan Ravalis. No, this was a gambit
of some kind, though she could not see the purpose behind it.

His easy laugh told Ovelia he'd nibbled at her bait.

"Fear not, my lady," he said, his words dripping with arrogant condescension.
"You are just as necessary to the war effort. Without *Hecatomb*, all will seem
lost. Your skyship will be ineffective in Low-City, but I would have you
remain in dock, continuing your repairs. Whether you again fly in this war
or we stop the horde now makes no great difference. Your contributions will
not be forgotten."

"Just what I ever wanted," Lenalin said drolly. "And so you will be king
again. Is that it?"

"We all have the triumph we want." Ovelia could practically see Lan's
insufferable grin.

"And what of the Frostfire in Low-City?" she asked.

That quieted his fervor. Lan had official reports, but Shard had gathered
rumors as well of a barbarian who used Frostfire in the streets. For her part,
Ovelia had merely *felt* the power.

"Superstitious ramblings," Lan said. "What do the smallborn know of
magic? I'm sure they simply saw barbarian trickery."

"And if not?" Lenalin asked, her voice soft. "If the Blood Queen has
returned?"

Lan set his jaw. "If Semana Denerre nô Ravalis has returned," he said. "I
shall simply kill her too."

Silence spread, and Ovelia held her tongue. She hoped it would not come to pass.

"If there is nothing else?" Abruptly, Lan turned on his heel as though to leave, then paused. "Though I must admit, I am confused why you refuse to ally with me. I could offer you—" But he trailed off with a strangled sound.

At first, Ovelia didn't know what had happened. She looked to Regel, confused, sure that Draca would have warned her if he meant to strike. But he looked just as stricken as she felt, his body taut and his hand on the hilt of his sword. He hadn't struck Lan or even moved.

She heard the whisper of the silk and suddenly heat swept through her. *No.*

"I see you are surprised," Lenalin said, her voice clear without a veil to muffle it. "Surely not struck dumb by my beauty, after your brother stole it from me."

Her face was bare.

Ovelia's heart hammered in her chest.

"Lena—" Lan's tongue slipped over her name. "Lenalin Denerre."

"Once, perhaps." She stood, awkwardly, using the table for balance. "For years, I sought to maintain her. To remain. To remember." She shook her head. "That woman is dead. That name is dead."

"Why—" Lan faltered again. Ovelia could practically see his mind spinning. "Why show me?"

"Because I have not forgotten, nor have I forgiven." Lady Shard raised her chin, and Ovelia could hear the smile in her voice. "And neither should you."

"You," Lan said, struggling to get out the words. "I am tied to you. You've returned me to the city. All of those around me—they are yours. I… This was a trap, and I am caught in it. I am at your mercy. And—" A sharp intake of breath passed his lips. He clearly had difficulty even looking at her, let alone reconciling the truth she had revealed. "We can make amends. Stand beside me. Be my queen. Nay—be *the* queen, and let me be your consort. I—"

Abruptly, she stepped toward him, and both Regel and Ovelia twitched forward as though to intervene. Lan, who had started to take a step back, abruptly drew up straight, terrified and trapped. Ovelia could feel the fear rolling off him in a deluge of stinking rain.

"Foolish boy. You have no power here, and certainly none to give me." She trailed her fingers like claws down his tunic. "Your brother took my face. My body. My position. My birthright. My pride. My self-worth. My respect. But you know what he didn't take?" She tapped her head. "My memory."

Lan stammered, nervous. "I—"

She cut him off with a raised hand. "I remember my wedding," she said. "I knew you were watching me. You like to watch, don't you?" She stepped very close to him. He tried to look away, but she caught his face and held it facing her. "You watched Paeter beat me. You watched him force himself on me. You watched us, and he watched you, to see exactly what he was doing to you."

"I never touched you," Lan said. "I never did anything."

"Did you want thanks?" she asked. "And yes, you never did anything. All those years, you could have proved you were a better man just by speaking, but no. Your brother was a gutter beast, and you were less than that. You aren't a man. You aren't a beast. You. Are. *Nothing*." She nearly touched her scarred lips to his. "How could you ever be worthy of anyone, let alone me?"

"What is this?" Lan's face burned. "Justice?"

"If you like." She drew her nails across his cheek. "Lenalin longed for justice. Cried out for it, with every silent scream." She sneered. "I prefer vengeance."

Lan made a little strangled sound. Ovelia knew him—knew the anger roiling inside him, but it had no outlet. He could not lash out, as Regel or Ovelia or both would have him dead before he landed a blow. Ovelia knew, in that moment, that as much as Lan hated the woman before him—as much as he hated Ovelia, hated Semana, hated every woman—he would not strike. He could not.

Lenalin had beaten him.

"Well." Lan did the only thing he could: he stood up straight and puffed out his chest with whatever pride he could still manage. His jaw worked, trying to chew and swallow the anger. "Perhaps when I lead our forces to victory and restore your homeland, you will think better of me."

"Perhaps." Shard inclined her head. "But I doubt it."

He turned on his heel and headed out the door, and Lady Shard gave Regel an almost imperceptible nod in his wake. Ovelia wouldn't have seen it, had not Shard grown so vivid in her shadowy world that her features could almost be discerned. Too shocked by what had come to pass, Ovelia could hardly process the gesture.

"What—?" she said. "Why would you do that? You were almost quit of him. Now... now he will find some way to strike back at you. He—" She shook her head. "I thought you wanted to be free of this. To leave this city as soon as possible. Why reveal yourself?"

"Because this is a war all of us must fight." Shard adjusted the veil back over her face. "And because he doesn't get to win."

The steel in her voice made Ovelia shiver.

As he strode through the rain of High-City, Lan's mind roiled. Lenalin Denerre—alive? And—Silver Fire, her *face*. Her eyes, full of cold hatred that had grown and germinated for so many years. He couldn't stop thinking about it all the way back to where the warriors rallied near the last remaining lift.

It never occurred to him to look over his shoulder for a relentless shadow.

A summerblood with a network of cuts and burns across his face came out of the gloom and saluted him as he approached. Lan fumbled to return the gesture. What was his name? Dane? Dain? Of a Thinblood, Lan thought—perhaps Blood Duldur. With those scars, he'd clearly seen battle already.

"Your Majesty," he said. "Your armor is ready. Do you pass well?"

"Well," Lan said, his voice cracked. "Well enough. Where?"

The warder pointed to a tent erected at the edge of the square, surrounded by dozens of armed warriors. Nearby, Lan could hear the hum of ornithopters and Tar Vangr's three remaining ironclads. The force mustered to push back against the Children down in Low-City was a meager one by any stretch, but they should be sufficient. If only he could feel confident.

Without another word, Lan stormed into his tent, where his power armor lay cleaned, burnished, and charged for him to don and lead his men into glorious battle. Always before, he'd looked upon the beautiful suit with pride in himself and his cause, but now it tasted like dust in his mouth.

Was this what fear felt like? Or perhaps it was shame?

As he adjusted the fingers of his right hand in Mask's blasted gauntlet, he felt a cold presence behind him and he could see Regel's icy eyes in the mirror.

"You're here to rebuke me, too?" he asked, awkwardly pulling on the gauntlet.

Regel said nothing, and Lan barely had time to muster another cutting word before he stepped up behind him, close enough to take him in his arms. Lan stiffened, surprised at his own reaction, and sucked in breath for an objection or perhaps something else. Something softer. Regel's face hovered over his neck, lips at his ear, close as those of a lover.

Then he felt the bite of cold steel slipping between his ribs.

"What—?"

Lan looked in the mirror, where Regel had plunged a tiny dagger into his side. He shivered at the splintering pain. Instinctively, he evoked the magic in the fire gauntlet, but Regel was behind him—he could not aim the deadly power.

"But I'm fighting for *Lenalin*, you rutting fool," Lan said. "For Tar Vangr."

"And now you get to die for her, too."

Lan gasped at a fresh spasm of pain and clutched at the shallow hilt. It was a punch dagger, just large enough to be held in two fingers. It probably wouldn't even show under his armor.

"Whenever you want to die, pull that out."

Regel left the dagger lodged in Lan's side and vanished out into the night.

The horns sounded, and Dain Duldur appeared in the entrance to the tent. "Majesty?"

Lan grimaced, trying hard not to show his pain. Regel was gone, and he could not go back. He gripped the handle of his sword hard and tried not to curse. Or weep.

BOOK FOUR: BETRAYERS

Two months ago—Autumn, 982 Sorceris Annis—The Free Isles

How long they spent together in that cave, neither could say.

At dawn while Mask sat, legs crossed and eyes closed, the ugly man leaned against the entrance to the cave, watching the sun rise over the open sea to the east. A black slick spread across the water, radiating out both ways like flames, but it looked remarkably peaceful. He listened to Mask's quiet breathing, slow and controlled, and tried to time his own to match. He'd never experienced a scene quite so tranquil, and he could almost imagine the world was a beautiful place.

He went out every morn, primarily to fish but also to watch for intruders upon their tranquility. He saw several ships during their time, though only once did one come close enough to count the masts or smell the trail of pitch smoke in its wake. A mad urge rose up in him to attract their attention, so that he could parlay with them or slay them and seize the ship for his own. So that he and Mask could set sail to some other place, where no one would ever find them. But that, he knew, was not to be.

As the sun rose high, he would cook the fish he had caught with his bare hands that morning, and they would eat together. Some days they would speak softly, and sometimes they would merely sit together in companionable silence. He felt her heart in a way he never had before, and he could read volumes in her eyes. She had never looked at him that way before, and it made him feel lighter.

He spent the downward slope of the day gazing down into the majestic beauty of the island rocks where they sheltered—the waves crashing at high-tide, laying slick the sharp spurs of stone far below their cave. He could climb and scuttle over the rocks, hunting and searching and finding new, colorful stones and small creatures of shapes he hardly knew.

Some evenings, as the sun dipped beyond the rock to the west of their cave, Mask joined him out on the overhang, and they watched the skies shift color from gray to a kaleidoscope of orange, red, purple, and yellow. As the season waxed, the great Eye of Ruin sank farther and farther south, which allowed them to see it almost entirely from their south and slightly east facing vantage. The brighter the sunsets became, the less often Mask came to join him. She avoided the light of the day, and he could see the tremor in her body that suggested she wasn't yet strong enough to endure the heat.

How had his healing affected her? He wondered, but he never asked.

By night, they lay fully clothed and huddled together in the cave, where the darkness brought a deep, bone-shivering chill. Her body felt small and frail against him, and he could feel her fever and her radiating magic. Her body was an oven cracked at the edges and leaking heat, and Mask curled into a tight ball as though to hold it in—or perhaps to hold herself together. He wondered if he could somehow enfold her totally and keep it inside her, or take it into himself. He wondered if he *should* do such a thing, or find some way to let the heat out of her.

It tore her apart, she told him once. When he asked what she meant, she only shook her head.

It stoked a spark of guilt, to feel at peace while she suffered. But deep within himself, he still hated her; hated what she had done to him for so long, what on some level she was still doing to him. Hated himself for what he did to himself with her. But he loved her too, and she loved him.

They were both broken creatures, and if they deserved nothing more, at least they had this.

⤳

Just as all things must pass to Ruin, so too did their time come to its inevitable end.

As the sun set, abruptly the Deathless stood in the cave, stooping slightly under the overhang. Gilt's loin-cloth and cloak did little to hide his perfect body, and that produced niggling doubt in the ugly man. What he wouldn't give to be a normal man, much less such a specimen. He had assumed Mask would be drawn to Gilt's beauty, but she seemed no more interested in him than any man or woman. Even now, when she looked up at him with fire in her eyes, it was only his face that she scrutinized.

"It is time?" she asked.

Never one to waste words, the Deathless nodded grimly, then looked to him.

"Yes," Mask said. "Tithian will accompany us."

After only the slightest hesitation, Gilt nodded. Silently, he padded out of the cave and up onto the rise. The ugly man looked to Mask, but she had settled back down beside their small fire. Her shoulders had stilled over the days they'd spent together, and he sensed no tremor in her. Whatever conflict she had fought in her mind and heart over their time together, she seemed to have resolved it.

The ugly man nodded to her and left the cave.

The Deathless waited at the highest point of the island, at the top of broken stone steps whose traversal sent tiny stones skittering. The ugly man marveled at Gilt's grace in climbing those treacherous steps: the fae had disturbed not a single pebble, as if he was a specter of smoke rather than a being of flesh. He stood now, gazing down at a nearby Free Isles ship that floated upon the Dusk Sea not too far off. The burly bodies of the pirates working the mast and rigging gleamed like burnished bronze in the last light of the setting sun. The ugly man ducked to hide behind a ragged outcropping of rock.

"Be not afraid," Gilt said, as though in reply to a question unasked. "They do not see."

"It is prudence, not fear." The ugly man straightened, but he kept an eye on the ship in the near distance. "I am but oone man, they are many, and their weapons are mightier than mine.."

"But not hers," Gilt said. "If they come, they will die. Do I lie?"

The ugly man had to concede that he did not. "Do you love my master, Fae?"

Gilt regarded him directly for the first time since they had met, and the ugly man found his black eyes unsettling in the extreme. "That is a thing I have forgotten," he said, his voice like distant thunder.

"Forgotten." The ugly man frowned. "Do you love her or not?"

The Deathless approached him, his body sculpted from living stone so very perfect in comparison to the ugly man's own. Another day, it might have set him on his guard, as it had many times before, but in that moment, he felt every bit as strong and vital as Gilt. Every bit as worthy.

The sun had set fully, and darkness surrounded them. The ugly man could see faint purple echoes of the day's illumination over the Sunset Lands far to the west, and a chill settled over the land. He stood against the cold, while Gilt seemed one with it.

"I am Deathless," he said. "That I might know death not, so too have I forsaken life. I wear the name of the last thing I have abandoned—the last happiness I knew as a mortal being." The black eyes blinked once, slowly, and the gesture was not quite that of a mortal man or woman. "Death is loss. I have nothing, I can lose nothing, I cannot die. That is the mystery of death."

"So you do not love her."

Gilt raised his perfect eyebrows. "Do you?"

They stood close together now, like mismatched images in a silvered glass. Mask was that mirror—the connecting tissue between the two of them. She was a mismatched mirror herself: the beautiful princess, with her hair like white gold and skin the hue of warm sand, and the callous assassin, with its black corpse shell and ragged voice like that of a dead thing. Thinking of her now, the ugly man could not say which reflection was really her face, but he knew one thing: he loved them both.

At length, the ugly man nodded.

"Then stand beside her," Gilt said. "For she will need you, as the days darken and ruin falls."

"What need of me, when she has you?" he asked. "You, who are so handsome—so perfect."

Gilt shook his head. "I will take you to the frozen city, but no farther."

"What do you mean?" The ugly man felt uneasy, of a sudden. "You'd abandon her?"

The Deathless's expression was far away. "I have traveled far and seen many things," he said. "A great calamity has descended upon my people, in the form of the Reaper of Men. The change he brought has been long in its birth, but it cannot be denied. Many things have changed, and I must return to see them through. I will leave her side, soon, and I will not return to the world of mortals."

"I think I understand," the ugly man said, which they both knew for a lie. "Does she?"

"She understands duty." By the Deathless's neutral expression, he likely hadn't informed Mask and saw no particular reason to do so. "And she knows I cannot walk her path."

"But I can." The ugly man considered. "You know where her path leads?"

The Deathless shrugged his mighty shoulders, which was about as much answer as the ugly man could expect. Finally, he nodded in reply.

"Then I had best walk it beside her."

~

Near midnight, when the ugly man descended back to the cave, Mask was still meditating before the fire. Her body seemed mostly relaxed, as though she had fallen asleep sitting up.

He sat across the fire from her, uncomfortably folding his weaker leg over the stronger one. His body had mostly recovered its strength since his ordeal in Luether and then Shard's prison, but he still felt weak—defeated. It hadn't been until their time in the cave that he'd realized exactly how hurt it had all left him, in his mind and in his heart. Looking at her now, his heart hung open, and somehow he knew the words they shared in this moment would heal him or destroy him.

They sat silently for a moment, while he grappled for something to say.

"Tithian," he said.

Her eyes flickered in the depths of her mask. "What?"

"Before, you called me Tithian," he said. "Are you Mask, or are you Semana?"

She considered a moment, then nodded. "Yes."

He wanted to ask more, but the longer he waited, the more he thought that was enough. Finally he nodded, and they sat quietly while the fire burned low.

SEVENTEEN

THE CLATTERING, CLANKING RIDE down to Low-City was agonizing. Every time the chains hit an imperfection and the lift buckled and bounced, Lan felt the tiny blade digging into his side and winced. Those around him chuckled or murmured relief that the lift hadn't fallen, but he almost wanted it to tumble from the sky. It would certainly save him this torment.

He hardly felt the blade when everything was still and he remembered to breathe shallowly. And he kept that side averted from everyone, hidden behind the warding shield on his left arm. He'd tested the arm in his tent in High-City, to see if he could lift the shield normally, and he mostly could, albeit with pain. It would slow him but not stop him—at least not at first.

Low-City Tar Vangr was a burning wreck. More buildings burned than did not, and the smoke mingled with the acidic clouds to produce the reek of corruption that Lan could feel suffusing his skin even through his bear-shaped leather mask with its golden trim. As the lift lowered, he could see the scarred and scorched network of streets and plazas that resembled a battlefield more than a city. That it could fall so far, so fast, staggered him.

At least the Children of Ruin were not an organized military force, and it would not be an arduous task purging them from the city. Lan expected a few battles here and there, and then they would come against whatever remained of the horde. Their exploits would draw the barbarians like moths to a lantern, and there, Lan would crush them and rout them.

At least, he hoped it would go thusly: the wound in his side would certainly lay him low before too long. If he was to die, he would die a warrior hacking with a sword, not an exterminator chasing rats.

A part of him wanted to go back, to mount some sort of effort to turn the city against Lady Shard—burning *Lenalin Denerre*—but he knew she had outplayed him. He could move against her, but with Tar Vangr's fleet lying in ruins in faraway Luether, they would be at the *Hecatomb*'s mercy. And even if Tar Vangr's fleet proved a match for her warship, she could simply fly away, leaving them to their fate. Or worse, she might stay, and the resulting civil war would see them all dead or vulnerable to the barbarians when they finally figured out how to get into High-City. And worst of all, perhaps she would reveal herself, muster the winterborn to her cause, and turn Tar Vangr against Lan and the Ravalis.

He could feel the scrutiny of Regel the Frostburn, who lurked like a shadow somewhere among the warders. Lan glanced back and saw him standing at the edge of the lift, the edges of his cloak whipping in the wind of their passage, blue magic leaking from around the hilt of the sword at his waist. Had he the confidence it would serve, Lan might have ordered the warders to turn upon him and rush him off the lift, but with that accursed sword, like as not Regel would slay all of them first.

No, the only way out was to redeem himself in Lenalin's eyes.

And honestly, he found he wanted to do just that.

As a boy, Lan Ravalis had not sought to become the monster he saw reflected in Lenalin Denerre's eyes. Quite the opposite, in fact. In his earliest memories, he played at knights and barbarians with beautiful Paeter, sometimes even letting clever little Garin tag along. Lan was always the biggest and the strongest, but he had always deferred to Paeter. His brother had showed Lan the proper and best way to be a man, and he had followed the model to the best of his ability.

Thinking on it now, Lan realized he had loved only one person in his life, and that was Paeter. And he had never told him. Not that he ever could, of course: such feelings between men were unseemly, let alone their expression. That had always seemed right and proper—natural—but now...

Now, at the end of his life, Lan was not so certain.

They arrived at the base of the lift, which settled with a shudder into the furrow in the stone, and Lan was the first one off. It might have been a heroic leap, but the pain in his side flared up at the sudden movement, and it became more of an awkward shuffle that put him on the muddy cobbles. If the warders nearby found it comical, at least they kept their mouths shut.

He could tell at a glance that the defense of the Harborside lift had been a bloody one. When Lan and his warparty arrived, it was not to a battleground but to something between a graveyard and a field hospital. The square lay littered with corpses piled three deep in places, and the defenders had only now proved able to recover their own dead. The injured screamed and cursed as weary-eyed warders loaded them onto the lift, and the living laid corpses in the red tabards of Ravalis or the black cloaks of winter warders near the edge of the lift, to be loaded as the warparty vacated. Flies buzzed everywhere, and the ongoing gibbering of barbarians in the near distance set Lan's teeth on edge.

It was grim work made sweaty and foul by the heat of the Narfire leaking through the broken square. He'd heard of some sort of magical catastrophe in the square, and it amazed him the fires hadn't erupted and destroyed the lift already. Low-City seemed like a thin veneer stretched over death, a patina cracking with the heat and pressure from below.

"Who leads here?" Lan raised his voice, but no one seemed to want to meet his eye. They focused on their work, like pallbearers who have no tears left to weep.

Murmurs spread through the warparty. Lan winced and touched his side. Probably, they took that as frustration at being ignored. "One of you, stand and speak—"

Someone among his party moved, and Lan realized the shadow that was Regel had stepped forward. He spoke to a woman, spattered with blood and mud and covered over with bruises. Lan watched for a moment as they interacted briefly and quietly, then turned to survey the square.

"Form up into squads, six strong," he said. "Each squad will take a street, sweep, then rejoin at the main thoroughfare." Lan had never bothered to learn the names of Low-City streets. He'd only ever come down here to indulge in his base desires, and those felt so far behind him now. What a waste. "Kill any barbarians you encounter and send survivors, if any remain, back to the square. We will regroup and repeat for the next set of streets. Squads of six means—" He counted his warriors. "Six squads. Move."

"Majesty," said Dain Duldur. "We should leave a squad at the lift, to secure our retreat."

The square fell silent, but for the cries of the injured and the faint sounds of barbarians in the city. Lan looked at Dain slowly and directly. "Do you question me, warder?" he asked, voice low.

Dain blanched slightly, but to his credit, he didn't back down. Rather, he straightened his shoulders and met Lan's eye, the scar across his face strengthening his resolute expression. Brave.

"I seek to advise, not to question," he said. "Majesty."

Lan winced at the stinging pain in his side. "You think these stout-hearted warders insufficient to face the rabble that might come against them?" Lan asked. "They've lasted so far."

"These folk have been fighting for many days, Majesty," Dain said, gesturing at the defenders. "Some of them were here that first night. Let us relieve them."

When Lan looked around, he saw it was true. He hadn't realized it at first, but the defenders seemed exhausted as though a modest wind could send them staggering. Only three of the two dozen ironclads sent to Low-City remained functional, and the warders had put them to use hauling bodies. For them, the war might as well have become a harvest, and not a joyous one.

"You are certain," Lan said, "this is not fear leaking from your lips?"

Dain stood firm. "I was there on the walls when the Children came," he said. "I know their brutality and I will not underestimate it. Neither should you." He raised his chin. "Your Majesty."

Lan laughed. Or, at least, he tried, until a spasm of pain ripped up his side and he scowled.

"Very well," he said. "Stay behind and ward our retreat. More—" He coughed, and the pain swept through his lower back. His voice came out deep and rough. "I'm taking the ironclads, though."

"Majesty." Dain nodded and offered Lan a short salute. "We will not let a single barbarian through, and the lift will be open when you return." *Or we will all be dead,* he left unspoken.

Lan nodded, and Dain turned away. There was a weariness to his movements—an earned casualness that spoke of the battle he'd seen—and Lan did not begrudge him the lack of formality. Antipathy or not, nobility or not, the man would do his duty.

"Majesty?" asked one of his attendants, but Lan flinched away before the man could touch him.

Silver Fire, had the Frostburn stuck him with a poisoned blade? Either way, he had only so long, and they both knew it. It made him angry, and also spiteful.

"Form up." He waved his hand. "After me. We're killing every barbarian in the city tonight."

To a chorus of cheers that overrode the anxious whispers, they marched forth, ironclads clanking in the wake of three of the squads. A small contingent under Dain's command remained behind at Harborside, looking small and weak without the ironclads, and Lan gave the man a last, meaningful look. Dain offered another salute and even a reassuring smile, as if to say that he would be waiting.

The blade shifted slightly in Lan's side, or perhaps his guts rubbed painfully against it, and he grimaced. Dain Duldur would be waiting a long time.

~

As the walking dead man dispatched his orders and argued with his lieutenant, Regel surveyed the gathered faces. Bone-deep weariness hung about them, hollowing them out to mere shadows of themselves. Pushing around Frostburn's unsatable hunger, he thought he knew exactly how they felt.

Then he saw a familiar face among them and stepped toward her. "Nacacia," he said.

At first, she did not seem to hear, but kept about her business with an empty gaze. He had to touch her shoulder, and still she tried to avoid him. It was only when he said her name again that she looked up, and her eyes cleared of blood haze. "Lord of Tears?" she asked, her voice small and cracked.

"Furious Nacacia." He touched his forehead to hers, and a tremble shot through her body at the touch, as though every muscle tensed and relaxed in an instant. She pursed her thick, split lips.

Lan was watching, but Regel did not care. He'd not thought to see any of his Circle of Tears ever again, not after his assault on the palace of Tar Vangr with Ovelia and Mask. Nacacia looked awful: physically exhausted, blood-and-soot smeared, and drained physically and spiritually, but he saw the old familiar strength in her eyes. She had not lost herself.

"My Lord." She licked her lips and winced. "My Lord, I lost her."

"Lost?" Regel frowned. "Who?"

Nacacia looked stricken, as though his words stabbed her in the heart. "Sarelle," she said.

Serris's daughter.

"In battle," Nacacia said. "I lost her. She—" She looked wanly down the street, toward a series of buildings burning smokily in the gloom. "We should go. We should find her."

She started to walk in that direction, obviously limping, but Regel caught her by the arm. Constant battling for so long had left her too weak to fight, and they both knew it.

"No." Regel felt Frostburn hunger at his side. "Rest. I will bring her back, if she lives."

Nacacia's eyes gleamed with unshed tears. She nodded.

They took their leave of one another, and Regel looked back at Lan, who had dispatched numerous squads of warriors to the corners of the square. He gave Regel a rueful look, and his face looked slightly pale. Perhaps he would survive the knife after all, but that seemed unlikely. Whether in battle or of that wound, Lan would die. It was only a matter of patience.

It reminded Regel unsettlingly of a year past, when he and Ovelia had taken shelter in a safehouse together, and he had delivered her an unerring poison. He'd thought her dead for sure, and yet she had survived. Perhaps it was not too late to save Lan as well, and considering their situation, would that not be the best course? Regel had acted on Shard's command, not by impulse, but now he wondered. The warders did not know they were following a dying man into battle. Was it not Regel's responsibility to stand beside them, to protect as many as he might?

Any of them might die this day, and the city might fall despite all their efforts. When the end had come and it no longer mattered what he did, what he did was *all* that mattered.

He did not join one of the squads, but continued to shadow Lan Ravalis.

~

The first hours of the assault to liberate Low-City went quite smoothly, as Lan had hoped but not expected. They'd come across a few isolated barbarians, and the squads had made quick work of them, reporting only minor bruises and one broken arm when they regrouped per instructions. The arrival of the *Hecatomb* seemed to have shattered the barbarians' morale and fractured their solidarity as an occupying force, just as he had thought it would. If this was the horde, they could win this.

Lan wondered if Regel was there, slinking along in the shadows where he could inflict the most harm. Mayhap he remained, to watch Lan—to continue his long, sharp judgment from afar, to make sure his vengeance was completed. Or his justice. Either way, Lan could not see him, and that was for the best. He still felt the pain of the blade, but it had subsided to a dull ache.

All of it changed at nightfall, when they found the barricade.

The barbarians had been in Low-City for some days between the breach of the wall and the arrival of Shard, during which time Lan had expected them to run wild like animals. And indeed, they had—building nests like rodents and leaving carcasses in the streets—but apparently, they also followed the instruction of someone wise and tactical of mind. The ramshackle collection of barrels, splintered shields, wagons, and harvested furniture that cut off the main thoroughfare attested to this truth.

Was it the hurdle itself that gave Lan pause, or was it perhaps the unexpected juxtaposition? To think these primitive madmen would even think to create such a thing, let alone actually do it?

"Majesty," said one of the warders near at hand, his voice trembling with uncertainty.

Only then did Lan realize what he was looking at, and a shudder passed through him.

Amongst the detritus, stacked and hammered roughly haphazardly in place, Lan saw bodies. Men and women and, indeed, children affixed to the barricade like mortal building blocks. Some had been nailed in place, others impaled on spikes or bound to the construction with razor wire. And as Lan and his warders approached, some of them perked up and started moving. They struggled feebly to escape, limbs twitching and mouths gaping open in terror and agony.

"Your Majesty, what—what is that?" The warder's dark, summerblood skin had gone the pale brown of freshly harvested maple.

The captives left to die were screaming now: they loosed cries of fear and pleas for succor or—mostly—they begged for death to relieve their suffering.

And as their voices rose in a cacophony of lamentation, so did an ululating cry from beyond the barricade. Lan watched, a tremor running through his body, as the distorted faces of barbarians appeared over the edge of the barricade, like hornets swarming out of a nest. Their cries for death matched the resonance of his own pain, making his whole side lock up in sudden biting torment.

"Majesty—"

"Fight." Lan put a hand to the hilt of his powered sword, reassured by the warm metal. He drew it with a hum. Flames wreathed the blade, illumining the street and casting sinister shadows on the taut bodies of the dead and dying. "Fight for your city! Fight for your lives! *Fight!*"

They fought.

At Lan's back, casters cracked in the night, and streaks of power sliced the darkness to ribbons. The volley exploded into barbarians who came scrambling down the barricade and into the tortured victims. Blood burst into the air and across the wood and metal, and then the barbarians were upon them. They smashed like charging boars into the front ranks of Lan's warders, whose armor discharged with enough force to knock them back off their feet. A wave of foul-smelling smoke rose over the front rank, and only a single warders took even a step back. The rest took advantage of the thwarted charge and pushed forward to spear the fallen with glowing ranseurs that pierced right through their patchwork armor. As horrific as the barbarians looked, they died just as efficiently and satisfactorily as anyone else.

They could win this.

Lan shook himself, winced at the pain in his side, and charged forward with a roar. A barbarian wrapped in rattling chains hefted an axe, and Lan cut right through it with his liquid-hot powered sword and down into the man's torso. The dust magic turned his sword to a miniature star in his hands, and it burned through the barbarian like a swath of flame. With a sickly grinding sound of metal on chain, it ripped out through the barbarian's opposite hip, and his body fell messily in half, sizzling.

"Forward!" Lan bellowed, and his warriors answered.

They drove another few steps, trampling the dead beneath their knobbed boots, and activated their shields once more to knock barbarians to the ground. The process resembled a wheel slowly turning and grinding the corpses of small animals under its tread. Flame from a heavy caster burst amongst the charging barbarians, blasting a knot of them apart and sending seared chunks of flesh in every direction. The barbarians weren't canny enough to turn and flee, so Lan's warriors slaughtered all the way to the barricade. Lan stood at its base, panting and wincing but with his blood on fire.

They should have pulled back—regrouped and assessed strategy—but how could Lan give that order? They were looking to him—the warriors of Summer and Winter. Blades singing, armor that crackled with electricity and flame, men and women of power and fury. Behind *him*.

"Forward." Lan sheathed his bloody sword, slung his shield around his shoulder, and pointed at the barricade. "Follow me!"

Climbing the barricade was more difficult than it seemed. The wood and metal were slippery with murk and blood, and the structure didn't seem to be built or stacked in a sensible manner. Only a deranged mind would have spawned such a thing. One man attempted to recover a prisoner of the wall, but any attempt to move the hapless victim only caused further agony. Blood poured from his mouth and he ceased his screaming. The summerblood who'd tried to free the man staggered back, gagging, and fell off the wall to the street some two paces below, where he lay groaning and retching.

"These folk are dead," Lan said as he climbed. "We cannot save them, but only avenge them."

Every time he pulled with his left arm, a spasm of pain locked up that side of his body. He'd almost managed to forget about the tiny knife in his side. It would not stop him. Not now. Not ever.

"Up," he said with a choked voice. He couldn't say if anyone had heard, nor did he care. "Up!"

Lan wasn't the first to the top of the barricade, but he stood among half a dozen others, looking down into the smoky ruins of the Low-City streets. Buildings lay crumbling or smoldering with greasy smoke, but the square beyond the barricade was surprisingly empty. Surely they hadn't slain *all* the barbarians in Low-City in that push. Right hand on his sword, he signaled with his weakened left and his warriors spread out in two threshing wings, shields at the ready. The square opened ahead of them, with no obvious obstacle to force their foes against. They would have to be cautious.

He willed the flame of his sword to subside and drew the weapon with a soft rustle.

Silence descended, impossibly, and smoke skirled around Lan as he stalked forward. The breath inside his mask near deafened him, and he could both feel and hear his blood thudding in his throat. His heart was a furnace, stoking the fire in his chest and drowning out the pain in his side with its heat. His vision blurred and he almost laughed. He was strong. He was unstoppable.

A shape loomed out of the smoke: a barbarian with shards of metal poking out of his arms and shoulders, facing away. The barbarian started to turn when Lan wrapped an arm around his neck and rammed his still-hot sword through his back. The barbarian shuddered and went limp, and Lan lowered him to the ground. By his face, the lad had seen perhaps five-and-ten or six-and-ten summers. A flicker of annoyance made Lan grimace: if he had to murder someone, it could at least be a man grown.

Then a gust of wind swept through the square, making Lan's cloak whip back from his body, and by instinct he put his arm up to shield his masked face. The smoke billowed away, sucked into the uncaring sky, and for the first time he could see clearly what they faced. At his sides and behind him, his warriors gasped or cursed or even prayed to the Silver Fire.

The plaza ahead teemed with barbarians—hundreds, if Lan could trust his eyes, or perhaps even a thousand. They looked weary, as though they had just marched quite some distance, but they yet rippled with muscle and bristled with weapons. Distorted faces and warped bodies leered in their direction, and Lan could see the delighted hate emanating from their bodies. His thirty or so warriors had no chance to survive such opposition, let alone defeat them. The barbarians began to laugh, the sound haunting and discordant, ringing in his ears like thunder.

Lan saw a familiar figure wrapped in black leathers floating above the horde, green lightning crackling around her slim body. Semana Denerre nô Ravalis. He could not see her face through the mask, but he could just imagine the look of contempt on her visage. She waved dismissively toward them, not even bothering to strike with her own magic.

Before anyone could speak, Lan raised his sword and willed fire into being around the blade.

"Charge!" he cried, and ran forward. "*Charge!*"

They were trapped, with an army at their front and a barricade at their back. There was no escape and no hope of victory. A younger Lan Ravalis might have admitted defeat, surrendered to hopelessness, and thrown down his blade in hope of parlay. By the Fire, he'd done so often enough in his life. But he was hurt, angry, and tired.

So tired.

The charge surprised the Children of Ruin, for certain, and dozens of them fell dead before the bulk of the force could so much as react. The warriors of Tar Vangr charged in with shields blasting and spears stabbing, and barbarians fell like stalks of grain before the scythe. It was laughable—less than two score attackers against over a thousand defenders—but the sounds of battle were not those of mirth. Blades sang and smashed into flesh and armored hides, and everywhere casterbolts exploded into the ranks of the barbarians. Men and women screamed in fury and in agony.

A barbarian with dagger blades instead of teeth appeared before him, and Lan brought up his shield in time to meet the man's axe sweeping down from above. The blade screamed off the shield, set to ringing by its fortifying magic, and vibrated its way out of the barbarian's hand. The man cursed and fell back, broken fingers twisting spasmodically, and Lan followed with a withering thrust that spitted the man like a hog. The barbarian fell, dragging the sword down with him, and Lan lurched down with a mild oath. The weapon caught in the man's ribs and refused to come free.

Something slammed into his back, but his powered armor deflected it with a sparking whine. At least half a dozen barbarians surrounded him, smashing down at him with axes and cudgels and other bludgeons, and Lan grunted and cursed, trying to pull the blade free.

It wasn't fair. They didn't deserve this victory. They weren't stronger or better or worthier than he, only more numerous. And he would die.

One of the strikes caught him in the side, and though the armor buzzed with power and deflected it, it jarred the knife in his side and veritably ripped him in half with pain. The agony turned to rage, and rage gave him strength. He sent forth wave after wave of flame from his gauntlet, driving the barbarians back long enough to take a grip on the sword with both hands. The sword blazed with power and Lan ripped it out of the corpse, which resembled a spitted and roasted hog. He whirled the blade in an arc that hacked one spear in half, took off a second barbarian's hands, and drove the others back. He cut a circle of blood, sword in his left hand, fire gauntlet on his right, carving himself breathing room.

Barbarians leered at him on all sides, jeering as he brandished his flaming sword in their direction. That wasn't fear—it was mockery. And why not? He had failed—as a king, as a man, as everything that mattered.

Beyond them, his warriors screamed and fought and killed, summerblood and winterborn alike. He wondered how many owed loyalty to the Blood Ravalis, and how many fought for Tar Vangr, and how many simply fought for themselves and those they loved. Regardless, they all died just the same, cut down by opponents that outnumbered them a hundred to one.

One barbarian strode forth, cheered on by the others, into the circle Lan occupied. The man had the stature and face of a bull, complete with massive tusks that grew out of his distended mouth. He hefted a spear hung with clattering fingerbones and bloody feathers, and in his other hand he held a hooked axe with several notches. It looked like he'd killed someone recently, and meant to claim another summerblood in power armor as his most recent prize.

"No," Lan said under his breath, ignoring the pain in his side. He shifted the sword to his right hand and readied his shield anew. "Not *you.*"

He was the Bear of Luether, the King of Tar Vangr.

He was Lan Ravalis, and he would not give his life easily.

The barbarian came at him, all posture and bluster, but Lan was ready. The spear jabbed at him, but he knew it for a feint—an obvious one. Lan casually batted it aside with his shield and struck in the same motion, not waiting for the axe attack he knew was coming. He hacked up and across and should have taken the barbarian's arm, but the man backed off with a hiss. The circle laughed loud and long.

"Toy with me, will you?" Lan coughed, and red spattered the goggles of his mask. Blood. He tore the mask off and faced them, bare-faced and unhelmeted. "I'll kill all of you savages."

They whooped and roared, laughing at him.

A second barbarian came forward, this a broad-shouldered man with two curved swords, and he whirled them before him in a scything wall of steel. The barbarians cheered, and Lan was ready for it. The instant the man with the swords shifted his attention away, Lan charged forward, putting his full momentum behind his sword. The barbarian saw the attack too late, and the sword took him low in the torso, stabbing right through his gut like a heated knife through a rotted pumpkin. The man's eyes went wide and blood streamed from his mouth. He spoke, but Lan was too busy roaring to understand him.

More blows rained down upon Lan, and slicing pain ripped through his right leg. A barbarian sickle had found the knee gap in his armor and carved a hot line through it. Lan ripped his sword free, disemboweling the barbarian he'd struck, but it hardly mattered. The others who had attacked him skipped back, jeering, and he staggered in a circle, warding them off. His side thudded with pain, beating in and out, as though the hurt was in his blood. It was part of him, and soon it would be all of him.

It continued in this way for some time—longer than Lan had thought possible, in fact. Several times, a barbarian stepped forward, shouting incomprehensible boasts to the growing crowd, and every time, they exchanged a few blows, leaving Lan weaker and tired, and then the barbarian fell back and rejoined the circle. Every time, Lan expected his body to give out, but every time, dull stubbornness kept him fighting. It became even a little funny, after a time, judging each barbarian and deciding which might be worthy enough to strike him down. Alas, every one of them disappointed him.

At some point, the fight became about preserving himself so that he died of the blade in his side, rather than any new wound. Lan did not know if Regel lived, let alone whether he was watching the struggle. Perhaps he'd been too wise to follow them over the barricade. It hardly mattered, but Lan hoped he was watching. If anyone got to kill him, it would be the shadow of the Winter King.

The sounds of fighting beyond their circle had died away, and even the cries of the wounded. All he could hear was the relentless gibbering of the barbarians. He wondered if the world made any other sort of sound. The latest challenger stepped forward, marked by her lack of lips and the many shards of steel thrust through her face to make her brows and cheekbones sharp as knives. She wore barbed plates of iron and had a small axe in each hand. A woman. Was this Ruin's final insult?

Lan raised his sword in an arm grown leaden with weariness. He had to fight to lift it. His left arm didn't work at all, and his shield fell limply toward the ground. He fumbled with the straps to free it, and it clattered to the cobbles with a dull thud. Not that it would serve any real purpose. He fought through the soreness and managed to cup the pommel of his sword with his trembling left hand.

The barbarian spun her axes and hissed like a snake. Lan realized she had fangs rather than teeth and it disgusted him. "Come on," he said. "Come on, you—"

She hurled one axe, then the other.

Somehow, Lan managed to interpose his sword between his face and the axe coming for it. The sword shattered as the axe skipped off into the crowd, and he heard a distant, satisfying curse of pain. Their laughter diminished, and that as much as the deflected axe made him smile, though bloody drool leaked out over his lips and chin.

He felt the dull pain in his midsection only belatedly, and didn't understand what had happened until he fell to his knees. He looked down at the axe buried in his guts, through his battered and cracked armor, and wondered why it didn't hurt more. Blood dripped down the blade, and Lan felt his strength leaving with it. His broken sword drooped and clattered dully to the cobblestones, its fire extinguished.

The barbarian rushed in eagerly, and Lan raised the blasted gauntlet toward her. Fire surged, encompassing her, and her scream cut off as she ran a few steps and collapsed to a smoldering heap.

"Come on!" he roared, spitting blood.

They circled around him as he knelt there, projecting flame in smaller and tighter circles until he no longer had the will. Lan slumped, his battle lost, all his soldiers gone. Dimly, he searched the barricade but saw no sign of anyone escaping. It disappointed him that the others had all died. He would have liked to have saved one person.

Hand trembling, Lan unbuckled his breastplate, and it fell ringing to the stone. Beneath, his shirt was plastered to his thickly-muscled trunk with sweat and blood. He looked down at the festering dagger wound, from which dark veins of infected blood spread, and made a disapproving sound in his throat.

"Hurry up, Oathbreaker," he said under his breath. "Or some beast will steal your glory."

The circle parted to admit two men, both of them young and neither sympathetic of visage. Indeed, one of them wore a grin that reveled in pain and death, and the other hid his face behind a mask made of bones. It took Lan a moment to realize why that mask was familiar, and finally he drew in a sharp breath of recognition.

"Tithian," he said. "You—"

The ruinscarred man shuffled to Lan and shoved him over with his club foot. Weak as a newborn, Lan could hardly resist. He fell back on the cobblestones, coughing and cursing.

"Who is this, Slayer?" The other man cocked his head to one side, studying Lan as might a hunting bird. "He seems to know you."

"No one, Dar-Karsk." Davargorn shrugged. "I have a name that is known and feared."

Lan felt it bubbling up inside his bruised throat, and he couldn't keep it at bay. The laugh sent shudders of grinding pain through his body. "You? *You?* Known and feared? That—" He trailed off, unable to draw breath for more words.

Dar-Karsk, whoever he was, headed back into the horde, which parted like water around him. He seemed to hold some sort of position of leadership among the barbarians, and Lan was beset by regret that he'd not managed to kill him. It might have helped Tar Vangr, yes, but mostly it was Lan's own stubborn pride. He hated to die thinking he'd accomplished nothing.

Davargorn bent low over him, eyes on Lan's festering wound. "Stabbed under your armor," he said. "Chose the wrong friend, did you?"

Lan swallowed a curse. He didn't have the words to spare. "Heal me," he said.

Davargorn considered him in a manner not dissimilar to that of Dar-Karsk. "What?"

"You have the power," Lan said. "Lay your hands on me and heal my body. Quickly, before"—he coughed—"before I cough myself to death, damn you."

Davargorn blinked, but Lan only saw his blue eye close. The white remained bulging and wide. "Why would I do that?" he asked. "You are an enemy to my queen."

Lan nearly choked on his bile and rage. "Rut your queen, good and bloody," he said. "What has she offered you this time? Love? Her body? Don't be a fool, Tithian."

"No." Davargorn shook his head. "You won't understand. You can't."

"Can't!" Lan snapped, and just opening his mouth made his whole body tighten in pain. He felt it in waves now, each one greater and duller than the last. His limbs tingled and his fingers went numb.

But he could speak, and so he did. For as long as he could.

෴

The dying man filled the next moments with every insult and slur he could think of against Semana Denerre nô Ravalis and Davargorn both. He slandered her character, cast her as sexually licentious and morally bankrupt, manipulative and vile, and assured Davargorn that, pathetic as they both were, he didn't deserve her. He poured all of it up at a seemingly insensible Davargorn, launching every barb like an arrow, as though his words could close around Davargorn's throat and strangle him with hate.

Davargorn had the sensation that someone was watching him, but when he looked around at the gathered horde of barbarians, no face stood out. Darak was there, yes, delivering some sort of speech to the gathered barbarians. Most of the monstrous folk had turned away from Lan, paying no attention to the rants of a dying man. So much noise without any substance—fury without force.

It all sounded like a condemnation of Lan himself, and of no one else. A life wasted.

In the end, when the Bear of Luether no longer had breath, Davargorn could only shake his head. Before, such aspersions on Semana's morality or "decency" might have upset him, but now? It all seemed so pointless. To his knowledge, Semana had never even had sex and probably never would—she had certainly never suggested to him any interest. And even if she did, why would that diminish her?

To see Lan desperately cling to that, in his last moments, seemed distantly sad. Davargorn had thought the man had something to say—to teach him. But now he saw he had been wrong.

At length, he reached down, making Lan flinch, but all he did was tug free Mask's gauntlet from his hand. Then he rose, filled not with rage but profound boredom, and turned to go.

Terror lit in Lan's eyes. "Wait," the king said, his voice barely a dry whisper. "Wait—"

"You couldn't live with dignity," Davargorn said. "It was too much to expect you to die with it."

With that, he walked away, and Lan's gurgling protests faded behind him.

He was pleased no barbarians cut Lan's suffering short with spear or sword. He meant nothing.

When Lan Ravalis finally died, it was slow and horrible and entirely unheeded.

EIGHTEEN

IN THE SQUARE THAT had seen the great battle that day, ash drifted like snow from a hundred burning houses, and a gibbering cry of triumph arose.

The Tar Vangryur launched no further assaults, and indeed, when the last of their folk had taken the lift up to the relative safety of High-City, they cut the chains. The last of the four lifts toppled down out of the sky with a shattering boom that shook the city. The buildings shifted on their foundations before settling once again into doomed quiescence. Abandoned to its fate, Low-City felt less like a living place and more like a corpse yard. Death spread through the streets like diffusing mist that settled into the cobbles and cracks in the stone, bubbling from the heat of the Narfire.

For the Children of Ruin, this was ideal. Death was their goddess—their perfect state of being. They considered it their sacred calling to bring the world to its grim destiny.

And so they reveled in it. They feasted on captured foodstuffs and guzzled stolen wine. They rutted in the streets, men and women and otherwise piled upon each other, grasping and embracing and thrusting with animal drive in the warmth from below. The dying Low-City became their paradise, and they took to their leisure with relish.

For Tithian Davargorn, the orgy of celebration lost any appeal it might have once offered. As a younger man, trapped in a cycle of slaying and secrets, he'd taken proffered flesh when he could find it, more with hopeless vigor than genuine enthusiasm. Now he just found it off-putting. There seemed to be something missing, and he thought that if he had not found it yet, they would not find it.

At his side, Semana seemed equally unimpressed. The black leather hid her face, of course, but he'd grown adept at reading her feelings from her body. Or, at least, what she chose to convey.

Slurred laughter caught Tithian's notice. Face red with drink, Darak staggered toward them, that pretty servant lad of his on one arm, and a mostly nude barbarian woman on the other. Tithian tried hard not to look at her mostly bared chest, nor at Crown of Fire's hungry look, directed both at Semana and Tithian himself. He hadn't lain with a man for some time, and the youth's good looks made his neck itch. The thought of sex always brought back up his self-loathing and put him in a foul mood.

"Greetings, my beautiful Blood Queen," Darak said. "Join us."

"You've had your fill of bloodwine, I see." Semana made a distasteful sound. "And smell."

A crooked smile spread across Darak's ruddy face. "And we've more to share," he said. "Come. Join us! This is a night of celebration for a great victory."

"How many of your horde were slaughtered in the streets this day?" Semana asked.

"Many," Darak said. "We should celebrate their glory."

The barbarian woman giggled and fidgeted, clearly displeased at the conversation. With a few words in their guttural ruinspeech, Darak sent her away with Crown of Fire toward a nearby alley. Tithian guessed he'd intended them to wait for him to join them, but from the sounds of things, that didn't seem likely. Darak's inebriated joy sobered slightly into a grimace.

Darak gave Tithian a questioning look, and Semana waved her hand. "Tithian Davargorn is my creature," she said. "You need fear no betrayal of your secrets."

"Not to anyone else but my *queen*," Tithian said. The clarification made Darak glare at Semana, but she offered no obvious reaction to his words. Tithian took that as encouragement.

Perhaps surprisingly, Semana had told Tithian the truth about Darak and herself—told him much about the time that had passed between their parting and this reunion. He knew the man was Darak Ravalis nô Denerre, but knew also that it was a somewhat guarded secret from the barbarians who supported his cause. Tithian only vaguely recollected meeting the prince once or twice in his youth, and he remembered a callous, supercilious prig of a lad who insisted on dominating every conversation he took part in. This Darak did not vary much from that one, though he'd grown somewhat subtler. In that, he saw the resemblance between Semana and her brother, but in no other respect.

"This is a great day, Semana," said Darak. "You should join us. Celebrate our victory."

"Victory." Semana scowled. "You consider this a victory, when you've lost thousands? How many froze to death beyond the walls? How many lives did you consign to the fire in taking Low-City? Just today, Lan Ravalis killed over a hundred with a handful of warriors and superior weapons."

"And now he is dead," Tithian said.

She cast him a look that made him shrug and look away. He continued to listen but cast his gaze outward at the burned-out buildings and smoldering barricade at the edge of the square. He couldn't say for sure what he sought, but he would be prepared for anything that approached.

"The Children do not mourn their losses, but celebrate those who have been honored with death. To refuse their revelry risks insulting them." Darak put on a waxy smile. "Have you not lectured me at length about embracing barbarian customs? And not without condescension, I should add. I'm the one who's lived among them half my life, after all. And yet, you do not listen to me?"

"Not interested," Semana said, refusing to take his bait.

"Sister." He moved closer to her, their faces only narrowly separated, and ran a hand up her arm. "Come. Drink. Feast. Take a lover, or three. Be a Child of Ruin for a night. You might enjoy it."

Tithian did not like the way Darak was touching her. He grasped the handles of his swords.

"Begone." Semana raised her chin. "Rut those creatures to your heart's content, or at least your little blade's. I'll have none of it."

The stern determination in her voice eased Tithian. He smiled beneath his skull mask.

Dimly, he saw a figure flow across from one of the alleys. If Tithian hadn't been watching at exactly that moment, he might not have seen the man. Little stood out about the shadow, except the ease of its movement. It didn't seem possible.

The boisterous barbarians near the center of the square laughed uproariously at some jest one must have made. Likely to do with killing, which seemed to be all these people found amusing. It distracted Tithian, and he lost sight of the shadow.

"My queen." Darak spoke low, his voice soothing. He laid his hands on her shoulders and whispered in her ear from behind. "Take ease. All proceeds as we have foreseen."

"As *I* have foreseen," Semana said. "Without me, you'd be dead beneath Carr's axe."

He stiffened slightly, but just as quickly he returned to his sycophantic charm. "And I've yet to thank you for that." He rubbed harder. "Thank you."

Tithian gave Semana a questioning look back over his shoulder, and she nodded.

"Fine," she said as she extricated herself from Darak's grasp. "I can bear your self-congratulation a bit longer. So long as you follow my path going forward from this."

"Oh yes, I recall." Darak made a face. "*Peace*. You really think anyone will wish for such a thing?"

Semana shrugged. "It hardly matters what they want," she said. "Only what they *need*."

Darak nodded and moved away. Tithian watched him go, and his barbarian woman giggled again when he approached. Cheeks growing warm, Tithian looked away to avoid losing his composure. Semana was watching him carefully, and Tithian was glad the mask hid his expression.

"He pushed that hard," Tithian said. "Your brother takes an unusual interest in your body."

"My brother is..." Semana waved that away and pointed to the alley. "I saw you watching them. You should join them. It might be your last chance for some time."

"I'll stay with you," Tithian said.

"I see." He thought he detected a trace of sadness in her voice.

They stood together for a few moments, the great unspoken conversation between them remaining so. As close as they had become, Tithian felt it now as an impassable expanse. He wondered how long he would remain at the edge of the abyss, when he knew it could never be bridged.

He might have said something more, or perhaps she meant to, as she drew in a breath at the same time he did, but a cry interrupted the moment. From the crowd of Children at the center of the square, Tithian heard the squeal of a small child. The fire was not too far away, and he could see the hazy silhouettes of folk scrambling about in some sort of fight. He glanced to Semana, but she was already flying toward the scuffle. Tithian loped along after her with his awkward, mismatched stride.

When they drew close, Tithian saw one of the barbarians holding aloft a child—some two or three winters of age, perhaps—the way one might a spring hog taken as a prize. The child flailed and slammed their small fists and feet ineffectually against the barbarian's massive, scarred arms. Their laughter died, however, when Semana appeared, hovering just above the ground like a specter.

"Stand and speak," Semana said. "What passes here?"

Perhaps they did not understand her tongue, but her stance was clear enough. All eyes turned to her, and Tithian saw confusion and more than a little fear on their faces. One of their number, however, kept his eyes downcast so that his cowl hid his craggy face. The man didn't present an obvious threat, but Tithian stepped aside to try to get a better look at his face. Unsuccessfully.

One of the barbarians—whose arm resembled a withered skeleton of a living limb—grated out something in Ruinspeech, and Semana responded in kind, the harsh language surprisingly smooth on her lips. She gestured to the child, whom the barbarians seemed to be arguing over, and the big barbarian holding the little creature barked out something that sounded like a challenge.

Tithian stooped and drew his swords with twin hisses that blended into a single hum. Bone Arm uttered a cry of alarm and raised her one-handed axe. Two others drew weapons while a third simply toppled over backward in a drunken fluster. The cowled man across the way tensed but did not draw a weapon, and he was the one Tithian watched. The four hardly seemed like a threat, but that one...

The barbarian holding the child spoke again, calling out some manner of challenge, but abruptly his body stiffened as though struck with a shock of lightning. Tithian's heart thudded in his head, and he'd felt the touch of blood magic often enough to know what Semana was doing.

With obvious effort and horror in his eyes, the massive man lifted one foot and took a step, then another, toward Semana. Within a pace of her, the giant of a man fell to one knee with the crunch of bruising bone, then the other, and bowed his head in abject submission. Still held aloft in both hands, the child continued to squawk in his hands, but their wails had ceased. The child looked fixedly at Semana with dark eyes that brimmed with intelligence and curiosity, but no fear. Remarkable.

Semana took the proffered child with surprising gentleness, and brushed a lock of pale hair out of their face with one withered black glove. Seeing her this way, he wasn't sure how to feel. He looked back to the hooded barbarian he'd sought out, but the man had vanished into the night. Where—?

With her right hand—the one that boasted the pitted war gauntlet he had reclaimed for her, the palm growing faintly red—Semana waved dismissively at the blood-bound barbarian and she emphasized the gesture with a click of her tongue. Abruptly unbound, the man fell back on his haunches and, big and strong as he was, scurried away like a terrified rat.

Tithian looked once more for the old man but found no sign of him. Another figure was approaching through the smoky darkness, however, and Tithian recognized Darak. His red-haired lustlad hurried along behind, disheveled and limping slightly, but the giggling woman was nowhere to be seen. Bare to the waist, his golden chest and belly smeared with black lesions, the barbarian prince glowered in simmering rage. It seemed anger had overridden his inebriation.

"What passes here?" He goggled at the child in Semana's arms. "What is that?"

"I believe this child's name is Sarelle," Semana said. "And she is under my protection."

Tithian wondered where he'd heard that name before, and it struck him suddenly: in the tunnels beneath the palace of Tar Vangr, that woman of the Circle of Tears had cried it out just before Lan Ravalis killed her. He'd only heard it the once, and that incident had passed in a blur of pain and rage, and yet he remembered it so very clearly now. Why?

"Eager, Barbarian Prince," Tithian said to Darak. "Finished your revelry so quick, eh?"

Darak sneered but otherwise ignored the question. "What need have you of a child?"

Mask shrugged. "None."

From Semana's protective embrace, Sarelle stared unwaveringly at Darak, regardless of how he glowered back at her. Crown of Fire smiled at the child, who blinked at him uncertainly.

"Why then?" Darak sneered.

"Because once I offered blessings to her mother," she said.

Tithian shared Darak's confusion. Semana was not given to sentiment, nor had she any sort of interest in children he knew of. But he'd come to embrace the uncertainty of Semana. He trusted her.

Darak seemed to lack that same flexibility or trust. Ultimately, he scoffed and took his leave of that place without a word, taking his attendant with him.

"You are *certain* that is your brother?" Tithian frowned. "He's barely an ally."

Wordlessly, Semana put the child—Sarelle—down on the ash and dust-strewn cobblestones. The little creature was filthy—clad in shapeless clothes little more than rags, skin coated with blood and dried mud—but her eyes were bright and determined. Tithian expected his horrific mask to frighten her, but Sarelle seemed at ease, if a touch wary. He remembered holding this very child hostage to force Serris to betray her master, and she hadn't seemed afraid then either. What was wrong with this child?

"Hark." Semana unclasped the mask, freeing her face for Sarelle to see. "Where is your—?"

She only got that far before Sarelle, eyes wide at Semana's revealed face, let out a small squeak and scurried toward Tithian. The sudden move surprised him so greatly that he had only just started to tense when the child shoved under his cloak and sheltered behind his gnarled leg. He felt Sarelle's little hands on the back of his knee, and the child looked out at Semana warily.

He realized, with an odd little wash of amusement, that the child found the mask more comforting than Semana's face of flesh and blood. Moreover, she seemed to remember him, and not as a menacing presence. A remarkable child indeed.

"It's well," he said. "She means you no harm."

"Indeed." Semana put her mask back on and greasy smoke flowed from her boots. "I'll leave the child for you to look after. See that she's yet alive when I return."

"Wait—"

Tithian started to protest, but Semana simply lifted into the air and floated away, off into the darkness. He looked down, and Sarelle was gazing up at him, curiosity in her dark eyes.

"Well," he said. "So it passes."

～

Regel watched as Mask settled atop one of the buildings. Traversal up the moldering ladder alongside the building proved no great challenge, but doing it silently slowed the ascent. At the edge of the rooftop, he paused to look out at the smoky square, full of blurry forms ambling about. Somewhere, Tithian Davargorn and Sarelle were hidden in the smoke, and doubt still gripped him.

He'd had a bare instant to decide whether to stay with them or to follow Semana, and this was the path he'd chosen. He hoped he hadn't sacrificed Sarelle in the process, but this might be his last chance to see Semana. He had to try once more to dissuade her from this path, if such a thing was now or ever had been possible. But if anyone could reach her, he thought it had to be him.

On the roof, the Blood Queen had removed her mask and sat at the foot of a short wall that bounded an herb garden, the plants long since withered or torn up. As he watched, she leaned back against the stone, letting ash drift down onto her upturned face. She looked profoundly weary.

"I see it, too," she said, so abruptly it seemed she addressed the Shadow. But no, she'd spoken to no one in particular. "The fire."

Regel's chest squeezed tight and he might have gone to her then, but of a sudden, something stood beside him in the darkness. He felt the cold presence behind him and turned, hand going to his weapon, but Gilt's black eyes were calm and empty of any threat. The Deathless fae did not strike, but instead merely watched until Semana rose, stretched, and took off again into the night.

Gilt shifted a fraction. Regel tensed for a fight before the Deathless vanished into the shadows and reappeared some five paces behind him, in the center of the rooftop. He held two glassy black blades like extensions of his forearms, fingers alongside the blades, one horizontal and the other vertical. The fae often used such a gesture to convey determination if not an actual threat. This confrontation was no idle thing, but it did not necessarily presage battle. Yet.

"Do you protect Semana?" Regel asked.

"The struggles of the living are no part of we, the Deathless." Slowly, the Deathless shook his head. "I should not have followed her as long as I did."

"Then why have you returned?"

Regel asked the question, but he knew the answer. They both did.

"The scythe must return with me," Gilt said. "It must be held in a place of safety and honor."

They both knew the words were empty, but they had to be spoken.

Regel drew Frostburn, illumining the darkened rooftop in its eerie blue glow. He raised it straight out from his shoulder, his arm faintly aching with the effort. He laid a second hand over the pommel and felt its cold energy surging into his arm. The magic of the sword swept through him, numbing him to the soreness and pain. All his worries and concerns fell silent, and the world shrank around them. Only the rooftop existed. Only the Deathless. Only Regel. Only his blade.

Gilt inclined his head. He extended the blades, one high behind him, the other low and pointed toward Regel. "I am honored," was all he said.

Then words had no further purpose.

Regel could not say which of them struck first. The fae's blades clashed with his, raining sparks and flecks of ice around them like tears. Gilt spun twice and thrice, hacking his black fangs down against Regel's defense, and the slayer swayed back and forth. Their bodies flowed together, against one another and in concert, centuries of training and wisdom against will and unshakeable determination. In truth, it seemed as though they had danced in this way for hours, this duel yet a continuation.

Blue mage-glass sparked off brick as they fought back against a wall, but the Deathless leaped over the attack and turned a flip over Regel's head. Drawn by the hungry power of the Frostburn, Regel followed Gilt, running straight up the wall and projecting himself back over the seeking black blades. The Deathless struck up at him, and Regel parried each of his strikes as he flew back and across. He landed in a roll, came up to his feet, and slashed back around to catch a fresh pair of strikes that sent him lunging to the side with their force. He rolled with the blows and dived under scything cuts that swept the air just a hair's breadth above his upturned face.

As the duel unfolded, Frostburn's power grew until the sword became a blue star in his hands, and he finally brought it up and toward Gilt like a talisman. Magic burst and roiled like an icy storm between them, and the

Deathless fell back and away, rimefrost shooting across his cloak. Shivering, he fought free of his cloak and looked down at the veins of blue ice tracing his muscles.

They stood facing one another, the Deathless's perfect body rippling in the fire and smoke and light of Regel's blade. His near-black skin had turned a shade of gray, and his eyes like chips of black ice gleamed with pain and with fury. He lifted his black blades, pitted and notched from parries against Frostburn. The weapon consumed all that it touched, and anyone who touched it.

"That blade," Gilt said, "is not yours."

Regel turned Frostburn in a slow circle. The bottomless hunger drew him downward and deep. It could never be filled, and it would consume him.

"It is a talisman of my people," he said. "It is our deathright. It is *us*."

Regel did not want the sword any more than Gilt wanted him to wield it. But he *needed* it, for just a little longer. He raised Frostburn anew and let it hang forward and down from the level of his eyes.

Gilt's expression hardly wavered, but Regel could see his distant sadness. "So be it."

The Deathless lunged for him, projecting himself like a casterbolt. Both blades hacked down at Regel's head, and he caught them both on the sword. The force of the charge smashed into him, carrying them both over the edge into the plaza below. Even as they fell, a black blade stabbed down, narrowly missing Regel's face and instead carving a line of pain along his jaw. That blade should have gone through his throat, but somehow, Gilt had missed an easy strike. Regel smashed an elbow into Gilt's perfect face, twisting his nose to the side. The cobbles hurtled up to meet them.

The world bent, shadows elongating, and they fell through the ground into a world of darkness. Regel rolled along blackened stone and finally came up to one knee, blade pointed toward Gilt. Around them, the buildings blurred, their stones seeming to boil and stretch in the smoke. Inky blackness flowed like a living thing, like mist but nearly as thick as blood. The city was a graveyard of its true self.

Regel nodded. Fitting that they might fight their duel in the Deathless world of shadow.

The barbarians swarming around the square had vanished, left behind in that other, broken world, but the dark place was not empty. Far from it. Regel could hear a faint, echoing rustle, and he looked up to see the shadow of the great mountain—and the great serpentine creature of darkness wrapped around it. A voracious beast that had just begun to stir, bigger and mightier than even the Frostfire dragon, whose scale dwarfed armies. It sensed them, and it would come for them. Soon.

"Reaper of Men."

Gilt rose, holding his cracked black swords wide. Had he wanted to kill Regel, he would have struck in his distraction. That told Regel what he needed to know.

"You won't slay me, and you know I won't return with you," Regel said. "You want to die."

Without reply, the Deathless came again, attacking with his right-hand sword, then slashing in with his left. Regel danced back, deflecting one, two, then evading aside. Gilt spun away, and for the first time his steps showed a hint of weariness. Regel did not feel tired in the slightest—he felt nothing through Frostburn's magic, but for a distant sadness.

Their duel resumed, and it stretched on. Blades flew and muscles strained, locked in perfect balance, each a match for the other. Gilt was a Deathless fae, the victor of a thousand battles against the finest of combatants, chief among them the sheer expanse of time. Regel was a mortal man, but he had the finest weapon the Deathless had ever crafted. Neither could win and neither could lose.

They fought for what felt like hours but Regel knew it was only moments.

Finally the beat varied. The Deathless lunged and Regel spun along the thrusting arm and lashed out in a glittering arc. Gilt ducked and tried to stab under his arm, but Regel was too fast. He eluded the thrust, slashed Gilt's shoulder open with Frostburn, and kicked the Deathless in the back, sending him staggering. He came up in a crouch, contorted to favor his wound.

"You cannot return, because you cannot leave her," he said. "And so you fight to die."

Gilt's eyes blazed with hopeless rage, such as Regel had rarely seen from one of the Deathless fae. It reminded him of the Deathless Rose's face, during their final confrontation. He'd never expected to see anything like that again.

The fae stood, blades raised, but Regel was on him, slashing hard and horizontally. The obsidian blades came up to block, and Regel hacked into them again and again, sending flecks of ice and chips of black stone hailing around them. Frostburn struck the blades, then the stone, then the blades again, leaving long, loping lines of rimefrost along the black stone underfoot.

Finally, Gilt threw forward his blades in an attempt to parry, and the Frostburn struck them like a hammer, shattering stone in all directions. The fae fell back, holding the jagged hilts up in a vague threat. Regel followed, though, and put the ice-blue blade of Frostburn against Gilt's throat.

"Free me," Regel said.

Gilt's black eyes were unfathomable. He made not the slightest move.

Small rocks clattered to the ground around them like rain. From above them, Regel heard the groan of breaking stone as the massive creature flexed and wriggled, coils pulling free of the mountain.

"Free me," Regel said, "or we all die."

"All." Gilt's expression wavered.

Regel drew the sword away from Gilt's throat. "I will save her," he said finally.

The creature roared, its booming cry like a city collapsing in a thunderstorm. The creature took flight and fell toward them. It was death, and it had come at last.

At length, Gilt nodded faintly.

NINETEEN

P EACE."
The way Shard said the word, as if speaking around a bit of grit in her mouth, told Ovelia all and everything about how she felt regarding the subject. She did not need to see Shard's face behind its veil, by which she appeared to all onlookers as a serene, anonymous figure. Ovelia, on the other hand, could feel the tension in her body from two paces away. It made her want to go to her—comfort her—but she remembered the harshness Shard had directed toward Lan Ravalis, and it gave her pause.

They stood in the entry hall of the palace of Tar Vangr, with some fifty or sixty councilors in the mage-city's government. Shard held a goblet of fortified wine, but she'd not drunk more than a sip or two, lifting her veil just enough to permit it. Such was not the case among the gathered throng, which had barreled straight into drunkenness without much pause. Ovelia recognized a few voices, but most were foreign to her. Lan Ravalis had not been a gentle or wise king in her absence, executing or exiling a number of influential and key members of the Council, and Tar Vangr's upper echelons yet reeled.

Now the king in exile had not returned, and rumor said he was dead. Tar Vangr was desperate.

So why would the Children of Ruin want peace?

"Peace," Shard said again, under her breath. "And we are to believe this?"

"I don't—" Ovelia bit her lip. Passions warred in her heart, and she decided to keep her silence.

Laud Ravalis, Lan's cousin and the king in his absence, gave an awkward little cough. At his sides, his chosen Ravalis warders rapped the butts of their powered spears smartly on the floor, sending a wave like rolling thunder through the chamber to attract the attention of all those gathered.

"Fellow folk of Tar Vangr," Laud said, his voice amplified to sound slightly metallic. "You've all heard the tales, so I'll not waste time. Representatives of the Children of Ruin—the barbarian horde that burns our city's foundations— have sent word that they wish to sue for peace. And I—I will hear them."

A stifled cry cut through the crowd, piercing the silence that had fallen like a sack dripping with water. Murmurs and protests flowed out in all directions, filling the hall with conversation, argument, and even a few tears. Ovelia could not see Laud, but she could tell by his smell and his breath that these

231

last days had treated him harshly. He was young, having seen perhaps eight and ten winters, and within his first year on the throne, half his city had fallen and as many of its people. High-City sought to accommodate far more folk than the place could safely house and feed. Between the remnants of the Blood Ravalis personal guard and the few survivors of the Children's push through the walls, Laud had little army left and even fewer war machines. They all knew the dire truth of the situation.

"We've no choice but to hear them," Laud went on. Ovelia detected the tremor in his voice, and suspected it showed in his stance as well. "Surely all can see this."

Shard just barely managed not to snort. "Oh, *surely*..."

Nearby nobles turned toward them, and Ovelia perceived them grow a little more substantial in their flush of distaste for Shard's blatant disrespect. Ovelia drew a little closer to her, and the movement prompted the babe to kick. She'd been so uncomfortable for so long, she couldn't tell if it had grown worse recently or if her tolerance had finally begun to slip.

"He seeks to protect your people." Ovelia whispered to Shard. "This is noble."

"*Noble*." Shard's raised voice held scorn. "Foolish."

Laud cleared his throat once more and addressed the pirate queen directly, his words muting the clamor. "What would you have us do, Lady Shard? Fight to the last? We are near to the last."

"At least it'll be quick," Shard said, sparking murmurs.

Laud cleared his throat. "They offer terms of peace. Should we not hear them, at least?"

Every eye in the hall turned to Shard in her black veil and her very pregnant warder. Ovelia had heard plenty of whispers about them, and she wished she were holding Draca drawn and ready.

Shard, for her part, only laughed.

"If you say so, lad," Shard said. "Yours are the shoulders that will bear the burden."

That she should speak so to the king of Tar Vangr, even young as he was, sparked a significant reaction in the chamber. One of the Ravalis cousins made a scoffing sound, and Ovelia wasn't certain if that indicated agreement or disapproval. Usually she was so good at reading others, but between her diminished sight and the babe's restlessness, she found it hard to focus.

"Then they will bear it." Laud straightened his shoulders. Shard's discourtesy went unaddressed, but Ovelia could sense Laud's resolve hardening to steel. "I called you here, Lady Shard, because I trust your wisdom—and yours, Lady Dracaris."

Ovelia bowed in acknowledgement, and only when mirth stirred faintly around her did she remember that she was wearing a shapeless dress, rather than the leathers or armor she preferred. The bow must have looked odd, but she'd never learned the habit of the graceful curtsy.

"I have spoken." The young king inclined his head. "Those I have called to attend these talks may remain. The rest, I would ask that you take your leave. The Children may yet plan some treachery, and I will put none of you in danger without need."

"Hope but do not trust," Ovelia said, just loud enough for her mistress to hear. Surely that, at least, Shard could not criticize.

"What optimism," she said. "Pity it'll be his doom."

Most of the folk filtered out into the outer hall or the cold sleet of the awful night. Ovelia gladly sat on one of the supplicant benches, and the babe soothed somewhat. Shard leaned against the nearby wall, her critical eye sweeping the chamber. For a mercy, she kept her harsh judgments to herself.

How Ovelia craved the release of sweetsoul just at the moment. She'd managed not to indulge since Luether, and even thought herself past her addiction, but the desire cropped up at the least opportune times. It left her body aching and feeling hollow.

To distract herself, she attempted to figure out who remained in the room.

Laud remained, as did his warders. He also kept most of the members of his Blood, which was not a surprise: of course a young king tentatively clinging to power would want his kin around him.

Ovelia picked out a figure in particular that she could see only faintly: a woman with a distinctively astringent smell, as though she'd washed aggressively with alchemical soaps, lingering uncertainly at the edge of the dais from which Laud had delivered his pronouncements. There was a small boy at her side: Caetus Ravalis, youngest heir of the Blood, if Ovelia remembered aright, who had a distinctive habit of mumbling incoherently under his voice. The woman seemed faintly familiar, but Ovelia would have dismissed her out of hand had she not taken that moment to walk purposefully toward her. Perceiving that the woman offered little threat and meant little harm, Ovelia rose, awkwardly, and only then did she know her.

"Laegra Ravalis," Ovelia said, stiffening. "My condolences for your loss."

Whatever the woman had meant to say, and clearly she had meant to say something, it died away in hesitation. "Vargaen," she said finally. "No longer Ravalis, now that my husband is dead."

Ovelia chewed at her lip. She could feel Shard watching from nearby, her attention curious.

"I—"

Laegra trailed off, and she gazed at Ovelia, taking in all her particulars. The sword belt and the storied blade she wore. The vibrant red hair she hadn't managed to brush since Atropis, let alone style. The linen dress straining to cover her swollen belly. Her belly, especially. What she must have thought…

"Aunt Laegra, are you crying?" asked Caetus, who must have accompanied her toward Ovelia. Strange that she'd not even noticed the lad, but then, her attention had been entirely on Laegra.

Neither of them spoke, but finally Shard interceded in her husky voice. "No fear, my lad," she said. "It is simply business between women grown."

"Oh." Caetus perked up, and Ovelia almost smelled his enthusiasm. "Is it true you're a pirate?"

Shard hesitated. "Yes," she said, a slight bemused smile in her voice.

"Tell me about your adventures! Oh please!"

Ovelia could feel Shard's hand brush reassuringly against her back, then the pirate queen passed beside her and moved away with Caetus. "Once," she said. "A rival captain had stolen my lady-love away, and sailed with her to the fiery mountains of ancient Angarrak."

"But aren't you a lady?" The boy sounded bewildered.

"Yes, what of it?"

"Well, Auntie says lads and ladies—"

"Don't be a fool, child," Shard said. "And don't interrupt."

Blessedly, she led him a few steps away where they could not intrude on Ovelia and Laegra's discourse. The two women faced one another silently, the tension boiling between them.

When she finally spoke again, Laegra spoke suddenly, the words spilling out as though a dam had broken. "I spent many years hating you," she said. "You were all my husband spoke of, his jealousy of his brother who got to have you, and—" She sniffed, and Ovelia realized she was crying.

Gently, Ovelia laid one hand on Laegra's cheek. She didn't say anything. She didn't need to.

"I'm free," Laegra said, her voice breaking between sobs. She indicated Ovelia's belly, though she didn't actually touch her. "Your child. It's not, ah, not his…"

"No." Ovelia took Laegra's hand and pressed the palm to her swell. "*No.*"

"Oh, thank the Fire." The relief flowed from Laegra's words.

Ovelia could feel her body relax as Laegra touched her. When she spoke again, Laegra did so in a whisper. "Then we're both free."

Ovelia smiled, doing her best to mean it. The woman seemed to know something about what Lan had done to her, but thankfully, she did not know all of it. She could not possibly know how Ovelia had felt: no one living could know that, except perhaps Shard, who was watching them carefully.

She might have spoken, but at that moment, a commotion from the end of the hall where the stairs led up into the palace drew their attention. A Ravalis warder Ovelia did not know hurried down the stairs, breathing quickly and heavily. He was flustered, she realized, and that made her clutch Draca's handle and take a small step in front of Shard.

"Majesty," the warder said, voice breathless. "The—ah…"

"What is the meaning of this?" Laud's tone brooked no hesitation, much like his cousin's manner of command. The man was gentler than his blood, but he was still a Ravalis.

The warder caught his breath, but Ovelia could feel the terror radiating from him in waves. "The barbarians, Majesty, they—" He swallowed hard and pointed a quavering finger up. "They've come."

Nervous and confused murmurs spread through the body of folk in the hall. Ovelia could practically hear Laud's confidence waver. At her side, Laegra covered her gasp with her hand.

Ovelia reached a hand toward Shard, and the queen squeezed her fingers.

~

In sleep, the child's long lashes fluttered faintly, and her cheeks flushed a little. Gone was the courage Sarelle displayed in waking, but she displayed no fear, either. She lay on a pallet of skins and furs and took sleep when it was offered, like any professional soldier.

Remarkable, how peaceful the child looked, despite the horror all around.

Tithian had taken over the shabby garret atop the cobbler's shop some days ago. It had only a single entrance, by way of an easily retracted ladder and a trapdoor that blended into the ceiling below, and he could make an escape across the rooftops at need. No barbarians had yet discovered their hiding place, despite frequently ranging past in the street or even in the building below, and the cobbler's shop was mostly made of brick, so they'd not bothered setting it alight.

What he awaited, he couldn't say, but he would wait.

He paused in lacing up his boots for the day's events and considered her sleeping face.

Bringing the child along on his forays for food and drink and other supplies seemed like folly. He might not have bothered, though, as Sarelle seemed an unusually quiet, circumspect child. On one occasion, three Children of Ruin had clustered in the shop below, boasting and breaking furniture and defacing the walls, and Tithian had crouched above, blade in one hand, Sarelle under the other arm, waiting. She'd not made a sound.

Was today the day?

Sarelle's eyes were open and gazing at him, Tithian realized, and he reached immediately for his mask, left unattended on the scarred table behind him. There was no fear in her gaze, and he hesitated. She found masks more appealing than faces, but unlike every child he had ever encountered in his life, she did not seem troubled at his distorted, ruin-twisted visage.

"Girl," he said.

"Man." She pushed herself to a sitting position.

They'd established early on that Sarelle was a girl. Had Serris referred to her that way, when they had met? He could not remember. Regardless, Sarelle had asserted her identity in no uncertain terms, and he respected it as a matter of course.

"Where are you going?" she asked.

"Why do you think I'm going anywhere?" Tithian leaned forward in his chair.

Sarelle glanced down at his half-laced boots, then up at him. Her icy blue eyes dared him to lie.

"Well seen," he said. "I need to replenish our stores. You want to eat, don't you?"

"I pass well." Sarelle's belly growled, belying the assertion, and she put her hands over it. She looked away, a touch embarrassed. She would learn to lie better, in time.

Tithian nodded. "You don't want me to leave?" he asked.

She looked back to him, eyes eager. "Take me with you."

He frowned. "You are a child. This is your third winter, perhaps?"

"*Fourth.*" She crossed her arms over her chest. "And I have two names. Sarelle Wolfsbane."

"Indeed." He raised an eyebrow. "You'll tell me that story, then?"

"Mayhap." Sarelle assumed an indifferent expression and glanced down at one hand. It was the gesture of a woman grown, and it almost made him laugh. "If you take me with you."

Tithian smiled, knowing full well how repulsive the expression always looked. Sarelle grinned in reply, and that made his heart lighter. "Well," he said. "You'll keep very quiet, yes?"

She grinned wide.

~

The trek up the steps to Tar Vangr's throne room took much longer than Ovelia remembered. In all the hundreds of times she'd climbed these very steps, often with her princess at her side as now, it had never seemed quite so long and difficult. Her breath came harder halfway up, and it grew increasingly difficult to carry her body. She felt bloated, uncomfortable, and foolish. What she'd said to Shard on the *Hecatomb* felt like a naïve exaggeration now. What could she even do, if it came to a fight? But Shard seemed determined to hear these barbarians, and Ovelia had to protect her as best she could.

Laegra accompanied them, head held high, and she towed Caetus along by one hand. Ovelia did not like it, but the boy had been adamant. He wanted to meet a real barbarian, and ultimately Laud had relented. Laegra would protect him, and Ovelia would simply have to protect them both.

And so the king and his band of Ravalis, Council members, warders bristling with casters and blades, one pirate queen, and one very pregnant warder climbed the steps to the throne room at the top of the mountain that supported the core of Tar Vangr like a spine. Boots tromped on the stone, teeth ground, and weapons clicked. For each of the thousand winding steps, they grew that much more tense and ready, until they might as well have been infantry charging an impregnable fortress.

When they reached the throne room, at the freezing height of the mountain, it was all many of them could do not to scream in challenge.

Whatever Ovelia had expected in the throne room, she did not find it. Frigid wind blew through the open balcony, setting banners to waving and pawing at the blue-burning candles all around the chamber. There was no barbarian warparty, but only four figures in mismatched armor wielding jagged weapons, who eyed the Tar Vangryur with more curiosity than any obvious challenge. Nevertheless, Ovelia could see them with a good degree of clarity, owing to the threat they posed.

One was clearly a man, his mostly bared and heavily tattooed torso attesting to that, and the slightest movement of his head made chiming sounds thanks to the tiny clicking blades woven into his long beard. A second was just as clearly a woman, bedecked in blasted leather, her face a mass of scars and a toothy sneer. Ovelia could not identity the others as clearly, but it hardly mattered: they looked just as dangerous, clad in woolens and furs caked with layers of blood that ranged in smell from old to fresh. No armor, Ovelia thought, which seemed odd. One of them seemed clearer than the others in her perception, glaring at her with obvious loathing from beneath a cowl of leather, and it gave Ovelia a touch more confidence. Perhaps she did resemble a threat, after all.

"Laud Ravalis, great-child of the Usurper," said a man's voice. "At last."

One other barbarian stood in the chamber, whom Ovelia had not before detected. Indeed, he was not standing in the throne room, but actually *sitting* on the throne itself. Now that he spoke, she could perceive him clearly, his clothes glowing with power. He was wearing—Silver Fire, that was Lan's golden power armor, stinking of blood but still carrying a dust magic charge. Who was this man?

Ovelia tried to get a better sense of him: a youth of some twenty winters, of moderate height and build, his face partly obscured under a hood. She could smell him intensely: powerful astringent soap and perfume, under which she detected the unmistakeable stench of rotting flesh. It was the voice, she thought: that voice seemed oddly familiar.

At her side, Shard stiffened slightly but said nothing.

"I am Dar-Karsk, Master of the Winter Horde," he said. "I've come to accept your surrender."

~

They made their way through the alleys and gutters of the occupied Low-City, Tithian nimbly sticking to shadowed hiding spots, Sarelle lashed in a leather pack on his back. They moved by night, rather than the day, counting on the warmth of the Narfire to fight off the winter's chill while the darkness granted them some safety.

They made a surprisingly effective team. True to her word, Sarelle kept quiet as a corpse, and only when she occasionally clutched at his neck for balance did Tithian even remember she was there. The first time her sharp intake of breath alerted him to a barbarian he'd not seen, he understood her value. He circled back to sneak around the dozing lookout, and once they were safe in an alley beyond, he and Sarelle worked out a system by which she could lend her sharp eyes to his business.

He found that it wasn't just Sarelle's senses he appreciated, but also her company. With Semana gone, instinct and wisdom told Tithian to keep clear of the other barbarians. He'd felt lonely for so long, and it soothed him to have someone at his side—a child, mayhap, but a thinking and feeling person.

Finally, as the moon vanished beyond the mountain and the sun just peeked over the horizon, he found it: the scent of cooked meat, wafting from a mostly-intact building off the Way of Telius, near the harbor district. He'd passed a dozen cookfires and appropriated roasting houses during the night but turned away from each until he found a likely target. He did a full assessment of the warders below, who were mostly sleeping off gorging themselves by night, and noted only two warriors who might prove an obstacle. Better to slip in and claim the remnants of their meal without confrontation—especially with Sarelle on his back—but he loosened his swords in their scabbards just in case.

Only now did it occur to him there was a very real chance he might have to kill a man in front of the child, but he dismissed the rising concern almost as quickly. They'd taken her from a gang of barbarians, and she must have seen plenty of violence to have survived in Low-City since their initial assault. It struck him as sad and grotesque, a blow so powerful that he paused in his approach.

"What passes?" Sarelle asked, her voice a faint whisper against his ear.

He unlashed the child from his back and set her down on the cobbles beside him. It couldn't have been comfortable, but she hadn't complained and didn't look about to do so now.

"Stretch your limbs," he said, and she did as he demonstrated. "Wait here."

Her little face scrunched up in disapproval. "I'm hungry," she said. "Take me with you."

"It's not safe."

She looked unconvinced. "Give me a sword," she said. "I can fight."

"Indeed." The request was so patently ridiculous he had to smile. He drew one of his falcata. "You think you can even lift this? Much less swing it?"

"Hrm." Sarelle may have been a child, but she was not given to exaggeration of her own abilities. She pointed one small finger at the brace of knives on his belt. "One of those, then."

"That." Tithian pointed to a good hiding place in a heap of rusting metal gears and wires.

"No," she said, reaching for the blade's hilt. "*That.*"

Tithian stepped away, surprised at her speed. "This is not an argument. You wait here."

"With the fang."

"With—?" Tithian sighed and shook his head. How did folk handle children daily? This was a greater challenge than any sword he'd ever crossed. "Well," he said finally. "It passes well."

He drew the dagger from his belt and was about to hand it to her, hilt first, when a muffled groan came from the house they were casing. His attention diverted, he remembered the blade only when pain lit in his hand, and Sarelle scurried past like a mouse.

239

He looked down at the line of blood she'd left in his palm, cutting up toward his wrist, and for a moment, he didn't know what to think. He looked up again, to see Sarelle scrambling through a missing pane in a low window. His foot twisted behind him, sending pain shooting up his leg, and he lunged after her—not fast enough. She was over and through, leaving him cursing in the alley.

Tithian nearly shoved through the window, heedless of the glass in his pursuit, but something else drew his attention. There, at the front of the building, the barbarian warders he'd noted had vanished. For a certainty, the half-dozen sleeping forms remained, but he saw no one standing up, keeping watch over their brethren. A breath later, he realized one of the barbarians now lay against the outer wall of the hall, gasping for breath through a spreading pool of blood, and the other was nowhere to be seen. What could have moved so quickly and struck them both down?

With a flicker of his will, he closed the wound in his palm and drew both his swords. The tender flesh still hurt against the leather wrapped handle, but he could bear it. He would need it.

The building must have been a collective living hall or inn, considering its furnishings: couches, tables, a cooking area with heating stone and sink, all arranged around a guttering hearth. The corpse of the second sentry lay halfway into the room, partly frozen to the floor with sheets of blue-black ice. Sarelle stood over the corpse, looking down in horrified fascination. Beyond her, stark black against the crackling flames on the hearth, stood the man who had killed them, ice spreading up his arm and down to the floor from the glowing blue mage-glass blade he held low.

Regel the Frostburn, Shadow of the Winter King.

They faced one another, and Tithian couldn't see an ounce of pity or compassion in the man's grizzled face. It might well have been chiseled out of iron, left to the cold and covered over with rimefrost. He may have drawn faint breath, but he did not live. Not truly. Tithian could see that.

"Oathbreaker." Tithian held his falcata wide—not overtly threatening, but not peaceful either. "Or is it an oath you mean to keep this time?" He tensed his muscles, making ready to spring.

"An oath." Rimefrost flaked from Regel's lips, as though he'd not spoken in days. "Yes."

Regel may have stood ready for a duel, but his attention hung chiefly upon Sarelle, who stood between them unmoving. She in turn stared up at Regel, terrified for the first time Tithian could recall. That strong sense of self-assurance and confidence bled out of her even as he watched, and he could see her small shoulders quivering. She seemed paralyzed, standing like a statue sculpted of glass—sharp but fragile, ready to break.

"Come back to me, girl," Tithian said. "*Sarelle.*"

She looked back with a start, as though she forgot he was there. She still held the knife, and Tithian saw his own blood drip off the end, already growing tacky. Her eyes narrowed at him. He'd lost her, but not because she feared him. Because she had learned all she needed from him.

"I swore an oath," Regel said to Tithian. "Stand away."

A year ago, he'd have jumped to the challenge. Welcomed it. Thirsted for it. Without question.

Not this day.

This day, he considered his situation. Even if he could defeat the Frostburn and his mage-glass sword, his chances of doing so without a significant wound seemed remote. He could heal himself, given time, but embattled Low-City Tar Vangr under barbarian occupation hardly seemed the place to lie wounded and vulnerable. But even if he stood down now, would the Frostburn allow him to walk away? The man stood with such determination and power, Tithian could not say for certain.

And so he said what he had to say.

"Semana," he said.

Regel, who had extended a hand toward Sarelle, hesitated, and his eyes fell upon Tithian directly for the first time. They looked like glowing chips of ice, burning with the magic of the Frostburn.

"Semana and her brother. They have gone to High-City."

Regel's face remained impassive. He clung tightly to the hilt of Frostburn. Tithian could tell by the spark in his eyes that his words had an impact.

Finally, he spoke a single word: "*Why.*"

"For the talks, of course," Tithian said.

"What," Regel said, then: "talks?"

Tithian forced himself to smile. "Peace."

Regel's eyes narrowed. "The Children's peace is death."

"Exactly."

Regel moved so quickly Tithian could barely follow, let alone evade or deflect. He wielded two swords against the Frostburn's one, but that didn't matter. Searing pain bloomed through his face, and the next thing he knew, he lay against the wall, blood flowing in his eyes. Frostburn had ripped through Tithian's mask of bones and leather, tearing it almost in half, so he discarded it unceremoniously.

It took a moment to heal himself of the damage to his face, but he had time. Regel was gone, as was Sarelle—rushing out to find a way to High-City, no doubt.

Even if he found such a route, Tithian knew he would be too late.

TWENTY

OF THOSE ASSEMBLED, IT was Laegra Vargaen who spoke first. Afterward, Ovelia would wonder, in a bittersweet way, whether it was their encounter below that gave her the courage to do so, or perhaps her newfound freedom in the wake of Lan's death. Either way, she stepped forward before anyone could stop her and challenged the man who sat upon the throne of Tar Vangr. It was, Ovelia thought, the bravest act she had ever seen from the woman—and ultimately a mistake.

"Who are you, barbarian, that you would dare to sit that throne?" Laegra asked.

"I?"

Dar-Karsk loosed a sound—a guffaw—that redoubled and built upon itself into a full-throated laugh. The peals of mirth grew mocking and hollow, until finally they cut off in a series of coughs that sounded like a man trying desperately not to choke on his own amusement.

One of the Tar Vangryur party made a move, but the barbarian honor guard responded in kind, and suddenly the tension redoubled. Weapons were brandished high, casters whined, and barbarians hissed at warders. Ovelia felt it all—took in all the information about the various combatants her power gave her—and paid special attention to the barbarian she had noted before, who had looked at her deeply. It was this one about whom Draca warned her, its smoke painting images of impending doom.

For his part, Dar-Karsk seemed entirely unconcerned with the tension. He finished his mirthful fit and waved one thick hand at Laegra, as though both to favor and dismiss her in the same gesture.

"I am disappointed but not surprised you do not know me," he said. "But you will. Oh yes."

At last, Laud stepped forward. "This display of discourtesy was irregular and unnecessary," he said, his tone diplomatic. "You should have come to the gates. You would have known welcome."

"Your hospitality flatters me." Dar-Karsk rose from the throne, his robes rustling about his powerful frame, and stepped toward them. "I preferred something more direct."

Ovelia understood, and she could tell Shard did too, by the way she tensed just behind her. Dar-Karsk had eschewed a formal arrival and avoided taking food and drink, and so he was not bound by the ancient laws and customs of hospitality. He had no protection from them, nor they from him. Surely Laud and his warders knew that and would not relax their guard.

Shard's hand touched Ovelia's hip, perhaps to restrain her or perhaps to draw reassurance from her. Either way, Ovelia strengthened her resolve to shield her mistress.

"Are you a Druid of the Children of Ruin?" Laud asked. "You speak on their behalf?"

Again the man chuckled, as though at a private joke. "Yes and no," he said. "The Children of Ruin don't want your city. They only want to destroy you. To bathe in your blood and weave your guts into their hair. Tan your skins to patch their cloaks and string your fingerbones into their necklaces. Me." He waved one hand dismissively. "I've a different goal in mind."

He looked to the throne, then back to them. Ovelia thought he was looking right at her, and she could feel the weight of his gaze without seeing it. That voice, from so many years ago...

"You come to discuss a peace between our peoples," Laud said, his voice a touch hopeful.

"True." Dar-Karsk ran his hand over the smooth black stone arm of the throne. Surely it was cold to the touch, but he evinced no discomfort. He caressed the throne as gently and warmly as a lover.

"Is this a thing you can maintain?" There was a note of unease in Laud's voice, as though Dar-Karsk's disengagement and indifference unsettled him. Ovelia knew it unsettled *her*.

"You doubt my power?" Dar-Karsk asked the question idly, still not looking.

"Yes." Laud raised his chin. "Would you do any different?"

Dar-Karsk gave a wry chuckle. "The Children are animals," he said. "If they are fed and corralled, they will remain under control. Just so, if their appetites will be slaked elsewhere, they will go. They will not remain to fight an enemy that has been defeated."

Behind her, Shard sounded oddly muted. "Lia," she said. "Lia, we have to—"

Something held Ovelia here. A confluence of duty and destiny.

"But not *you*," Laud said. "You speak of the Children as though you are not one of them."

Dar-Karsk shared a look with the barbarian who had glared at Ovelia. "I am, and I am not," he said. "I have a greater destiny than what Ruin offers."

"Lia..." Shard's voice seemed to come over a vast distance. "Lia, please..."

She could hear Dar-Karsk smile. He was drawing this out. Savoring it.

"I am the child cast aside," he said, his voice echoing. "That which you sought to abandon." He grew brighter even as she watched, his features sharpening until they had almost become distinct. "The exiled prince, thrown to death in the snow but reborn by the power of the Worldfire."

He raised his arms, and the air around him wavered. With her shadowy sight, Ovelia could see the magic forming and pulsing around him, and she recognized it for what it was. Since that terrible night six years ago when the Winter King had begged her—almost forced her—to run him through, and she had seen Orbrin's power flare to life and die as his own lifeblood slipped away. *Frostfire.*

"I am Darak Ravalis nô Denerre, King of Tar Vangr, and I have come to purge my city at last."

As the words resonated, before anyone could speak, his escort, the one who had looked at her with such intensity at first, raised their hands. *Her* hands, Ovelia realized too late, which had become almost entirely articulate in her smoky vision. Magic burned through the air, unraveling the barbarian's cloak and adornment, leaving skin-tight leather in its place. Hungry green magic burned around the figure, flaring from the death's head mask.

Mask.

Darak casually glanced to the sorcerer and spoke a single word. "Now."

Smoke boiled from Draca, and Ovelia ripped it from its scabbard.

~

When the green slaying magic began to stream out from the broken dome atop the palace of Tar Vangr, Regel the Frostburn almost lost his grip and had to scramble to cling to the sheer slope. A tiny squeak came from over his shoulder, and he could feel Sarelle's body shivering tight against his back.

He was too late.

That day, the climb he'd made as recently as six winters before seemed impossible. Wind howled around him and the snow melting on his upraised face burned like fire. He could not feel the chill, not with the power of Frostburn enfusing him, but the acid left tracks across his unprotected face. Perhaps he should have found a mask, but he hadn't had time.

And now he was still too late.

Regel strained to reach another handhold, but his body locked up and couldn't quite extend so far. He pawed at the stone, his fingers slipping, then swung back, his anchor arm aching with the effort to hold him up. He grasped the mountain with both hands and panted as he hung there, cursing at his weakened body that couldn't seem to accomplish this climb.

His lungs heaved and his heart hammered in his throat. His arms and legs burned. He should have taken more time. He should have thought, not just acted.

The girl made a tiny, incoherent noise. Regel had sworn to protect her, and even if he reached High-City, which was not at all sure, would the child survive the journey? He did not think so.

Regel looked up once more at the summit of the palace, where magic flashed like the fireworks he remembered on a long-ago Ruin's Night. His heart slowed and sorrow welled within him.

The stone he clung to shuddered, and Sarelle squeaked in surprise. Before Regel could react, a jagged chunk of the mountain tore away beneath him and they fell through the smoke and clouds.

Semana stared out at the gathered Tar Vangryur, who stood frozen in place like statues carved of living stone. Or not quite *frozen*, for they moved very, very slowly, like glaciers sweeping down the mountains, little by little over centuries. The warders slowly brought their weapons in line with the barbarian honor guard. The barbarians roared in response and brandished their axes and swords. The Ravalis boy king, his face lit with a kind of terrified confusion, raised a sword to point at Darak, who basked in his impending victory. Laegra Vargaen, whom Semana remembered from her youth in the palace as a sallow and bitter woman, turned to flee, a scream on her lips. Lady Shard, wrapped head to foot in black silks as always, stood straight and stared at her. Ovelia Dracaris, a strip of crimson cloth over her eyes and a linen dress straining to cover her swollen belly, raised her burning sword.

It was upon the Bloodbreaker that Semana fixed her attention. She moved faster than the others, almost but not quite as fast as she should have. Why did Semana perceive the world in this way, caught between one moment and the next, and why did Ovelia inhabit that same world with her?

"Semana..." The word started slow and accelerated to almost a normal cadence. Darak's voice, distorted as the moment stretched. "What are you waiting for...?"

Abruptly the world passed normally, and Semana became aware of herself standing in the throne room, chest heaving, blood pounding in her head. She had hesitated. She—

Casters barked, and power ripped across the throne room. One of the barbarians flew back, burning, to smash against the far wall, and Semana watched as a casterbolt ripped the arm off another in a bloody burst. A casterbolt sizzled past her ear. Laegra's scream flooded the chamber.

"Now, sister," Darak said. "Now!"

What had happened? Why had she hesitated? Half a dozen Ravalis stood before her: the last, most powerful members of the Blood. She could wipe them all away without effort. But why——?

A starburst of light dazzled her just as a massive force struck her in the chest, sending her pinwheeling back through the air. She hit the floor hard on her backside in an explosion of jarring pain. The world blurred for a few heartbeats, and when she came back to herself, she saw smoke rising from her breastplate. The shielding magic had protected her, but that had been a cast to the heart.

"Sister!" Darak was shouting.

Semana managed to lever herself to a sitting position. Chaos had erupted in the throne room. The barbarians had leaped upon the warders, closing the distance and negating the efficacy of their casters with brutal efficiency, but the numbers stood against them. Two of the Ravalis warders were down and one nobleman of the Blood, but now blades and shields crashed and slammed together in a stalemate of blood. One of the Ravalis men had fallen to his knees, a massive cut across his forehead, and blood poured down his face as he screamed in agony and terror. As Semana watched, a caster fired wildly, its deadly bolt of fire smashing into the wooden boards set in place of the glass above. The flames smoldered and caught. Darak kept screaming, but she could no longer hear him.

She might have sat there, stupefied, but then she saw Ovelia Dracaris, her burning sword darting like a snake. The woman's movements emphasized caution and the conservation of energy, even more than usual, but even encumbered with her late pregnancy, she was a fine warrior. She cut down one of the barbarians, sending the woman screaming to the ground with a bloody furrow carved through her chest, and silenced her with a backhand slash that took her head off.

Seeing Ovelia—alive, vibrant, and powerful—filled Semana with rage. She raised her hands and sent lances of green power snaking toward the combatants. The plaguefire struck one warder and boiled away the middle third of his body into brown, putrid muck. A second bolt arced around the collapsing corpse and cut down a gray-haired Ravalis, ripping rotting holes through his back and out his chest.

Semana felt them die—felt their vitality fill her with power—and she wanted more. *More.*

She climbed to her feet, power lashing all around her. She slew Ravalis after Ravalis, from those in the chamber to those who came rushing up to aid.

247

Boots pounded on the stairs and the doors flew open to admit new warders, who she cut down just as readily. Fire or lightning might have struck upon the protective dust magic ensorcellments of their armor, but the plaguefire cut right through them heedlessly as though their shielding plates of steel were made of snow.

Every one of them wore the face of her father Paeter, or else gave her uncle Lan's leering grin, or else stared at her with the disapproving eyes of Demetrus Ravalis. They were all her enemies. All of them wanted to destroy her and her family. Slaying them felt so entirely *right*, and the power filled her with an unstoppable righteous fury that would brook no doubt.

Reflected green flames danced in the remaining sheets of glass of the dome.

Laud Ravalis appeared, sword raised in a shaking hand, and he reached out toward her. How he had come so close, Semana couldn't say. She could barely hear through all the screams and loud crack of caster discharges, and she could see nothing outside of the faces and shuddering corpses of her victims. But Laud was there, eyes wild, blood trickling from his mouth. Someone was screaming her name.

Perhaps he meant to kill her, or perhaps he meant to surrender. Either way, she turned her power upon him, and watched as the green spears of power transfixed and rotted his body. Gray lines spread across his flesh, turning it to muddy offal. His eyes turned yellow, then red as blood drowned them, then popped as his skull folded in on itself. The reek washed over her, so powerful and fetid that she choked and thought she would die as well. Laud Ravalis died the instant the power touched him, but Semana ripped every ounce of life away before she let his desiccated corpse drop to the floor.

A scream drew her attention, and she saw Laegra Ravalis cowering at the door to the stairs, unable to make herself get up and wade through the corpses and the flashes of killing magic that filled them with death. She was curled around something—*someone*, Semana thought: a young boy, who had the distinct brown skin and red hair of a summerblood. Another Ravalis, perhaps even Lan's child? Hatred flared in Semana—hatred for Lan Ravalis—and she sent a storm of plaguefire toward the woman. Laegra bore no ensorcelled armor to protect her, and so that power would slay her when—

Abruptly, the power arced away from the cowering woman, hissed across the battlefield, and dissolved into the flaming blade of Draca. Ovelia stood, legs wide, face slick with sweat, and held the sword like a shield. Dimly, in the eerie green shadows, Semana saw Lady Shard standing behind her.

248

Semana screamed and drew on the power of her silver glove, meaning to wrench away one of the pillars of the chamber to hurl at her. Let the Bloodbreaker try to block *that*.

"Semana!" Darak held up his hands. "Hold."

Through the panting rage, Semana just barely managed to control herself, heaving.

The throne chamber of Tar Vangr was a moldering battlefield, riddled with corpses and choked with the smoke of discharged slaying magic. It had ripped bodies apart and splattered their guts, painting the walls with gore. Blood and bile dripped from the ceiling ten paces up. Those faces that still existed were nightmare masks of greenish flesh painted with trails of blood and foam from every orifice. Ovelia stood smeared in blood and viscera, her crimson hair plastered to her face and neck. The fire of the sword alone served to mark her out, and that power flickered—drained, perhaps?

Somewhere, a child was crying, and Semana could hear a woman weeping. Laegra? Herself?

The havoc of the plaguefire made it impossible to say how many lay slaughtered, with all the remains mingled. Dimly, Semana recognized limbs and a severed head belonging to the barbarians they had brought as their honor guard. Semana wondered how many she had killed with her reckless slaying magic. She'd just been so furious. So sure. And now, in the cold-numbed face of reality, she felt...

Nothing.

She wanted to scream, and might have, given another moment.

For his part, Darak made snuffling sounds that Semana recognized as the attempt to hold in laughter. Ultimately, he failed and loosed a triumphant guffaw.

"At last," he said. "The Blood of Ravalis is broken. Greatfather." He looked down to the stone and spread his arms wide. "Greatfather, you are avenged."

Semana blinked, trying to understand what had happened. She'd finally caught her breath.

Boots sounded on the steps, and more folk appeared past the heaving, panting Ovelia. They moved with caution, most armed but some empty-handed and aghast. They came to bear witness. Distantly, Semana recognized some of the faces from her childhood—folk she dimly recalled from royal decrees, Council gatherings, and other such functions. She saw no Ravalis faces among them. Had she broken the Blood of Summer entirely? But no, Darak lived. And *she* yet lived.

They had won.

Heedless of the many eyes upon him, Darak strode toward the moldering husk that had been Laud Ravalis. He stooped down to reach into the charnel pile and wrapped his fingers around one of the tines of the Diadem of Winter, which gleamed from amongst the offal in the first rays of the rising sun. He drew it up, awkwardly as though it carried surprising weight, and gasps emerged from the shocked onlookers. Semana realized belatedly that the rotted remains of the young king's head had stuck in the circlet and drooled pus down toward the floor. Darak pulled an annoyed face and slapped the heel of his palm against the circlet a few times until finally the head squelched free and dropped to the floor. There it split open like an overripe fruit, spewing blood and brains that smelled of rotting fish.

Somewhere from among the group of horrified onlookers came vomiting sounds. More cries of disgust and alarm rose when, heedless of how disgusting it was, Darak pressed his nose and lips to the crown as though to inhale the fragrance of a sweet apple. He tasted the silver.

"I am Darak Ravalis nô Denerre," he said. "First and true heir to the throne of Tar Vangr. I expect my coronation to transpire before nightfall. You may bow."

The shock held the silence. Of them all, only Ovelia presented any real threat, but she had yet to move a single step in their direction. She meant only to protect Lady Shard, Semana realized. Why?

Suddenly, a vision came upon her: a thoroughly mad thought of what Ovelia's stance might mean. But surely that made no sense. Surely it was only a product of her excited mind.

And yet she knew what would come to pass with frightening surety, and knew all was lost.

"Why do you hesitate?" Darak asked. "Am I not the eldest blooded heir of Tar Vangr's last true king? I demand your acknowledgement. And your obeisance." He raised his left hand to point at them, and more than one of those gathered flinched away in terror from the mere gesture. He extended one finger, pointing toward the floor at their feet. "Kneel."

A tremor passed through the group. It did not pass immediately, but at length one of the winterborn warders lowered his weapon and sank to one knee. It broke the others' resolve, and they knelt in a wave. A handful, a dozen, and then all of them showed their obeisance to the Winter King's heir. And as each of them knelt, Darak's smile grew a little wider—a little more powerful. This was the moment of victory he had spent half his life working and waiting to achieve.

Semana looked to Ovelia, who did not kneel. Her crimson hair spilled down around her, gore dripping onto the floor, and Semana realized that she trembled. Afraid, perhaps? Yes, but not of Darak, and not of Semana. No, Ovelia had foreseen what would come to pass next, just as Semana had.

"My lady," she said over her shoulder. "My lady, do not—"

Semana realized Lady Shard yet stood, very aware of Darak's command but refusing it. She stared across at him with a stance coiled into determination and power. Semana could not see her face through the veil, but she thought that if she could, she'd have seen a face of triumph, not fear.

"You," Darak said across to Shard. "You are the skyship pirate, I think. Perhaps you think yourself not under my rule. That I must make further allowances to—"

"No," Shard said, the word so sharp it cut through the tension in the room like lightning.

For three frenzied heartbeats, Semana found herself falling into her mask and her other relics, ascertaining how much power yet remained. The plaguefire mask was almost exhausted, and her silver glove had lost much of its charge. The gauntlet still boasted most of its power, and her flying boots. She had enough to get away, but why had she thought of escape?

"No?" Darak blinked rapidly three times. "No, we need not negotiate further, or—?"

"No, I'll not bow to you," Shard said. "Not ever."

Then she reached up to pull her veil aside. And her face...

Semana caught her breath, and Darak made a little strangled sound of surprise.

The face was mangled, as though from a hundred razors. A dozen deep pink scars pulled at the woman's features, pinching her right cheek, carving off part of her nose, and giving the left end of her lower lip a distinct downward curl that exposed the hint of teeth. One eye bore a mask of scars all around it and the eyelid drooped halfway over the silvery-blue iris. One ear was almost entirely gone, and she wore her silvery blonde hair in scar-outlined tufts from the pale skin of her scalp. The marks of old stitches and sutures left raised, angry red welts across the side of her head. Her eyes gleamed vividly at Semana, however, and there was not a trace in that horrid visage of hesitation or fear.

And despite the ravages of cutting glass and the long years of imperfect healing, Semana knew that face immediately. Darak did as well, but in his case he found his voice. He stammered slightly as he'd done in his boyhood, prompting looks of sympathy from grown folk and sneers from youths.

"Mother?" Darak asked, breathless.

And in that moment, Semana's unnameable dread came to pass.

"I am Lenalin Denerre," she said, her voice scratching like fingernails upon rough-hewn stone. "The king is dead, and so you shall have a *queen*."

Darak's breath caught, strangled halfway between a gasp and a scream of hatred.

The world ceased to make sense for a moment then, and Semana could not track what was happening. Lenalin, somehow alive after so many years gone, glaring upon her with dark righteousness. Darak, with whom she had only recently reunited, suddenly cajoling her to kill their mother. Ovelia bearing witness without sight, the crimson band that protected her burned eyes impenetrable. Ovelia, who even now began to stalk forward, sword held between them like a talisman.

"Up," Lenalin said, the word a thunder peal that filled the room. She was not talking to Semana or Darak, but to the gathered Tar Vangryur. "Up and draw steel, cowards! Defend your realm!"

"Semana!" Darak was saying. "Semana, you rutting *wretch*! Semana!"

It was Ovelia who had let her regain control before, and it was Ovelia who did so again.

With a cry, Semana drew upon the magic of her silver glove and sent a blade of force slashing toward Ovelia. Draca parried it, though it struck with enough force to make her stagger. Even as she did, Semana brought her gauntleted hand forward, pouring forth a gout of flame that should have burned them all—all but Lenalin, who stood back enough that the battle would not touch her. But all that power went into Ovelia's sword, the flames consumed by Draca's flames and dispersed to nothing. The legendary warding blade of Blood Dracaris glowed a brilliant scarlet with power, and it struck Semana as oddly tragic that Ovelia could not see the sun rising in her hands.

With a cry, Darak thrust his fists into the floor, and great furrows churned away from him through the stone. He was using the Worldfire, and not to great effect: the power of Ruin held less sway over stone worked by the hands of men and women. She heard him gasping and cursing to call the power forth, and he sent a shockwave through the floor strong enough to throw most of their would-be attackers off their feet, and spoil more than one cast sent in their direction. Casters cracked and bolts sailed past them. One smashed off the waning protective magic over Semana's right shoulder, making her arm go numb from the force and dropping her fire gauntlet to her side.

One struck true, however: Darak's leg shot out from under him, and he fell face first into the muck. The Diadem of Winter bounced off his head and rolled, despite his flailing attempt to catch it.

"No," he said, sobbing with pain and frustration. "*No!*"

"Semana," said a warm, compassionate voice, and she realized Ovelia was approaching her, sword held to one side to shield from magic, but the other hand extended. "Please, Semana—"

None of this made sense. Semana could barely think, and she thought she wavered on the edge of madness. Who could stand in this place, as she stood now, and keep their mind intact?

She moved, hardly aware of what she was doing, and tried to pick Darak up with her silver glove, but she didn't have the power remaining. Instead, she seized his blood and forced his body screaming to its feet despite his leg. Darak cried out for mercy and cursed her name, but she forced him to put his arms around her. Another gout of flame discouraged would-be pursuers, and Ovelia hung back to drink the flames into Draca. Some of the warders were singed, however, and fell cursing to the floor.

Semana sent a wave of force smashing into the wooden scaffold erected to rebuild the great glass dome after she had shattered it the previous Ruin's Night, blowing a massive hole in the side of the throne room. Rain turned to sleet poured down upon them, and stung where it touched exposed flesh. Darak was screaming. Semana thought that at least with her Frostfire she could not feel the chill.

She turned one last time, and found Lenalin gazing out at her, through the haze and smoke and carnage of the battlefield. Their eyes met, and Semana was once again a child: a girl living through her third winter, experiencing what would become her earliest and most cherished memory.

The child Semana buried her face in her mother's skirts and inhaled her sweet perfume, hiding as she did from the specter of death that was the Frostburn. She had never liked him as a child—never understood why her warm, beautiful mother would spend even a heartbeat in his ugly, cold presence. But Semana could cling tight to Lenalin's leg, and look up into her face and see love. Tenderness. The only such she had ever known in her young life.

"Mother," Semana said, though there was no way Lenalin could hear over that distance.

And yet, somehow Lenalin heard and understood. She narrowed her good eye and pulled back her lips in a grimace of pain and disgust. There was no love, not even long-lost love. Only hate.

"Not my child," she said. "You are not my child."

A scream rose in Semana's throat but she choked it back.

She threw herself and the cursing Darak out into the winter night, her boots streaming smoke and murk as she bore them both far, far away.

TWENTY-ONE

A S DAWN WAXED OVER Tar Vangr, light finally broke through the thick gray clouds on the distant horizon. It was, perhaps, the first time since the start of winter that unfiltered rays of sun fell upon Tar Vangr, illumining the smoke rising to shroud High-City. The city stood, teetering but unfallen, scarred and gravely injured but alive. Whether the hurts would prove mortal, the next days would determine.

The light lingered for a moment, then vanished when the clouds massed once more and strangled it. Ruin would not let hope remain for long.

Standing on the balcony of the throne chamber, her unbound hair streaming, Ovelia felt the fleeting warmth on her face, and could not shake the feeling that she would not experience it again.

Her stomach stung as the child kicked, and she well understood their frustration. After such a long time, no wonder they longed for freedom.

"Not long now," Ovelia said, her voice a faint whisper. "But the life I wanted for you…" She shook her head. "It's too late now."

"Is it?"

The hand that touched her arm should have surprised Ovelia, but she had known it was coming. She had seen all this, even if she only remembered it now.

"You know there are folk in there advising me to break the support spells and drop a quarter of High-City on the bulk of the barbarians?" asked the Queen of Tar Vangr, in a conversational tone. "It's madness. These folk are mad."

"This was all your plan," Ovelia said. It was not a question.

Lenalin Denerre—she had officially shed the hateful name "Ravalis"—stiffened at Ovelia's side. Gone were the black silks that shielded her body head to toe, and she wore instead some manner of gown appropriate to a highborn Tar Vangryur. Ovelia could see her only faintly, and not the colors of her garb, but she suspected Lenalin had chosen white and silver to honor her Blood.

Anything less would hardly do for the Queen of Tar Vangr.

No doubt the expedited coronation had been lovely: banners and gowns hastily gathered, musicians recruited from the refugee masses, and the like. Not that Ovelia, standing at the side of the throne as they crowned Lenalin, had seen any of it. They'd even made an effort to cleanse the mess Semana's magic had left of most of the Ravalis and their inner guard, but Ovelia could still smell it. She couldn't stand that chamber, and she'd left as soon as she could. Even now her stomach turned, and her child seemed to like it even less. They'd been kicking steadily for some time now.

"This was your plan from the beginning," Ovelia said. "Taking back the throne. As soon as you saw me in Luether. Mayhap before."

Lenalin responded only at length. "You were the one who brought us here, not I."

Ovelia shook her head. "How many years have we known each other, Lena?" she asked. "You always made your own choices, even if they were bad ones."

At first, the queen seemed about to argue the point, but she merely chuckled. "Speaking of bad choices," she said. "Do I seem like the sort to sail to my death?"

Ovelia acknowledged the irony. They were, after all, trapped.

Icebergs had closed over the dock, blocking Tar Vangr from any passage by sea, and the thick drifts of snows prevented any attempt to traverse the surrounding lands. They were frozen in place, trapped in an icy chrysalis at least until spring, if not forever. The *Hecatomb* still could not fly, though the thaumaturges had assured the new queen they would have it air-worthy as soon as possible.

Again, Ovelia shook her head. "You'd not throw your life away. You came here with a plan."

The world shifted slightly around her. Draca loosed puffs of smoke, and she thought suddenly that it presaged some threat. Only then did Ovelia realize the balcony behind them had filled with folk. Treachery? A coup attempt, when the queen had just ascended and would not expect it? She braced for an attack—humming swords or the whine of casters—but none of them had drawn steel. Perhaps she had a chance to escape with Lenalin. She appraised the situation in precious heartbeats, searching for the opening to carve a path. She reached for Draca.

As she reached for the sword, Lenalin caught her hand and held it firmly.

"What—?" Ovelia started, but Lenalin's lips touched her own, cutting her off.

"What," Lenalin said, "if *you* are my plan?"

Ovelia's stomach lurched, and she thought her child was laughing. How could that be?

A soft grunt of effort sounded, and Ovelia realized Lenalin had lowered herself to one knee. "My father should have done this all those years ago," the queen said. "I will make this right."

"Done what—?" Breath caught in Ovelia's throat.

The gathered folk were not here to attack, but to bear witness.

"I know what you did for my father—for my Blood," Lenalin said. "And I know what you have done for me." She took Ovelia's hands. "Stand and lie beside me. As I am queen to Tar Vangr, so shall you be queen to me." Her eyes appeared in Ovelia's shadowy world: pure silver pools. "Be mine."

In that moment, Ovelia saw how this would all pass. She saw her path and Lenalin's; she saw Regel and Semana and Tithian Davargorn, and the part they would all play. She did not know how it would end—there was still time enough to make those choices—but she saw what was needful. That darkness would come, yes, but for now, for this moment, perhaps she did not have to face it. Perhaps—

"Yes," Ovelia said. "*Yes.*"

Only when the cloth over her eyes felt damp did Ovelia realize she was weeping.

Lenalin rose and wrapped her arms around Ovelia. "You are safe, my beloved," she said.

A pleased gasp went through the gathered folk, and applause and praise rose. Warm in Lenalin's arms, Ovelia leaned her head against the woman's shoulder and no longer tried to stop the tears.

This, for now, was enough.

⤳

In Low-City Tar Vangr, in his tent of tanned hides staked out over the Narfire warmed streets, Darak Ravalis nô Denerre gave voice and action to his fury as never before. Nothing was safe. He rent totems and tribute given him by the clans of his horde, pounded weapons claimed from fallen foes on the cobblestones, and shattered bottles of fine liquors of every color and taste one after another. He hefted a crystal decanter nearly the size of his head high into the air and brought it down with a thunderous crash, sending wine splattering and broken glass scattering across the tent.

He'd come so close—slain all his rivals, sat upon the throne of Tar Vangr, even worn the Diadem of Winter—and yet.

To come so far, only to fail. And not through his own actions—because of *her*.

Darak's mind burned too hot to identify exactly which "her" he meant—Lenalin, Semana, perhaps even Ovelia—and he didn't care. It was all of them. They had conspired to deny him his due.

He meant to kick over a fallen pot, but he'd put all his weight on his injured leg, and it abruptly buckled and put him flat on his backside, sudden pain blossoming up his back. The power armor had kept the casterbolt from shattering his leg, but it still hurt awfully.

There he sat, furious and rubbing at his sore leg.

Darak had always understood his father's distrust of women. He had failed to engineer his mother's death, and the horrible woman had forced Paeter to banish him from the city. He'd seen, at that moment, how his father had been unmanned. He was weak. Subservient to a woman.

He'd hoped to escape that same curse among the barbarians, but to no avail. If anything, it was *worse*. There, women had restrained Darak at every turn, frustrating his every attempt to propel himself forward. Afferath had held him back. The Circle had rejected him. Even Carr, the most mannish woman he knew, had stood against him and he had been left no choice but to drive her away after her defeat.

But it was not until this night that he saw the reach of the curse they presented. Not until he stared into the ruined face of his mother and saw the death of all his dreams.

Never shall a woman rule over a man. That was a truth of the Ravalis, and he should have cleaved to it more closely. If he hadn't trusted any of them, mayhap he wouldn't have come to this end.

Semana. His sister had arrived ostensibly to help, and he couldn't deny the use she had proved. But she had counseled delay and worked to undermine his every decision. And now, tonight, she had spoiled all his hopes—first by her damned hesitation, and then secondly by failing to slay their mother.

Lenalin rutting Denerre. Ruin burn her. Burn them *all*.

A sharp intake of breath alerted him to the presence of someone at the flap of his tent. He looked, ready to scream at Semana, but it was not her. Instead, there stood Crown of Fire, who looked at the ruin of his chief's tent with shock and confusion. Behind him stood Fellis the Night Wolf, her face hard in the muddy darkness.

"Oh," Darak said. "It's you."

Another day, seeing Fellis's glare might have made him wary, but just now, the fury wouldn't let him think through the implications. Let her try to ingratiate herself with him. He wouldn't mind a little stroking of his ego, and perhaps a few other things. She would remind him of her power and purpose, and he would pay lip service to her value. Sometimes literally, but in most cases she only liked to watch.

As it passed, however, such was not her aim.

He felt the power swelling around her, filling the air like a living, breathing thing. In his weariness and anger, he casually pushed back against it as at an irritating fly, thinking it would pass as always. When he rebounded from a wall of heavy air around her, he ended up on his backside amongst the ruins of his tent. He blinked away his dizzy surprise.

"This is a leavetaking," Fellis said, her voice sharp and certain. "You have failed, Dar-Karsk, and the Circle will no longer condone such weakness."

"Wait—" he said, but abruptly his body felt like it was on fire. His blood coursed hot and fast and sweat poured down his face. He could barely pant, much less speak.

"This is not a conversation." Fellis strode toward him, past a quaking and terrified Crown of Fire. She towered over him as he sat, struggling to breathe, and her eyes gleamed crimson in the firelight. "Your weakness has led us all to our doom, and now you must pay the price in blood."

Pain such as he had never experienced locked Darak's body in a mute statue.

Darak choked out a reply, one word at a time. "We... rule... this... city."

"Rule?" Fellis looked unimpressed. "The land has closed, and the sea is cut off. We are prisoners, not rulers. We should have left with Carr, but we stayed, believing in your promises. Now you have trapped the horde within these frozen walls with no hope of escape until the spring, with our enemies safe above us." She shook her head. "You condemn the horde to its death, through your foolishness and your false pride. You have betrayed all of us."

Her last words sounded so powerful and dark they made the air tremble. Behind her, Crown of Fire gave a little strangled gasp. Darak was surprised he had not pissed himself and fled already.

"You..." Darak managed to fight off the pain. "Don't care... for them. Only... yourself."

Fellis gave him a grim smile. "Mine is the power of the Worldfire," she said. "I will endure, and I will leave this place. But you." The smile turned venomous. "This place is your tomb. I shall see to it."

For the first time, Darak became aware of what she was holding. He'd often seen her with the ashwood bow inlaid with bone, but he'd never seen it pointed directly at him. The arrow that stretched the string gave off faint wisps of black smoke, and he saw that the head glowed red with heat. He'd seen her kill men before with this power, and it had never occurred to him to wonder what it must look like to her intended victims. It was oddly beautiful.

She loosed her arrow, but her aim went wide. Darak felt it hum past his cheek and stab instead into the ground near the edge of the tent. Instantly, it burst into flames that licked at the water-stained skin. Darak looked up at Fellis, whose expression had changed from one of hate to one of surprise. As he watched, a trickle of some dark liquid ran down between her eyes, and Darak realized it was blood.

She coughed, and blood flicked from her twitching mouth and onto his face.

Then her eyes rolled, her face slackened, and she collapsed to the side. There was an axe buried in her head, and attached to its handle was Crown of Fire's hand. The two men stared at one another over the body of Fellis the Night Wolf, which lay in a spread pool of deep red blood. Crown of Fire looked wide-eyed with terror and far, far too young. Vulnerable.

Darak thought his slave might have seen more winters than he, but until that moment hadn't understood them nearly as well.

The tent, Darak realized, had caught flames. He saw their flicker reflected in Crown's eyes and felt the heat at the same time. With a glance over his shoulder, he saw that Fellis's conjured fire had clung to the walls of the tent and was even now consuming it with raging hunger. As Crown half-sat, half-stood, flames had leaped from the tent to his sleeve, and he could only stare. The fire had become a living thing, furious at the death of its mother and desperate to avenge her.

It might have done so, had not Darak seized Crown of Fire by the collar of his robe. He hissed the lad's name, startling him from his stupor, and Crown began screaming in sudden pain. Darak hauled him bodily out of the tent and they collapsed to the slushy cobblestones of the square. Behind them, Fellis's magic consumed his shelter in a raging howl of fury and promises of doom. He thought he could see her face in the flames, screaming wrathfully but, ultimately, impotently.

He sneered at the fire. This was *his* destiny and his alone.

Belatedly, Darak remembered Crown of Fire's burning arm. The man rubbed the arm futilely in the wet and muck, but the flames still raged up toward his face. It took a heartbeat's consideration, but Darak determined the slave still held value. He drew Worldfire into himself and used the increased strength to lift Crown and dash him into a nearby snowdrift that had only started to melt at the base. He forcibly rolled the man around, like a thrashing dog pushed into a bath, and the flames went out.

A moment later, Darak took note of the fifty or sixty barbarians gathered around the burning tent, staring at him intently. Crown of Fire lay in the snow, weeping and shivering, his arm a red and black mess. Likely he would live, but Darak did not much care. He'd served his purpose.

"Come," Darak said. "We will find my sister, and I will show you all is not lost."

After the ceremony of joining, in which she was invested with the full powers and dignity of the queen of Tar Vangr, Ovelia felt something she'd not expected. A sensation she'd not known in, well, she didn't remember how long. Perhaps she hadn't felt this way since before King Orbrin had asked her to kill him and Semana had disappeared. Before Paeter had sent Lenalin crashing through a mirror. Before the day the Ravalis and Denerre had joined their Blood, and Ovelia had seen their world falling to pieces.

As she lay upon the queen's bed, she felt, in a word, *happy*.

She felt a faint pressure in her lower body, reminding her of her babe. It seemed unfair, that she could lie here happily, when worthier folk like Garin were dead and gone. She wondered where she might find Regel, whom they hadn't seen since Lan led his assault on Low-City. Logic dictated he was likely dead, but Ovelia hadn't let herself believe it. Perhaps it was her sight, or perhaps it was her guilt. If she'd outlived even Regel, that gave the lie to any sense of justice.

Not that she was completely happy. Her body had disappointed her time and again, and it grew worse by the day. She felt uncomfortable all the time. She could endure the frustrating discomfort, however—after today, she felt she could endure anything.

But even so, she might have allowed herself this happiness. She could have ignored her guilt and embraced joy, at least for now. Silver Fire knew she had done so enough times in the past: justified the hardest sacrifices and the worst actions for the sake of doing what was right. But there was something else: a dark thread that ran through the tapestry she wrapped over herself to keep the coldness of the world at bay. And she had to know.

"Why?" Ovelia asked. "Why me?"

"Hmm?" Across the room, Lenalin inspected her scarred face in a silvered glass. She hardly seemed aware of the question, but Ovelia knew she had heard her well.

Lenalin herself had become very clear in her shadowy sight, growing more and more opaque as time passed. Anyone else might have considered the events of that day proof of Lenalin's good intentions and support, but Ovelia had grown intimately familiar with her sight and how it functioned. She knew what this meant, even if she feared it.

She knew.

Ovelia rose from the bed and wrapped a blanket around her swollen body. "Why take me as your companion?" she asked. "Why bind your life to mine?"

"Expediency," Lenalin said. "Binding you to the Blood of Denerre exculpates your infamy."

Ovelia crossed to the side of Lenalin's desk, feeling her way along the edge. "I am still a pariah in Tar Vangr," she said. "My Blood has no power in this city anymore. I can't offer you anything."

"Your magic, then." Lenalin looked to her, voice calm. "You see things I cannot and shall not."

"You've ignored my counsel," Ovelia said. "I didn't want you to remain in Tar Vangr. I didn't want you to go to meet with the barbarians. You have your own plans. You don't need me."

"I had a duty to you," Lenalin said. "I know what you did for my father."

Ovelia shivered, but she would not be distracted. "He never owed me a debt, and what I did, I did freely." She laid one hand on Lenalin's arm, and the woman grew still under her touch. "So why?"

She shouldn't ask this, Ovelia knew. Lenalin had just learned that Darak yet lived, and had come to Tar Vangr to throw down the city. She was dealing with enough darkness. Surely Ovelia should be a rock of support, not a source of challenge. But she had to know.

"Why did you choose me?" Ovelia asked.

"Because I love you," Lenalin said.

They both knew that was true, and they both knew that was not the reason. Lenalin loosed a long, sad sigh, and she grew even sharper in Ovelia's perception. Ovelia could almost make out Lenalin's disfigured face: the scars and tightened muscles and torn features she had only been able to feel with her fingers and lips.

"I have need of you," Lenalin said, because of course she did.

"To fight your war." Ovelia felt a pang in her belly. Certainly the baby wasn't ready to come—it was too early, yet. It must have been something she ate at the feast. "Please reconsider. The *Hecatomb* isn't fully repaired. If you try to fly it—"

"There is no more time," Lenalin said. "We have been casting down climbers for days now, and sooner or later we will run out of casterbolts. The Children are bleeding us of our resources. All our other skyships are crashed or have abandoned us. The Narfire is our last, best option."

So. Lenalin would unleash the Narfire, as the Ravalis had done twenty years ago, as Luether fell. It would burst forth from the mountain of Tar Vangr and destroy everyone and everything in its path.

"It's death," Ovelia said. "It's mass murder."

"It's war." Lenalin sighed. "But this is not what I mean."

Ovelia nodded. "What must I do?"

"You—" Lenalin bit her lip. "Does the Frostburn live?" she asked. "Have you seen this?"

"Yes." Ovelia did not hesitate.

"Then I will ask this thing of him," she said. "Not of you."

Ovelia started to protest, but the queen took her hand in both of her own.

"It can wait," she said. "It should wait. Until your child is born. I do not—" She shook her head. "I do not want this darkness between us. I want something good."

Ovelia saw the future spiraling out ahead of them. She smiled.

"Then you shall have it."

❧

She stood at the blasted and blackened threshold of the Burned Man tavern, staring down at her hands, which trembled in the dawn light. Her hands that were spotless but slaked in blood.

How much time had passed, Semana could not say; it all seemed to blur in her mind. She'd longed for a vision or perhaps madness to set in—for some sort of release—but instead she only perceived her hands, trembling slightly, and beyond them the wreckage of the building.

Part of one wall yet stood, covered in the ugly bruises of fire, and the heavy posts that formed the front doorway. Otherwise, the once-powerful edifice had become only rubble and ash. A yawning cavity in the cobblestones marked the remains of the basement, where the Circle of Tears had hid in the wake of the Ravalis's destruction of their base of operations, then fled before the invasion. Semana did not know if the Ravalis or the horde had found the basement, but it was little more than a black festering wound now.

She remembered laughter and bravery and strength in this place, which was now a graveyard.

In a way, she could say much the same of Tar Vangr itself. The last Mage-City, which had stood so proud among the clouds, now crumbling and all but succumbed to Ruin. Not that Semana had much love for her homeland or the city that had claimed her youth, her greatfather, her mother...

Her mother.

Not my child, Lenalin had said. *You are not my child.*

It still hurt. As though the woman had stabbed her in the middle and left the knife there, the hilt standing up from between her ribs. Semana reached up to feel at her leather-shielded stomach and knew dim surprise when she found no such weapon. She was exhausted.

"All things die," she said under her breath. "All things fall to Ruin."

She had practically no magic left in her relics, having used it all in the treachery in the palace, and then to get Darak and herself safely down from the mountain. If someone attacked her now…

The sound of a boot scuffing on stone behind her seized Semana's attention, and she spun, calling slaying magic into her hands by instinct. Tithian's masked face peered at her from the depths of his cowl, and the instant she recognized him, she let the magic dissipate and drain away.

"Master," he said.

"You're hurt," she said, noting his limp and the way he carried himself.

"Temporarily," he said. "You?"

Semana's heart pounded in her chest. She, who had never been at a loss for words, couldn't manage to speak. With a titanic effort of will, she made a tiny movement toward him, just half a step.

That was enough. He stepped forward and put his arms around her in a warm, firm embrace that both supported and protected her. Had his arms always been so strong? For the first time since the cave in the south Dusk Sea, she felt safe.

Semana indulged in the feeling for a long moment, then could no longer ignore the world around them. She pulled away and looked around him.

"The child," she said. "Sarelle."

"Gone," he said. "Claimed by the Frostburn."

She nodded. She'd not *known* that would come to pass, but it did not surprise her. Regel the Frostburn still had a part to play in this, that she knew.

Tithian was looking at her very closely, and abruptly Semana felt ill at ease. Her arms tingled where he had touched her, and she hugged herself, rubbing at the leather in a vain attempt to scratch that itch. It was strange indeed to touch him in that way, after so many years fearing that he would not understand. Even now, after what they had shared in the cave and beyond, she was not entirely comfortable. She wondered if she ever would be.

Tithian's eyes had hardened, and Semana realized his gaze had settled over her shoulder. She turned her head halfway, peering out through the eye slits in her own mask, and took in the group of barbarians heading her way, along with a bandaged and whimpering Crown of Fire. Darak was at their head, and she could tell at a glance they split the difference between honor guard and death dealers. And by her brother's pale face, she got the distinct impression which course they favored would depend on what came to pass in the next moments.

At her side, Tithian tensed, blades drawn, but Semana touched his wrist gently to keep him at bay. She thought she could draw upon her Frostfire, not that it would even touch Darak, and her Blood magic felt far away. She tried to get a taste for his blood, but it eluded her. She felt so tired.

"Dar-Karsk." She looked to her brother, who seemed wary but not anxious. The man had a damnable self-confidence to him she found very unsettling. "What brings you to—?"

Before she knew what had happened, Darak moved across the intervening space and clouted her heavily on the cheek with Worldfire-powered force. She came back to herself on her backside on the ground, the world spinning and apparently gone mad.

Tithian had burst into motion and even now held half a dozen barbarians at bay through force of will and brandished blades. Darak was loudly declaiming something Semana couldn't make out: her ear rang where he had struck her, so she could barely make out what they said. Crown of Fire was nowhere to be seen, but she thought she could hear his voice calling her name, just a whisper against all the cries and shouts. Her heart pounded in her head and her limbs tingled, half numb from the blow.

No one had ever struck her like that: so casually and without any warning. It had taken her utterly by surprise, and she hardly knew what to think.

Darak's attack seemed to have increased his standing among the barbarians. They clamored around him, raising their axes and spears and swords, and he stood with his arms raised like an angel that strides upon the earth. Like one of the lost gods, who had abandoned the world to Ruin long ago.

"I am Darak Ravalis," he was saying, she thought. "The true king of Tar Vangr, and you will all kneel before me. Together, we shall throw down this city…"

Now that her mind had come back into focus, shock turned to anger, rage built within her, and Semana tasted Darak's blood hot in her mouth. The Blood magic came easily now.

She would slay him, however weak she felt. Slay him and…

He turned to her but she could barely hear him, his words distorted as though through flames. She could hear it flickering around her, speaking with a thousand tiny voices. She thought if she strained, perhaps she could hear them, and so she did. The words seemed familiar, but she couldn't quite—

The ground rumbled beneath her and she fell to one knee. None of the barbarians shouting at her seemed to have been affected or even to have noticed. Completely unaffected, Darak kept shouting until his face turned purple. Semana reached toward him, as though to bat aside a noisome fly, and saw that her hand was bare and wreathed in silver flame. She waggled her fingers, watching as the flames danced around them. It reminded her of watching the Frostburn dance a coin across his knuckles.

Around her rose a column of silver flame. The Narfire grew all around her, flowing around her body and into it, fusing with her bones. Stifling a cry of surprise more than pain, Semana realized she was pulling in the Narfire and it fueled her magic. Her fingers shook and her teeth chattered at the effort required to control even this taste of it.

She was invincible. Immortal. All powerful.

The column of silver fire risen around her burned away suddenly into an inverted tower of windows, all of which depicted a different scene. She saw wind-swept mountains and barren deserts and islands amid vast blue oceans. Cities she saw as well: streets of cobbled stone overshadowed by brick buildings that leaned together in their age and damp contrasted with shining edifices of steel and stone where folk flew about on chariots in the sky. Such wonders—worlds upon worlds beyond this world—if only she had the power to seek them out.

A voice spoke to her, like thunder rising from the depths of the earth below. It made her bones shiver and her heart tremor and she knew, somehow, that it was her own voice. Not hers as she spoke now, but hers as she might speak, if she had the power of the Narfire. If she could channel the full power into herself, from the heart of the Silver Fire…

"*Come,*" it said.

Abruptly the vision ended, scattering away like the fragments of a dream upon waking, but this time she remembered it. She knew the way she felt. She knew, at long last, what the visions meant.

What she was to do.

And looking at the glittering eyes of the gathered barbarians, Semana knew how to achieve it.

BOOK FIVE: DESTROYERS

Eighteen years ago—The third day of the year, 964
Sorceris Annis—Tar Vangr, City of Steel

THE FIRST TIME LENALIN Denerre nô Ravalis laid eyes on the little silver-blonde headed child—as she sat in the gazebo at the heart of her garden, overlooking the wide, stunning view of the Dusk Sea laid out before them—she could hardly stop herself from vomiting in disgust.

"This is the whelp, is it?" Lenalin took care not to slur her words.

Ovelia stiffened, the harsh tone cracking against her dutiful expression like a casterbolt fired within a dozen paces. Standing just ahead of her, Orbrin Denerre in his silver and white robes smiled broadly. Trust her father to take even the harshest barbs in stride.

"This is your second child, indeed," he said, nodding down to the babe swaddled in his arms. "Semana Denerre nô Ravalis."

Her husband's name further soured Lenalin's stomach, mingling with the entirely too much wine that she had drunk already that morn in preparation for this meeting. She was exhausted and weak.

"The creature has a name already, does it?" Lenalin asked. "At least our name comes first."

This all seemed so needless, with Paeter away at war. Better to say her babe had perished in the birthing bed. No doubt he would be glad of it, and Lenalin herself would certainly be relieved. Bad enough that she had to ward Darak: the little beast was lingering at the edge of the gazebo, watching this meeting with cold, appraising eyes. So like his father in that way, if nothing else.

"Well." Lenalin's fingers twitched toward the jug of wine half-hidden behind her divan in the gazebo, but she dared not drink in front of her father, the king. "Let me see the little creature, then."

Orbrin approached, looking down at her and the child with the same indulgent smile, making the wine sloshing in Lenalin's stomach threaten to come back up. She'd been in the birthing bed two days gone, and ate nothing but drank much ever since. Whatever it took to blight out those horrid memories. The screaming. The agony. The monstrosity.

Orbrin presented the babe for Lenalin's inspection. "Your child."

266

It was nothing in the little child's face that prompted Lenalin's visceral loathing. Indeed, the child was quite comely, with the fine features of a highborn scion of winter and warm skin with a yellowish tinge. They were definitely winterborn, though their coloration was notably darker than Lenalin's own skin. The pigment suggested heritage from both winter and summer. How appropriate. The child even had a short mess of silvery-blonde hair, which almost made Lenalin gag at the similarity to her own.

"And what is it, this child?" Lenalin asked. "Boy or girl?"

Orbrin looked startled at the question. "But—that is not—"

Behind him, Ovelia's cheeks glowed with red pinpricks of hot blood. "Lena—" she said.

"Well, if they are to be the child of a Summer Prince, then should they not be born in the culture of Summer?" Lenalin asked. "Forced down a single path and shamed for it?"

She refused to be the only one who suffered that indignity.

Orbrin shook his head. "That is not the way of Winter," he said. "Do not—"

"A girl, then." Lenalin held up a hand to stay Orbrin's objection. "If, as she grows, she finds we were wrong to name her so, I will accept it with a loving heart."

She almost hoped such would come to pass, just to watch Paeter squirm.

"A girl, then." Orbrin sounded only a little unsettled by his daughter's declaration. "Would you name her, then? She *is* your child."

Lenalin glared at him balefully. "Do *not* ask that of me."

They struggled for a tense moment, father and daughter, without words. Finally, Orbrin relented and nodded in deference. "So shall she be, Semana Denerre nô Ravalis, Princess of Tar Vangr, Heir to the Blood of Winter and Summer both."

Ovelia released a relieved breath. "So shall she be."

Lenalin carefully kept her features schooled. *To satisfy your own political ambitions, Father?* she thought but did not say. The indignity of it all. The gall.

For a heartbeat, she considered lurching to her feet, grabbing the child, and hurling her from the battlements. Watch Orbrin's face fall in horror, and perhaps even hear Ovelia scream.

But that would be cruel, and though Lenalin had cruel thoughts, she would not act upon them. She was a target of Paeter's cruelty and a receptacle for Orbrin's cruelty. She could endure this.

Darak made a small noise, and Orbrin looked up to see him. Greatfather and child locked eyes, and the Winter King smiled gently. "Come," he said. "Meet your sister."

267

Darak hopped down from the stone planting box where he had perched and ambled over. He was a precocious child of only two or three winters—Lenalin hardly remembered anymore—but he had the shrewd, cruel features of the summer blood. His face split into a smile upon looking down at the tiny little child, and Lenalin forced herself to smile.

"Sister," Darak said. "My sister. Mine."

A happy domestic scene. Praise the Nar.

If only Paeter had left to go on campaign before learning Lenalin was with child, this could have been avoided. But he was always watching her—tracking her courses and insisting on what she could eat, what she could drink, and especially whose society she could seek. Paeter had known of her pregnancy even before she had. She had laughed that day, three seasons gone, when he insisted she see Maure to confirm his suspicions. Then she had wept bitter tears as he laughed back at her.

Privately, that night, weeping alone after Ovelia had betrayed her, she realized she was glad Paeter had insisted on having his way with her before he left. It was the first time she had ever welcomed such a thing. Bad enough that she had no one to tell—not after seeing Ovelia with Orbrin, and her own terrible mistake with Regel. It was that last night Paeter finally broke her.

"That's enough," Ovelia said at length. "Both princesses need to rest."

She gave Lenalin a longing look, which went steadfastly ignored. Lenalin could hardly stand any of these two-faced snakes around her any longer.

"Yes," Lenalin said. "Leave me. Go play with your pretty princess somewhere else."

Perhaps she would throw *herself* from the battlements when they had left. But no—she did not want to give them the satisfaction.

If she had left it there, much might have been different. Perhaps they would have gone forth and all of this would have gone aright. Paeter would return from the war and welcome his new daughter. True, he would be disappointed to have a girl child, but Darak was well enough, and so it would not trouble him over long. Semana could go unnoticed, and perhaps even grow up happy, free from her father's abuses and torments, at least for a time. Lenalin would envy her that, yes, but in time she too would learn to at least tolerate the child, perhaps even love her.

But she could not forget the horror of that night: the squalling, monstrous thing they had pulled from between her legs, and the bitter tears she had wept at the pain of it and the betrayal of her own body. And when Maure had come to her, face grave, and said they had a solution.

Another child.

"Oh, Father," Lenalin said as they were going. "What a lovely child, do you think?"

"Yes." Orbrin smiled, relieved, and spoke the reply that came automatically to any who bore the blood of Winter. "Blessings upon her mother."

It was only then, catching sight of the look of sick agony on Ovelia's face, that Lenalin understood the truth. Understood whence this child had come.

It was all she could do not to scream.

TWENTY-TWO

Low-City Tar Vangr under occupation was not a safe place to be. The Children of Ruin had dealt the city a mighty blow with their invasion, but the rulers of Tar Vangr had inflicted arguably as much or more damage by abandoning the common folk in their hour of need. Now even the barbarians had largely burrowed in for the winter. From the outside looking in, Low-City resembled a graveyard.

Those who knew where to look, however, saw the stirrings of life that remained. Folk survived like rodents, hiding beneath burned out buildings and scurrying through the shadows between points of safety. Fully a thousand Tar Vangryur had survived that initial assault and burrowed deep beneath the city's streets, where the Narfire made them sweat even as snow swirled above.

In the aptly named Rat Cellar, beneath the cobbles down by the docks, fully twenty folk squeezed into a space made for eight. Most of them lay in threadbare blankets and nursed wounds that slowed or entirely prevented their mobility, while tired folk with teardrop tattoos moved among them, ministering as best they could. The young man called Erim supplied water in shallow swallows to a woman burning with fever. Afterward, he slumped down beside Daren, who put a reassuring hand on his thigh. Erim leaned his head upon Daren's shoulder, taking peace and solace in that moment.

At Nacacia's order, the Circle of Tears had suspended their war of resistance and instead turned to protecting the folk of Tar Vangr in their hour of need. And thus did spies, courtesans, and assassins become protectors, chiurgeons, and rescuers. The same hands that had done violence now turned to healing, and caresses meant to seduce turned to gentle comfort instead. The rage of the horde was a dull, throbbing echo in the ground above the basement.

In the face of overwhelming hate, only kindness would allow life to endure.

So many folk crammed into the Cellar, weary from minstering to the wounded and afraid, that at first no one noticed the man in the gray-black weather cloak lurking just inside the secret stairs that led down to the cellar. He stood, silent and still like one of the roots of Tar Vangr. Finally, Erim perked up and bolted to his feet, albeit with a twinge born of fatigue. Another of the Circle of Tears saw his reaction—Krystir, a warrior who'd earned their name through quick, decisive action—and stood beside him, eyes narrowed. Then Daren joined them, hand near the handle of his caster but not upon it.

The man in the darkness neither spoke nor moved, but he was suddenly more there than he had been, as though taking note of his presence made it stronger. More concrete.

One by one, every face in the basement turned toward the stairs, and those who could rise did so. Nacacia—half her face a livid purple bruise, one eye swollen shut—approached the man silently. His face was a cold, frost-raked mask, and it offered not a hint of his thoughts. Nacacia's lower lip moved slightly, but she hesitated to proffer a word. Her eyes asked the question instead.

Slowly, he pushed his cloak wide, revealing a small child that clung to his leg. She was tiny, perhaps two or three years of age, her skin cold-pale and her messy straw-colored hair soaked through with half-melted slush. She shivered, but her bright gray eyes were clear as she scanned the room. Finally, she settled on Erim, and a relieved smile spread across her face. As though she'd been holding herself by the thinnest of reins, she sprang forth like a casterbolt and hurried across the chamber. He reached out, uncertain, and she threw her arms around him. "Erim," she said, the word warm.

Erim tried to speak but could not, and his swelling emotions showed upon his face: warm and cool at once, loving and bittersweet.

"Thank you," Daren said, giving voice to those words Erim could not. "Thank you for bringing Sarelle back to us, Lord of Tears."

The man nodded. The name seemed to apply to him. He had another, if only he could remember it. Perhaps he would remember something else of import.

Abruptly, the room returned to its various businesses. Coughs, wheezes, quiet weeping, and soft, soothing words filled the space. He was neither foe nor master but friend.

Nacacia drew close to him, her one good eye filled with unease. "Pass well, Regel?" she asked.

Regel. Yes.

He shook himself, and tiny ice crystals fell away from his body and his mind. He touched the sword lashed to his back, and it sent reassuring cold through him. At the same instant, his movement prompted all those gathered in the chamber to grow tense. More than one hand went to a weapon, and any grace he had earned by sending the child to her ostensible protector dissolved in that moment.

Nacacia reached out as though to touch Regel's arm, but her hand stopped short. Faint mist, like condensation boiling free, rose between her fingers and the sleeve of his coat.

"You haven't returned to us," she said. "Not yet. There is more for you to do."

Regel nodded. He looked up as though he could see through the earthen roof of the cellar, up through the darkness and clouds to the glittering city perched atop the mage-glass. His destiny lay there.

Of a sudden, the world trembled and the earth rumbled. A man who lay injured cried out in sudden terror and a woman sitting near him fell writhing to the floor. Some groped about for balance, and Nacacia had to catch herself up on Regel's shoulder. Bits of stone and earth drifted down like sifting rain from the ceiling of the cellar, and a crack spread through the stone.

Regel's own voice surprised him, sounding after so long silent. Dark. Cold. Unsure.

"Get them out," he said. "This place. It—"

Then another tremor struck, and the ceiling began to collapse.

~

Far above, the tremor struck High-City just before dawn, making the city sway on its mage-glass supports. Ovelia would have fallen to the floor had not Lenalin seized her and held her up.

"Pass well?" she asked, and Ovelia nodded weakly.

The building shuddered all around them, and Lenalin heard the groan of mage-glass straining to hold up its burden. Folk exclaimed in confusion and startlement, and a pair ran past them in the hall.

"What was that?" Lenalin turned to the window, where great plumes of smoke and snow roiled through the air as though from an explosion. She could see nothing through the haze.

Again, the building around them shook, and this time Lenalin could see spires waving madly outside the window. Structures that had stood for centuries came loose of their moorings, dancing like tall grasses in a breeze. Chunks of stone exploded off the dark mountain at the city's heart—Tar Vangr's spine—and Lenalin made out a shallow crack running up its length. A rock jumped out of the mountain at the end of the crack and she watched as it spun listlessly in the air, sailed toward High-City, and just barely skittered over the edge of the mage-glass. She could see it spinning down in the courtyard.

"How can this be?" Lenalin asked aloud of no one.

She already knew the answer.

Lenalin grasped the silver surcoat of a passing orderly. She didn't know his face or function, but it didn't matter. "Fetch my commanders," she said. "Go. *Now.*"

She was the queen of this city, and she would protect it. She would gather together the people who could get things done. Start the recovery efforts. Set the defense.

This was an attack. It was the final assault.

Another tremor ripped through the mountain, and this time all of High-City shook on its moorings. Out the window, across the courtyard, stone and bricks and roof slates fell like volleys of casterbolts, vaporizing snow and scratching and cracking the mage-glass in their wake. Across the way, Lenalin saw one section of the city shaking more wildly than the others. It trembled on its anchors and—

Then it tumbled down the mountain, carving massive divots and rents in the stone as it fell. She could hear the thunder of the mage-glass city cracking and crumbling to pieces.

Around her, folk responded in shock. Some stood covering their mouths in utter surprise, while others cried out in their horror. Who could say how many folk had perished in that collapse?

Lenalin reacted with purpose.

"Lia," she said. "Lia, we need to—"

She reached down as though to touch the woman's shoulder, but Ovelia grasped her wrist with sudden strength. Lenalin might have chided her, but what she saw when she looked down stole her words away. With her other hand, Ovelia clutched at her skirts between her knees.

Damp and bloody, Lenalin saw.

Silver Fire, her pregnancy. It was so sudden. And too soon.

"I'm sorry," Ovelia said. "Lena, I don't understand."

Lenalin's heart lurched but she set her jaw. She squeezed Ovelia's hand, then pulled free of her grasp. "You," she said to a woman in a guard's livery. "Take Lady Dracaris to the chiurgeon. Quickly."

"Lena—" Dazed, breath thread, Ovelia struggled meekly as they led her away.

Lenalin suppressed the shiver that ran through her. She had no choice. She had to protect her city, and that meant she had to move quickly.

"I'm sorry, Lia," Lenalin said under her voice. She raised her chin and set her jaw.

She would protect what was hers.

~

In her dream, Ovelia saw the fire again. It burned around her and through her, whatever she did. If she ran, if she hid, if she tried to shield herself, it did not matter. The fire consumed her. The fire destroyed her. The fire was her world.

But in this dream, she was awake.

In this dream, she was awake and in agony.

How much time had passed since they'd taken her from Lenalin's side, she could not say. Nor could she describe the blurry journey from the overlook to the cramped, sweaty birthing room. Lenalin's touch was all she remembered, as though her fingers had burned blackened scars into her wrist. In her shadow world, she could almost see the marks on her skin.

Her vision had otherwise all but disintegrated. Shadows moved around her—half a dozen folk with blurry, distorted faces like nothing human—and she could not follow what they were doing. Hands prodded her and voices murmured. Someone forced apart her legs, and she hadn't the strength to resist. The pain was intense, radiating in waves that tore up through her body, and every one of them made her awareness crack and splinter. It felt like something was ripping her apart from the inside.

This wasn't right. She knew that from the past and from the future.

Everything around her was fire, and she shrieked and tried to flinch away from it. Fire inside her. Fire around her. She was burning and burning and it would never stop.

She tried to scream, but her teeth were gritted hard and the sound couldn't escape.

Words drifted into her awareness. "Lady Dracaris. Do not fear."

She knew that voice.

"Maure?" she asked, hardly able to speak.

"Aye." The old nurse put a soothing hand on Ovelia's forehead. "Me, lass. Once again."

"I—I can't see you, Maure," Ovelia said. "My eyes…"

"I know, child," Maure said. "Listen."

A tremor shook the room, knocking objects clattering from tables and throwing more than one of the attendants off their feet. Folk cried out or muttered in surprise.

"Lass." Maure clutched Ovelia's hand. "Listen to my voice. Trust me."

Ovelia's heart thundered in her head. She felt unmoored—adrift in a dark world she could not make out—lost. She swam in a sea of silver flames.

"Lass, I need you here," Maure said. "Your child needs you here."

Ovelia's world came back into focus. Her senses returned. Her body was in agony, trying to thrust itself in different directions at once, but she knew herself again.

"What," she asked. "What do you need… from me?"

Maure's voice was calm. Reassuring. "I need you to calm yourself. Your heart, it races too fast."

Yes.

Slowly—agonizingly—Ovelia wrestled her lungs under control. The pain persisted, but it had lessened. She could reign over her body again. Ovelia forced herself to breathe through the pain. "This is wrong," she said. "It should not be this way. It's… it's too soon."

"It will pass well," Maure said. "I am here with you. I will guide you. As I did once before."

Yes.

Again, a vision crossed over Ovelia's perception: she held a squalling babe, her head fringed with soft down that would lighten as she aged. Her eyes, slitted open, burned like ochre pools. The only time Ovelia would ever hold her, just that brief, merciful moment, before she gave her up. Gave her to…

"Lena," she said. "Where…?"

"Rest," Maure said. "The queen will be here when she can. We are under attack."

Ovelia saw a flare of light in her shadow world—an arc of magic so angry and powerful she could perceive it through stone walls. Power battered the mountain of Tar Vangr, lashing it again and again like whipcords of flame. And she knew the source of that power.

"Semana," she said, gasping.

~

The obelisk lay on its side, broken off at the base, in the Square of the Fallen. Before that night, it had stood unmoving vigil over the passage of time, a silent watcher that paid homage to those who rose up to rule and then fell, as all things must, to ruin.

Now, the centuries of tragedy the obelisk chronicled lay half obscured in snowfall and slush, and boots of rough-boiled skins trod upon the delicate carvings until they became muddy and illegible.

Above the fractured history of Tar Vangr floated Semana Denerre nô Ravalis, Blood Queen of the Children of Ruin, energies arcing from her hands and lashing out against the mountain spine of Tar Vangr. She channeled the

275

Worldfire in all its power and majesty, ripping into the earth and tearing at the foundations of the last mage-city that stood in the World of Ruin.

Just below her feet, a small horde of wounded, feeble Children of Ruin gathered, clamoring to touch her foot or her calf. When one of the barbarians succeeded, their body arched and went taut as though caught in an electric current. Their skin paled, their muscles loosened, and finally they collapsed, to be replaced by another of the insane creatures, who scrambled over the fallen heedless of fragile limbs and faces. This seemed wrong, but she understood the sense of it: they were wounded and impaired, and this was the best way to serve the war. They lay senseless and weakened, gripped with profound fatigue that would last for days or more.

With every drained body, a current of power rushed into Semana, and she used it to strike the great mountain, loosing earthquakes and carving out what she desired. The tremors collapsed buildings and brought fragments of mage-glass raining from above. If she continued to strike with all the power at her command, she could bring down all of Tar Vangr if she wanted.

But that was not her plan.

She'd originally come upon the idea when the dragon's blood had shielded the Children of Ruin against the elements. If power could be transferred to mundane folk through blood, it stood to reason that a skilled blood sorcerer could claim it directly. In her case, it was not so difficult to draw life energy, freely offered, from one or two or even scores of supplicants. The Circle had used the Worldfire thusly for centuries, drawing power from their servitors at times of need. She simply took it a step further.

She smashed their lives into the mountain, one by one, carving flat divots out of the stone. She tore apart a mountain that had stood for millennia, from which her blood had emerged in the Prophecy of Return, which had stood since before the World of Wonder, from the birth of the world. All things made by women and men would one day fall to Ruin, without exception, but upon this day, so too would a work of the world itself. With this power, Semana could not fail.

Somewhere deep in her heart, a voice cried out against this, but the raw power she channeled drowned it. The Worldfire burned through her, like fire in her blood, scalding every vessel in her body. She could taste the barbarians sacrificing themselves for her—their hearts beating entirely for her—and it thrilled her. The power over them and over the world. She never wanted this feeling to end.

And she wanted more.

There, pulsing in the heart of the mountain of Tar Vangr, she sensed the burning Narfire: the lifeblood of the World of Ruin. It had called to her—drawn her to this place—but when she had reached for it, it burned her fingers. She knew what she had to do: to reach the locus of the Silver Fire, where she could control it and draw it into herself. All this time, all the powers she had mastered—all of it had prepared her for this day. She had the power and knowledge and will to absorb the Narfire. All of it. She would drink the power of Ruin and incorporate it into herself.

And with that power, she could transcend this world. She could reach that spiraling column of windows into other worlds—other times—and travel to them. She could become more.

She could become *all.*

Semana happened to look down, to where Darak was shouting up at her, his words drowned in the roar of shattering stone. How quaint and harmless he looked, like a little boy shouting into the storm. But she would remember his use—and the danger he posed.

"Enough," he was saying. "Enough!"

She might have ignored Darak, but there stood Tithian, staring up at her uneasily. She could not see his face through his skull mask, but she'd learned to read his emotions in his stance just as easily.

They were right. She had to rest.

Semana sent one last scything blast of lightning into the stone, then let the dust and haze clear. Snow swirled around the vortex of her power, then boiled away into vapor. Semana sweated and heaved inside her armor, but not out of weariness or pain—wielding such fury was pure ecstacy.

Glowing with heat, great stone steps stood in the solid stone of the mountain. Each was at least a pace in height, but a strong woman or man could climb up them without too much trouble. The work of half an hour had produced one long stair, and she had begun to carve a switchback to continue the climb. By the time the sun rose on this, the last day of the year, the barbarians would reach High-City.

Hair wafting around her, she floated back down to the cobbled streets, her body weary. It felt as though she'd spent all morning lifting jar after jar of heavy oil, and she felt the fatigue in every muscle. But at the same time, she burned with the desire to do it again. *More.*

Dust whipping past his mask, Darak surveyed her handiwork and uttered a disapproving sound. "I still think we should have made tunnels." He pulled off his mask and wiped his nose on his sleeve. "The defenders will loose bolts upon us as we climb. We'll have to fight for every step."

"Tunnels," Tithian said, "run the risk of collapsing the mountain, killing us all. Is that your aim?"

Darak sneered at him. "When I want your opinion, squire, I'll command it."

Semana could see the two of them marching toward each other, ready to meet in a duel at any moment. She saw how it would unfold, blow for blow. And while she did not much care for the outcome, it would not serve for them to fight yet. Soon, it would not matter.

"If I destroy the city, what throne will we sit, brother?" she asked, as though she cared even the slightest bit. "I will carve the steps in a snaking pattern, and favor sides of the mountain hidden from view. Fewer defenders will be able to strike those points."

Darak scowled and secured his mask anew. "Rest as long as you need, but no longer," he said. "The usurpers must not escape."

Darak droned on a bit, but she wasn't really listening any longer, and she barely noticed when he went away.

Tithian stood at her side, his hands raised a little between them, as though he wanted to touch her but didn't dare. "Pass well?" he asked. "You seem weary."

"I pass perfectly well," she said, even as she felt the weakness swelling up inside her.

He seemed wary at first, but if Semana had learned nothing else over the last six years, it was how to lie to Tithian Davargorn. He finally nodded and went on his way.

Semana gazed up at her handiwork, and at the barbarians swarming up the newly carved steps. Distantly, in some part of herself she'd thought left far behind, she remembered the rugged beauty of this mountain, admiring it on one of her ornithopter tours of the city. As a child, she had wondered how far its shadow truly extended, whether there was truth to the tales of a dragon that lived in its depths, and if she might find treasure in the ancient tunnels. Now that she had defiled that childhood memory—scuffed the beauty of those dreams—it seemed even further behind her.

This day, she would finally put to death the woman she had been.

She would become what she *must* be.

TWENTY-THREE

A S THE SUN ROSE high on the last day of the year, the earthquakes finally stopped, and Lenalin loosed a sigh that had been swelling in her chest since before the sun rose. She surveyed the damage to the mountain from the height of the palace overlook, gazing straight down the slope to the swarming mass of blood-crazed lunatics ready to march up and destroy High-City. That they had waited even this long spoke of significant restraint on their part, or—likelier—extremely tight control on the part of their Blood Queen. Lenalin had seen personally the forceful will of the woman who had been Semana Denerre nô Ravalis, and if anyone could command such a legion, it was she.

"Your Majesty," one of her generals said at her elbow. Coriff Yaela. "My Queen?"

"I heard you," she said, though she hadn't listened. She rubbed at her sore hip.

The morning had been an exhausting one. She'd spent it riding one of the few remaining ornithopters through High-City, supervising rescue and evacuation efforts. Whole swathes of the mage-glass city could no long sustain residents, and fully half the buildings had been assessed as unsafe. When the Blood Queen ceased her assault, hundreds had been trapped in their homes and communal halls. That, unfortunately, was only the beginning of the difficulties: More than a dozen buildings had seemed safe at first, only for unseen weaknesses in the structures to necessitate further evacuations. Until the mage-engineers could get down to assess the damage to the supports, buildings would tremble and collapse in an unexpected pattern for only the Nar knew how long. The logistics, she'd come to understand, were a nightmare, and it left the High-City entirely off-balance.

The uncertainty and suffering played exactly into Semana's hands. Lenalin could feel it in the way the folk looked up at her, faces smeared with dust and sometimes blood, eyes wet with tears or dry and filled with hate. They knew whom to blame for their misfortunes: their new queen. Lenalin knew few so much as acknowledged her, let alone loved her. Blood and pain had marked her reign thus far, and many of them saw no reprieve in the future. Hope drained away as the hours passed.

Lenalin remembered one crowd of children, their clothes scuffed and soaked with the heavy snows, parading through the street to a new location as mages tried to keep their building standing. As a child, she would have seen love and hope in those gazes, but now she knew better. That was confusion at best, but more likely blame that would turn to hate in a few years. Those children would grow up remembering the horror of this day, and to them, the Black Queen Shard would be responsible.

She, after all, was the one who had failed to protect them.

To see the folk of High-City Tar Vangr, so secure in their privilege and power, suddenly facing hardship and difficulty and pain… It was all so familiar. She had been them, long ago, both in their ignorance and in their suffering. At once, she sympathized—knew full well the pain of such suffering—but at the same time there was distance in her heart. She could not help but see in the folk of High-City the same weakness that had put her in Paeter Ravalis's bed and under his fists. These people had looked the other way when he had beat her, over and over again. Then, when he had attempted to murder her in his rage, not only had they failed to punish him, but they had elevated him. They were foolish, fickle, and entirely undeserving of salvation. And yet.

Her hip ached.

Lenalin stood upon the balcony of the palace and breathed deeply. Her advisors had begged her multiple times this morning to abandon the palace as unsafe, but years as a skyship pirate had given her excellent balance. It was an empty thing, anyway: nowhere in High-City was safe, as this morning's tour had proved. That, and Lenalin wasn't about to concede defeat.

"Majesty, we need to pull the mage-engineers to the defensive lines." Yaela spoke gently but firmly. "We cannot wait any longer, if we're to hold for even a few moments."

Yaela was a decent woman. Lenalin remembered her from her youth—a lesser heir, one suited for coin-counting and figures rather than charisma or leadership. Lenalin had never found her all that impressive, but sixteen years had wrought significant changes in her. That, and the murder of many of her Blood's leaders last year, which had required her to rise to the occasion. Now she was the matriarch of her Blood, and Lenalin could see the responsibility weighing on her shoulders. The Pirate Queen of Atropis knew about putting on a mantle she'd thought ill-fitted.

"The placements will have to hold," Lenalin said. "The efforts of the engineers are pivotal."

"Majesty." Another of her generals—the less impressive Vees Duldur—sounded irritated, as usual. He stroked his white-laced gray beard. "There will be casualties."

She gripped the rail hard. "There have already *been* casualties."

The earthquake had collapsed parts of High-City, dropping them into Low-City. An entire ward of the city had fallen and slid down the mountain to obliterate the eastern end of the docks. Lenalin's quick response in sending rescuers to the outer reaches where the vibration had the worst effect had saved hundreds, but Lenalin imagined plenty of folk had fallen with that section of High-City. They still didn't have numbers, and likely wouldn't for days.

She understood Duldur's point. The mage-engineers she'd assigned to rebuilding could be at the front, strengthening the fortifications, powering defensive projectors, and charging heavy caster emplacements. All but the last of Tar Vangr's ironclads had vanished in Lan Ravalis's doomed charge, and only infantry and a few ornithopters remained to halt the barbarians' advance. Without the mages, the defenders would be at a significant disadvantage, with only the bare minimum of weapons.

"The barbarians could march any hour, Majesty," General Duldur said in his patronizing way. He often spoke to Lenalin as though she hadn't the least idea what she was doing. As though she hadn't ruled over her own mage-city full of pirates for over a decade. "We need to—"

"You need to trust my command," Lenalin said. "Or I can replace you."

She did not actually say that she could throw him over the bannister, but Aeldad's glare conveyed the threat. Lenalin was not a physical woman—she had her first mate for such practical purposes. At the same time, intimidation secured only limited gains. Better to ply a different tactic.

"Duldur," Lenalin said. "I know your child is one of the defenders."

The old man sputtered for a second, surprised.

She understood her generals were wary of her, and why wouldn't they? She had vanished nearly twenty years ago, apparently to her death, and now she returned, a pirate and scoundrel captaining a powerful, gleaming skyship that none could credit. Even now, that air of menace and mystery surrounded her, from her black veil and gown to her brutish crew to her chosen consort, the infamous Bloodbreaker Ovelia Dracaris. It was like something out of a tavern tale, one that most wise people would not consider for even a moment.

Lenalin reached up and pulled her veil back over her face, revealing her scarred visage to her generals. Duldur recoiled slightly, which was a reaction she was well accustomed to. Yaela looked vaguely sad—again, something Lenalin well understood. She reached across and touched Duldur's hand.

"As I understand it." Lenalin continued, looking over at him. "That was his choice, not yours. We all must take risks, or we stand no chance in this."

Duldur held her gaze as long as he could, then nodded. "Of course."

Inwardly, Lenalin nodded to herself. Intimidation only went so far; building an empathic connection would serve far better. She looked down at the carved staircase leading up the mountain, and at the caster placements waiting in the lower platforms of High-City.

Why were they waiting? Now was the moment. The toll the earthquake magic had taken on Tar Vangr was devastating. The defenses were weak. High-City reeled, ready to be crushed, and yet the Blood Queen had not marched. She had to be waiting for something. But what?

"My Queen!"

A woman ran toward her. Aeldad reacted immediately, raising her spear over her arm, but Lenalin waved a hand. She recognized her old nursemaid Maure, albeit a bit wider and grayer than fifteen years ago, and knew she posed no threat. At her beckoning, the old woman drew closer, but she abruptly hesitated, unsettled. Lenalin knew the look that crossed her lined face: had seen it rarely enough, but she recognized it all the same. And she wanted pity from no one.

Another day, Lenalin might have delighted in the unease her face seemed to cause Maure, but she didn't want to see that expression any longer. She covered her face again. "What is it?" she asked.

"Ovelia," she said. "Her child…"

In the heat and terror of the morn, Lenalin had almost forgotten. They'd taken her queen to Blood Yaela's castle, which the engineers had assured Lenalin would be safe from further tremors.

"Well?" Lenalin asked. "Speak on."

"Her child is a difficult one," Maure said. "She is resting, but it will be hours yet. Perhaps all of this day. Will you—" She bit her lip and nodded. "Will you go to her?"

That… Lenalin expelled a slow breath. She shook her head. There was no time.

The old nursemaid nodded somberly. "If there are changes, I will send word, or come myself."

Lenalin waved and turned back to the rail. She gazed down the mountain slope, cursing the barbarians for their hesitation. March or leave, she just wanted them to act. Something else was happening here. Semana was preparing for something.

It was time.

"Aeldad," she said. "The resonance spell."

Her first mate nodded and handed her a thaumaturgically enhanced projector. The device was about the size of her hand, and she held it up to her mouth to speak into. Duldur and Yaela stood proudly at her sides, though the former looked dubious.

"Tar Vangr," Lenalin said.

Her voice resonated through the city. It coursed through the mage-glass and echoed everywhere it touched. Everyone in High-City could hear, she knew, and many in Low-City as well. She knew the Blood Queen was listening, and she shaped her words accordingly.

"Folk of Tar Vangr, City of Steel," she said. "I am Lenalin, the Black Queen, daughter of Orbrin Denerre, last King of Winter, and the rightful heir of the Blood of Winter. Your liege."

The folk in the main square, below the balcony, looked up to see her. Hundreds of people, some carrying weapons, other baskets or children slung across their bodies. These were the ragged, suffering, scared folk who remained of the City of Steel.

She should use this speech to reassure them, she knew. She should sympathize with their struggles, challenge them to stand strong, but she did not have those words. She remembered the faces of the children in the streets and she had no lies to offer.

"The hordes below us, who will march upon us at any moment," she said. "They are people, just as you and I. Foolish, deluded, and monstrous people, who want nothing more than to kill and rend and destroy. But they are not faceless monsters. They are like us—fallible, weak, disgusting. They have their own desires, just as pathetic as yours and mine. They are cowards."

Silence gripped the overlook, but Lenalin could hear Duldur struggling to contain his objections. Aside from a surprised gasp, Yaela held her tongue. When Lenalin glanced to her, the woman nodded slightly. The back of Lenalin's neck prickled uncomfortably, just where she couldn't reach.

Even from this remove, she could see confused faces in the crowd of Tar Vangryur gathered to hear her. Warders of the city, common folk simply seeking to survive, all of them looked to her for reassurance and guidance. But she only had what she had to offer.

"I will not lie to you," Lenalin said. "I will not deceive you. The Children of Ruin are but mortal beings with mortal wants and desires. They have no grand destiny to face us—to destroy us. They do not even hate us. They simply follow the commands of one who does. One who..." She paused to collect herself. "One who would see our city burned to the ground and torn asunder if he cannot rule it. He is a petulant child, unworthy of you or this place. He is a coward and a fool. Even I, who turned from the crown as long as I could, wouldn't piss on that worthless wretch were he burning at my feet."

That made Aeldad chuckle. Duldur look at her, horrified.

Lenalin could hear it, the murmurs rising—the folk in the street perplexed and confused.

"Will we win the day?" Lenalin shrugged, though few could see the expression. "I doubt it. They are many, and we are few. Our weapons are near exhausted. And in truth, after centuries dropping our filth and scraps to the poor of Low-City? We do not deserve to win. We deserve to die."

Duldur's head seemed on the verge of exploding. Yaela maintained cool confidence.

"But this is the World of Ruin, not the World of Wonder," Lenalin said. "*Desert* matters not. *Justice* matters not. The only matters I know are the strength of your arm and your will to keep fighting. The Children will try to kill us, and we will kill them first. Every one of you, from man to woman to child and all who stand between: find the best weapon you can and fight. I do not care how many you kill. I do not care whether you falter on your first strike. I do not care if you run and hide. My opinion does not matter—only yours does. You alone matter, and you alone must live with what you do this day."

She did not say, "or die with it," but the implication was clear.

Lenalin closed her hands into fists on the railing.

"Do not fight for me. Do not fight for this city. Fight for yourself and..." She thought of Ovelia then, and her voice cracked. "Fight for those you love."

Only then did it come to pass. Only then did Lenalin see the stirring of the folk below. It was not hope, exactly, that spread among them, but anger: righteous fury that burned and demanded retribution. These folk were not noble; Lenalin had ceased to believe in nobility fifteen years ago, when a supposedly noble man had thrust her through a mirror and left her for dead. There was no good left in this city, if there ever had been. But there were people, and those people would fight to survive.

Her generals relaxed, and Duldur even murmured encouragement, but Lenalin wasn't listening. She waited, hands clenched on the rail, for the reaction. She knew what would happen.

She had not long to wait.

Stone roared as the mountain trembled under a fresh strike, and Lenalin had to grasp the rail to keep her balance. High-City trembled, and Lenalin could see the buildings swaying like trees in the breeze. Some of them collapsed. In the square below, folk stumbled or fell off their feet.

Darak, no doubt, had pressed for a march.

"That boy is but a boy," Aeldad said.

Lenalin nodded. It was as she had intended: if Semana wanted to delay, she meant to draw out the attack before the Blood Queen was ready. Lenalin knew full well that Semana was the true threat.

Below, Lenalin watched the castle of Blood Yaela waver, then collapse. *Ovelia.*

"Ware!" General Yaela pointed down the slope, to tiny figures swarming up the carven path.

The invasion had finally begun, and Lenalin could only stare.

"Your Majesty," Duldur said. "Your command?"

Lenalin gazed down at the attackers, who looked like insects at this distance. They climbed with remarkable alacrity, as though they'd marshaled for this moment. Already the lowest tier of defenders—those brave souls who'd lashed themselves to the great mage-glass buttresses that held up the floating High-City—had begun to loose casterbolts at the enemy. It resembled children hurling stones into the encroaching tide. The barbarian horde numbered in the tens of thousands, and Tar Vangr boasted perhaps two or three hundred trained warders, and ten times as many denizens who would fight to defend their city. Fight and die in vain.

Duldur was veritably shrieking at her. "Queen Denerre!"

Ovelia.

Chills passed through Lenalin as she realized this was a feint. A distraction. Lenalin could be wrong, but that was how she would execute this invasion. And the Blood Queen was her, not only in face but in will. All of this passed according to her plan, and Lenalin saw no way Tar Vangr could survive.

"I must go," she said, thinking of Ovelia.

"Go?" Duldur said. "Your Majesty—"

"Yaela," she said, and her general immediately attended her. "I am going to the dock. You will command the defenses until my return."

Duldur spluttered an objection. "Your Majesty," he said. "Surely—"

Lenalin raised a hand to cut him off. "I know your seniority," she said. "You've thirty years of tactical experience to your name. Coriff Yaela was but a child when you served Cassian Ravalis in the City of Flames. You protected both Demetrus Ravalis and my father, and only through your efforts did they escape the fall of Luether. You acquitted yourself valiantly when the Children invaded Echvar; it was not your fault that war could not be won. Surely you should wear the mantle of command. Yes?"

The old general could say nothing. Every word was what he might have said.

"But Coriff Yaela is a child of this city," Lenalin said. "She was born here. She spoke her first words here. Took her first steps here. Took friends and lovers among its people. She loves Tar Vangr. She—" Lenalin swallowed. "She *is* Tar Vangr. And she will do what must be done."

Neither Yaela nor Duldur spoke a word, nor did any of the warders who stood around Lenalin. They knew the words were not meant only for Coriff Yaela.

"And I do not wear the name Lenalin Denerre," she said. "You will address me as Shard."

Duldur shivered. "Yes, Queen Shard."

Lenalin took her leave then, trembling.

She wanted to run. To flee this dying place, as she had before.

Not this time.

TWENTY-FOUR

I N THE DARK BEFORE dawn on the last day of the year, as the last tremors of Semana's ritual finally ended, Prince Darak Ravalis nô Denerre, Dar-Karsk of the Children of Ruin, the first male druid to stand among the Circle, was wroth.

He roared insults and curses, tore up scrolls, smashed tankards and stools against the warmed cobbles, and otherwise destroyed everything in sight. His Worldfire magic lashed out around him, making the ground tremble like one of Semana's earthquakes, albeit much smaller in scale.

"How dare she." He growled like a rabid dog. "How dare *she*!"

The man's rage, Tithian noted with cool detachment from just outside his tent of stitched skins, had grown dramatically over the short time they'd spent together in the fallen Low-City of Tar Vangr, but he suspected it had built for years. He hadn't seen its birth or its adolescence—ironic, for nothing about Darak's rage seemed remotely mature. He threw a child's tantrum, breaking inanimate things and asserting his petty displeasure as though anyone would care.

For instance, now he pushed himself out of his tent as though to roar in rage at anyone nearby, only to pull himself short when he saw the half-dozen or so Children of Ruin who stood ward there. They were each of them his superior in size and strength, and he backed down immediately under their bemused looks. A coward and a weakling, indeed.

His eye found Tithian and narrowed. "You there, slayer," he said. "Find Crown of Fire and bring him to me."

Tithian frowned, though his bone-covered mask hid the expression. He found Darak beyond pathetic, but he obeyed, regardless. Presenting himself as a useful servant had so far made the petulant barbarian prince tolerate, if not actually like or respect him, which allowed Tithian to stay close. The instant the man posed a threat to Semana, Tithian would cut him down.

Out in the daylight, he passed among the barbarians marshaled at the foot of the mountain, hood low and gait uneven. Free of Sarelle, he could walk freely among them again. They whispered a word at the edge of his hearing, and while he did not understand their language, he recognized well enough the respect and even awe in their voices. He had nothing to fear from them. As the morning sleet slaked the cobblestones around him, he pushed on down the Way of Spidercatchers toward the hall where he expected to find Darak's lad-servant.

Tithian well understood the barbarian prince's rage. He was the sort of man who loathed being under the thumb of a woman, and so having to bow to Semana grated upon him. Without her, would Darak even be here, let alone command? Tithian thought not. And now that Lady Shard had become queen of Tar Vangr in his place, foiling his plans? No wonder that enraged him.

Tithian wasn't sure whether Shard was really Lenalin Denerre, miraculously alive albeit terribly scarred and crippled, but he didn't much care. She was their enemy. *Semana's* enemy.

That was all that mattered.

He came upon the open doorway of what had once been a large alehall and now played hosted to the crude hospital to support the barbarians' efforts. Tithian was given to understand the Children of Ruin held the wounded in contempt, leading them to leave their fellow barbarians fallen on the field rather than waste energy hauling them back to safety. This was one of the worthwhile changes Darak had made to their strategy: a hospital, even crudely staffed, reduced the horde's losses. Only now did Tithian realize that if he had come here to work as soon as he arrived in Tar Vangr, like as not he could have saved hundreds of lives with his magic.

Not that he or Semana much cared. Indeed, Semana had taken many of the wounded to perform her blood magic ritual, and the hospital seemed sparsely populated just now.

Sure enough, there he found Crown of Fire, tending to the wounded, just as he had observed him on many nights previously. Going from bed to bed, bandaging wounds, massaging hurts, and soothing hearts. The man, who Tithian thought had likely seen as many winters as he had, looked generally quite pleased to go about this work. Tithian couldn't help but feel a touch of, well, not sympathy, but at least understanding. He had lived that way most of his life.

"Scarlet," he said, his own secret name for the man, for his fiery hair.

Crown of Fire looked up and offered a genuine smile. He looked weary but also content. "Shadowchild," he said, which was his secret name for Tithian. Apparently, he reminded the barbarian of the Frostburn, who had spent some time among them. As recently as a season before, Tithian would have killed anyone who compared him to that man, but now it did not bother him. That, and Crown of Fire had a certain charm that excused such gentle mockery.

"Have you come for me yourself?" Crown sighed and wiped a bloody forearm across his brow, leaving a greasy red smear in its wake. Then his face fell. "No, you haven't."

Tithian nodded his head once.

"When my master calls, I answer." Crown's expression narrowed, lines appearing around his young eyes. He must have been quite handsome, before Darak's brutality and this war left him with so many bruises and scars. He looked exhausted at the mere thought of his master.

He went back to the barbarian he'd been working on, who lay moaning and bleeding on the pallet. Tithian stood gazing levelly at Crown, waiting while he checked the patient's wounds and replaced the bandages with cloth that was, if not quite clean, at least cleaner. He thought their injuries relatively minor—more bloody than deep—but he had to admit his magic gave him a distorted view of such things. He'd shrugged off far worse hurts than anything he saw in the hall.

Eventually, Crown looked up once more. "You're still here."

Tithian nodded. In truth, once he had delivered the message, he had felt his task complete, but he'd lingered to watch. The care with which Crown attended the barbarian's wounds soothed him. Not at all like his own healing arts, which burned and tore and consumed like fire. He nodded.

"We'll go now?" Crown nodded. "Yes."

They walked through the haze, as barbarians streamed around them to take up positions at the base of the pathways carved into the mountain. The assault had not yet begun, and Semana's insistence on delay surely angered Darak even further. Crown was a slight man, narrow of build and more wiry than muscular, which might have brought harassment from the other barbarians, Tithian thought. But as Darak's favored servant, he could expect relative safety among the horde—at least so long as the barbarian prince remained in power. Tithian suspected that would not last forever, and he wondered what would become of Crown of Fire.

For his part, Crown walked with shoulders slumped, sadness in every step. The despair wafted from him like a perfume. It could not be easy, being the petty tyrant's slave and the receptacle of his lusts, but what about this day made it worse than any other?

"Shadow," Crown of Fire said as they paused outside Darak's tent. "Give me your hand."

Tithian said nothing, but did as the man asked. They stood there unmoving for a moment, eyes shared and hands joined.

"I wish we had met in another season," the man said. "Before the coming storm."

"You would not have liked me in my youth," Tithian said.

That made Crown of Fire smile. "Perhaps."

The man pulled free and stepped into the tent.

For a heartbeat, Tithian felt certain someone was watching him. He looked about, and the nearby barbarians averted their speculative gazes. Perhaps it had just been that: rivals searching for a moment of inattention or other weakness, where a strike might stand a chance.

Regardless, Tithian waited a ten-count before following Crown of Fire.

What he found was not a surprise: Darak sitting in place, inside a tub of curled wood, while Crown of Fire ran a curved blade along the fleshy curves of his arms and bare chest. The rigors of the wild had sculpted him a fine body at the same time his magic had eroded it. Semana had spoken to Tithian of the tumor-like lesions Worldfire produced, which resembled fuzzy black worms that grew from his flesh. Tithian wondered what it would feel like to touch Darak with his magic. Horrific, no doubt.

"Why do they follow her, and not me?" Darak asked, though he clearly did not expect an actual answer. "I am the one who has lived among them. I am the one who has adopted their disgusting ways. I've eaten their food, lived among them. I've rutted their folk and been rutted in return." He scratched at the sickly pink skin where Crown had scraped one of his black lesions away. "And yet, they follow her, not me. They love her, not me. *Why?*"

Crown of Fire wisely said nothing, but merely let Darak continue ranting about the Children of Ruin to one of those Children. *They. Them.* Not *you.* He could have asked Crown of Fire for his insight into his own culture, but Darak made it clear these were not real questions. So caught up was he in his own self-importance he did not even acknowledge his servant as a person.

Tithian sighed under his breath. He'd known within five breaths of seeing Darak why none of the barbarians respected him, let alone loved him.

"They are fools," Darak said in answer to his own question. "I offer them a place in this city, once I am king, but instead they owe their loyalty to a whore child who—"

Only then did he realize Tithian stood inside the tent, and he closed his lips before he uttered another slander against Semana. Pathetic.

"I am bound for my master," Tithian said. "If you have a message for her, I will—"

Darak spoke right over him. "Tithian Davargorn," he said. "Hard to believe that sickly little boy my sister carted around grew into, well, you." He raised his chin. "Take off that mask."

At first, Tithian did nothing, but Darak casually reached out and caressed Crown's neck. The gesture might have seemed peaceable, but Tithian could read the threat in it. He had no great love for the red-haired barbarian, but in that moment, he didn't want Darak to take that satisfaction. With an exhalation of disgust, he reached up and pulled his mask up over his face and onto the top of his head. In the stuffy interior of the tent, he was extremely aware of the bristly hairs over his deformed jaw and his large, luminous white eye that was almost blind in the filtered daylight through the tent flap.

Crown of Fire stifled a little gasp, and it made Tithian's throat tighten. Darak caught the sound too, and he smiled. "You've not seen his face, my slave?" he asked. "By all means, look. He's even more hideous than when he was a child."

"Master, I—" Crown started, but Darak caught him by the chin and squeezed his cheeks.

"I said *look*," Darak said, turning Crown's face in Tithian's direction.

The flame-haired barbarian did so, his eyes wide in a combination of fear and apology. Tithian was accustomed to the scrutiny. It stung, but the hurts such looks inflicted had long since ceased to linger. "Satisfied, your Highness?" Tithian asked after a moment.

"Well enough." Darak released Crown and waved him back to scraping him clean. "My sister tells me you wield magic. Is this so?"

Tithian hesitated. Would Semana really have revealed his secret in that way? He'd only recently come to see her for who she truly was. He considered, and thought it unlikely. "A marginal talent, Highness," he said. "Derived from relics, as Mask wields. Nothing of interest to you."

Darak weighed him for a moment with cold, judgmental eyes, then dismissed him with a scoff. "Cheap dust magic, born of a world far before ours," he said. "Nothing like the power we wield."

"*We*, Highness?" Tithian could not stop himself reacting. His contempt screamed forth.

Darak scowled. He slapped Crown's hand away and rose up to his full height in the tub, the robe falling down to obscure just his middle. He raised one hand, and silver flames licked along his fingers. "The Frostfire in our blood," Darak said. "The Worldfire we have both learned to wield. We are the same—masters of the force of Ruin."

"Masters," Tithian said. "You could carve out a mountain with your power, then?"

He knew antagonism was foolish, but the barbarian prince had well earned his ire. Perhaps he might provoke the over-stuffed fool into attacking him, and hence cut him down without hesitation but with satisfied prejudice. His hands veritably trembled on the hilts of his falcata at the thought.

Darak looked deeply offended, indeed. The Frostfire in his hand burned brighter.

Whatever Darak might have said—and from his face it would have been quite the curse—none heard it, for at that moment, the mage-glass around them began to hum and tremble with sound. Low-City had less mage-glass than High-City, of course, which was practically built of the stuff, but mage-glass reinforced the buildings around them, shone with light overnight to light the streets, and traced the cobbled roads to provide nigh-unbreakable rails for horseless carriages and wagons. Tithian had only heard this effect conjured once before, long ago as a child, announcing the death of Lenalin Denerre in a terrible accident in the palace. What a bit of fine fate that the voice he heard was that of Queen Shard.

And the words she spoke made him veritably cry for joy.

There was no sentimentality or kindness in her words. If anything, she sounded profoundly contemptuous of Tar Vangr and its people—not like a queen at all. And why not? Tithian knew little enough of Lenalin Denerre, but Lady Shard he knew: a hard woman who had no mercy for anyone. He had knelt in the woman's presence and knew she held only darkness and cruelty within her.

It only grew better, though, when she spoke of Darak and his incompetence. Tithian could see each word stab into the boy, causing his features to widen and the pulse to beat harder and faster in his throat. Coward. Petulant. *Child.* The bit about not pissing on him if he were burning almost made Tithian laugh aloud despite himself. Those were not the words of a woman in fear, but rather one in power—one who had nothing but disdain for her would-be rival.

And Tithian watched it work *perfectly.* He had spent much of his life in the presence of a cruel, manipulative woman, so he recognized what Shard was doing. By the end of the speech, Darak stood wide-eyed and furious, his arrogance extinguished and his rage pushed to the point of madness. His body trembled and his lips worked but no words emerged. His face had flushed nearly purple and he could hardly breathe. The man looked so much younger and so utterly pathetic, and why? Because Queen Shard had spoken the same words that were in Tithian's own heart.

And now Tithian did laugh, because he couldn't keep himself from scoffing.

Darak glared at him, but that only made Tithian laugh again—harder this time. He couldn't conjure up the slightest shred of fear for Darak Ravalis or whatever he called himself. In that moment, he looked more a clown than a barbarian, let alone a prince.

And the effect on Darak, of hearing laughter directed at him, was explosive.

The air around him blurred and sizzled and a hurricane of winds whipped about his body and upward, ripping the tent apart around them. Tithian cringed in the sudden flash of light, which dazzled his dead eye. It was sleeting, but the wind of Darak's Worldfire kept it off them. He roared in outrage, a sound like that of a yowling hyena, and the earth shook around him. It was a local tremor, nothing like what Semana had accomplished, but Tithian had to clutch a nearby crate to keep his balance.

"March!" Darak screamed. "Up! Out steel! On your feet! Up the mountain! Go!"

The hundred or so barbarians within the reach of his voice only stared at him, confused. They stood ready to march: Semana intended them to march at dusk, under cover of darkness, on Ruin's Night. They waited, for Darak's voice was not the one they obeyed.

"You—" Tithian stifled a laugh. "You have no power here."

"Power," Darak said, his voice like the growl of an animal. "I will show you power."

He reached out and grasped Crown of Fire, who had started to draw away, and pulled him close. Tithian shared a look with the red-haired barbarian, but he could not cross the intervening distance in time. The fingers of Darak's free hand lengthened and bristled into claws like those of a bear, and they flashed across to rip the young man's throat and chest open. Blood poured forth and Darak bent his head against the flow. It was so sudden and unexpected that Tithian couldn't even react.

Crown of Fire made a gurgling sound that snapped Tithian back into the moment. His heart lurched and he pulled one of his swords. His head felt fuzzy, his senses distorted. A sickness in his head.

Power crackled through Crown of Fire's blood, flowing into Darak and around him. It was not Blood magic—at least not as Tithian had ever seen or felt it practiced. It was crude and disorganized, allowing sickening energy to flood in all directions. Tithian was not the only victim of the power: he saw half a dozen nearby barbarians stagger and wave their limbs about as though without control.

"Mine," Darak said, blood pouring out over his lips. "*Mine!*"

A flare of burning power shot up through his body and slammed into the foot of the mountain, sending a tremor through Tar Vangr, much like the chorus of quakes Semana had caused with his magic this morn. It roared up the mountain and set High-City to trembling on its supports. How he could wield such power, Tithian could not say, but clearly he had little control. The steps Semana had carved with her own magic cracked, sending pieces of rock skittering down the slope. Had he struck again, he might have collapsed the paths entirely, but Crown of Fire's life allowed him only that one strike.

And there did not need to be another. The barbarians saw the display of Darak's power, raised their weapons, and roared his name. As one, they streamed onto the passes and up the mountain, beginning the assault upon Tar Vangr. They marched against Semana's orders, heading up hours early. But there was nothing Tithian could do to stop them.

Darak let Crown of Fire's pale, limp body fall beside him. It bounced and slid to the ground, one listless arm caught over the edge of the tub. Crown's hand clutched at Darak's leg, as though in a last, belated attempt to supplicate him for clemency. The barbarian prince himself looked over at Tithian, his face smeared with crimson blood, his eyes wide and triumphant.

In that horrible moment, Tithian realized that he might have misjudged Darak Ravalis.

"Well," Darak said. "Do you need a command, ugly boy?" He pointed toward the mountain.

Slowly, Tithian put his sword away, the better to move, and he joined the march.

TWENTY-FIVE

THE FIRE WAS IN her dream and in her waking.

Ovelia was blind, but she could see much.

She saw beyond this chamber—beyond this time and place.

She saw Regel as a younger man, stalking across a darkened chamber to nearly behead a man in a single bloody slash of Frostburn.

She saw Garin, reaching for her, just as a terrible explosion ripped his hand apart and sent his body tumbling back.

She saw Semana astride a massive, rippling beast with three jaws and dozens of eyes that sailed through the sky.

She saw Lenalin bathed in silver light, her skin flawless and smooth, her scars healed, fire streaming from her hand.

She saw...

She startled at the feel of cool water at her lips, and it splashed all over her face. She gasped, sure she was drowning. For a heartbeat, Ovelia forgot herself and tried to stand, but pain erupted at her core and put her flat on her back. Anxious hands held her in place.

"Lass," Maure said. "Calm yourself. You're safe."

Ovelia pulled herself back to herself, her face coated in sweat. The air felt icy cold, and her body burned as though her heart was a furnace. Her lungs heaved and she felt so, so tired.

The nurses and attendants had been working on her all morn, their hands of frozen stone making her flinch at their every touch. She had no privacy anymore, no ownership of her own body. It felt like her destiny was no longer in her hands, if it ever had been.

But she had to keep seeing it. Her visions came faster and faster, and she saw across time and space and everywhere. Semana, blood running down her face, leading an army of screaming barbarians. Regel gradually slumping to the ground, cut down by a thousand foes. The great mountain of Tar Vangr collapsing, High-City crumbling in flames and falling stone. A skyship crashing into an army of barbarians, turning them to dust as it ripped through the earth. Cracks ripping through the planet, and Silver Fire rising to burn and destroy everyone and everything.

It all spooled back to the same moment, where she stood at the locus of the Narfire, with a shadow falling across her. She turned, Draca flaming in her fist, and looked into the eyes of Semana.

"Ovelia, lass—" Maure's voice cut through her visions again. "Your child will not turn on its own. I've tried to move it, but I don't have the leverage. I need you to climb onto all fours."

Her insides felt like they were pulling apart. The pain below her belly was intense.

Someone spoke, but Ovelia's ears felt like they were full of water. She parted her cracked, parched lips to snap a curse, but somehow her rage transcended such petty insults.

"First I cannot move, now I *must* move!" Ovelia growled. "*Decide!*"

"The babe must move," Maure said. "On your hands and knees, lass."

"Well!"

It hurt—Silver *Fire* how it hurt—and she had to force her limbs to cooperate, but she managed to shift onto her side, dragging one leg under her. Her belly felt like a burning hot mass of knives, and whenever she touched it, the pain redoubled. If she lay down on her front... No. She could not bear that.

She thought fleetingly of Garin Ravalis, who had put her in this situation, and imagined his cocksure smile. "Cheer up, Lady," he would say to her. "You don't wield a sword between your legs, do you?" And she would laugh at his absurdity and feel better.

Silver Fire burn you, Garin Ravalis, she said in her head. *Why did you have to be kind?*

Finally, she supported herself on all fours, propping herself on her elbows. She pressed her face into the sweaty pillows, inhaling the smells there, and tried not to think about her backside hanging in the cold air. The last time she had borne a child, had it felt so demeaning? The last time...

"Yes, lass, well. Just—"

Ovelia felt Maure's hands on her, one strong palm on her bulging belly while the fingers of her other hand felt at Ovelia's nethers. Vaguely, Ovelia could see two shadowed figures standing near her at the head of the bed, and she glared her defiance at them. She had won harder battles than this.

"The babe is turned, lass," Maure said. "You can lie back."

"Mayhap..." Ovelia grunted as a fresh pang shot through her. "Mayhap I prefer... ugh, this." Her back certainly appreciated the relief, though it made her elbows ache to hold herself up.

"On your back. *Now.*"

She knew better than to argue with that tone. Maure had been her nursemaid as long as she could remember. The woman had attended Ovelia's own birth, and done somewhat to fill the void left by Ovelia's own mother. There was love between them, trust also, and right now, *command*. Ovelia had not given herself over to someone else for years, but just now, she had no choice.

With a series of heaving breaths and gasped curses, Ovelia turned and lay back. Her midsection was still a beating mass of pain, swelling and contracting and seeking to tear her apart, but at least she could breathe. A hand pressed a cool cloth to her brow and she allowed herself a relieved sigh.

Someone was speaking. She could faintly hear the words surrounding her, as of someone delivering an address just outside the door to the chamber. She could not make out the words, but she dimly realized the identity of the speaker. Lenalin sounded strong. Powerful. She did not need Ovelia beside her—not now, perhaps not ever. And that only made Ovelia's heart pound the harder.

Perhaps that was why Regel had faded in Ovelia's heart: he needed her so badly to be what she was not. By contrast, Lenalin did not need her, but chose to share her life and bed with Ovelia anyway. They saw each other for the people they were, good and bad alike, and loved despite it. *Because* of it.

It all seemed like nonsense now, as she lay bearing a dead man's child in a city about to perish. But she had to believe these things mattered, in the final analysis. When the story was told and done.

"Not long now," Maure said. "I can see a bit of hair. Red, like the child's mother."

"Like their father," Ovelia thought she said. The world seemed hazy, not quite fitting together.

Garin. She had loved him, after a fashion: loved his spirit, his will, even his stubbornness. He had been a good man, flawed but important. What Luether and the World of Ruin needed. Would their child—a babe that never should have been conceived—be the same?

Ovelia knew with an inexplicable certainty that she would not see it for herself.

The world shook, and at first Ovelia thought it was just the pain and confusion. Only when folk started falling over did she realize it was another tremor, like those that had ripped through High-City this morn. Maure fell against Ovelia's side, clinging to her protectively. The bed upon which she lay began to slide, its feet scraping loudly against the stone.

Then they were falling.

In her world of shadow, Ovelia could barely make out what was happening. Ewers of water and various implements sailed past her, alongside tumbling bodies with no place to hold on. Maure crushed her down on the massive bed, which at least mostly held its place in the center of the room through sheer mass. But as the tower in which they found themselves listed to the side, it began to slide in the direction of the tilt. Ovelia gritted her teeth against the pain, bracing for the inevitable—

The bed smashed into the wall in the direction of the slide, and in the impact Maure bounced up and off Ovelia. If she had not thrown her arms around the old nurse, she might have lost her forever right then. Bricks rained around them, smashing into the wall-turned-floor, and one smashed numbingly into Ovelia's leg. Dust rushed around them and the roar of the collapsing building tore at Ovelia's ears.

"Hold to me!" she screamed, not knowing whether Maure heard. Or whether she yet lived at all.

The tower cracked like an egg, the wall buckled, and they fell through darkness.

TWENTY-SIX

THE EARTHQUAKE AT HIGHSUN was the signal. The ground shook under his feet, a far greater tremor than any the Blood Queen had lashed through Tar Vangr that morn: entirely uncontrolled, without any focus, causing reckless damage in all directions. More segments of High-City shifted and tumbled, and dust and shards of mage-glass rained down. Through it all, the Children of Ruin cheered and screamed their fury up to the cowering folk and the empty heavens above.

Regel the Frostburn took shelter from the falling detritus where he crouched in the shadow of an abandoned building off the Path of Spidercatchers. His body was battered and covered in dust and blood, and he did not properly remember how he had come to be here. Dimly, he recalled flashes of folk scattering as earth and stone fell upon them, and he—no. Not him. The *sword*.

His eye fell to Frostburn in his hands, its wavy length gleaming bright blue. Hadn't he sworn off this blade? It felt like so long ago now. He could only dimly remember a time when he had not carried this weapon. It felt like a part of him: an extension of his very arm. His very soul, if he had one.

It no longer mattered. He had a quest to fulfill. And Frostburn *hungered*.

The earthquake literally shook him from his dissociative fugue, and he snapped back into focus. Time flowed strangely, but he stood once again at a specific moment. A crossroads of destiny.

Regardless, the Barbarian Prince, swollen with power and smeared with blood, was beyond his reach. Not only was Davargorn there, but Regel counted eight heavily armed barbarians watching over him. They were, even now, strapping the golden power armor that Lan Ravalis had shed after his fall in Low-City. He was too hard a target, and not even Frostburn could overcome so many.

Abruptly, Darak said something to Davargorn, and after a heartbeat's hesitation, the deformed man turned and headed toward the mountain, as though to join the press. Without even properly thinking about it, Regel sheathed Frostburn, slipped out of the shadows, and pursued.

Again, as often in his life before, it came down to one man with one blade.

~

Passing among the barbarian horde was not so difficult. Regel had not looked at himself in a silvered glass in some time, but the thick bristles of his beard itched and his clothes had grown ragged even before his time in Low-City. Those Children who even noticed him required only one look at his grim face before they delivered a grunt of acknowledgement and left him to his own devices.

He had become a Child of Ruin, in all the ways that seemed to matter.

His scuffed and tattered cloak swirled around him, pressing hard against his body and scarred face. Had he worn a mask before? He didn't have it now, but perhaps that was for the best. The barbarians did not wear masks, after all: they preferred to let the cruel elements of Ruin weather and strip their distorted faces. Most brandished their weapons and screamed as they climbed, and Regel slipped among them, unassuming and silent.

The climb was the hardest part. The rough-hewn stone steps were slippery and steep, at least half his own height, and he had to mantle and scramble his way up the mountain path. Had he attempted the climb alone, it might have passed well enough, but he had to contend with thousands of screaming barbarians all trying to climb up the path with him. They pushed and shoved and trod upon each other, some faster than others, many slower. They climbed at a snail's pace, seeming disoriented and confused after just a short way up the mountain. It slowed the climb to a crawl.

Regel looked ahead, to where Davargorn's dark-cloaked form cut through the snow like a hunting wolf. If not for his clubfoot and awkward gait, he'd have already vanished from sight. Regel put his head down and focused on each step ahead of him. At least Frostburn shielded his body from the chill.

Snow fell all around them, billowing in their faces and dusting them with a thick layer of slushy grime. At Regel's side, a barbarian latched onto the next step and slipped free. She gasped, scrabbling at the rock and everyone nearby, and caught hold of Regel's arm. She overbalanced, teetering on the ledge, and he managed to twist free of her hold before she went over. He moved without awareness, and then she was gone, her body smashing against the slope on its way down to the cobbled street.

He stood for a moment, considering his arm where she had grasped. In the moment, he had reacted as though to an attack, and only now did he realize she'd only meant to save herself. Could he not have pulled her back up onto the path?

He realized his quarry had got further and further ahead of him. He had to keep moving.

Halfway up the slope, some hundred and fifty paces above the streets of Low-City, the barbarian horde encountered High-City's defenses.

They didn't attack until Regel came just within their range, after some two hundred barbarians had already entered it. A rain of casterbolts fell upon them, lashing out from the mage-glass supports of High-City and from the city itself like lances of lightning and fire. A score or so caster wielders had climbed down the ladders that normally serviced the gears and chains that carried the great lifts between the levels of the city, but of course the Tar Vangryur had cut the chains shortly after the invasion began, meaning that the ladders now hung, all but unsupported and purposeless, in the cold, whipping wind at that height. Even in his youth, Regel would have considered that a harrowing climb, and he was surprised more warders had not tumbled to their deaths.

He applauded the wisdom in delaying their ambush. They'd waited until the bulk of the horde had climbed within their range, thus trapping hundreds on the mountain path, unable to climb up or down. The will to cling to one of those ladders in the freezing wind for so long, and then to hold while so many barbarians drew close enough to hurl spears at them? Remarkable.

And hurl they did. Spears, axes, even rocks—any weapon the climbing Children could find, they sent arcing toward the defenders on the ladders and mage-glass buttresses. Regel saw one caster wielder take a spear through the chest, gurgle an aborted scream, then fall away into the snowy air, their weather cloak flapping like the wings of a dying bird.

With the line of fire clear, Regel pushed forward to the next hunk of stone that offered cover from the sentries. Rock exploded around him and dust and snow burst into the air with enough force to knock him staggering—lucky, because a casterbolt cut past and ripped his hood free. If he'd still stood, that bolt would have bored a hole through his throat. Instead, it struck a barbarian climbing behind him like a blow of lightning, knocking the man howling and flailing off the mountainside.

At just that moment, Regel saw Davargorn looking back, and their eyes met over the expanse of snow and bloody rock. The younger man crouched behind a natural crenellation for cover from what looked like a rainstorm of casterbolts cutting apart the part of the horde that had climbed ahead of him. The sentries directed volley after volley at the barbarians, staggering their attacks to keep the invaders pinned down and unable to strike back lest they expose themselves to a casterbolt. These warders had particularly good aim, and the path lay littered with crushed and mangled bodies.

301

For the two of them, however, none of that mattered. The world drew down to Davargorn and Regel, and the snow fell slower around them, its descent slowed to a glacial crawl. The sound of folk screaming and dying became a faint, muted curtain that buzzed in his ears. By his face, Davargorn stood in the same world. Slowly, he pulled his mask back, revealing his distorted face and crooked smile.

They both knew that if one of them was to die this day, it would be at the hands of the other.

Then Davargorn smiled, braced, and mantled the rock to run across the field of slaughter.

The suddenness of it startled Regel, and by the time he started forward, Davargorn had made it halfway across. He moved with remarkable speed despite his deformities, bobbing and weaving to avoid the bolts raining down at him. He had no weapons to strike back, nor did he have any interest in making the attempt. He simply ran for the far side, where he could find cover from the casterbolts.

Regel threw himself forward, heart pounding in his head. He was not a young man. He could not move that quickly or that wildly. There was no way he could survive that field. And yet, he did not hesitate. He had no choice. He had to—

A black shape cut up through the air, blocking the caster-wielders, like a dark bird of prey. Lances of green energy snaked out like lashing whips to stab through the sentries, making their bodies burst into bloody husks that plummeted into the snowy sky. Chunks of mage-glass showered down like rain, their edges splintering and rotting away as they fell.

Mask the Blood Queen spun a half circle in the air and rose up, arms stretched wide, the better to survey the mountain path. Her army had climbed perhaps halfway up the mountain, and it was doubtless that it was *her* army. Surely she would see Regel, but her gaze swept past him.

A casterbolt arced toward her, but a shield of blue light sprang into being over her chest and the bolt shattered off to spin listlessly into the snowy sky. She flew on, mayhap to find a better place along the path to protect the march, mayhap to a greater destiny.

Davargorn, Regel realized, was nowhere to be seen.

"Forward!" came a voice from below and behind.

Darak was marching with the army, wielding a spear that seemed to be shaped of three twisting branches. He wore his uncle Lan's golden power armor, smoking with power as it aided in his climb.

"Push forward!" Darak cried. "For Ruin! For Death!"

Regel considered waiting to ambush the barbarian prince, but between the armor, that spear, and the warders that surrounded him, he didn't favor his chances. Nor did he have time to wait, with barbarians streaming up through the gap and surging around him up the path.

Before they arrived, Regel took up a javelin from a dead barbarian, as well as a small, sharp knife he could throw. The weapons must have made him look more convincing as a barbarian, because none of the invaders who noted him took a second look. He pressed forward among the horde, keeping his eyes on the snowy sky for signs of snipers or a leather-clad sorcerer.

At the higher reaches, the mountain pass became rougher and less stable, as Mask had carved these steps faster and from a distance. So too did the winds become fearsome the higher one climbed, and now Regel could feel as well as hear the wind howling, loud enough to drown out even the screaming lunatics all around him. Warriors stumbled and staggered, and a few fell over the sides in their exhaustion, to tumble down the sheer slope and out into the snowy gloom. But for every one that fell, at least ten pushed onward.

Though these barbarians worshipped only death and destruction—though they longed to bring ruin down upon Tar Vangr—they were caught in a struggle against the World of Ruin itself. A world that did everything in its power to force them back. He shivered and forced his limbs to operate, even if the cold could not touch Regel. His life balanced upon a knife's edge. At any moment, he could slip and fall to his death, or walk into an ambush.

Striding into the storm of death, he realized that he had forgotten what it was to be alive.

~

Regel had been climbing for hours, though he could not say how many. His body fought him with every step, and his legs felt increasingly heavy. Had Frostburn not shielded him from the cold, he would not have lasted even this long.

The barbarians were strong and vital, but the farther they climbed from the Nar-heated streets, the more warriors succumbed to the cold. Folk simply collapsed, sinking into snowdrifts riddled with muddy bootprints, and others trod upon them, pushing their bodies deeper into the snow. Whether they clung to life or the cold slew them, no one had the time to recover them or the interest in doing so.

Regel knew the Narfire beat in the heart of the mountain, but it was contained—trapped within tubes of mage-glass constructed more than a thousand years ago. It could not radiate out to save them.

For some reason, that thought lingered in his head and distracted him, nearly to his ruin.

He felt the tremor before he saw the boulders and snow sliding toward him. The avalanche was small, though he knew it would grow in speed and strength as it swept down the path. The world slowed, and snowflakes drifted around his face. He knew he could do something about this, but perhaps he should not. Perhaps, if he wanted to thwart this invasion, he should do nothing—let the avalanche sweep him away, as well as some bulk of the Children of Ruin.

But even if he would have chosen to sacrifice himself in such a way, the sword did not let him.

Frostburn slithered into his hand, gleaming azure against the swirling snow, and he was once again in the collapsing Rat Cellar, surrounded by some of the few survivors of fallen Low-City. At his side, Nacacia scowled and cried out a warning while Erim loosed a terrified scream. At his side, Sarelle Wolfsbane watched Regel with judging eyes, as a child who has seen death before she should. Death had come for her, and she could face it.

Frostburn was in his hands again, and now as then, blue power swelled around him. His hair rose and his cloak billowed. The icy power flowed forth in a shielding wave that struck the advancing doom and froze it in place. One barbarian had the misfortune to stagger into the wave of magic, and his flesh abruptly turned to ice, leaving him a blue- and white-encrusted statue.

Smoke rose all around Regel, and he veritably choked on the miasma of his own magic.

That was when Davargorn ambushed him, sailing out of the snow and smoke like a lancing bird of prey, one sword extended and the other held back, ready to swing. Regel had no time to think, but only react. He danced backward and threw up a firm parry as Davargorn landed in the snow where he had knelt a heartbeat ago.

His blades smashed, one after the other, into Regel's parry, and Davargorn pushed forward with a thrust of his good leg to shove Regel backward. Somehow, Regel kept his balance despite Davargorn's assault, and they broke apart amongst the horde.

Davargorn gave Regel no time to find his balance, but instead surged forward like charging cavalry to spear him on his swords. Regel managed to knock both aside with hard parries that knocked the blades just wide, and fell back rather than take the opening it left. Davargorn pursued, cutting high and low and thrusting straight ahead, pressing for a weakness. Seeking. Unhindered.

A barbarian stumbled into Regel, and he twisted around the man to use him like a shield. The tip of one of Davargorn's blades burst out the man's back, splashing red blood into the snow and only Regel's cloak as he moved. Davargorn whirled right, opposite the direction Regel countered, and ripped his weapons free of the dying barbarian only to run another one through. Regel smashed into a third barbarian, and the two nearly went down together. Instead, Regel twisted free, losing his cloak in the process, and the barbarian fell squirming and shrieking in rage to the ground.

More barbarians tried to seize either or both, but Regel and Davargorn turned their attacks against would-be interlopers, cutting them down before refocusing on one another. The flow of invaders was not a threat to them, but merely a hazard—no more dangerous than a flowing wind or drifting snow. Some of the invaders paused to watch their battle while others pressed on, heedless of the titans clashing in the snow. It was not a flashy combat, but a brutal exchange of efficient thrust and parry and counter and elusion. Blades flashed and caught and pressed, back and forth, sometimes like a wrestling match, sometimes like a fencing bout.

Twin falcata smashed into Regel's sword but he pressed right through, nearly skewering Davargorn's mouth. Were it not for his mask of bones arranged into the visage of a skull, that wild attack would surely have killed him. Instead, it tore away the lower half of the mask in a shower of leather, bones, and blood. He fell back, sputtering and cursing, and tore his mask from his face. He and Regel faced one another, their faces bare to the elements. Hatred burned wildly between them.

Regel had to win this duel. For Lenalin and Ovelia. For Tar Vangr.

Regel and Davargorn fought, clashing and grappling back and forth, carving arcs and jagged lines in the snow with their feet and blades. They should have slowed by then, panting and heaving, but they drove themselves past the point of exhaustion. Regel could feel magic rising up within him, flooding his limbs with new strength, and he could see the same happening in Davargorn. Their mirrored power reflected one another and grew stronger. Neither could kill the other, and so neither could die.

The horde chanted and cheered. Some might have recognized one or the other of the duelists, but that wasn't the point. Regel caught a glimpse of Darak among their ranks, his face mostly hidden behind the golden helmet. Whether he knew Regel or not, he made no move to intervene. Indeed, he drummed his spear in time with the chant. Perhaps he was more of a barbarian than he pretended.

The horde bore witness to the rage of Ruin, visited down upon Tar Vangr this day, reduced to the tiny world between these two men. One fighting for life, one for death. Only—

Only that wasn't true.

It occurred to Regel like a blow of lightning—so abrupt and powerful he nearly missed a parry and came away with a slashed arm for his trouble. Davargorn pressed, but Regel slammed a shoulder into his chest, driving him back and separating them for a heaving heartbeat.

Nearly single-handedly, the two men had brought the invasion to a crawl, as more and more barbarians stopped to watch their battle. They were chanting, and Regel could faintly make out the single word they repeated over and over: "Death," they cried. "Death! Death! Death!"

All his intentions, all his rage, and what was he doing? Fighting. Shedding blood. For what?

And in that moment, the world seemed to slow. Davargorn dived toward him, swords raised for Regel's heart and stomach, his mouth contorted in a screaming snarl. The barbarians around him caught mid-chant. Darak's eyes blazed in the darkness of his mask. The snow drifted lazily past Regel's face.

In that moment, Regel stood in a snowy field far removed from the mountain of Tar Vangr, facing the Deathless Rose as they danced for the final time. She looked upon him, and there was a smile in her eyes. She knew something he had not, but now, he started to understand. Too late.

As the blades came scything for him—one to spit his heart, one to disembowel him—Frostburn fell limply to the side. Regel was defeated, in part by Davargorn, but mostly by Ruin itself.

Then light flared into being behind him, so bright and powerful Davargorn screamed and faltered. He fell and covered his lidless white eye. Regel turned, though he knew from the feel of the wind rushing around him and the hum of mage-engines what he would see.

Great golden rings scythed around the *Hecatomb* as it loomed out of the storm toward them, narrowly navigating the remaining mage-glass buttresses. Its great lights flared to life only when it was too late for the barbarians to flee. Behind the mage-glass of the bridge of the skyship, Lenalin's eyes burned with wild hatred, and he thought he could see the teeth of her angry smile gleaming.

Then the *Hecatomb*'s weapons poured forth a storm of death upon the horde.

TWENTY-SEVEN

IT WAS A DESPERATE plan, one that should have yielded only mixed results. The massive *Hecatomb* could hardly fit under High-City, and it clanked and groaned as it flew. No one could have imagined it would escape notice among the invaders, but the thick snowfall had built into a raging blizzard as the day lengthened, covering the approach of the skyship as it flew dark. Thus, when it fell upon the invading force, they knew no reason to avoid congregating in a single place.

Thus, hundreds upon hundreds of lives boiled away in a roaring storm of fire, lightning, and lancing casterbolts. The *Hecatomb's* own weapons caused the brunt of the damage, while a dozen of Lady Shard's elite pirates fired with discretion and accuracy. Any barbarian who took aim with a javelin or a caster of their own caught a blast in the chest that knocked them tumbling back through the snow.

The *Hecatomb* killed over a thousand people in heartbeats. No hesitation. No mercy.

This was Queen Shard's plan. This was who she was.

The white flurry became red and ashen, the mountainside reduced to a smear, as the skyship pressed upon the spine of the horde in an effort to break the back of the invasion.

And it might have succeeded, had not a wave of green tendrils of power swept across the deck, rotting them away into moldering, skeletal corpses at a pass. One of the pirates caught a green blast tearing across his stomach and right arm, which dissolved into dessicated bone and pus while he collapsed gurgling to the deck. Pirates leaped for cover, crying out in alarm and terror.

The Blood Queen swept up inside the Hecatomb's scything rings—inside the reach of the skyship's main weapons—faced the mage-glass windows of the bridge, and locked eyes with Queen Shard, who stood in the mage-pilot's place.

"Hail, Mother," Semana said.

Shard could not have heard her words over the roar of the storm, of course, but she responded as though she had. The words struck her like a blow and she screamed through the glass.

The *Hecatomb* abruptly surged backward, so suddenly that a stream of fire from one of the cannons swept just short of Semana's hovering feet. She narrowly dodged the scything rings, floating outside the skyship's corona, just at the edge of its firing solution. Smoke poured from her boots, projecting her forward, and she spiraled up and toward the retreating craft. Proximity was her only safety, but that also opened her to the attacks of Shard's pirates. One leaned out from cover to loose a bolt with a mighty *crack* in her direction, and it narrowly missed only because of the skyship's wild flight.

The *Hecatomb* roared back through the storm, and Semana flew after it. The skyship snapped a mage-glass buttress like dry kindling, sending shard of glass flying in all directions. Semana narrowly dodged one significant chunk, and used her silver glove to throw herself wide of a shock of lightning. She sailed forward after the retreating skyship, which did its best to bring its weapons to bear. But when she drew too close, one of the pirates loosed a bolt that smashed into her leg with a numbing impact.

In this way, they danced through the forest of mage-glass supports under High-City, smashing many of the supports aside like shattering ice. The *Hecatomb's* weapons fired up at Semana like heavy casters trying to cut down a sparrow, while her own sickly Plaguefire carved smoking scars across the craft as they flew. Somehow, Shard's evasive piloting minimized the strikes, and one of the rings always interposed itself between Semana and the bridge in time to deflect any of her blasts. She felt like an angry fly attacking a bucking horse—one that lashed out with hooves and teeth and tail made of flames.

With a burst of energy, Semana threw herself inside the rings just as they scythed around, missing her trailing ankle by a hair. She alighted on the main deck, and immediately fell behind a half-melted bulkhead where her magic had carved a path of destruction. It felt odd, cowering behind cover like this, the way Tithian might have done during their time together. But her magic was running low, and she didn't have enough to spare to shield herself from bolts she could avoid. Her lungs heaved, and she tried to calm herself with an effort of will. Until a bolt shattered off the bulkhead a thumb's length from her head, at least, at which point she ducked lower and panted.

She leaned out from cover, and a bolt reflected off her cover and sparked off the shield that sprang into being around her shoulder. The impact struck through her shield, and her shoulder burst into pins and needles of numbness as pulled back. At least she'd had the chance to count the opposition: four of them. And they were the best trained or at least had the best instincts, because they remained behind cover and took turns discharging their casterbolts in her direction. They knew how to fight together, and they would defend their captain to the death.

She reached out with her senses for their blood, but another thunderous discharge stole her focus, and she couldn't get a taste. Also, with hundreds of folk gathered in close proximity, finding these four specific bloods felt like trying to scoop up drops of oil floating in an ewer of steaming hot water.

Semana looked around and sent tendrils of Plaguefire toward one of the massive storage crates behind which one of the pirates hid, hoping perhaps she could destroy it. But that caused only a little damage and got her a casterbolt to the arm for her trouble. She could feel the power draining away from her breastplate, and suspected she could only suffer one or two more strikes like that.

How did anyone fight like this? She didn't have the experience or training for this. Tithian was the one who knew how to fight like this. If only he were here…

Semana pulled the last of her Worldfire to stiffen her body, making her flesh like stone. Her body became heavier and sluggish—slower to move— but she might survive a blow if her breastplate's magic failed. She felt the moderate charge left in her mask and glove, and decided it would have to do.

A sparking casterbolt passed overhead, leaving the stench of burning air, and she moved.

Semana ducked from behind cover, starting to stand but only as a feint. She ducked low and took three steps, until she could see just a bit of one of the pirates—the edge of their boot—and loosed her magic. Even as a casterbolt struck her in the thigh, which went limp under her, she snatched that boot with the magic of her silver glove and wrenched upward. The pirate gave a wild cry and sailed upward, dragged aloft, until Semana cut him in two rotting pieces with a whip of Plaguefire. The top of the corpse sailed away into the storm of snow, lightning, and flame.

For a heartbeat, Semana saw Lady Shard reflected in the window at the end of the deck, behind all the pirates with their casters, and she hurled the bottom half of the corpse—still held in the grasp of her magic—right at the bridge. The pirate's armored form smashed into the mage-glass and didn't make so much as a dent, but Semana heard the scraping sound it generated. It slid free with a sickly squelch, leaving a thick trail of blood and viscera smeared across the glass.

Semana looked up in time to see Lady Shard's first mate—Aeldad, was it?—pointing a heavy caster in her direction. She loosed bolts from both slots of the caster, one of fire and one of lightning, which slammed into Semana with enough force to fling her wildly back against the rail. There she lay stunned for a heartbeat, certain the bolts had penetrated her body and nailed her to the bulkhead. She coughed and there was wetness on her lips—blood or spittle, she didn't have the chance to check.

Aeldad could have loosed upon her again, but instead she ducked right back behind cover. The other pirates were doing likewise—taking cover and bracing on the snow-strewn deck as the Hecatomb plummeted, its velocity pulling downward. Down toward—

Semana chanced a look over her shoulder as the skyship swung crazily back toward the mountain, and she saw the burning stone and sizzling snow looming closer in her view. She summoned the power in her boots and projected herself up and away in a swirl of foul-smelling smoke just as the skyship scrapped itself with crushing force against the mountain. Another instant, and the *Hecatomb* would have wiped her off itself like a splattered insect.

Semana flew crazily, uncontrolled without her silver glove's stabilizing power, and avoided a blast of flame from the *Hecatomb's* main cannon by sheer luck. She felt the intense heat and smelled her leather burning. She tumbled and flailed in the air, desperately trying to keep wide of the ship as it scraped. Chunks of stone and corpses showered around her, and she flew crazily back and forth to avoid being crushed. One particularly large boulder broke free of the mountain and tumbled toward her, and she blasted herself aside just as it ripped past on its bouncing descent toward Low-City.

Was Lady Shard insane? Did she mean to *destroy* her own city to save it?

If that was indeed her plan, it was proceeding apace. Semana caught a brief vantage on the situation, and it was not encouraging. The barbarian army was in shambles, effectively halted on the mountain path and swarming like an angry, half-dead beehive. The bulk of the remaining force had halted just outside the range of the warders up in High-City, who could pick off the vanguard at their leisure. She cared little interest for the Children of Ruin, the invasion, or Tar Vangr in general, but something about the destruction and death set her teeth on edge.

It felt like such a waste—so unnecessary and foolish and disgusting.

She heard it then—dimly, mostly blocked out by the surging storm and the scream of the damaged skyship, but there: screaming. The folk of High-City cried out in terror, and the weapons of their warders turned to new targets: the barbarians who came boiling out of the very palace itself.

While the bulk of the force braved the icy climb, a hundred or so had delved into the twisting dark of the passages that honeycombed the mountain of Tar Vangr. This had been Semana's initiative, one Darak argued stringently against at first, but he'd have to concede now. If he even yet lived.

She'd seen him on the field of battle, hadn't she? Just before the *Hecatomb* had attacked…

Semana bit her lip to bring herself back to the battle. Her whole body ached and she felt immensely tired, but if she lost focus, she was lost.

The *Hecatomb* pulled up, its rings grinding and sweeping barbarians free of the path, then tore free of the mountainside. It shook and trembled but propelled itself upward, the scything rings trailing smoke, blood, and snow into the air. Semana, hanging in the air none too far below where it had crashed, looked upward, panting. Did Shard intend to fly to High-City's rescue? Or mayhap escape?

Only one thing was certain: the day was not lost yet.

Semana poured power into her boots and pursued, launching herself into the blurry storm. She had to confront Shard. Finish this.

As she passed the ledge, a dark form hurtled out of the snow and latched onto her, knocking them both into a stuttering spin. Semana almost hurled her uninvited passenger into the snow with her silver glove, but the weight was somehow familiar and reassuring. At a glance, she recognized Tithian's mottled face, and even more so, the determination in his eyes. They exchanged a glance and a nod, Tithian tightened his arm around her waist, and together they shot up through the storm after the *Hecatomb*. He felt almost frozen, but she hardly had time to think on that now.

Shard steered the skyship out from under High-City out over the bay, its propulsion rings trembling as they scythed around it to keep it aloft. The craft listed slightly to starboard, clearly wounded but not yet incapacitated. It only seemed more dangerous to her, especially now that she'd seen how much Shard was willing to destroy that she might win.

Semana flew them after the ship, darting into its unpredictable ring cycle about where she had landed before. This time, however, she dropped Tithian, who hit the deck at a roll and came up behind the same block of cover she had previously occupied, and alighted just beside him.

Semana screamed to be heard over the howling wind and the rings. "Can you get to her?"

Whether Tithian understood her or not, he nodded, and was off like a shot. His blade he held under his tattered snow-scarred cloak, and a frosty trail seemed to follow him as he ran.

This was his element. He kept fine balance on the rolling deck, dashed between points of cover, and cut one down before they even knew what was happening. The remaining two directed their fire that way, and Tithian crouched low to avoid their bolts.

Semana saw her chance, and she took it.

They were far enough away from the horde that she could taste individuals' blood: Tithian's, hot and salty and carrying a familiar taint to it, and also the two pirates guarding the deck. One of them tasted very strong—the blood of a warrior twice her weight and strength, clearly Aeldad—while the other she could take hold of more easily. She reached out and grasped at that pirate, and one of the two warders abruptly cried out as his body seized up, against his own control.

Suddenly, she was two people—herself and the smaller pirate—sprouting limbs that she could only numbly control. Dully, she heard badgering cries from Aeldad, whose blood beat faster in her ears. Semana held a caster in the hand that was not her own, and she started to raise it.

Unfortunately, without the slightest hesitation, the woman loosed a casterbolt right into Semana's borrowed chest, and the sorceress lost her connection, clutching at the false pain.

It gave Tithian an opening, though, and he rushed across the rolling deck, seemingly leaving a trail of frost as he ran. He leaped as Aeldad brought the caster around to cast at him. He dodged, mostly because he had thrown himself forward and aside as she loosed, and the bolt skipped harmlessly past. He rolled to his feet, right into the butt of her spent caster, which struck him in the left shoulder and sent him sprawling to the deck.

As she loomed over him, the first made cast the caster aside and wrenched her mask open to reveal her hard, powerful face and wild eyes. "You face the Crushing Aeldad, Ravalis dog," she said, voice booming. "My mistress should've killed you when first—"

Wordless, he drew a handcaster and loosed from the deck, catching her in her thick midsection. She staggered back another step, her expression one of shock. She looked down at the wound, wrenched the quarrel free and dripping, then grinned at him as he climbed to his feet.

"I agree," she said, drawing a huge axe from off her back. "No words."

Tithian gave her a faint nod, then fell back into a fighting stance. He pushed his cloak away, revealing his drawn sword glowing glacial blue in the stormlight. Semana drew in a sharp gasp.

That was *Frostburn*.

How he had obtained Regel's sword—her father's sword—Semana had no idea. But she knew its fearsome power, and terrible hope erupted inside her. They could win this day.

Aeldad did not seem to know the danger, or perhaps she did not care. She leaped upon Tithian with a roar, axe whistling and blood sailing. Perhaps he had expected the legendary weapon to give her pause, as he seemed surprised at her ferocity. He fell back, narrowly knocking her axe just wide of his arm. Frostburn traced lines of rimefrost through the air.

As she caught her breath, Semana took a moment to watch them. Their duel drew her in, hypnotic despite its lack of grace or beauty. The two of them hacked and pushed at each other like laborers at a fallen tree they meant to reduce to kindling. Again and again Aeldad struck, keeping Tithian constantly on the defensive. He had fought enough axe-wielders that he knew not to block the axe with something as comparatively fragile as a sword. And she swung that weapon so hard and so fast Semana doubted even the legendary Frostburn would survive a direct hit. Aeldad hit his block halfway, making their weapons scream, and he fell to his backside before her, faltering.

"Tithian!" Semana screamed, and threw a bolt of Plaguefire at Aeldad's back.

The pirate anticipated the strike, and turned halfway to interpose the bracer on her left forearm between herself and the magic. Semana gasped as the ropey green tendrils flowed harmlessly into her bracer, dissipating into acrid but harmless smoke. She felt the bracer drawing more magic out of her, in fact—sucking greedily at her mask. She took an involuntary step forward before she managed to wrench the magic free of the bracer, letting it writhe randomly and cruelly across the deck, leaving rotting scars in the iron and wood. Only then, panting, did Semana see that Aeldad had drawn a handcaster and pointed it in her direction. The woman cast, and Semana's blue shield rose to protect her—mostly. The bolt put her flat on her back, head ringing from the impact. She tasted blood where she'd bit her tongue.

Tithian uttered a wordless cry and threw himself at Aeldad, sweeping Frostburn at her head in a scything blue arc, but the woman was quicker than such a massive body had any right to be. She thrust out with the butt of her axe, catching him with bruising force in the center of his chest. Semana could hear his ribs groan even from so far away. He slid back, his bad foot dragging, and stayed on the defensive. Her axe slammed into Frostburn again and again, trailing rimefrost through the air.

At least they two were fighting again, but the duel was decidedly one-sided. No fantastic, nigh-mythical sword could overcome such an obvious disparity in strength and reach. And Tithian was exhausted, having climbed most of the way up the mountain and then fought Regel himself. Whereas Aeldad seemed all but fresh. Even with his magic spurring him on, Tithian could not last forever.

"Go," Tithian said between strikes. "Find—Shard—"

He was right. The *Hecatomb* had almost righted itself, now poised above High-City. If they did not stop Lenalin now, she would thwart their attack, and possibly bring the mountain down in the process. With Aeldad occupied, Semana could get past her to the bridge. But she couldn't move her body. She just sat there, exhausted, watching the battle unfold, demanding more magic flow into her drained relics. Who had she been, to think she could single-handedly defeat a skyship?

She had to help him, but her magic was failing her.

She tried to use her blood magic to seize hold of Aeldad, or at least slow her, but again her bracer flared with bright light and Semana's magic distintegrated into nothing. Until that bracer was overwhelmed, she could not touch Aeldad with magic, and she did not have enough power to defeat it. She could do nothing but watch as Tithian kept giving ground, seeking shelter behind caster placements and dust magic batteries, and Aeldad pursued him doggedly, hacking him down, shoving him—where?

Toward the railing, Semana realized, where he would have nowhere else to go.

Her heart leaped into her throat as she saw Tithian desperately parry the axe aside, leaving both weapons helplessly wide, and Aeldad kicked him square in the stomach. He slammed back into the loosened railing, which gave way under his weight and tumbled out into the storm. Tithian caught himself and hung halfway off the skyship, Frostburn dangling among the furious winds—it seemed to have frozen to his hand, and that was the only way he kept hold of it. The golden propulsion rings of the *Hecatomb* spun not too far below him, and Semana had a terrible vision of Tithian sliced in half by intersecting rings. Her heart thudded in her throat.

Why couldn't she move? Why couldn't she—?

Aeldad stood over Tithian, mist rising from the head of her axe. Her bare face was all but feral, her eyes blazing, and bloody spittle drooled down her chin. A drop fell onto her axe, which was shot through with icy lines, and froze into a bloody teardrop. She lifted the axe over her head.

Semana put the last of her will into her silver glove, demanding it unleash a spark of power to knock the axe from Aeldad's hands, but the most she could muster was a tiny flicker. It was little more than a flick of a finger, but when it touched her axe, the frozen corner of the blade snapped off and flew away into the swirling snow. The pirate didn't seem to notice.

"Tithian," she said. "The axe—"

There was no way he could have heard her. Not over the roaring storm and the shuddering mage-engine clanking away beneath them. And yet, somehow he knew. The axe came down, and Tithian brought up Frostburn to parry with only one hand on the hilt.

The axe should have plunged clean through the mage-glass blade and thence into Tithian's chest, but instead, the frozen steel shattered into a hundred shards that flew in all directions. So many strikes against Frostburn had weakened the axe, and it snapped like ice.

Driven by the momentum of the clashing axe, the sword cut down, cleaved through one of Aeldad's arms, and halfway through her chest. The pirate looked down at Tithian, her expression caught between frustration and surprise, then staggered forward, scrabbling for him with her one remaining arm. They struggled, but he slipped free of her weakening fingers, and her bulk tumbled over the side of the skyship into the obscuring storm.

The paralysis that had gripped Semana finally lifted, and she ran forward to Tithian's side. He took her hand, and together they pulled him back up onto the deck. Frostburn glittered in his hand.

"Pass well?" she asked, pulling her mask back on her head.

He returned a curt nod. He pointed to her silver glove, then her mask.

"All but exhausted," she said. "Yours?"

He grunted. He held Frostburn far from his body, as though the blade stung him at its proximity. And sure enough, Semana could see trails of ice creeping up his arm.

One doom at a time.

Together, they looked to the bridge of the *Hecatomb*, and shared another nod. The time had come, Semana knew, to confront her mother. She would be ready.

～

In an increasingly cold world, he found it difficult to think clearly.

His Master was there, so distracting with her warm flesh. He could see the steam of her breath, the tiny flush in her cheeks, and especially the cold fire inside her body. That, most of all, drew him to her. He longed to hold that power inside himself, that it might marry with the power of Frostburn and...

What? Increase his strength? Turn him to ice forever? He did not know, and yet he relished it.

"Tithian," Semana was asking. "Tithian, are you with me?"

That was a name that indicated him. He clawed down the sudden urge to run her through with Frostburn—an image that filled him with inescapable horror—and nodded. He swallowed the lump in his throat but still could not speak. Instead, he nodded.

She looked relieved. "Together, then."

He nodded, still unable to speak. His lips felt frozen shut. His *teeth*.

They had paused at the door to the skyship bridge, and other than the clanking mage-engine, the world had gone eerily silent. The *Hecatomb*'s

315

weapons had stopped firing, and even the storm seemed to have eased somewhat. All around them, the snow fell in soundless white flakes that gave off only the faintest of sizzles when they touched their exposed skin. Tithian could feel the cool flakes melting on his unmasked face, but he felt no pain. Mayhap his magic swallowed up any damage before it could register, or mayhap Frostburn protected him—deadened his flesh so he felt nothing.

Nothing but cold.

"I'll open the door," Semana said in his ear. "You move first."

He nodded, mostly because it barely occurred to him to argue. Her hand trembled slightly as she reached for the crank, and it took some effort to turn it. The stout door of black metal showed burns and scorch marks from many battles, tarnishing its shining newness that seemed so alien to his eyes. Tithian had watched the *Hecatomb* rise from the pit less than a year ago, raining fiery death in its nigh-celestial majesty, and now it looked well worn upon the path to becoming just another battered relic of a forgotten age. All things, he recalled, must pass to Ruin.

The latch clicked and Semana pulled the door open to admit Tithian's darting form. He ducked low and rushed forward, fully expecting a casterbolt to come sizzling for his head. No such attack befell, however, and he ran through the cold, frozen world and pressed up against a blocky altar-like pedestal that grew from the floor, emblazoned with glowing red sigils and a thin coating of grime from the magic it was putting off. A skyship control column. It simmered with something bubbling hot and powerful atop its surface, so Tithian peeked around the column instead of over.

There in the center of the room, surrounded by six such columns placed equidistant around her, knelt Lady Shard, Queen Lenalin of Tar Vangr. She wore her familiar black robe with the hood mostly hiding her face, but Tithian could see the flash of her cold eyes in the light of the burning altars. Channels of magic power flowed from her hands into the pedestals, propelling the ship and controlling its armament, and a glowing star of crimson energy surrounded her on the ground, the pedestals anchoring its points. Tithian had seen mages pilot skyships and caravels before, but this one seemed grander and more complex than any he had witnessed. Most mage-engines only required inputs to a single control pedestal, but the *Hecatomb* must have been powerful indeed if it had six.

"I see you," Shard said from the center of the magecraft star. "You need not hide from me. Come, daughter of Denerre—" She sniffed in Tithian's direction. "And her hound."

To his surprise, Semana did exactly as she bid. She strode into the room, pulling back her mask to face Shard openly. "You have lost, Your Majesty," she said. "All your—"

"All my warders are dead, even Aeldad?" Shard sighed, and Tithian could see the sweat dripping from her nose. "I knew that as soon as you opened that door. Did my first mate die well, at least?"

Tithian heard the faintest bit of emotion in the question, but only because Frostburn made him hyperaware of his surroundings. He could sense the vibrations of strain in her body from the effort of piloting the *Hecatomb*. He could smell the sweat coating her robe. She stank of desperation.

"She—she did," Semana said. "A fitting end for a fitting warrior."

Tithian glanced to her, confused at the hesitation in her voice. He'd never heard Semana quaver in that way, and wondered at first if she was wounded. Only then did he see the moisture brimming in her eyes. Tears. He had never seen her weep—at least, not genuine tears. He grasped Frostburn tighter.

"I suppose you expect me to surrender," Shard said. "Now that you have defeated me."

"Mother, I—" Semana took a step toward her, then abruptly froze in place. Tithian immediately saw the cause: a light caster in one of Shard's hands, pointed at Semana's face.

"Don't call me that."

Shard reached over with her free hand and pulled her hood back, revealing her mangled face: lop-sided cheeks, mouth drawn up on one end and down the other, one eye swollen half-shut, her nose little more than a pair of nostrils. She was a horror. In his frozen world, Tithian felt nothing.

"I'm not your mother, lass," Shard said. "I'm not the Princess of bloody Denerre or the Queen of frostbit Tar Vangr. None of it, but especially not that."

"I don't—" Semana choked on the words. "I know about Regel, mother. I know—"

"You know *nothing*." She emphasized the word by shaking the caster at Semana. "*Nothing*."

Tithian crept around to flank her. She hadn't seemed to notice him. All her attention lay upon Semana, who had advanced a step closer. Just a little farther…

"The Frostburn told me the truth," Semana said. "He told me you bore him a child, and—"

"Ha! Ha *ha*!" Shard threw back her head and laughed. "Poor childish fool, taken in by the lie. The bloodbroken *lie* my father told everyone. And you believed it. And so did Regel. Ha!"

Semana looked utterly confused. "But, your child—yours and Regel's—"

"A deformed monster that nearly killed me, ripped from my womb by… *Father*." Shard's caster trembled. "Oh yes, I rutted Regel, and I bore his ruinspawn child, but not you, no. You're not mine."

Semana's eyes went wide. "But—"

Shard sneered, like a beast rather than a woman. "No child of mine!"

And abruptly she loosed her hold on the *Hecatomb*'s mage-engine. The skyship gave a lurch and Semana stumbled. Shard fell too, but her aim was true. Her finger squeezed the trigger of her caster.

Tithian was there, grappling to knock the caster off-line. The bolt discharged toward Semana but Tithian couldn't see her: grappling with Shard consumed all his attention. She proved surprisingly strong and agile despite her torn and ruined body, and he succeeded only in tackling her against the wall. There she fought and squirmed, locking her jagged teeth on his wrist. With Frostburn's aid, he didn't feel the pain, and simply pushed her head back against the metal wall and slid his hand down to seize her throat. Frostburn was an icicle in his hand and he put the point against her side.

"Hold."

Semana appeared at Tithian's side, a streak of blistered skin across the side of her face where the casterbolt must have just missed her. Her eyes blazed.

"What have you done?" she demanded, pointing to the fading crimson star of power.

"I've done what your mother couldn't do," Shard said. "I've killed you." She leered at Tithian through bloody teeth. "And your dog as well."

Out the big, scorched windows of *Hecatomb*'s bridge, Tithian could see the mountain of Tar Vangr approaching. He could feel the skyship dipping under their feet and listing slightly to the side. Undirected, without control, they would crash into the mountain in mere moments with a thunderous cacophony and then utter silence.

His only thought, in that moment, was for Semana. Could she escape this doom?

"Right the ship," Semana said.

"Or you'll slay me?" Shard shrugged as far as Tithian's arm permitted her. "I don't fancy it."

Tithian nearly drove Frostburn through her in that moment, but his arm wouldn't move. Semana, he realized, had seized him with her blood magic, and he hadn't even felt it. When had she taken hold of him? And why hadn't Frostburn warned him in some way? It seemed as if the sword had actively suppressed his senses, so that he couldn't even begin to resist her control.

Deep inside, an angry monster roared and flailed at her shackles, but in vain. Frostburn enclosed it in an icy prison, built of his blood frozen all around him.

"Right," Semana said, eyes flaring red. "The." Shard's body went taut, and Tithian could feel her muscles flexing to their limit. "Ship." Her body swelled, heart racing, about to burst. "*Now.*"

"Torture... is it?" Shard said, her voice a strangled gasp. Her eyes were wet and angry as she looked at Semana. "I told you... no daughter... of mine."

Semana's lip curled in a snarl or else a cry of despair. "You'll kill hundreds or thousands of your own people, why, just to kill me?"

Shard's eyes fairly bugged out of her face and she coughed blood. "Whatever... I must..."

Tithian could see the pleading on Semana's face, barely beneath the surface, restrained by years of pain and loneliness and regret. *"Mother, please!"* A younger Semana might have said. But it was too late, now. And in her pain, cracks spread through the bloody ice enclosing his heart and mind.

"She won't," Tithian said, finally able to speak. "You must fly."

Semana sucked in a breath. "I will take us both."

"You have enough magic for that?"

From her gutted expression, he knew the answer before he had even asked the question. "Tithian, your magic won't be strong enough," she said. "You must—"

That heartbeat of distraction was all it took to push back against her control. The arm holding Frostburn moved, but not to kill. Instead, he shoved the pommel of the mage-glass sword into Semana's chest, forcing her to stumble back a step. He pulled away from Shard and pointed the sword at Semana.

"Go," he said. "Fly."

"Tithian—"

They must have shared a gaze for only heartbeats, but it felt like hours. Tithian could see the pain on Semana's face—barely restrained, about to burst at any moment. Blood vessels stood out at her temples and the vein in her forehead seemed ready to pop. Even in his icy prison, he felt a raw, hot flood rising to thaw Frostburn's awful power. Then, as violently as the emotions had appeared, they retreated behind a cold mask of frostbitten stone.

"Who." She looked back to Shard. "Who is my mother?"

"You already know." Her face a mass of weeping scars, Shard drooled blood and snot. *"Sister."*

Eyes startled, Semana opened her mouth to question or protest or something, but at that moment the *Hecatomb* smashed into one of the tallest keeps in High-City, sheering the building in half and throwing them all down in the tremor. The mage-glass windows of the bridge shattered around them, sending shards flying like deadly knives in all directions. Semana shrieked and ducked to avoid the shrapnel, but Shard took at least one piece in the side of one arm. She hardly seemed to notice.

Tithian landed on his backside, and the gagging Lady Shard scrambled away from him, gulping in air. She reached for the fallen caster just as Semana did, and the two of them knocked it skittering across the deck. Semana reached for it, but Shard caught at her leg to draw her back. They wrestled, and Semana dealt Shard a desperate elbow to the face, allowing her to stagger away. Shard caught herself on the nearest control pedestal, hand atop the searing hot surface as though it didn't harm her.

The caster slid to Tithian's feet, charged and ready to cast again.

The *Hecatomb* went into a lazy sideways spin, and Tithian saw the view of the mountain slide around from the front windows to those off the port bow. The deck sloped as the ship drifted, listless but picking up speed, toward the mountain. Semana had to go, and soon, or she would be crushed as surely as the rest of them. Semana was screaming at Shard, but Tithian couldn't understand the words.

Everything went cold for him as he picked up the caster, took aim, and cast.

A clap of thunder and the sizzle of lightning, and the casterbolt blasted straight into Semana's chest. Her flaring blue energy shield absorbed some of the blow, sending her flying backward. Tithian saw her eyes widen as she tumbled out the far window of the bridge and out into the storm.

Clinging to the pillar for balance, Shard loosed something like a gurgling laugh and ran one hand through the sweat-soaked tufts of her silver-blonde hair. "Amazing," she said. "You *do* love her."

The mountain loomed, and Tithian thought he only had heartbeats. He tossed the caster aside, climbed up the pitching deck, and stood over Shard. She looked up at him, defiant and furious.

"Kill me then," she said. "That's what you're good for."

Tithian shook his head. "Not today."

He laid his hands upon her mangled face, and she screamed in surprise and frustration.

They hit.

BOOK SIX: IMMORTALS

Eleven years ago—Ruin's Night, 966 Sorceris Annis—
The Palace of Tar Vangr, City of Steel

L ENALIN DENERRE HAD NEVER liked children.

And this one in particular—Semana Denerre nô Ravalis—this one she hated.

She sat alone in her darkened chamber, windows shut against the snow outside. It couldn't quite block out the sounds of pyrotechnics celebrating the cycle of doom and rebirth outside. It was Ruin's Night, she thought, which seemed fitting.

Bad enough that duty to her Blood and her people had prompted her to bind herself in servitude to Paeter Ravalis, the worst man she had ever met, and bear him a child. Even worse that Lan had given the child a name immediately—*Darak*, of all things, which sounded like a dog's name—and insisted on calling them a boy from their birth. It was uncouth, it was ignoble, and if Lenalin had cared even one whit about the little monster who crawled kicking and screaming from between her legs, she'd have...

What? What would she have done?

"Nothing," she murmured to herself as she looked in the full-length mirror. She selected a small bottle from the side table and applied rouge to cover up the bruise developing on her left cheek.

She did nothing when her father paraded her before the Ravalis boys: leering Lan, who drooled over her and Ovelia both, and Paeter, whose cold eyes made her uneasy. She did nothing when her father insisted on this "marriage" to unite Denerre. She did nothing while she carried Paeter's disgusting child, only to give birth to the wretch on the day of Luether's fall—the day her mother died.

She *tried* to do nothing and let Darak perish, but fate had chosen otherwise. Cruel, cruel fate.

She had played the role of a dutiful "wife"—that was the term the Ravalis used, for a woman sold into slavery to a man—and never crossed her "husband" where others might see. She wouldn't want to undermine *his* self-confidence, after all. That, she could not do.

The first time she had refused him, the night of their bonding, he had punched her in the stomach where a bruise would not easily show. It had been so sudden and so violent—so unexpected—that Lenalin hadn't known how to react. He'd hit her again and again until she finally gave in. The beatings continued regardless, though if she offered herself to him, it would not be so bad. This night, she nursed several hurts, particularly on her left arm and hip—two of his favorite spots to hurt her. That arm had been broken so many times she wondered if she should bother having it splinted.

And she'd done nothing.

Perhaps it was fear, or perhaps it was contempt, for herself as much as anyone else.

A gentle rapping at her door announced a servant come to address any needs Lenalin might have. She remained silent, and eventually the servant went away. They were trained to do so, after all: if no reply came, all knew not to bother the Winter Princess. It was for the best, as Lenalin couldn't say whether she would scream or cry at someone who came upon her now.

Contempt, she thought, lacquered nails scraping at the cold stone of the small table.

It was definitely contempt, and not *just* for herself.

Semana, too, they held in contempt, and so did Lenalin. They made her parade around and pretend the spawn was of her own flesh. They shared blood, oh that was true, and by the *Fire* had she raged at that ignominity. But to force her to feign love and affection for the little urchin made Lenalin sick. And that it had taken the only thing she cared about—her sister at heart, Ovelia—who was utterly lost to her now. How perfectly horrible. It was her own fault, of course. Her own stupid, avoidable fault.

Because she had finally done something.

Regel the Frostburn, her father's kept slayer. Her shadow and devoted warder. Of *course* he had loved her, why would he not? And she had used him; in a moment of weakness, when Paeter had reduced her as far as he could. It was petty—it gave her something to hold over Paeter, if only in her own heart. She wouldn't dare speak of it in his presence. She was no fool.

Or maybe she *was* a fool, because she had taken a monster to her bed and borne him a child: a ruinspawn just as twisted and vile as her mistake.

Of course, the Ravalis couldn't have such a creature as their heir, any more than the Blood Denerre could, and gossip would doom them all. Everyone knew the ruinspawn were the result of forbidden affairs—perverted, grotesque creatures that came from equally deplorable acts. Paeter would never have accepted that thing as springing from *his* sainted loins.

And so, the lie.

Now Lenalin regretted it, albeit less for the harm it would do Regel—*had done Regel*—than for the position it put her in. Having to pretend Semana was her own child in public and in private, having to spend her own capital and favors to stop Paeter or the rest of the monstrous Ravalis from targeting the little beast, and, worst of all, having to endure the constant reminder of Ovelia's awful betrayal, every single day… It had only been two years thus far, going on a third, and Paeter had been away at war most of that time, though that did nothing for his host of perverse Blood relatives.

At least Ovelia looked as miserable as Lenalin felt, so that was something.

How had her life become this… this *horror*? It had seemed so gentle and exciting, exploring the tunnels in the mountain with Ovelia by her side, gossiping about handsome lads and lasses they wouldn't mind kissing in some forgotten corner of the city, sneaking out of the palace to have ink carved into their backs in twin dragons—Ovelia's red, Lenalin's silver.

They'd been girls together, inseparable, but now they were nothing, and there was no way back.

Lenalin was trapped. Doomed.

She heard the door scrape open and scowled. "I told you to go—"

Quick footsteps approached and a thick-fingered, brown hand slid around her neck, stifling her words in a sudden, quick intake of breath. It came by long practiced instinct, as she'd long ago learned to take in air when she could under her husband's loving attentions.

In the mirror, Paeter's burning eyes looked over her shoulder. "My winter flower," he said, toying with a lock of her hair. "It's been so long…"

"Since last night, you mean." Lenalin pulled out of his grasp, letting her disheveled hair slip back down around her neck. She took up a bone-handled comb from the side table.

"Nay." He laid one hand, palm open, against her neck, and she froze, comb half raised to her head. His low purr made her queasy. "You may have given me the lover's kiss last night, but I was away at war for years before—"

"I brought you off with my mouth," Lenalin said. "No need to give it such eloquence."

She wasn't sure what had given her the courage to be so defiant, but the startled expression that crossed his face gave her pleasure and further strength. She ran her comb through the hair he had despoiled with his touch, and that felt like a powerful blow.

"Honestly," she said. "Do you fancy yourself charming when you cannot call a thing by its name? False modesty ill becomes you."

"As vulgarity suddenly becomes you, my love?" Paeter grinned. Lenalin had never liked his grin: far too predatory. Cruel. "Mayhap you've changed in my absence."

Become more myself, you mean, Lenalin thought but did not say. The hot rush of defiance cooled to a simmer. She continued crushing out the tangled knot his fingers had made of her hair.

Paeter continued, undeterred. "Yes, in my drunken stupor, I allowed you to… bring me off with your mouth, 'tis true." He brushed her hair aside from her face and traced his fingers around her neck, caressing the lines of her throat. She stood taut as a charged wire, her every nerve alight with tension. "But surely you don't think that's the proper way to welcome your prince after so long away."

She almost gagged trying to speak, but still she felt that thin line of strength, pulsing between them like a vein. She was pulling power from him and into herself. She clung desperately to that tiny string, hoping that she could pull herself free with it—or else strangle Paeter.

"No?" Lenalin asked, voice choked. "What would you have instead? Ask."

Paeter paused. Even now he couldn't put a name to his own desires. She wondered how deep his shame ran, and she realized that was why he hurt her. Not that the reasons mattered now.

"You cannot, can you?"

Truly pathetic. He had all the power here, and yet he could not speak his desires or his needs. Everything he had, and it was not enough to reassure the pathetic little child inside him. Lenalin's lip curled and she could not stop herself. She did what she should not have done.

She snickered.

She chuckled.

She *laughed* at him.

"What—" He choked on the word. "What are you doing?"

She could not help it. As soon as the laughter started, it would not stop. Years of loathing and fear and despair came bubbling out in great peals of mocking mirth.

"Stop it." His hand tightened on the back of her neck. "No one laughs at the Jackal of Luether—"

That only made it worse. She brayed a guffaw that nearly doubled her over. Why had ever she feared this sorry excuse for a man? He did not warrant the terror he had always held over her.

Her mind must have split then, for if she had any sanity left, she'd not have laughed at him so. She wanted to tell him exactly what she thought of him, and of his children—the one true and pathetic, the other false and far superior—both of whom she hated. She laughed, loud and long, like a maniac. She would die anyway, why not have a laugh at it? All things must pass to Ruin.

She wondered if this was how the Children of Ruin saw the world.

"Stop it!" He was screaming at her now, but she didn't remotely care.

She wanted to rail against him for the awful ruin her life had become, and his part in making that happen. But she did not, for if she exposed her misery to him, it would only soothe and reassure him. It would please him that he wielded such power over her, and she would not give him that. She would not give him a moment of power over her.

Never again.

He put his hands on her, trying to seize her, but she twisted free and raked her nails across his face. The laughter stopped instantly, and she stared at him with wintry eyes wide and furious. A cold rage swept through her, like the Winter Queens of old.

"Don't you touch me," she hissed at him.

She was no longer a woman. She was snow. She was ice.

And by the Fire, he recoiled. Oh, that was fear in his eyes, and she found it *delicious*.

"How did I ever find you handsome?" She turned her back on him once more, so that she could only see his grotesque face in the mirror. "I hate you."

Sudden pain as Paeter shoved her against the mirror, and she heard the glass crack under her weight. She caught the edge, which bit deep enough into her palms to draw blood. She pushed back.

"I *hate* you!" Lenalin screamed at him. "I hate you and I will see you *dead*—"

Even as she spoke, he kicked her face-first through the mirror.

At first, she didn't even realize what had happened. She lay in a pool of glass shards that stabbed and slashed and ripped her flesh. Something snapped in her hip and her left leg went numb. For a heartbeat, she felt almost whole, and then blood welled from her flesh from hundreds of wounds. She tried to speak but could only choke out something like a plea, she wasn't too proud to admit.

Paeter didn't aid her.

He put his booted foot on the back of her head and ground her face into the glass.

The pain was enormous. Blinding. He kicked and stomped, driving her down into the cutting morass. Hurts sprang up in places that she had never even thought could hurt, and those parts of her *screamed* in agony. She could feel the glass unmaking her, her face and body and mind unraveling.

It became too much, and she found herself outside herself, looking down at a cruel little man grinding a woman beyond recognition. She watched with a kind of detached indifference, unsure exactly what was happening, how she could escape it, or how she could have prevented it.

Her thoughts flashed through everything that had led her to this point—all the years spent wasting away under Paeter's thumb, doing her duty, climbing deeper and deeper into the trap he laid, and for what? So she could be rewarded this way in the end?

It seemed to go on forever, but the attack couldn't have lasted more than a moment. Finally, it was over, and she knelt beside herself, looking down at her mangled body on the floor, something that didn't look like a woman at all. Paeter stood by her for a time, listening to air come bubbling up through the spreading pool of her blood. The bemused expression on his face—as if he was contemplating something he'd never properly considered—filled her with a special kind of horror.

Even in her extremity, she hadn't told him the truth, other than that she hated him. Even as everything else drained away, she took one sliver of pride in her strength.

Years ago, she might have wondered if the truth would save her, but she knew him too well.

Then he rose, leaving her wheezing and gurgling, and meticulously cleaned his slippered foot on the fur rug. He looked like he would speak, then simply walked away. The door scraped shut behind him.

And then she was alone in the dark room—alone with her body and the spreading pool of blood.

Time passed, and the pain dulled to a dim, distant roar like thunder, thence to a foggy numbness. So long as she didn't try to move, it didn't even hurt. She just felt... cold. Apart.

A discreet knock came on the door: the servant returning to see if she needed anything. This was her chance. If only she could...

She mustered all her strength to call out, unlocking new, unexpected fires of pain all down her throat and chest. Her face felt like it was on fire, twisting apart and splitting. Then, when she managed to open her mouth, only a choked gurgle came out of her throat. She could barely hear the sound she made. Blood bubbled in front of her nose, and that was that. The servant received no reply, and so went on their way, as they'd been trained to do.

Dimly, Lenalin considered her own role in crafting this doom. Isolating herself, pushing away anyone who could have aided her. But indeed, the more she reflected on it, the more inevitable it seemed. The Ravalis wanted Tar Vangr, and they would stop at nothing to have it. Paeter had always hated her, no matter how biddable she had been to him. She had tried defiance, she had tried acceptance—it did not matter. The Ravalis prince only loved himself and tormenting her.

Perhaps she should have asked Regel to slay Paeter, or simply allowed Regel to do so when he offered it. Why had she taken an oath from him to leave Paeter in peace? Because her world would have ended, yes, and her Blood destroyed. But just then, lying there in the mess of her own blood and shredded face, she would have taken it all back. Let Regel slay Paeter and run away with him, if he'd asked. Or perhaps she and Ovelia…

No. Her life had been over long before this moment.

Perhaps an hour passed, and she realized she was still alive. She must have slept for a time, for when she woke, the world came back in tingling pain. She felt gutted—hollow—and so weak that she could not so much as move her head. She wondered if she would drown in her own blood.

The scrape of wood on stone told her the door had opened behind her, and she heard a voice as if from across a great distance. A voice of compassion and horror. Maure, her nursemaid.

The older woman stooped over her, dimly asking all sorts of questions that Lenalin heard as though through water. Her ears had stopped functioning as they should. Lenalin took some comfort in Maure's voice, at least. She would die hearing the voice of one of the few people in the World of Ruin who cared about her.

Then Maure touched Lenalin to move her, and the world erupted in a cacophony of pain. Her flesh lit all over with fresh, tearing pain, and every muscle in her body jerked taut. She came away from the floor with a sucking sound, blood dried to jelly parting with protest. It felt like her face was tearing off as she went. Lenalin had not wept in years, but she did now, bloody tears sliding onto her cheeks.

"Easy, lass, easy," Maure said.

"Kill me," Lenalin tried to say, but it came out as a wet gurgle.

"Paeter cannot do this," Maure said. "He cannot—"

He already has, Lenalin thought but could not say.

Slowly, agonizingly slowly, Maure helped Lenalin's corpse onto the bed, where she wrapped her in blankets. Just breathing had required too much of Lenalin's attention to realize she was shivering. Every tiny motion sent bolts of fresh pain surging through her. The old woman looked as though she had aged twenty years in the space of as many heartbeats.

"I'll fetch a chiurgeon," Maure said. "And your father. The king must…"

Lenalin caught her wrist before she could leave her bedside. "No." Her voice burbled through her ruined lips. "Not… my father. No… no one…"

Maure's eyes were grave. "But the chiurgeon," she said. "Them, I might bring."

Lenalin nodded. That much she could allow. Not Orbrin, not Ovelia, and certainly not Regel. They had all betrayed her, left her, or failed to protect her when she needed it most. She was alone, and she preferred it that way.

She laid back and gargled out a breath that was a struggle to get free. Lenalin Denerre was dead, cut to pieces in a sea of glass shards.

But now, if she survived this night, she would be free.

And if she ever returned to Tar Vangr, it would be to destroy it.

TWENTY-EIGHT

WHEN THE *HECATOMB* CRASHED into the mountain of Tar Vangr, slew hundreds of barbarians, and rolled end over end down across the city in its ruin, the day was all but won.

Hecatomb's deadly final assault had destroyed much of the invading army, and after its crash, a good three quarters of the city lay destroyed, but Darak Ravalis no Denerre—Dar-Karsk the Mighty—counted it a victory.

After all, his had been the plan that had sent a sizeable force through the tunnels, where they had never been caught in the *Hecatomb's* firing solution nor its suicide rush. Tar Vangr's greatest weapon lay spent and ruined, while plenty of its foes remained to take the fight to the streets, blade to blade and spear to caster. The City of Steel had loosed its greatest strike, and it would not be enough.

As the horde streamed out to engage the last remnants of the winter swords, dustknights, and whatever remained of the Blood Ravalis's warders, Darak inhaled the acrid scent of destruction and thought it good. Even the storm had let up, mostly burning off in the hail of destruction brought about by the *Hecatomb's* furious assault. The destroyed city lay open for all to see, and for Darak to take.

Semana would claim the credit for this masterstroke, he was certain. Her idle suggestion had brought it to his mind, yes, but he was the one with the knowledge and experience of those tunnels required to plot a course, as well as the tactical mind needed to see its utility.

Ruin had fallen upon Tar Vangr, both low and high, reducing many of its buildings to skeletons of themselves that leaned out over the rubble-strewn streets. Barbarians streamed out around him into the city, slavering with the desire to destroy it as they had Low-City. Darak found himself not only indifferent to the destruction, but somewhat pleased by the thought. Indeed, he might have joined them in their orgy of violence and death had more pressing business not drawn his eye.

"You there," he said to one of his warders. "Attend me. You and your cadre. A score should do."

Darak strode toward the object of his impending victory, tapping his buzzing spear on the ground with every step. All of this had passed as he had foreseen—as he had engineered. The city could be rebuilt and peopled with folk more amenable to his rule. But a moment such as this...

The *Hecatomb* lay before him, as battered and ruined as the rest of Tar Vangr. The skyship had crashed into the mountain, then slid and rolled across High-City, leaving a swath of smoldering rubble, cleaving low buildings in twain, and flattening everything in its path. The destruction had annihilated the bulk of the barbarian army, but at grievous cost. Now the skyship lay on its side, poised near the east edge of the city, hanging a little over the mage-glass edge.

As Darak approached, the skyship groaned and leaned toward the edge, and for an irritated breath, he thought gravity might deprive him of his triumph. But no: the shifting skyship released the remains of one of its propulsion rings, which tore free and plummeted toward Low-City. Freed of its burden, the *Hecatomb* righted itself once more to rest on its base, exposing the crumbled bridge.

Darak loosed a breath he hadn't realized he'd been holding and smiled wide. "Go," he said to his escort. "Search the wreckage. Bring me whatever remains of my mother—"

"Stop."

The voice cut through the cold air like a knife set on a red-hot anvil. There, materializing out of the dust and gloom, stood a waterfall of gray shaped like a man. His tattered cloak hung thick with dust and half-melted snow and his skin was choked with black grime. But his eyes picked up the dawn light, drawing all their attention to his frosty gaze. The power of his visage held them all in thrall, and none could move forward.

"Not another step," Regel the Frostburn said. "Not one."

TWENTY-NINE

A ROAR LIKE THUNDER woke her, and Ovelia burst into the throbbing, dizzy gray with a gasp.

The world was a disorienting blur of pain, panting, and cacophonous roars from all around. Her body felt bruised and battered and tingled all over. Wind whistled against her face and she smelled the acrid smoke of burning flesh and heard the ring of steel alongside the screams of the wounded. She groped all around herself and found only rubble and chipped glass, and some sort of edge upon which she sat. Her legs dangled freely over open air, and acidic snowflakes burned her sweaty face.

What had happened? Where was she?

Not too far away, she saw familiar crimson smoke rising from where Draca lay, impossibly, half buried in a snowdrift. The blade's lingering heat had turned the snow to melty sludge, which dripped in rivulets against the scorched and cracked mage-glass. Not that she felt in any state to fight.

She tried to move—to reach the sword, or at least shimmy back from the void—but only fearsome pain greeted that attempt. It felt like a pyrotechnic exploding inside her body, centered on her heart. Her chest heaved and she sucked in breath after breath to no avail. It felt like something heavy sat on her chest, crushing her down, but when she pawed at the air just above her, she found nothing.

Nothing, that is, but for a shard of mage-glass sticking up out of her flesh just below her right breast. She tried at first to pull it free, and the pain that ripped through her torso nearly tore away her senses again. The shard had thrust up through her, affixing her in place. It was on the wrong side of her body to pierce her heart, but it must have collapsed one of her lungs. She lay there, impaled and gasping, trying hard not to disturb the shard.

Her belly lurched and seemed to burst, as though someone were repeatedly jabbing a rusty blade outward through her stomach, but it was too dull to pierce her flesh and rip free. It might have been a mercy if it did.

Her child. Had something happened to her *child*?

A fresh pang struck her, making her whole body shiver, and she almost sat up despite the shard of mage-glass affixing her to the scaffold. Her child *was* the pain, tearing its way out of her by claw and by tooth, and there was no one to help her through any of it.

Panting seemingly to no avail, Ovelia lay back down and struggled to breathe. Below, she could faintly see trails of noxious smoke—the residue of a massive discharge of dust magic—and she could see flashes above. She must have fallen into the network of supports that held up the floating disks of mage-glass. Now that she focused her senses, she realized further that she lay at a precarious drop-off, and if not for the glass stuck through her, she might have slid right off to her doom.

Maure. Her attendants. What had become of them?

What of Lenalin? Ovelia didn't see the massive shining light of the *Hecatomb* anywhere. Had the queen crashed? Was she dead? Was all lost?

A fresh pang of agony wrenched through her, chasing those thoughts away. She had to focus.

First, she had to get away from the edge, and that meant pulling free of the shard of mage-glass.

Another contraction would come soon, she knew, so she gritted her teeth and tried to get her arms or at least her elbows under her. Gushes of red-hot agony ripped through her at the slightest movement, but she blocked it out as best she could. By the time the pain of birth struck her again, Ovelia had managed to half-sit, pulling herself perhaps a thumb's breadth up along the shard. That whole side of her body grew weak, but she demanded that it move. She had to time this just right.

Her body tore at itself again, and this time, she was ready. She clenched in, despite the nigh-overwhelming urge to push her child free, and waited a five count, then ten, then fifteen… It kept going, each count dragging out longer than the one before, and a scream built, demanding to wrench free.

Finally it was over, as though it had taken an eternity, but she was not done. Even as pain gave way to soft warmth as her body tried to soothe itself, she shoved up and forward with all her might.

This time Ovelia *did* scream. She screamed in escalating pain and horror as she pressed herself forward, bit by tiny bit, the mage-glass slicing roughly through her flesh.

Then it lodged against one of her ribs, and strength abruptly drained from her arms. They trembled, about to collapse. No—to have come so far, only to fail now?

Fear and terror gripped her heart—fear for herself and for her child, terror of losing all her work and the pain of doing it again.

No. No, she had to—

Ovelia pushed past her breaking point. She clenched her fists tight enough to draw blood. The world shivered and lightning crackled like veins through reality. The shadows swirled like parting mist, turning red like blood. Her body stretched and pulled itself apart and the pain was coming back like rolling thunder in the distance and…

Finally she ripped free with a tiny squicking pop, and fell tumbling to the side, away from the shard. Instantly her strength fled, and it was all she could do to stop herself rolling right off the edge. There she lay on her side, face pressed in the tingling snow, sobbing and choking, while another contraction swept through her. She reached down to touch at her bulging belly, and her hand came away slaked with wet, either from the nail cuts in her palm or the wound in her chest that was steadily seeping her lifeblood onto the snow around her.

A shadow moved over her, and at first, Ovelia thought it must be Regel. Of course he would come in her hour of need. He always had before.

Indeed, as he grew closer, she felt the intense cold of Frostburn in his hands, and she saw the blade in the shadows, like a sliver of bright blue light. She would know that sword anywhere.

But it was not Regel who bore it.

The man who stood over her shuffled toward her with a very distinctive gait—step, slide, step, slide. His one eye bulged big and white, and she could see it clearly in her vision, swimming with magic.

Tithian Davargorn.

Ovelia sucked in a breath, wheezing, and crawled backward as best she could. Her lower half was bloated and paralyzed, and she dragged herself on her elbows until she reached the edge and could go no further. She tried to speak but couldn't—all she could do was stare as Tithian approached.

She understood the heat rising from him—could read his intentions even without her eyes. He couldn't just let her die. Not when he had the means to make her death *excrutiating*.

"Daughter of the Dragon," he said. "I owe you this."

Then he plunged Frostburn into her belly—a quick thrust, in and out. Then he was gone.

She understood. And she did not hate him for it.

The pain, which she had expected to be enormous, was almost non-existent. The blade itself numbed her nerves and it felt simply like much of her body had turned to ice. She looked down, dimly perceiving through the swirling shadows, as icy veins spread across her body from the wound.

Frostburn's dark magic, she realized. All was lost.

Then another contraction came, and the babe kicked at her hand. It was alive. Somehow, Davargorn hadn't slain it. Ovelia gritted her teeth, weeping in frustration and despair.

As time passed, her sobs became rhythmic breathing. Ovelia screamed at herself to get up, but she didn't have the strength. She was losing too much blood. She'd spent too much energy, and she didn't have enough left to turn herself over. She could do little more than lie there and whimper—lie there, whimper, and push, however feebly.

At least—at least this child might be born safely.

By the Fire, she prayed she could do that much.

THIRTY

THE SILENCE STRETCHED LONG in the plaza of Tar Vangr, at the foot of the wrecked *Hecatomb*. Finally, Darak rolled his shoulders as though shedding a heavy mantle.

"You have no power here, Shadow of the Winter King," he said. "You have failed. The proof of your failure lies in ruin all around you." He raised his spiked war gauntlet, the barbed fingers limned in flames. "The last kings of Winter and Summer are dead, and their city lies in ruin. Even now, the Children of Ruin reclaim this place for their great goddess. You have no purpose any longer."

The old man did not move. He did not shrink away, nor show any sign that he had even heard. At Darak's side, his warders shook a bit free of the paralysis Regel had inspired, but they still looked upon him warily. Of course, he thought with more than a little irritation: the Frostburn was one of their mythical heroes, wielder of a blade forged by the Deathless they worshiped and feared. This disgusting superstition caused him no end of trouble. If only he didn't have to rely upon such fearful primitives.

"This is your angel of death, is it?" Darak asked, fouling his tongue with crude Ruinspeak. "This pathetic old wretch? Are you such cowards as to soil yourselves before a mere man?"

Regel raised his hand ever so slightly, though what the gesture meant, Darak couldn't be bothered to guess. It pushed his cloak aside, revealing his open, empty hands.

"No sword." Darak spat. "He is old and weak. He can barely stand. Strike him down."

The twenty barbarians at his back still stood fast and only murmured amongst themselves.

"Well." Darak nearly spat the word. He thumped his ensorcelled spear on the scuffed mage-glass underfoot, and it loosed a vibrating wave that made his bones shiver. "I shall slay him myself."

He stepped forth, spear humming. His uncle's power armor had kept him surprisingly warm and comfortable, even without the power of the Worldfire to bolster and carry him. He had never felt more powerful than in that moment, and he would make the barbarians understand that. His limbs fairly shivered with the urge to splatter Regel's withered corpse of a body all over

High-City. This was his moment—this, *his* day. The first of this new year and the birth of a new empire, with Darak at its head. No useless old man would deny him what was his by right of Blood and conquest.

Darak strode down a narrow slope, where the mage-glass had bent under the impact of the crashing skyship. It groaned precariously but held firm. He strode toward Regel, a smoking cloud of power, and Regel could only stare at him.

"You are a broken old man," he said when they were close enough. "I don't know how you survived the mountain, but I shall kill you with a single blow."

Regel made no reply, and his sheer lack of expression infuriated Darak. How *dare* the old fool ignore his power. He stabbed his empowered lance at Regel without much thought, driven by his rage more than any attempt at martial flourish. He shifted aside, the old man, fast enough to elude the blow but not quite enough to escape the cutting wave of force that split the very air around its point. Regel fell away, the skin of his cheek rippling, and Darak saw bloody streaks appear from the line of his jaw to his forehead. He hadn't even hit Regel, and still his power had nearly ripped the old man's face off.

Darak whirled the spear around, and Regel narrowly ducked. The force exuded from the spear pushed him into the ground, and he rolled with the blow to stay shakily on his feet. The proximity of the spear's dust magic was hurting him, even if it did not strike him directly. He coughed spatters of blood, his breath pink-tinged steam in the cold morning air. He was exhausted. He had almost no strength left.

And yet, he simply would not fall.

They fought, there beside and beneath the ruined *Hecatomb*, a battle that was more a dance than a duel. For years, Darak had drilled with the spear, devoting at least some time every few days to the art, but he felt like a graceless fool in comparison to the Frostburn's fluid movement. He lashed the spear at him, tracing clouds of inky smoke like ribbons floating in the air, but not a single strike caught Regel. The man moved like a shadow in a room with a spinning lamp, narrowly eluding every attack.

Every so often, Regel would produce a small knife to counter, but invariably it scraped off Darak's powered armor to no avail. He was otherwise unarmed and should have fallen quickly, but instead he dragged out the duel, his body slowly crumbling under the spear's force. He wasn't trying to win— he couldn't possibly win—but he made Darak feel the fool indeed. And with that healing power of his, no doubt Regel could keep this up far longer than any man should.

In the back of his mind, Darak heard Afferath's cruel little laugh as she mocked him for his half-hearted efforts in the training round. The memory filled him with rage, and that drove him on.

"You could not save my greatfather!" Darak thrust, and Regel dodged. "You could not save my mother!" Again, Regel dodged, but narrowly. "You could not save my father!"

For some reason, Regel replied to that particular barb with a faint quirk of his mouth. Almost like a mocking smile, if the man were capable of mirth. It stoked Darak's fury.

Regel had lost this duel. How dare he drag this out, just to *mock*.

This time, Darak struck low and hard, and the spear sank into Regel's thigh. It wasn't a deep stab, but the reaving force in the spear burst forth and sent flecks of flesh splattering around them. The wound it left was deep, and blood poured forth onto the slushy mage-glass under their feet. Regel fell, his ruined leg unable to support him, and loosed a groan equally pained and disappointed.

"Finally." Darak raised his spear over the stubborn old man. "You've nothing left?"

At that, Regel looked up, eyes bloodshot and unfocused. He tried to chuckle but only succeeded at a cough, blood trickling down his chin.

"What?" Darak was almost screaming. "What is it, you rutting *shit* of a man—?"

The old man grinned, his teeth smeared with blood. "I killed your father."

Darak paused half a breath. He supposed he should be angry at that, but he felt... what? It seemed so far behind him, part of a different world—a different life—and yet, he felt a faint spark of something deep inside. Not rage but sadness. He tried to speak, but the words would not come.

In his slight hesitation, Regel managed to get wide of the spear. He half-limped, half-dragged himself away from the crashed skyship, out into the open space where a light snow had begun to fall.

With a contemptuous click of his tongue, Darak stalked toward the bleeding wretch, spinning the spear as it drew on the last of its charge. He left a bloody trail in his wake, and his ruined leg smeared it in a wavy, unpredictable path. Ultimately, Regel made it only so far before exhaustion and weakness made him stop, panting and bleeding copiously into the slushy snow. If he'd made Darak look pitiable, then this surely made him look far, far worse, did it not?

Darak looked up for confirmation, to his twenty barbarians standing silent vigil over the battleground like pillars rising out of the snow. They bore witness to the fall of their myth. Their faces were impassive and unreadable, but for some reason, Darak felt judged. Reviled. Pitied.

This was meant to be *his* moment.

"It has ended," Darak said. "How will anyone carry your legend forth, Oathbreaker, when you've picked such a lonely place to make your last stand?" His lip curled. "Your last *crawl*."

Regel caught hold of a jagged piece of metal, which sliced through the worn leather of his glove and bit into his flesh. Heaving, he pulled himself gradually up, at first leaning on the ruined skyship. Then, somehow, he managed to stand under his own power. His flinty eyes flashed in the morning light.

"Not so lonely," he said.

Then the crack of casters discharging chased away the last of the morning mist, and barbarians started screaming in sudden pain and fear. Half his escorts fell in that first breath, cut down by casterbolts that came scything out of the surrounding rubble. The survivors found themselves in quick, vicious duels with folk who had crept up on them, cold steel hidden under their cloaks. Most wore masks against the elements, but Darak saw one of their faces—a dark-skinned woman with scars and a fearsome aspect—and noted the black teardrop inked under her eye.

The Circle of Tears.

They were Tar Vangr's last defenders, a ragtag band of some dozen or so. Cowards who ambushed a superior force, now caught in a deathly struggle. Even as he watched, one of his barbarians seized one Tear by the throat and hurled them flailing into the wreckage of the *Hecatomb* with a crunch. They were terribly overmatched, and other than that first, cowardly strike, they would fall quickly. It was ultimately a failure—essentially, they were throwing themselves on the spears of Darak's forces.

Regel made a move, reaching for the spear as though to seize it for his own use, but Darak was faster. He caught the old man about the neck and held him aloft, strength enhanced by the suit and his own Worldfire. With that power, Regel's weight was basically nothing.

"You've wasted enough of my time, Oathbreaker," he said, dragging Regel up the slope of the crashed *Hecatomb*'s deck. "Now you get to watch."

He strode up the leaning deck, wood and metal groaning under his steps, toward the bridge.

"I'll make you watch while I crush whatever remains of my mother and thus become your king," Darak said. "Will you break another oath, I wonder? Will you serve he who slew the woman you loved, because he is her son? What a dilemma."

338

Regel said nothing, only drooled blood and glared.

Considering the gradual slope and slippery wood of the deck, it was slower going than Darak would have liked, but at length he arrived at his destination. The ceiling of the bridge had buckled inward until it hung nearly level with the deck. The whole chamber within must have collapsed into the fuselage of the skyship, flattened into it by the rolling impact. It seemed unlikely anything had survived, but he had to be certain. The dented metal looked thick and heavy, but with the Worldfire, he could strengthen himself. In his hand, Regel could offer no resistance.

Darak had no free hand to pry up the ruptured ceiling, so he slammed Regel down onto the deck and drove the spear through his already bleeding leg with such force that it sank into the gnarled wood. The old man offered only a faint grunt as the shaft went in, nailing him in place to the deck.

"Watch as the proper ruler of Tar Vangr seizes his crown," Darak said.

He bent, calling forth his power to let him wrench the bent iron up from the cracked planks. He would unearth the corpse of his mother, the false Queen of Tar Vangr, and then...

He heard it before he understood what it meant: a whirring sound like rumbling thunder below his feet or—and he realized this only too late—like a mage-engine cycling beneath the ruined deck. He heard it and furrowed his brow inside his sweat-humid power helmet.

Then a massive metal fist crashed through the deck and struck him full in the chest. He flailed unsuccessfully for the haft of the spear to balance himself and toppled back on the deck with a grinding, groaning sound of metal on wood. With its slope, Darak slid some twenty paces before he could finally arrest his movement. Who *dared*?

An iron-clad warmachine clawed its way up from the bowels of the skyship, breaking through the splintered deck and steaming magic into the morning light. It reached across and ripped the spear out of Regel's leg and the deck, freeing him to slide and roll down the sloped deck. Sunlight glinted from the towering war suit, half again as tall as the highest towering barbarian and nearly as wide.

"This is my city," Lenalin Denerre said over the iron-clad's projectors. "And you will not have it."

THIRTY-ONE

S EMANA STARTLED AWAKE. A sound dispersed through the wintry air around her—something like a shout or a scream—but she only caught the tail end of it. Perhaps she had loosed that cry herself.

Heat and spent magic distorted her vision. All around her stood the burned husks of trees and collapsed stone towers, and stone crenellations marked numerous tiers that ascended some distance up from the main street. She was in High-City, of that she was certain, but Tar Vangr barely seemed like a city any longer: such had been the ravages of the barbarian invasion that she had helped lead.

It all seemed so long ago, though she could still hear the song of steel and cries of terror. The war sounded nearby and yet distant, without purpose or relevance to her.

She was vulnerable, she knew. Her black leathers lay in smoldering ruin around her, their magic expended. Her defensive shield and breastplate had stopped the casterbolt Tithian had put in her chest, and apparently saved her after her crash into the garden, but it was depleted and all but destroyed. The armor felt like so much detritus on her now, like chapped and peeling skin.

Only when she saw the silvery stem of a winter flower between her fingers did she realize where she lay: in her mother's garden. Here, she had found a kind of peace as a child, until treachery turned it to ashes in her mouth. Here, she had seen her brother for what she thought was the last time, until he came back into her life, horrible and vile as Paeter Ravalis had ever been. Here she had stood exactly a year ago and allowed Regel the Frostburn to whisk her away from this city and her birthright.

As she stared, the flower withered between the metallic fingers of her war gauntlet, its life drained away and extinguished by the foul magic leaking forth from the relic.

Her heart lurched, and suddenly her skin itched all over. Wherever she wore the black leather, it burned her. Breathing hard, she fumbled off the barbed war gauntlet, hurling it to sink into a snow drift some paces away. She tore at the remains of the leather jerkin, which helpfully crumbled in her grasp and peeled away from her like a shed skin. It caught on her left wrist, and only then did she remember the sliver chain glove. She flicked her hand, trying and failing to dislodge it, and finally had to pry it off, one finger

340

at a time. On her knees, upper body all but bare, she unthreaded her belt with trembling hands, then stripped off the leathern breeches. She'd already lost one of her flying boots, and the other came off easily enough, though it caught and strained at her ankle. Finally, she lay back mostly naked in the snow, not feeling the cold, and exhaled in relief.

When her breath rasped in and out, she remembered that she still wore the mask.

Tentatively, Semana touched the mask, her fingers barely caressing the cool leather and strips of metal that gave it shape. She'd ripped everything else away, but the mask felt like a part of her face. A part of her. Could she...?

Heart thudding in her throat, she clutched at it and pulled, but the buckles caught at the back of her head. She clawed at them, her shaking fingers awkward and clumsy. Her breath quickened as she fought to get the cursed thing free, until she was sobbing with the effort. The last buckle came free, but it stuck to her face, refusing to come free. Had it adhered there? Had the fire she could not feel melted the leather to her skin? She just wanted it gone. Just wanted it—

Cords of green lightning sprang from the mask, clinging to her body, and it felt like a spider clutching her face rather than a piece of clothing. Semana cried out in terror and pulled harder. The magic stabbed into her, making her body shake and tremble with pain and weakness. If she would not wear the mask, it would slay her, consuming her strength in preparation for a new bearer...

"No," Semana said, managing to choke out the word. "*No!*"

Finally, the mask came free with a wet pop as she wrenched it off, and she hurled it to the ground in front of her with a cry. Her throat felt dry and cracked. The mask lay in a spreading pile of greenish muck, as its latent energies melted and corrupted the snow around it.

Tentatively, Semana felt at her face, and it seemed whole and intact. The spots on her body where the green magic had struck seemed pure and unblemished. Had she merely imagined the assault?

Chills scratched at her bare shoulders, and she clutched herself against an unexpected wave of cold. Her Frostfire felt far away, its protection all but faded. The snow around her felt wet and made her skin tingle, and she realized that stripping off her armor might have been a poor choice. The scorched and torn leathers lay in a ruined heap all around her, and it hardly looked like anything she could wear. Only the mask remained intact, and that... Once, not so long ago, she could barely stand to go without the mask for more than a few moments, but now, she could not bring herself to touch it.

The world faded around her. It seemed thin—nearly translucent, like a fleshy membrane stretched over a candle flame, and mere heartbeats away from melting through. Everywhere she looked, she saw the emptiness behind the world—how hollow it all seemed. Her armor had shielded her from Davargorn's caster, but she almost wished it hadn't. If she was dead, she wouldn't have to see this.

A foot scuffled on the snowy snow not twenty paces from her, and she looked languidly in that direction. It was a warrior—man or woman, barbarian or Tar Vangryur, she could not tell—and they stared at her with wide, bright eyes through a mask of blood. The mark of battle fatigue lay engraved deep upon the warrior's body, and they bled from half a dozen wounds into the driven snow. How they had come to this place, who could say? Certainly neither the warrior nor Semana cared to speculate.

Ultimately, the warrior charged at her, spear raised, some sort of incomprehensible warcry bellowing around the garden. Semana watched them come for a few heartbeats. The world seemed to slow, and the warrior ran as though through water, then slushy ice, then froze entirely. Their eyes bulged and veins protruded on their exposed face, and they gasped for breath. It was only when blood ran from the warrior's mouth that Semana realized they were in the grip of blood magic.

Had she done that?

She must have, though she could only dimly taste the warrior's blood in her mouth. It carried with it so many memories—so many hopes and terrors—but she did not bother to search them. They were like dreams to her, remembered poorly and dismissed easily. None of it mattered.

This person was not real. This world was not real. This story was not real.

The warrior choked and finally collapsed to the ground, panting and sobbing. Semana had not killed her attacker, but neither did she much care about their fate. The beginning did not matter, the middle could not hold, and the ending was a fantasy. What did it matter, if none of this was real?

Only she was real. She, and...

She felt it, then: a rumble of power that sent her to her knees, gasping for air. Instantly, her focus snapped to the mountain at the heart of Tar Vangr, from which smoke rose and buildings crumbled. The palace, built into and around the mountain, had fallen into ruin as barbarians had invaded it along secret tunnels that she and her brother had revealed to them. Even from this distance, she could see the glass-enclosed throne room at the height of the mountain lay in ruins, and she felt nothing. All her life, she had dreamed of sitting that throne, after taking her revenge on the Ravalis who had murdered her blood and destroyed her life, but now? Now her eyes went elsewhere.

It rumbled again, and she felt it in her blood. It was like a beating heart, calling to hers and matching her own pulse, but rather than blood it was magic. It pulsed through the ground beneath her.

The Narfire. The lifeblood of the World of Ruin.

Its song resonated from the walls of crumbling buildings and the stones of the mountain. Simultaneously a balm and a poison. It threatened and it promised.

This. This was the purpose that had drawn her to this place. She no longer cared for any throne, nor for her brother and his doomed cause. She cared nothing for vengeance or hatred. She was the daughter of power, and there she would find all the power she would ever need.

Semana rose, snow flaking from her damp shift, and started toward the palace, slowly but with purpose.

The mask she left where it lay.

THIRTY-TWO

WHEN LENALIN STRUCK, SHE struck with all her rage.

So many years she had run from this—this destiny that had taken her in its jaws, chewed her up despite her cries, and spat out a torn wreck. So many nights she had spent sobbing in pain, trapped in a body that would never heal, cursing the names and faces of everyone she had ever known. She hated this city, hated its people, wanted nothing to do with Tar Vangr. She had never meant to return here, never meant to reveal herself, never meant to fall in love and make questionable decisions.

Damn you, Ovelia Dracaris, she thought. *How dare you make me better.*

She should not have involved herself, or else she should have joined the fight *alongside* the barbarians. Or she should have died in that skyship crash, which a not small part of her must have intended all along, if only Davargorn hadn't healed her.

But deep inside, there was some spark that she'd thought long extinguished. Some shred of the woman she had been—the queen she would become—the warrior no one believed she could be.

And just then, right in that moment, piloting a massive ironclad warmachine against the would-be usurper and master of the barbarian horde?

She felt powerful—righteous—for the first time since she could remember.

Darak's strengthening magic let him take a blow that would have reduced a human body to so much bone-studded pulp, but she felt his nose buckle under the Lancer's fist. The power connecting her to the ironclad let her feel its sensations, and that blow sent a thrill up her arm and to her heart.

"My city," she said, her voice echoing over the outward projectors. "Not yours."

Darak scrambled up to his feet and groped for the spear, a look of utter shock on his face. Lenalin was aware of his barbarians, but she didn't care. She had eyes only for him.

"Not so easy when your opponent can fight back," she said.

She extended her senses, and the Lancer became her body. She was strong. She was fast. And she had a fully charged magic battery. She tore the rest of the way free of the *Hecatomb*'s fuselage.

"Mother?" Darak asked, his voice choked in disbelief. Hoping he was wrong.

As her wayward son staggered down the slope of the crashed *Hecatomb*, Lenalin sent the Lancer lunging forward, fist raised high. She brought it down like a hammer, and Darak narrowly eluded the crushing force. Her fist smashed into the *Hecatomb*'s fuselage, bending it inward with a groan.

"Why are you running, King Darak? This is what you wanted." She spread her arms wide. "If you want this city, come and take it."

That gave him an instant's pause, and Lenalin took full advantage. She lowered the Lancer's left arm toward him and discharged a blast of white-hot flame that tore across the space between like a living creature that wanted to rip and tear. Darak summoned power and declaimed words in the guttural tongue of the barbarians and waved his spear, shattering the wave of fire with a burst of wind.

Lenalin knew enough Ruinspeak to recognize pleas to the Goddess of Death. She smiled madly.

Just like his father: his body was strong but his will was weak.

"You call upon a goddess, and yet you name yourself a man?" she asked. "Pathetic."

Darak's face reddened. He lashed out with the spear, crackling with power, but the thrust went wild and clipped off the Lancer's left arm. It still struck with a clap of thunder, knocking the Lancer to the side. Lenalin gritted her teeth as her left arm went numb under the discharged magic.

The magic of the Worldfire was a wild, disruptive thing, and its power diffused that of the ironclad. Lenalin was no alchemist or scholar of the various forms of magic, but the raw power of the druids of Ruin seemed to trump the artificial workings of dust magic.

Lenalin spun the Lancer's right fist in a wild arc, and it smashed into Darak's magic-strengthened body. At first it seemed like his power might absorb the blow, but the Lancer's strength won through and Darak staggered back, waving his spear desperately at her as though it were a shield. Just as she had expected, he was easily rattled. If he hadn't disabled her weapon, she might have killed him right then.

"How dare you?" he cried. "I am the King of Tar Vangr! My will—"

Something broke inside her. Something freed itself from years of self-loathing, buried under more despair than one woman could bear. There was no more pain—only herself.

Lenalin could feel it.

Herself.

Her.

Lenalin propelled the Lancer forward, barreling right into the boastful barbarian prince and cutting off his words. They went down in a heap, and he somehow managed to avoid being crushed by the massive ironclad—or at least so she assumed, because he did not scream in agony. The mage-glass scratched and scuffed on the ruined skyship fuselage, reducing her visibility to half.

The suit rattled and clanked all around her, and Lenalin growled and cursed as she tried to get her bearings once more. The roar of the mage-engine propelling the ironclad filled her ears, and beyond that, the sounds of battle. Would Tar Vangr even exist at the end of the day? She did not know, and only a small part of her cared. Sweat poured down her face and she wiped it away with her left hand.

She had come to finish a task, and she would do so.

There. She saw Darak squirming out from under the crook of the Lancer's left elbow, trying to find distance. That, she knew, she could not allow. If he had a free moment, he could get away from her and find his balance—call upon more of his power or rally folk to his side. Ironically, perhaps he could have defeated her if he'd stayed and stabbed with that spear while she lay there, but his natural cowardice won out.

This was their duel, and she would not let him get away.

"No," she said. "*No.*"

The Lancer's left arm refused to do more than twitch, and the right possessed a pincer rather than a weapon. It would have to do.

"This is your master?" she called out, not expecting a reply. "This pathetic child?"

She lashed out at Darak and managed only to tear away some of his fur cloak, exposing the smoldering golden armor he wore beneath. Lan Ravalis's power armor—of course. Lenalin should have had Lan executed and that armor kept in High-City, but alas. That, she realized, was what had allowed Darak to survive her strikes. Had he been protecting himself solely with his own magic, he would have to be a sorcerer to rival Semana's talents. And that, Lenalin doubted.

"Ahh!" Darak wrenched his leg free of her claw and dealt the ironclad another stout blow with his spear. The discharge was less this time, but it was still enough to send tingles up Lenalin's arm.

She grasped at him again, but the right arm had only a diminished capacity, and he eluded it relatively easily. He stared back at her with wide eyes and scurried and scrambled up and away. The terror on his face told Lenalin something important, and that was that he did not know the effect his spear had on the ironclad. Perhaps she could use that somehow...

Whatever she did, it had to be soon. Even aside from the disruptive hits, the warmachine's dust magic charge ran low, and she could only pilot it for so much longer. She tried to move toward him, but the Lancer protested and refused to stir. She did not have the magic left for a charge.

Now or never.

"Darak Ravalis!" she cried, and the projectors made the sound so loud Lenalin could feel the dead skyship quake beneath her. "You hide behind stolen armor and stolen power? Your father would be ashamed of such cowardice."

It didn't serve. He just kept walking the other direction, heedless of her attempt to draw his attention. Perhaps he was a bit stronger than his father in that way.

"Your father hated you," she said.

That gave him pause. "What?"

She nodded fiercely. "Why do you think he exiled you from Tar Vangr?"

"Because I tried to seize control of my own destiny, as you failed to do." Darak's fingers tightened on the spear. "Father learned of my treason and he sent me away..."

"He sent you away because but you were a spoiled, violent little shit we couldn't stand to have around," Lenalin said. "I hated Paeter, but on this point, we agreed. Of course he finally sent you away. I only wish he had killed you then and have done."

Darak stood up straight, leaning on the spear, and looked back with a murderous expression. His black eyes held nothing but hatred, and even as Lenalin watched, his skin sprouted fresh black splotches and lesions she had not seen before. His flesh rotted before her eyes, and Lenalin hesitated. She thought she understood the Worldfire, but this was a manifestation she had never even heard of.

"You..." Darak started toward her, caution forgotten. "You disgusting wretch of a woman. Why could you not have the good grace to die when father pushed you through a mirror?"

"We are Blood," Lenalin said. "You think Paeter made you brave? Nay. *Mine* is the spite that brought you back only to fail here. To embarrass yourself before all your assembled legions."

"Me?" Darak pointed the spear at Lenalin. "I will kill you and everything you love."

"Oh? And what if I love *you*, child?"

Darak threw back his head and laughed. "We are Blood of Ruin," he said. "We cannot love."

Lenalin thought of Ovelia, and just for a heartbeat she took pity on her cruel, monstrous child.

347

Just for a hearbeat.

He came close enough to see, his visage a horror. His face puffed out and swelled, as though it might slough off at any moment. Black furry burrs grew all over his flesh, such that she could barely see any actual skin. He moved with poorly coordinated, shuddering movements. He would kill himself drawing on the Worldfire, but not before he struck. Mayhap they would die together.

Just a little closer, and she would put that claw through his chest and end it.

But just when he came within a step, he abruptly lifted the spear and hurled it directly into the shoulder joint of the Lancer's right arm. Lenalin barely managed to pull in a shuddering breath before she screamed at the sudden pain. The sharp crack of magic knocked the Lancer on its back, and she lay staring up at the snowy sky, not comprehending what had just happened.

Then Darak appeared above her, peering through the scored mage-glass of the Lancer. His lewd face looked particularly hideous and his voice was a cold rasp.

"That was your last weapon, yes?" Darak asked. "You may think I am fooled, but I know warmachines. The Children have used them for generations—stolen or captured or cobbled together from old battlefields." He leaned down toward the mage-glass. "Or did you think you were clever?"

Lenalin snarled up at him, but the Lancer wouldn't move. She willed it forward and goaded it, but the Worldfire had done too much damage. She wanted to scream in frustration.

Darak rose up and looked around. The battle around them had fallen to a lull, and many eyes turned their direction. An audience—exactly what Darak craved.

"See now your fallen queen!" Darak raised one fist high and power coiled around it like a gathering storm. He would bring that fist down and shatter the glass. "Watch her fail to protect you!"

At least he had inherited his father's love of his own voice. He should have shut his mouth and killed Lenalin already, but instead he stood over her, bragging and mocking her. It gave her a moment.

That moment was what she needed.

"Now, Mother," he said. "I shall take my place—"

Air whistled around him as the cockpit of the Lancer abruptly burst open, and Lenalin exploded up toward him. Whatever he might have said was lost when she put her hands around his throat, choking off the words. And her scream drowned out his words anyway.

"M-muh," he managed, until she adjusted her grasp. The sapping power of the Worldfire had left her arms tingling with numbness, but she felt stronger than she had in years. Shard hardly knew where it came from and hardly cared. She pressed her thumbs into his windpipe.

"No more," she said. "No! More!"

His eyes bulged, terrified and confused. He looked so alone and afraid as all his plans crumbled, hardly understanding what had happened. Good.

"Do you see it?" she asked. "The ruin of all your dreams?"

They stood together perched atop the damaged ironclad, itself partly wedged into the broken deck of the crashed *Hecatomb*, at the center of the last city of civilized folk, crumbling to Ruin.

But in that moment, none of that mattered.

"How does it feel, to know all you've hoped for comes to nothing?"

She choked him until his hand fell, the magic he had summoned unraveling.

"Do you understand, you monster?" she asked. "Do you understand what you've done?"

His knees buckled and he sagged down, and she went right along with him. This should have hurt—her knees and hips hardly bent this way anymore—but she felt only strength. She joined him on the ground, continuing to squeeze for all she was worth. His choked pleas for mercy enraged her.

"You took my face," she said. "You broke my Blood. You destroyed my *life*!"

Darak's eyes rolled up in their sockets and his mouth formed a single word: "what."

"Burn you, Paeter." Spittle frothed from her mouth. "Just rutting *die*, you piece of shit!"

Her arms burned with the effort of strangling the heir of Ravalis. Her lungs heaved to pull in breath. She felt like she would come apart, but not before she would destroy this pathetic little man.

Her strength had begun to flag, and he managed to draw half a breath. "Nnn," he said. "Not..."

This waste of a man who had—

Darak managed two words—"not Paeter"—and then lost consciousness.

In that moment, as his purple-black face bulged, Lenalin stared down at Darak's face and he looked... like her son. Darkened, distorted, and rotted, but her own child, the product of her own body.

And none of that really mattered, except that Darak was not the man she hated.

"No," she said. "You are not Paeter."

She released him, and he crumpled to the ground with a wheezing sigh. Rotted flesh drooled from his face and his teeth were covered with blood. He was utterly defeated.

349

"But you are like him in one way," she said. "The only way that matters."

Sense came back into his eyes and he blinked up at her, sputtering to breathe. "Wh-what?"

Lenalin looked around at the battle. Hundreds of Tar Vangryur had rallied and looked to her for inspiration and courage. And now that she had defeated Darak, the tide had turned against his horde. All around them, casters discharged and blades clashed as the folk of this city took it back from the barbarians who sought to steal it. From a distance, she heard horns and while she did not know what they meant, they filled her with hope and strength.

"I do not need to kill you," Lenalin said.

Then she walked away, leaving him drooling blood and sobbing.

THIRTY-THREE

EXACTLY HOW LONG SHE lay there, Ovelia could not say. At first, she counted her breaths, but when her attention faltered, she lost track. Perhaps the dripping blood would provide a better measure, but even that seemed to blur as time alternately crawled and skipped along. The pain in her lower half grew impossible, then throbbed. Her body had exceeded its capacity, and now she felt only a dull ache.

The pain seemed far away, as though the agony had driven her outside herself.

Her thoughts drifted to her another time, years ago, in a darkened chamber. As though thinking of it made it so, she found herself standing in the Winter King's privy chambers, watching herself deliver the child that would go on to be her best friend's daughter. Standing over her other self, Ovelia peered down with eyes that had no trouble seeing. By the Fire, she looked so young—her face slaked with sweat and her unscarred face taut with concentration and hopeless optimism.

Perhaps her life would not spiral entirely out of her control. Perhaps, if she did this thing, she would hold a part of it fast. Perhaps all would go well.

That night had seemed like the hardest thing in her young life, but now it felt like a paradise by comparison. She had persevered, out of love and obligation, and it had set her on a path that defined and doomed the rest of her life. Had she known then what would befall, would she have chosen else? She could not honestly say that she would.

She saw a different time and place, then. She stood before the Winter King, the first time they were equals, and considered what he had asked of her. At first, it seemed she would refuse—that she would scream at him and protest and fight and do whatever she must to keep her child—and for that drawn out heartbeat, Ovelia hoped that she would, even though she hadn't. At length, she dipped, as though the weight of the world crushed her down, and sank to one knee. She bowed her head in acquiescence. Then, when he was gone and she was alone, she wept big, bitter tears.

At least, Ovelia thought now with the virtue of age and wisdom, Orbrin had asked. He cared at least that much. In the cold, lonely years since, she had told herself over and over that he had merely used her, but she saw now that he had loved her, after a fashion. Just as she loved Regel, in a way, and used him too. They used each other.

That was what this world was, she had always thought. Folk using each other.

She saw again that horrible night, years later, with her tears that would find no audience. The Winter King dying on her blade, offering her one last smile. At the time, she had denied the tiny spark of pleasure in her heart, but now, looking down upon herself as she slew Orbrin, she saw it on her face.

No wonder Regel had come to hate her.

Something shifted in the snow around her body, and it drew Ovelia's attention back to the world at hand. She felt so cold, and realized it was her lifeblood spreading in the slush around her. Blue veins had spread out from her belly, down her legs and up across her chest and to one arm. Frostburn's curse, working upon her. She looked down upon her pale face and body, and wondered if she was even alive.

She felt it, then: the pulsing beat of the silver fire within the mountain of Tar Vangr. She could see it coursing beneath the stone like blood. The mountain was an artery and a vein both, power surging up into the palace and back down into the core of the World of Ruin. It spread out as it coursed, though, like blood seeping through ruptured lesser vessels. The mountain, damaged in the invasion, had become a bruised husk, filling up with power and swelling, like her own body.

By the Nar, it was going to *burst*.

Someone moved in the swirling snow, and she recognized Regel. He looked terrible—exhausted, beaten, and worn past his own breaking point. But he kept moving, shimmying and sliding down the snowy slope to find her. He landed in a half-crouch, managing to arrest his movement before he went over the edge, and knelt over her. He placed his hands on her chest and she saw his power swell.

"Ovelia," he said.

Her heart fluttered to see him. Too many years and too much pain had passed between them, but that all felt far away now. She put out her hands and touched his face, or might have, had she truly stood there. But instead, she stood over her dying body, unable to touch or speak to him. She would have to relinquish her eyes once more. Perhaps she would die. She did not know.

There, between her legs, a child squalled. She had done it. Surely that was all.

Ovelia looked up once more at the mountain full of silver fire and knew what she had yet to do.

She relaxed her power and became herself once more. Pain crept up around her again, as though she had slipped into once-boiling water. She felt little of anything, but for a dull ache in her head that must have sprung from her body trying to preserve the last vestiges of life. The last embers, that Regel might coax them back into flame.

Oh Regel, she thought. *Why can't you let me go?*

They drew close once more, as they had a year before. She felt him—every tiny hurt in his body, every beat of his heart—and they knew an intimacy deeper than any lovemaking. Once more, Ovelia found herself in a scarred and dying body, and once more, Regel poured his life into her. In that moment, it was not only reminiscent of the time he had saved her—it was the same moment. They knelt together in the destroyed throne room of Tar Vangr, after she had failed, and he gave her one last chance. A new light for an old, broken world.

Then the pain returned in full, and she coughed and sputtered, spattering Regel with blood. He'd revived her, certainly, but the experience was not pleasant. She shuddered and quaked, her body seemingly poorly fitted. She should not be here, and every time he returned her to life, she felt it deeper and longer. She couldn't move, and it felt like the world was crushing her.

"Ovelia," he said in her ear, and only then did she realize he had embraced her.

Neither seemed to have expected him to act thusly, and finally he drew away, seemingly confused. She could see him well enough, marked by burning rage and an inherent violence. But now he seemed indistinct—shaken and unmoored. She understood something about him that had always seemed so elusive.

"Ovelia, I cannot heal you—not fully," he said at length. "I know this wound. This magic. Frostburn is stronger than me. I—"

She touched his lips. "I know," she said. "I have seen it."

A mewling sound drew her attention to the child between her thighs. Somehow, even as she had died, she had accomplished this last task.

"Ovelia," he said. "Your child."

She had to smile at the wonder in his voice. All those years spent dealing death and the power to heal at his fingertips—his healing hands—and Regel the Frostburn knew awe at the simplest things.

"Let me hold them," Ovelia said.

A faint protest of flesh greeted his knife, and in a breath, he placed the squirming child against Ovelia's breast. She half-sat, half-lay in the snow, and pressed the tiny face to her own. She could not see her child, and yet she knew their face—knew their body and soul and path from this day forward. Though she would never see it.

"Will you bring light or dark?" she asked the babe. "Will you try to protect this world, or will you bring it to ruin, as my daughter always has?"

"Your daughter." She could hear Regel's startled inhale. "But…"

Ovelia wasn't listening. She considered the tiny life in her arms. How she would have loved to live that life with them.

"I will get you to safety," Regel said. "You and the child. Then I will go and put an end to this."

In that moment, Ovelia felt so tired. Tired of all the fighting, all the hurting, all the loss. She almost said yes. But she had one thing left to do, and she could not do it if Regel stood in her way.

"No." Ovelia caught Regel by the hand, her grip slippery from blood and weariness. But she held him firmly as he tried to move away. Regel did not resist, but nor did he relent.

"Ovelia." He gripped the hilt of his borrowed sword tighter. "I must do this. You know I must."

She lacked the words or the strength to stay him. Instead, she seized his hand and pressed it to her cheek. The unexpected gesture caught Regel by surprise, and his words faltered. She nuzzled her nose against his rough palm, not unlike the way her child nuzzled at her breast, and sighed.

"No," she said, her voice almost a whisper. She adjusted the child curled under her arms. In a world of shadows, she could not see them, but she knew they were beautiful. The comforting warmth of her child reassured Ovelia of this course. "We will not win your way. Your way is done."

"Do not stay me," Regel said. "She must be stopped."

"She will be."

Careful of the child, Ovelia shifted her grip on his arm and pulled herself fully to her feet. She stood close to Regel, the swaddled babe and the weight of too many years between them. She had never had difficulty seeing Regel, with so much blood on his hands and violence on his mind, but the way he looked upon her now, his face seemed indistinct and fading by the moment. She almost smiled.

Slowly, she took Draca from Regel's hand. He did not resist, though his fingers seemed to extend for it even as it moved beyond their reach. A part of him would always long to inflict pain: on his foes and himself both. But that time was over—for now.

"Here." Ovelia pushed her child into Regel's arms, and he took them awkwardly, entirely unaccustomed to holding such a thing. "This is the heir to Tar Vangr and Luether both," she said. "The union of their blood and the end of their feud. Garin's child and Lenalin's child."

He looked up at her, his face blurry. "And yours."

The words all but stabbed Ovelia, and she almost turned back. Right then, she almost turned from her course. She and Regel would leave Tar Vangr to its fate, and find a safe place to live in peace. They would rekindle the love they once bore for one another, and they would raise Ovelia's child together to be strong and wise—cunning and kind. She would spend every year of life she had left watching her child grow: make mistakes and be disappointed, find love and be happy. All these things she knew would come to pass, if she only turned back, and she almost did.

Almost.

"And mine," she agreed. "You will keep my child safe. I know you will."

"Does your child not need you?" Regel asked.

"Yes." She looked to the coursing veins of silver fire at the heart of the mountain. "But my other child needs me too. I must stand between her and the fire."

Regel saw the understanding on her face—the determination and sadness—and he had no argument. He leaned forward to kiss her forehead, his chapped lips coarse but his touch surprisingly gentle. He leaned back, and in that moment, he vanished from her view, never to be seen again.

Ovelia turned to the path she had chosen.

THIRTY-FOUR

SEMANA DENERRE NÔ RAVALIS walked, her vision distorted by the haze of flames and leaking magic pollution. Bodies lined the streets, two or three deep at times, as well as broken arms and armor. The mage-glass underfoot was scratched and blackened from discharged casters and slaying spells run wild.

To Semana, it all seemed secondary. She drifted like a ghost through the frostbitten, gory streets, drawn inexorably toward the mountain and the heart of the Narfire beating within.

She knew what she sought, even if she had never seen it in the flesh or even heard it named, let alone described. She knew it from her dreams, both sleeping and waking. She knew it was there, and knew what power it held. Power that would be hers.

Those who saw her walk the streets that day would describe something impossible: a young woman, her skin of pale gold and her hair like molten silver, ambling without a care through killing streets and around explosions. Casterbolts flew in her direction and mortar charges as well, but no matter how close they came, she showed no sign of harm other than her hair wafting faintly before her face. She seemed almost naked, clad only in torn silks, but she was still stronger than any warrior.

Power had boiled her down to her essence, and now nothing else existed.

Without fail, wherever she went, the Children of Ruin paused in their business to observe her passing. Some turned their backs on forgotten foes, only to fall bleeding to the ground as their opponents had not forgotten *them*. Others turned upon her as though to strike this newfound and seemingly easy victim, then bowed in submission at her visage. Still others bowed and placed their heads against the mage-glass ground until she had gone by, then rose and went looking for more Tar Vangryur to fight, or else they fought each other for the Blood Queen's favor.

Semana did not mark any of them. She hardly perceived the world around her as real.

One shadowy figure moved along behind her, shuffling with an odd limp. He dragged one leg through the snow and dribbled blood and spittle as he went. He was a wreck, but he followed her. He followed mostly at the same pace she walked, but sometimes he made up ground accidentally. Once, he stumbled down a street and slid, making up a few paces. All the while, she drifted on, oblivious.

Only when Semana paused at the foot of the palace of Tar Vangr, at the opposite end of a long mage-glass thoroughfare, did the man catch up with her. He reached forward with one bloody hand, the skin rippling in the freezing wind, toward her silvery hair, which swirled wildly at this height. He was about to touch her when she turned abruptly and her red-hued eyes settled upon his face.

"Brother," she said.

Darak was a mess. His skin swarmed with black-furred lesions, which looked like spiders clinging to every length of his skin. He trembled, one leg clearly broken, one arm curled against his chest in obvious pain. Mottled purple bruises smeared across his throat and his face looked like so much spoiled meat. When he opened his mouth to speak, he sounded like a days-old corpse.

"Semana," Darak said. "Help... me..."

Slowly, she shook her head. His cause did not concern her—mayhap it never truly had. She sought something greater now, and he might as well not exist.

A confused light filled Darak's eyes, then it became a manic sort of hope. To his mottled, blood-filled eyes, the shake of her head seemed a gesture of sympathy—a rejection of the World of Ruin that had betrayed him so completely. A cruel world that had dealt him a seemingly winning hand, tempting him to wager all his resources and belongings and his very life upon his victory, only to snatch his glory away when he stood upon the verge of accomplishing his goal. His sister, at least, would not deny him. She would understand. She shared his blood and his destiny.

But no. She had not expressed her sympathy for his plight, but rejected its power over her.

And that filled him with rage.

How *dare* she. Did she not understand what was at stake? Did she not see his pain? Did she not know her place? Clearly she did not, and that he could not abide.

He grasped her upper arm to restrain her, nails biting into her skin. Had she paid him any attention—acknowledged him at all—she might have fought, but she just looked at him blankly, as though he didn't matter in the slightest. That look of utter contempt unmade him. *Unmanned* him.

He hit her. Dragged the back of his good hand across her face as hard as he could muster. The Worldfire had all but burnt itself out in him, but he had enough strength to knock her into the snow. There she lay, seemingly dazed, and looked up at him, her face slack, and her eyes glazed over.

"You were to be my queen," he said. "We were going to rule this world. But you—*you*—"

He ran out of words. They choked in his throat and refused to spill from his lips. His quest had failed. His destiny was gone. His mind fell silent. All he had left was rage, and he vented it on the foolish woman before him. That she was his blood no longer mattered. That she could slay him with a flicker of her own magic did not factor into it at all. At least he still had her.

And he would take her.

"No," she said, calmly and flatly, as though that mattered.

Darak fell upon Semana, snarling and growling more like an animal than a man. He tore at her silken shift, and slammed his fist into her face when she resisted. Blood streamed from her nose.

"No," she said again, more forcefully this time. "Stop."

It didn't matter. Her will didn't matter. She was a weak woman, and even hurt and weary, he could overpower her easily enough. He needed this. This scrap of power. Of control. Of domination.

Her body trembled under his, her skin so impossibly smooth compared to his own lesion-ridden waste of flesh. She had wielded the Worldfire, had she not? What right had she to maintain such beauty—such purity—when the power had corrupted him past recognition? He wanted to tear her skin with his teeth—sate himself upon her and then torture her until she was little more than tender meat.

He hated her. He *hated* her.

"This will be," he said. "You are mine. You have always been mine. You will—"

Then he started choking, and it was not because the words wouldn't come. Instead, he could feel the blood thickening in the veins in his neck, choking off his air.

Semana pushed herself up on her elbows, breast bare to the ice and snow. Her hair swirled across her face and her eyes were pools of blood. "*No*," she said, in a dark voice barely her own.

In sudden panic, Darak flailed at her. His fist had almost no strength, but he managed to connect with the side of her head. She fell to the side and scrambled away, and the pressure in his head eased for a heartbeat. He grabbed her ankle and pulled, trying to drag her back, but instead they both tumbled into the snow upon the bridge, the storm swirling around them.

"No," she shouted—not frightened, but angry. "*No!*"

They struggled, wrestling in the burning snow. Darak could hardly feel the chill—his Frostfire saw to that—and Semana seemed unaffected as well. He ripped at the rags shrouding her perfect body, jealous and angry and lusting to own her. Blood leaked out of his eyes and his nose and his mouth but he did not care. This. This was what it had to be.

He punched and snapped and slapped at her, while she desperately pushed and shoved and kicked at him. She was not a trained fighter, and he was too weary. They fought as they had when they were children, in the artless way of youth, with more ferocity than skill. But what he intended to do was anything but play, and she knew it.

She kept screaming at him. Begging him to leave her be. To stop this.

But he could not. This *was* Darak. This was his world. If he could not have her, he had nothing.

In the end, perhaps it had to pass this way: brother against sister, trying and failing to assert his will over her, and she finally would take no more.

He lunged for her, clutching at her arms, and his footing faltered on the mage-glass bridge. A sharp pain cut into the arch of his left foot and his leg slid over the edge. There Darak hung, barely holding onto Semana, whose hands tangled in his garb. They held each other, huddled together over the gap, and Darak clung desperately to her.

"Semana," he said. "Semana, wait—"

In the end, she simply let go.

As her hands eased their grip, Darak overbalanced and fell backward. He fumbled at the ratty silks that still clung to her body, but they tore when he tried to cling to them. His grip was too weak on her wrist and he slipped free. As he fell backward into the swirling snow, he knew regret for the first and last time in his horrid life.

Then he was gone.

～

Semana sat on the snowy bridge for a time, as the flakes tumbled around her. Her fingers twitched spasmodically, grasping for something that had long since slipped through them.

At the far end of the bridge stood her destiny: the tunnels that led to the sanctuary of the Nar, where all the power of the World of Ruin collected. She could see it now: a kaleidoscopic column of worlds shifting indistinctly around the mountain, centered on one spot accessible to mortal folk. There lay a temple, where in older, less enlightened times, the terrified folk so recently emerged from the stone after fulfilling the Prophecy of Return, had worshipped the Narfire as a god itself. But Semana knew it was no god, and there was nothing of divinity here in the World of Ruin, and would never be.

Not until she bathed in that silver flame and took their power for her own.

But she could not make herself rise, let alone cross the bridge to her destiny. She felt empty, hollowed out by grief and tragedy and utter failure.

Above, lightning crackled and the storm raged. The World of Ruin lashed at Tar Vangr as though to shake the fractured mountain at its base. Any other person caught in the open in that swirling blizzard would have been killed, their flesh frozen and stripped away by the lashing, acidic snow. But not Semana, with the Frostfire to protect her. She wondered if Lenalin, her false mother, lay dead this day. If so, had she broken her own Blood, in killing her brother?

Something deep and powerful stirred inside her, where she had buried her feelings long ago. As a child, she'd had to choose between despair and survival, and it had seemed so simple then. Now as a woman, she didn't know what she felt, let alone what to do with it. It bubbled and roiled inside her like a stew left too long to simmer. It burned and tore at her insides but she had no idea how to get it out.

And so it was that another man came upon her, this one also limping through the snow. His cloak hung in tatters, his leathers torn and rent and seared, but he moved with alacrity despite what must have been crippling wounds. Unlike Darak before him, when this man approached Semana, he did so peacefully and with respect. He stood over her for a time, gazing into the void where Darak had gone. He understood without asking, just as he always had—just as he always would.

As he stood with her, he took his tattered cloak in his hands and tore free the few razors still attached to its lining. One by one, he flicked them into the void, where they sailed off into the snow like glittering-sharp raindrops. Once, Semana heard one of the razors clatter against the stones below.

When he was done, he took the cloak from around his shoulders and wrapped it around her. The warmth was welcome but entirely unnecessary.

"I don't need it," she said.

Tithian Davargorn shrugged. "For your modesty, if not your cold."

Semana shook her head, but she pulled the cloak tighter about herself. Why not?

They watched the snow for another moment before she wet her lips to speak again.

"My eyes are open," she said.

"I know." He nodded grimly.

"You're afraid."

Again, he nodded, but this time he did so silently.

The moment stretched. Distantly, Semana heard a man cry out in pain. The battle was still raging—the last struggle for the World of Ruin's last mage-city. Before the day was done, all would fall to Ruin, whoever won, and there would be no city left. It hardly mattered now.

Tithian tried one last time. He knelt beside her in the snow, his mismatched eyes weary.

"Turn from this." He touched her cheek gently. "Remain yourself. Stay with me."

The hot mass inside Semana trembled and cracked but it was not enough. She shook her head. "You know I cannot."

This was her course—had always been and ever would be—and she had walked too far along it to turn back. From this moment hence, she was lost to him. All the lies, all the manipulations, all the darkness between them was at an end. Only one thing remained.

For a heartbeat, Tithian's face betrayed the truth inside him. The years they had spent together—as friends by necessity and siblings of circumstance, as something much more and something much less—all their shared history hung between them for that heartbeat, and Semana saw something utterly foreign on Tithian's face. She knew kindness and contempt, even if he had never expressed either—she recognized lust and desire, even if she had never herself felt either. But the expression on Tithian Davargorn's face was something new: something that made her heart ache for him and break both at the same time. And when he gave voice to it, she knew it was true.

"I love you," he said.

Semana smiled faintly.

"I know," she said, almost whispering. Which was a lie.

They turned from one another, then, their paths forever parted.

361

THIRTY-FIVE

BLESSEDLY, THE FAMILIAR ACHE in her hip hadn't yet returned, but by the time the sun set on Ruin's Day, Lenalin Denerre's body had become one walking bruise. Her legs were branches filled with rotting grubs that barely held her weight, and the smoke seared her already burning lungs. Her skin itched and her clothes stabbed at her. Her mask felt stuffy. Pain and discomfort had rushed in after her victory, and every breathing moment reminded her that her body could not tolerate such punishment.

The woman at her side was speaking, but Lenalin could hardly hear the bursts of casters and song of swords, much less words. Her mask muffled the voice, but in truth, she was hardly listening.

She should have rested after her trials of the day, but instead she had rallied what warriors she could and led them street to street, purging High-City of the Children of Ruin. The fall of their warchief had broken the horde, but with no one to take command, the barbarians had given into their wild nature and even now ran wild and uncontrolled through the city. It made them easy enough to defeat, in their isolated groups, but not always easy to find—they scurried like rabid vermin, foaming at the mouth and interested only in murder. Without leadership, there was no plan anymore—only chaos.

"Majesty?" the woman said again, her tone tinged sharp.

"Nacacia." Lenalin regarded her, this fierce, dark-eyed woman with her cropped hair and scarred leather cuirass. The teardrop under her eye told Lenalin she could be trusted—to a point. "What is it?"

Her field general bared her teeth. Lenalin had only known her a few hours, but she knew Nacacia was not the sort to mince words or hesitate to deliver awkward news. She liked that about her.

"Our hunters encountered a knot of two dozen barbarians," she said. "A clan or a tribe, under a giant of a man called Bellows in the Deep—a lieutenant of your..." She paused. "Of Darak Ravalis."

Lenalin shrugged. "And your purpose in telling me this?"

"The barbarians are marching this way, with the intent of parlay," Nacacia said.

"Parlay." Lenalin raised an eyebrow. "They used that word."

"Yes, Majesty." Nacacia nodded. "He wishes to bring suit, to negotiate for peace."

"I'd have thought most of those words beyond the ken of a Child." Lenalin pronounced the slur with no teeth. She'd met plenty of clever barbarians in her time. "Do you think them honest?"

Nacacia spat in the slush by way of reply.

Lenalin understood. It mattered less whether Bellows meant to betray them, and more whether they could repel him if he did. She looked around at the ragged defenders arrayed around the square in High-City: men and women and others covered head-to-toe in scarred, pitted leathers and plates, burned and scoured by Ruin, bent and yet unbroken. Some of them were palace warders, who had joined the fray, but most of the warriors Lenalin had commanded this day were common folk, highborn and lowborn alike. She had ceased to see the difference years ago, and now no one could.

Lenalin doubted this weary, wavering rabble could repulse a score of barbarians. She doubted they could withstand a stiff wind.

"I suggest we move," Nacacia said. "Evacuate this square—"

"Let him come." Lenalin waved over her objections. "Let them all come."

Nacacia nodded, her expression resolute, and went away, calling out instructions.

By reflex, Lenalin reached down to caress her hip, though for once, it didn't hurt more than the rest of her. She had to wedge her fingers between joints of the steel plates they'd convinced her to strap to her body. They'd wanted to put her in the full, gold-steel armor one of the Ravalis kings might have worn, but Lenalin adamantly refused. She'd rather die from a stray casterbolt or bit of shrapnel than array herself in that accursed Blood's colors. Unpowered armor had served her just fine—mostly, it just weighed her down and drained her energy.

And that was precisely how Lenalin felt: drained. She could not remember the last time she had slept or thought about anything other than war. Her mind felt light and hollow, wandering through a fog of weariness and heartache and frustration. There was something that danced just at the edge of her awareness, but she couldn't name it. Something that should have left her screaming with madness. Perhaps her mind had purposefully blocked the image, to preserve her own sanity. If so, it was a small kindness on a day with little enough of that.

She remembered that the folk who had put the armor on her had treated her body with utter deference, not the least bit unsettled. She couldn't remember the last time anyone had treated her that way. Not since... but she couldn't call up the memory.

Nacacia returned, her face grim. She checked her caster's charge twice over.

Lenalin did not have to wait long before a score of barbarians stumbled into the mage-glass square. They looked haggard and weary, like cornered animals. Their weapons were filthy and cracked, their armor stained with blood and dust and scorched with acid snow and slush. Too many days of battle had smeared their flesh with an indelible sheen of gray, and even with her mask, Lenalin nearly gagged at their reek from this far away. The day had been filled with such stenches.

Lenalin's warders bristled with casters and swords, standing ready to strike at the first provocation. Many had taken positions behind cover or inside the doorways of buildings. They looked just as forlorn as the barbarians. This was war as Lenalin had always understood it: equally terrified forces flailing at one another until someone wiser gave them permission to stop.

"I understood there to be four and twenty," Lenalin said to Nacacia.

"Perhaps not all of them wished to come," the woman said.

Lenalin nodded gravely. If he had killed four of his own for refusing to follow him, that told her several things about her would-be suitor, none of them reassuring.

"Giant of a man" failed to capture the physical truth of Bellows in the Deep. Lenalin was no slip of a girl anymore, but Bellows was at least thrice her own size and twice as big as any man she had ever met: a towering mass of muscle and gristle and fat. Half his face was a burned mass out of which glared a milky, bloodshot eye. The butt of a hafted weapon protruded over his shoulder while his bulk hid its head. Lenalin recognized the style by which the Children of Ruin wore their weapons: reversed, both to conceal their faces and also to make them more dangerous to the bearer.

A woman hung on his arm, from whose head stood sharp bristles of hair like spikes. Lenalin could tell she was just as monstrous as Bellows himself, not just because when she smiled, every single one of her teeth ended in a filed point. She wore her weapons more openly—a pair of axes whose heads flared wide of her hips like spurs that produced from her flesh.

"I am Bellows in the Deep," he said. "This, Rending Gnash."

"Nash?" Lenalin asked.

The barbarian woman glared at her, making a low hissing sound that reminded her of a serpent. Her gash of a mouth looked like a bloody wound. Thirty years ago, Lenalin might have found such antics and styling amusing—even intriguing. But not today. She smiled mirthlessly in the depths of her mask.

As they approached, she pulled back her mask to expose her face, on the chance that perhaps her horrid visage would win some respect from these ugly people. Alas, they reacted with scowls, just as most folk did to her face.

"I am Queen Lenalin Denerre, Blood of Winter," she said. "I am told you would treat with me."

His companion looked confused, but Bellows in the Deep nodded seriously. "This is the remains of my clan," he said. "I will depart your death-trap of a city. We will spill no blood. Yes?"

The request was crude and unsophisticated, but it seemed honest. Lenalin could sense the earnestness in his stance and hear the uncertain waver in his tone. He was afraid, she realized, and not just for himself. He feared for all his clan. He was a competent leader, for a barbarian.

"You do not wish your Blood broken," Lenalin said. "This I understand." She held out a hand.

At first, Bellows in the Deep only looked at her hand, wary of the gesture. Lenalin could not blame him: she was half or less his size, horribly scarred and mottled, clad in bits and pieces of steel plates. Who knew what sense she must have presented? It was hardly an ideal situation for such diplomacy, but if it prevented more bloodshed, then so be it.

Finally, he raised his hand as though to clasp hers. This was the moment, Lenalin knew, when all would be decided. If the barbarians intended treachery, plenty of blood would be spilled. Had she chosen wisely or wrongly? She would soon find out.

Crack.

The discharge of a caster split the air, and Lenalin flinched in sudden terror. She recoiled as though struck, but on a quick inspection, her belly was unbroken. Instead, Bellows in the Deep fell back, clutching at his chest, where she saw a smoking quarrel protruding perhaps a hand's width from his flesh. He turned to the side, and she saw the point of the casterbolt tenting the armor over his back.

Shadows fell over them as folk descended from above, casting with grim focus into the small fraction of the horde that remained. A thunderstorm of discharging casters sent barbarians screaming to the mage-glass beneath their feet. Blood spurted like a mist into the air. Rending Gnash caught a caster quarrel to the face, and she arched back and upward, then collapsed limply to the ground.

Bellows turned back to Lenalin and roared in fury and anguish. She took a step back, staggered, and would have fallen had not Nacacia been there to support her with a ready arm.

Lenalin shivered, confused. She pulled her mask back over her face. It made her feel more secure, even if it would do little in the case of an attack.

The barbarian reached for the queen, his grasping fingers smeared with his own blood, and Nacacia discharged a bolt of flame from her own light caster into his chest. The impact knocked him staggering back, but he still kept his feet. He fell to his knees and leaned back to howl up at the sky. The sound that emerged from his mouth now was low and pained—mournful.

Then another casterbolt took him in the throat, silencing him in a burst of blood.

All around her, the warders and soldiers were shouting in surprise and confusion. Amongst the chaos, Lenalin put out a hand to Nacacia to still a response and looked to the sky, where the snow had started to clear. A dozen folk in golden armor were descending, upside down, crimson cloaks spread out around them like the petals of flowers. Above them, parting the clouds, came a dark vessel, crimson rings spreading around it. The skyship was a small troop carrier, with a complement of perhaps a score of swords, many of them floating down even now. All were women, Lenalin saw from the shape of their armor and how they carried themselves. They wore the colors of Ravalis dustblades, and Lenalin restrained her visceral loathing only out of her superior sense of caution. These folk had the upper hand and the initiative; if they were foes, they would have slain Lenalin and her folk before now. Sure enough, when they had landed, they fanned out in a protective circle around Lenalin. She stood, waiting, knowing better than to disturb the entrance unfolding.

After a moment's hesitation, three more figures appeared from the vessel and floated down with the use of ensorcelled cloaks as well: two of them red, one golden. That last Lenalin watched in particular, crossing her arms as the woman descended like a triumphant angel. She landed before Lenalin, pulled her mask back, and shook her head in relief.

She was beautiful, this savior from the skies, with the deep brown skin and russet red hair of the Ravalis. She had the statuesque figure of a warrior and wore fitted light armor of leather dyed red and inlaid with gold that complimented it quite well. She kept her hair very short and not terribly well appointed, and Lenalin thought she might have shaved it all off sometime not too long ago. She had apparently come to battle fully painted and made up for a ceremonial procession, which told the queen of Tar Vangr that she had planned on this very arrival, rather than actual fighting. There was a golden dagger at her belt but no other obvious weapon. She had her two appointed warders for that.

Lenalin knew her immediately, though she had to admit she had not expected her.

"Alistra Ravalis, Daughter of Summer," she said. "I had thought you dead."

"Lenalin Denerre, Daughter of Winter." A cruel smile drew across Alistra's sharp features. "I wonder which of us spent more time dead," she said. "And now, here we are, both queens. You of a city in need of aid, me of a city able to offer it. A reversal of twenty years gone, no?"

"So it would seem." Lenalin reached up and caught at the edge of her mask. She pulled it free, revealing her face to Alistra. "That we might see one another and know peace."

Alistra's eyes widened slightly in surprise, a reaction Lenalin was well accustomed to. She didn't look horrified or disgusted though, only somewhat confused perhaps.

It was enough. At her side, Nacacia braced for an attack, and Lenalin hesitated to call her off. She knew the Spider of Luether, albeit not well, but she knew enough to be wary. If Alistra meant to kill them, a sudden strike might be their only chance. They paused, the three of them and Alistra's two warders, sharing a tense moment where many hands lingered on the hilts and handles of weapons. Lenalin's breath remained surprisingly calm, and she wondered why her heart wasn't racing.

"Something on my face, Queen Spider?" Lenalin asked.

The jest broke the tension. "Let me greet you, cousin." Alistra reached out and laid the back of one hand against Lenalin's cheek. It felt unexpectedly smooth and gentle. "Your city is safe, the threat purged as we speak. All these things, I have done for you and for peace between our Blood."

Then she leaned in and pressed her lips to Lenalin's in a kiss that was about more than greeting.

It lingered for a time, the kiss, and Lenalin did not even try to resist. Alistra Ravalis tasted of warm fruit and of ash—of warm summer nights and the pain of the mornings after them. She was sweet and promising and dangerous.

Nacacia made a disapproving sound, but Lenalin held up a finger to stay her.

When they parted, Lenalin looked up at Alistra warily. The self-proclaimed Summer Queen smiled in a very enticing manner. Her fingers caressed Lenalin's cheek.

"For peace, eh?" Pleasant as the kiss had been and warm as the touch felt, Lenalin shook off Alistra's hand and glared reproachfully at the woman. "And I am to take the word of a Ravalis?"

If the self-appointed Queen of the Summer City took offense, she hid it well. She gave Lenalin a faint smile. "We have both lost much to the men of Summer," Alistra said. "Let us end this useless feud before our cities lose more. Queen of Winter." She extended her hand again, this time palm up, in an offer of friendship. "Let us go forth from this day as sisters."

Lenalin considered the gesture for a moment, then laid her hand in Alistra's. The two women held the grasp for a moment, then drew apart, but remained closer than before. How very unexpected.

Something tickled at the back of Lenalin's mind, but she focused on the task at hand.

"Well," Alistra said. "I am relieved. I was worried this meeting would come to blows. But we daughters are more reasonable than our fathers, yes?"

Lenalin pulled her mask back in place against the cold. "You've dispatched your troops throughout my city," she said. She did not make it a question, nor did she do more to hide the "without my consent" other than leave it unspoken.

"Indeed, I have." Alistra made a beckoning gesture, and one of her warders gestured up at the floating ornithopters. "The ice floes prevented my mage-caravels from entering the bay, of course, but ornithopter carriers have proved sufficient to the task. Many barbarians attempted to flee by means of the broken wall, and my forces were on hand to hunt them down. We even took some prisoners, at least one of whom should be of interest to you."

"Prisoners," Lenalin said. "And I should pay you a ransom price, I imagine?"

"My bracing Ice Queen, I am amused," she said. "They are a gift."

Lenalin did not like it, but she did need the aid. "Surely you want something," she said.

"Surely." Alistra looked around the square, seemingly disappointed. "And here I had hoped you would have prisoners of your own to exchange. Perhaps a ruinscarred wretch I think we both know?"

That sparked Lenalin's interest, as did the way Alistra spoke it: smoothly and without obvious emotion, but with deep sentiment beneath the warm, perfect surface. There was a story there.

"I have seen such a man, and recently," she said. "If I should see him again, what would you advise me, Queen-Sister?"

Alistra allowed the faintest hint of a smile to crease her brown countenance. "Use him as you will, but with caution," she said. "If he yet lives, he must be a subtler blade than when last I wielded him. Methinks someone must have sharpened him somewhat."

"I see." Lenalin recognized the sentiment. "I shall watch for him."

"I thank you, Queen-Sister." Alistra took Lenalin's hands. "I suspect we should be great friends."

Allies, perhaps. Friends, unlikely. Something more? Lenalin wondered.

Other ornithopters were setting down, now, sometimes atop the bodies of slain barbarians. Urbane as Alistra presented herself, she didn't much seem to care for the sanctity of the dead.

"Rescue efforts are under way," Alistra said. "Though if you could aid us, it would serve well. Many of your folk are… less than enthusiastic about strangers from the south coming to save them."

Lenalin nodded. She wondered how many lives would be lost this day because of prejudice or simple, understandable paranoia. People who had spent days upon days hiding and fighting for their lives could hardly be relied upon to trust the extended hand of a stranger.

"I will issue a decree," she said, then immediately saw the difficulty of such a plan. The mage-glass through which she'd given her speech to rouse the city hung in ruins down to the slums.

"Mayhap the Queen of Winter could dispatch some of her swords alongside mine?" Alistra made the suggestion a cool, light one. "Mayhap friendly faces would cool some hot blood."

"A fine idea." Lenalin grimaced slightly, though she turned so Alistra could not see the expression. The last thing she wanted was to seem like she took orders from a foreign queen in her own city. She waved a confirmation to Nacacia, who did not make any attempt to hide her contempt.

"I like your little cat," Alistra said, watching Nacacia relay the order. "If you ever tire of her…"

Lenalin was no longer listening. Her eyes fell instead upon the skyship carriers, and the folk climbing out of them. Their ranks included haggard Tar Vangryur warriors in grimy apparel—Ravalis dustblades, Swords of Winter, and other soldiers—but most of those climbing off the transports were common folk, lowborn and highborn alike. Her notice fell chiefly, however, on an old man debarking with the aid of a muscular dark-skinned soldier, careful to shield a bundle strapped to his chest. She recognized Regel's grizzled face and gray eyes immediately and her heart lurched. Something clawed at her mind and her hands started shaking.

"Winter Queen?" Alista asked, a note of concern in her voice.

Without waiting for an escort, Lenalin shoved past Alistra and her warders and to his side. She caught the collar of his tattered cloak. "Frostburn," she said. "What is this? Where have you been? What—?" She looked down at the babe swaddled against his chest. "What is that?"

Regel's chapped lips parted. "Ovelia's child," he said, his voice little more than a groan.

And suddenly, Lenalin remembered the thing she had put behind her all that day. *Ovelia.*

"She—she's alive," she said, hardly able to believe the words.

Regel's face remained grim, but Lenalin didn't care. Her heart soared.

"Of *course* she's alive, and she birthed her whelp," she said, as if to reassure herself. "That woman is made of steel and sinew. It would take all the ruin in the world to kill her."

She looked down at the child, whose ruddy face peeked out from amongst the black fabric swaddling them to Regel's chest. As ever with newborns, she felt no affinity for the babe, but this one reminded her of Ovelia, from the ruddy brown skin to the tiny fringe of crimson hair crowning their elongated head. As she watched, the child opened their eyes, and they were the same amber-hazel color Ovelia had. Lenalin's knees felt weak, and not just from weariness.

"Lenalin Denerre," said the man beside Regel, sounding startled. "Your—your Majesty."

She looked to him, this huge summerblooded man who dwarfed Regel in broadness of shoulder and thickness of his arms, and he pointedly looked away from her. It was a behavior she'd seen many times before, but it jarred her because no one had recoiled from her all day.

As though he could sense her displeasure, the man fell awkwardly into a kind of bow. Lenalin let it persist a three-count before waving dismissively for him to rise.

"And your name, warrior?" she asked.

"Dain," he said. "Dain Duldur. I was a warder on the wall under King—" He swallowed. "Under Lan Ravalis." A shadow passed over his face at the mention, and Lenalin realized it was not her face he dreaded, but this revelation. Somehow, she felt even more insulted.

"Oh nay, *nay.*" Alistra appeared. Dain Duldur took one look at her cruel face and blanched. "Let us not speak of my dead kin as if he was something to be feared. He was but a spoiled child."

Duldur lowered his head, unwilling or unable to speak.

"These two," Alistra said, "we found shortly after we pushed into Low-City, perhaps an hour gone. Deserters seeking to flee the city, we thought, but mayhap you have a different idea?"

Lenalin ignored her and focused on Dain. "You were part of Lan's last charge, were you?" Lenalin asked. "And now you wish to serve me?"

He nodded.

"Not Luether, the city of your heritage?" Lenalin asked. "Queen Alistra seems to have reclaimed the City of Flames. Would you not be happier there?"

"Luether is the city of my birth," Dain said. "But Tar Vangr is my city. I shall stay. If—" He bowed again. "If you permit it."

"Yes." Lenalin nodded, then looked to Alistra, who sighed and waved. "Very well."

Dain brightened. "Your Majesty," he said, bowing to Alistra. "Is there among you a warrior known as Berric? He sailed south with Lan Ravalis, and—"

"Dain?" came a call from behind them.

Abruptly another man was there. He had the pale skin of a Winterborn, thick black hair nearly burned away on the left side where a casterbolt must have narrowly missed him.

"Berric!" The joy on Dain's face upon seeing him made even Lenalin's bitter heart soar.

The two men embraced and kissed, as pleased to see each other as though they'd been parted by great distances, many years, and possibly even death. Seeing it made Lenalin's heart ache anew.

"How absolutely disgusting," Alistra said.

Lenalin narrowed her eyes at her. "How's that?"

"Why, one of those lads serves me, and the other just swore to serve you," she said. "When you find love, you should cling to it." She glanced sidelong at Lenalin. "Do you not agree?"

The words made Lenalin's skin crawl. She hadn't thought of Ovelia at all, that day, keeping her purposefully from her mind. Seeing the keep in which she had gone to give birth collapse, she hardly knew what had come over her. Grief. Madness. Murder. It all seemed like a blur until she stood here, now, in her besieged city. Tar Vangr lay in ruin, but the tide had turned. Now they might win the day, and Ovelia had somehow not only survived, but borne her child. How mad did that seem?

She had never intended to win this war—never even *wanted* to win. Lady Shard would not have stayed to fight, but Lenalin Denerre?

"For you, Ovelia," she said under her breath. "For you."

She looked to Regel, who had removed himself somewhat, as was his wont. He had slipped some sort of carving into the hands of the red-haired child, who gummed it contentedly.

"Where is she?" Lenalin asked. "Where is Ovelia? I must see her at once."

Only now, when he returned a dire expression, did she start to waver in her joy. She realized that this was not merely Regel being Regel, but that he had dark news.

"What is it?" she asked. "Speak quickly."

Regel wet his chapped lips. He explained, in short, clipped sentences, what had come to pass between them. How he had come upon her wounded and almost dead, how he had aided her in giving birth to the child. His story became fuzzy after that, with details he left unaddressed, but one fact stood out among all the others. Lenalin ground her teeth.

"You *left* her?" she asked. "Then and there, you let her walk away into the snow?"

"She said…" Regel seemed uncertain, but he nodded. "She said her daughter needed her. To stand between her and the fire."

"Her daughter." Lenalin blinked at him. "But…"

At that moment, far above them, silver fire burbled forth from the mountain at the core of Tar Vangr, like the first wave of an impending eruption. Lenalin knew that sound and sight: she had seen it in Luether, twenty years past. And now, someone sought to loose the Narfire upon her city as well.

"Come." Heart in her throat, Lenalin grasped Regel's hand. "*Now!*"

Her tone brooked no argument, and he made none.

THIRTY-SIX

T HE HEART OF THE Narfire at the core of Tar Vangr mountain was a sacred
place. According to legend, it had saved the folk of winter, trapped in
the long centuries between the violent end of the World of Wonder and the
promised safety of the Prophecy of Return. The shrine erected deep within
promised peace and contemplation in a place of raw, barely contained power.

The power, Semana sensed in abundance, but she found no peace.

As she crept through its passages, heat and steam filled the air around her,
and without her Frostfire, she might not have been able to breathe. Semana
traced her fingers idly along gleaming powerlines that pulsed with silver
fire, and had to pull away as the raw power singed her fingertips. Deeper in,
ancient horns bleated a vain warning that told Semana she should turn back.
Not that she could, of course.

The snow had long since melted off Semana, and now steam rose from her
skin and the tattered remains of her shift to mingle with the smoke in the air.
Underfoot, the stone trembled and cracked under the growing pressure of the
Narfire contained within the mountain.

As she ventured deeper, Semana heard a new sound—clashing and
grinding, like the crash of steel against glass—and her stomach turned over.
Somehow, she knew the source of that awful sound, and cursed herself for not
anticipating it. She picked up her pace.

Semana emerged from the tunnels into the deep core of the mountain,
where the planet's lifeblood rumbled. Silver fire licked the walls, leaking from
glowing pipes that channeled it away and down into the city. The Narfire
was the lifeblood of Tar Vangr, of all the mage-cities, but the damage to
the mountain had crippled the mechanisms that harnessed it. The magical
protections were crumbling, the pipes that carried the fire overheating, and
soon the fire would burst forth to consume Tar Vangr and all within it. The
fire churned and redoubled behind the mage-glass barrier that kept it at bay.

And all that stood between Semana and this world-ending power was a
haggard Ovelia Dracaris, smoke streaming from her family's bloodsword,
hammering the mage-glass with her last strength.

She had borne her child, Semana saw immediately, but she did not look
better for it. Blue veins of ice criss-crossed her body like scars—the Frostburn's
curse. Mechanically, she raised Draca, making Semana's breath catch, and

brought it around with shattering force against the mage-glass wall. Tiny shards of glass flew forth, and the cracks around her strike zone spread a little farther.

"Stop!" Semana meant to scream, but she managed only a choked whisper.

Ovelia, who had lifted her sword for another strike, looked over her shoulder. She had lost her crimson blindfold somewhere out in the snow, and her murky hazel eyes gazed out at Semana.

The two of them stood there, regarding one another.

Semana reached out for Ovelia's blood, hoping to seize it and hold her back, but she could hardly even taste her presence, much less control her. Not through the protective magic of Draca, which would stop her Frostfire as well. Even when she discarded all her relics, she had not felt so powerless.

Ovelia moved again, making Semana shudder, but she merely put her hand on the mage-glass wall between them and the Narfire. Her chapped, bloody fingers spread across the glass.

"I've seen this in my dreams," Ovelia said. "This moment."

"So have I," Semana said.

"Yes." Ovelia took her hand away, smearing a bloody print, and turned fully to her. "I know."

"You know," Semana said.

Ovelia nodded. "Yes."

"Because of that?" Semana pointed to Draca, whose shadows told Ovelia what would come to pass. No doubt she had seen every possible permutation of this moment in its flames, and so Semana could not catch her by surprise. But even as Semana said it, she knew it was not so.

"No." Ovelia held out the sword between them. "Not this."

Shakily, she placed her free hand over her heart.

"You know we share this power." Semana swallowed a lump in her throat. "You know because you are my mother."

Ovelia's throat visibly quavered. When she spoke, she produced only a whisper. "Yes."

The weight of that secret hung like a curtain that shrouded the rest of the world around them, finally parted to allow them to see each other.

"Why," Semana said, her voice barely a whisper.

Ovelia blinked but said nothing. Blue veins had started to creep into her dull hazel eyes.

"*Why*," she asked again, louder.

Ovelia had only a sad, blind gaze to offer her. Curls of smoke crept up her neck toward her face.

"Why, why, *why*?" Semana shrieked by the end of it. "Why would you do this to me? Why?"

"Because you are all that matters."

"No." Semana almost snarled at her. "*No*. I will not accept that. You don't get to tell me that."

Ovelia recoiled as though Semana had struck her. Her face was heartbroken.

"Why not tell me the truth?" Semana asked. "When I was a child, I understand. You could not tell me then, but why not a year ago, when I took off my mask? When I revealed myself to you?"

"And what would I have said?" Ovelia asked. " 'Oh dear child, I am your mother, that you have hated all of your life, for killing your father'?"

"My father," Semana said. "But I thought Regel—" Her eyes widened and she raised her hands to cover her mouth. "No."

Ovelia's head dipped slightly, as though in shame. "I have made so many mistakes," she said. "Know that Orbrin ordered me to kill him, to protect you, and when I refused, he begged me." She raised the sword to strike the barrier once more. "All that I have done, I have done for love of you."

"Then why!" Semana cried out, and Ovelia paused once more.

Shoulders heaving, Semana gritted her teeth. "Why bar my way now?" she asked, tears in her eyes. "You say you love me, and yet you would stop me having that which I want?"

"It is *because* I love you. This." Ovelia gestured with her shaking hand to encompass the cracked wall. "This will destroy you. I know this."

"You underestimate me at your peril," Semana said. "I can absorb this power. I can wield it. I can become the goddess of this world and every other. Please." She stepped toward Ovelia. "Let me try."

"I know you can succeed." Ovelia shook her head sadly. "That is why I must stop you."

She drew back Draca to strike the barrier once more, but abruptly Semana threw her arms around Ovelia, making the blind woman stiffen. Tears stinging at her eyes, Semana buried her face in Ovelia's chest. Her mother was so cold—so tired—and yet, when Ovelia raised her arms tentatively and wrapped them around Semana, there was warmth there. Semana did not recognize the feeling of welcome and comfort. To her knowledge, she had never experienced something quite like it before.

"I accept you, Mother," Semana said. "I name you Mother."

Steel clattered to the stone as Draca fell from Ovelia's nerveless fingers, and she embraced Semana tightly. Their bodies melted into one another, so warm and powerful that Semana wondered if she even existed as a separate person. She was once again a child, staring up from the puddle into which she had just fallen, blood oozing from her skinned knee and her hands covered in mud. But instead of a supercilious, distant mother who hardly seemed to acknowledge her pain, much less care, there stood above her a warm presence that opened her arms wide. She welcomed Semana into her embrace, and against her breast, all of her pains and worries seemed to fade away.

Semana saw without seeing, and she knew that Ovelia could see it too.

They saw a life together—a life they had never lived and could not live. A life where Ovelia had been Semana's mother not just in blood but also in name. She stood at Orbrin's side, and Semana had a father who loved her—who took time from holding court to hear her childish grievances and heartsick utterances, who snuck her sweets when no one was looking. Even her sister, Lenalin Denerre, old enough to be her mother, always had a radiant smile for her. There was no jealousy between them—no rivalry. Together, their Blood became something rarely seen in the World of Ruin—something redemptive that could stay the tide of crumbling death and inevitable doom.

A family.

Tears fell from Ovelia's face onto Semana's forehead and slid down to her cheeks.

"I am so, so sorry." Ovelia whispered the words in Semana's ear.

"I…" Semana's voice choked. "So am I."

Then Ovelia's body stiffened. She tried to grasp at Semana, but her fingers were not her own any longer. Neither was her mouth when she tried to speak, and she managed only a guttural moan.

"So am I." Semana held up her hands, fingers curled into claws. Ovelia's blood hammered in her throat and she could taste it on her tongue. She was sick—dying from Frostburn's poisonous magic—and the sensation was bitter gall. Semana swallowed it anyway.

Without Draca's power to protect Ovelia, there remained nothing in Semana's path.

With a flick of her wrist and a twist of her fingers, Semana pried Ovelia away. The woman fought her control, but she was old and weary. She had nothing left, and the Blood magic was everything. Power and strength surging in her veins, Semana dropped Ovelia to her knees in the chamber like a doll she'd grown tired of and put her hands on the mage-glass wall. The power resonant within the core of the mountain sang to her, and the flames coalesced around her fingers on the other side of the glass.

"Do not," Ovelia said. "Do not do this…"

Semana could barely hear her. She saw it again, the column of windows into other worlds. A whole limitless swath of realities bounded only by the power of her imagination. An infinite progression of sights and feelings and experiences to savor. And to conquer.

The power surged in response, fire flowing into multiple streams into her hands through the glass. In moments, these streams joined together into two great rivers of silver fire. It swept through her body like a rising tide of molten stone, burning and cleansing her from within. Light streamed from her eyes and her mouth.

She understood that if she did this—if she claimed this power—she would drink this world dry. Without the Narfire to sustain it, the World of Ruin would cease to be, and all upon it would perish.

But she did not care. How could she? The power was too intense, the taste too delicious.

Some part of her rallied against this—screamed at her that she should turn back—but it was too late. She had come too far and sacrificed too much. What was there left for her in this world? Nothing.

She hated this world and everyone in it. She hated Tithian Davargorn, who had refused to follow her. She hated Regel the Frostburn, her false father who had tried to steer her. She hated Lenalin Denerre, her false mother who had never loved her. She hated Ovelia, her blood mother who had abandoned her. She hated herself. She...

She lost touch with the world around her. The Blood pulsing in her head and in her veins was abruptly silent. Her body shook under the onslaught of the power. She felt as much as saw herself rising from the stone, born aloft like an angel. Like a goddess.

Then the ecstasy turned to pain. White-hot searing pain that stabbed outward from every tiny stretch of her flesh. Her heart hammered desperately in her chest, crushed under an impossible weight. Her bones stretched and came apart, grinding against one another as though sharpened. She tried to pull her hands away in shock, but she could not. Her flesh was seared to the mage-glass as the voracious, destructive power of the Nar burned through her.

Only then she realized that as much as she hungered for the power, so too did it hunger for her.

"Help... me..." she said between teeth chattering so hard they would break.

She saw the windows to the other worlds exploding inward, shattering and lost.

What had she done?

It was too much. Suddenly, she was just one young woman, and this was a world's worth of magic. It had powered the World of Wonder until its downfall, and now it kept the World of Ruin limping along. How could she contain such force? No—it would overwhelm her. It would consume her, then burst forth to shatter the world. It would end another age, and the world would not recover this time. She would fail, and the world would still be destroyed.

Unless.

Then a shadow moved at her side, and Semana perceived with burning eyes that it was Ovelia. The woman stood; battered, exhausted, blood drooling from her mouth and nose and her blinded eyes, her skin almost entirely turned to ice, and yet she stood. Her skin was cracked and blistered, her hair singed, and the sinews stood out ready to pop in her neck. One of her eyes had turned to bluish glass and the other was unraveling. She gave Semana a wan smile as best her chapped face could deliver, and hefted Draca with obvious effort.

~

Ovelia had all the answers but could give voice to none of them. *Because you will die. Because you will kill our world. Because you will destroy all the worlds that only you and I have seen.*

Because this is not who you are.

Not that she could speak through the blood magic.

Somehow, she had regained her feet. She had taken hold of Draca, too late for its power to shield her, and used it to lever herself up. Power surged into Semana, who stood watching her. Ovelia could see her as clearly as if she had never lost her vision. She looked so frightened. So alone.

Slowly, though it took all her strength, Ovelia reached toward Semana's face. She raised her arm against crushing force, pouring all of herself into that one, small gesture. Semana could have brushed her aside or smashed her with her magic, but instead all she did was stand, trembling and waiting.

Shadows emerged from Draca, speaking of what was to come, but Ovelia could not look down to search them. Nor did she need to. They both knew what would come to pass.

Ovelia touched Semana's cheek, her fingers tracing the contours of pain and sorrow and anger there, and in that instant, Semana was soothed. She made a little sound—like a choked gasp—and her eyes lost their burning crimson rage, softening once more to their own beautiful amber-hazel. The same color as Ovelia's own. They stood and gazed upon one another, honestly and openly for the first and final time—parent and child, mother and daughter.

"I love you," Ovelia said.

Something shattered. The blood magic fled from Ovelia and the Frostfire flared from Semana to surround them both. Her connection to the Narfire lessened—not severed, but weakened.

"Mother," Semana said, hardly able to breathe.

Ovelia knew what she had to do.

Semana closed her eyes, trembling.

With the last gasp of her breath, Ovelia brought Draca around once more and smashed the cracked mage-glass barrier. The glass shuddered, then burst toward them in a torrent of flame and cutting shards. Semana screamed and reached for her—perhaps to pull her away or else to strike her—but Ovelia stepped forward and shoved Semana aside. Her body took the brunt of the wave of the Narfire, and for an instant, it seemed she might withstand it.

Then she pressed Draca into Semana's hands, and its protection surrounded her instead.

The heat was sudden and overwhelming. Even as Ovelia's clothes burned away and her skin reeked of roasting meat, she looked to Semana, with her burned eyes that could not see but yet knew more than could be seen, and bowed her head.

"I love you," she whispered again.

Then the fire exploded forth in its full force, and Ovelia was gone.

THIRTY-SEVEN

S ILVER FIRE BURST IN gouts from the fringes of the mountain of Tar Vangr, and tremors swept through the city only awkwardly attached to its side.

"There," Lenalin said, her voice raised over the whirring. "Put us down. Hurry!"

The Luetharr mage operating the ornithopter followed her directive and brought the craft down on the platform outside the entrance to the shrine at the mountain's core. The fluttering prayer flags caught Regel's eye, curling and crisping in the intense heat pouring forth. The wind was intense, and the ornithoper nearly crashed more than once, but the pilot managed to land safely. The rings had just barely stopped rotating when Lenalin threw one leg over the side, fumbling to climb out. Regel reached over to help, but she slapped his hands away. The look on her face was one of terror and anger.

She hit the snowy ground in a flounder, sending up steam and skirls of snow around her feet as she hurried in her shuffling run toward the entrance.

"Lena—" he said, and reached out for her.

A great rumble swept through the air and the summit of the mountain cracked open, splintering the palace, and a great column of Narfire rose up into the sky. Power poured forth from every pore in the mountain, including from the shrine entrance before them. Lenalin pulled up short, startled, but Regel was still moving. He lunged forward and caught her, wrenching her away from the rushing flames. He shielded her with his body, hoping the wet weathercloak might absorb some of the blast.

The intense heat washed over them both, and Regel's body quaked from power within and without. His healing gift suddenly flared like an exploding star, and his awareness blossomed all around him. He knew every tiny thumb's breadth of his body as if he were staring at it: he felt every trickle of sweat, the tiny pressures of blood beating in his veins, the dazzling light refracting in his eyes. He counted the roots of his hair and felt the raised swelling of old scars and fresh wounds. He could say precisely how much blood coursed through each of his extremities, and he knew precisely how much longer his heart could continue to beat. He knew himself with a focus and detail he could not have credited, and his mind broke at the influx of knowledge.

It was only through focusing outside himself that he maintained some semblance of sanity, and when he did that, he became perfectly aware of the life all around him. The Narfire itself was life, pure and burning and scouring, and it fed the tiny vines that clung to the mountainside and the snow-blooming flowers that sheltered in its rocky shallows. He felt the crew of the Luetharr ornithopter, all of them knocked from their feet by the intense wave of magic. He knew which of them were men, which women, and which neither though their world forced them to pretend otherwise. He felt the blood in their veins and the tasted the wind in their lungs and smelled the bile rising in their throats. He knew their hopes and their pains and their fears. He knew them all with a fearsome intensity, though he had never met any of them before, and had not even bothered to count them.

And he felt Lenalin.

Oh, how he felt her. He knew suddenly everything about her, just as he had known his own body a breath ago. He felt every pulse of her heart, tasted the adrenaline-tinged blood roaring through her arteries, and breathed with her quick, shallow breaths. He felt every inch of her skin as though he were touching her with his fingertips—as though he had an entire afternoon to caress and explore her body, all in the space of a single moment. And when he found hurts, he eased them. He poured his life into her and purified her and for that moment, he *was* her.

Their bodies were one flesh, in a communion neither had invited nor wished.

And when that moment ended—when the wave of magic passed, and he was left trembling and gasping for breath that seemed impossible to catch—what he felt was an overriding sadness. There was shame in what he had done—what he had felt—but more than that, he understood her pain. He knew the years of loneliness and loss and understood, as he never had before, what had befallen her. And he knew that he would never leave her side. Not until and unless she bid him go.

"Lenalin." He caught up the edge of her mask and drew it over her face. "Lena, are you—?"

He stopped, startled. Awed.

She blinked up at him. "Frostburn," she said. "What?"

Movement at the opening to the shrine caught their attention, and both looked up to see a slender, wan form approaching out of the darkness. She was nearly naked, dressed only in tatters of cloth and covered head to toe in a thick, chalky patina of ash. Her eyes opened, gleaming ruddy amber in the dim light, and she stared out at them seemingly without seeing. There was something in her hands: a wavy length of steel similarly covered in grime but issuing tiny plumes of smoke.

"Lia?" Lenalin shoved Regel off her and stumbled forward, only to come to an abrupt halt. "No."

Semana turned her focus upon Lenalin and Regel, as though she had not seen them before. In fact, she looked as though this was the first time in her life she had ever seen anyone or anything. Moisture filled her eyes and she shook her head almost imperceptibly.

"Your face," she said, her words wondering. "Mother, your—"

That word. It was that one word—mother—that snapped Lenalin out of her hesitation. She flew at Semana with a fury, snarling like a beast as she charged forward. The queen of Tar Vangr strode toward the fallen Blood Queen with a murderous stride, and Semana took a hesitant step back. Had Regel not restrained her, surely she would have throttled the young woman.

"What did you do?" Lenalin's demanding words seemed to strike Semana like the blow of a hammer. "What did you *do?*"

Semana raised the blade, and ash fell away to reveal the gleaming crimson-tinged steel of Draca. At the sight, Lenalin abruptly stopped once more, and fell to her knees like a puppet whose strings had abruptly been cut. Her hands clasped Regel's arm tightly.

"You killed her," Lenalin said, clasping her hands in front of her heart. "You *killed* her."

"I—" Words failed her, and Semana looked down at the ground. "She saved me." She slipped to her knees on the stone. "She saved all of us."

The tears brimming in her eyes fell down her cheeks, tracing paths of clean skin. It was the first time Regel had ever seen her ashamed.

They remained like that, the last heirs of the Blood of Winter, both weeping: Semana letting the tears fall as she knelt alone, Lenalin sobbing into Regel's shoulder.

Regel did not know what to do. With a blade, he was unstoppable—a phantom slayer who could destroy any foe. But with the heart, what was he? A mere novice who had never survived a duel, much less vanquished an opponent.

He made a series of choices then, and only the years to follow would judge any of them wise.

~

It seemed impossible.

They had won the day, but at such a cost. Lenalin had lost the one thing—the one person—she could not bear to lose. How could this come to pass?

She had chosen wrongly. When Ovelia had begged her to return to Tar Vangr, she had foolishly relented. And then, after the disastrous initial assault, she had let her lover persuade her to stay. To keep fighting. To reveal herself, after so many years hiding her face and heritage. To care about this corpse mound of a city that had given her nothing but heartache.

Regel was speaking as though across a great distance. Lenalin couldn't make out the words.

And now Ovelia was dead, sacrificed for the daughter she never should have had, who had never loved her or her supposed Blood or anyone. A selfish, ungrateful wretch who deserved death.

Slowly, careful not to startle Regel or give herself away, Lenalin forced a smile on her face and nodded along to whatever nonsense spilled from his lips, all the while unbuckling the hand caster at her belt. He didn't seem aware of her intentions, not until she had aligned the caster with Semana's chest. And then it was too late.

A *crack* split the air, and Semana fell over backwards as though struck by a blow of lightning. Abruptly, Regel hurried to Semana's side, leaving Lenalin where she knelt.

No, not Lenalin. She'd been a fool to claim that name again.

She was Lady Shard.

Shard tottered shakily to her feet and walked toward Regel and Semana. The younger woman lay on her back, her soft brown face turning paler as Shard watched. Regel knelt at her side, his hands on her, and white magic fell from his hands into her body to heal the wound. Blood pooled around Semana's compact body—which looked so small and frail—and her face looked surprisingly peaceful.

Shard wanted to blow her face apart to end that peace. She wound her hand caster for a second lightning-empowered quarrel.

It was then that she caught sight of the gleaming steel of Draca, on the blasted rock near Semana's hand. The sword ignited and blazed with all the power she had ever seen it put out: a miniature star that should have burned a hole through Semana with its heat but did not. The steel reflected her face like a mirror, but it should not have been able to show her as much detail as it did. She must have seen something in the sword's flames, the way Ovelia always had.

She saw Lenalin Denerre: delicate cheeks, deep blue eyes, full, heart-shaped lips, pale silver-blonde hair, skin like porcelain, entirely unbroken. Beautiful. Perfect.

At first, she thought it only a vision, but when she reached up to touch her face, she felt the truth. This was her face—restored to what it once was—and her body with it.

Lady Shard was dead.

"I tried to tell you," Regel said. "The wave of fire—Ovelia's last blessing. It—" He touched her smooth cheek. "It must have healed you."

A scream surrounded them, like an ongoing peal of thunder. Regel shuddered and looked as though she'd struck him. Lenalin realized only at length that she was the one screaming.

She scrambled to her feet and fled, scratching at her face.

~

When Semana came back to herself, it was to the feeling of soft hands cupping her cheeks in the gloom. At first, she thought surely Ovelia knelt beside her. Surely her mother—her true mother—had drawn her from the darkness, and for a fleeting moment, Semana thought they would be happy henceforth, and all this pain would remain forever in their shadow.

Then she saw the cold eyes of Regel the Frostburn and she remembered the truth.

"You are not my father," she said.

"No." Regel narrowed his eyes. He rose from where he had healed her. "Leave this place and never return," he said. "There is nothing left for you here."

And with that, he rose and walked away. He took Draca as well, leaving her cold and alone.

Semana wanted to call out for him. To scream after him. To beg him to return. But she did none of these things.

Because when he had told her there was nothing left for her, he was wrong.

"Yes," she said. "Yes there is."

It would take the Narfire time to replenish itself. Years, perhaps, or even decades. The World of Ruin would endure, and in time it would recover. And when it did, she would be there.

She would succeed.

It was her destiny, and the destiny of this broken world.

~

EPILOGUE

THE TINY BABE GIGGLED at the long brown fingers caressing his forehead, then his chin, then his chest. The hand, skin stretched taut over its veins and sinews, hesitated, then drummed two fingers over the child's heart. The child pawed at the fingers and gave a warm smile.

"This is it, then," Alistra Ravalis said. "My little cousin. Last heir of our tainted Blood. Hmm."

"My lady?" asked one of her warders, but Alistra waved her to silence.

As she stood looking down at him in the temple of the winter god—as one of the last buildings that still stood in Low-City Tar Vangr, it served as her ironic temporary base of operations—Alistra had one simple thought over and over: that he seemed an unlikely hero.

He seemed so small and fragile, this tiny spawn of heroes. Ovelia Dracaris, The Thrice-Dead Dragon, and her sword that drank magic and told the future. She, who had broken one Blood and brought it back to life. Garin Ravalis, the Fox of Luether, who had brought down two empires—both the guise of Luether and the truth beneath it. He who had birthed a death machine of perfect destruction into this world that had enough of that, but which had saved one Mage-City and destroyed another.

What would their son become?

"Will you take the child?"

Alistra wasn't surprised to hear that cold voice. Of course he had come upon her before either of them left Tar Vangr. It would likely be the closest he would come to her for years, or perhaps as long as their lives would last. Alistra wondered if one of them would end before they left this chamber.

"This is her son, you know," Alistra said. "Ovelia's son."

"Her child," the man said.

"Yes." Alistra realized he had meant to correct her. "Of course. You are a child of winter, I suppose. This child will be what it will be."

She turned slowly to Tithian Davargorn, who stood across from her in the worship chamber. He looked terrible: his clothes a shredded mess, his cloak gone, his skin a mass of bruises and scars. The look on his face was one she did not know, and she felt it like cold water coating her skin. The feeling was not entirely unpleasant and she shivered with something like delight.

"My warders?" she asked, seeing no one beside him. "Do they live?"

385

He shrugged. She saw then that he bore a sword like a wavy icicle, held low diagonally alongside his knee. Steam rose from the icy sword, but she saw no blood on the blade. Reassuring.

"And now you have the Frostburn's sword," she said. "Do you take his name as well?"

"No." The word was cold but not bitter. "I will transcend him."

"By claiming my Blood first?" Alistra asked. "A fine start to a promising career—"

He moved then, faster than she could have expected, and held the sword at her throat. His rush pressed her back, up against the altar upon which she'd laid the babe. His body pressed hard against hers. The stone was hard against her lower back and her fingers scrabbled at the stone. She had to hold her chin up, looking into his face.

"I'd not hate you, Tithian," she said.

The blade was so cold at her unprotected throat that her neck and face lit with tingling, numbed pain just from the proximity. If he cut her now, would she even feel it?

But a moment passed, their mingled breath steamed the air, and he had not killed her.

"What do you want?" she asked. "You are free now. No one will stop you."

She felt the blade's intense cold, but her magic-dead flesh protected her from its power. Anyone else likely would have died from such proximity, but to her, Frostburn was but a sword. What interested her more was Tithian Davargorn.

He felt so cold against her, but she could tell there was heat there. Desire. She could not deny that it burned in her as well. When she had met Tithian Davargorn, he'd been a foolish lad, easily manipulated and used to her whim. But now—now he was a *man*. And it was not the violence or the rage or the power that told her this. It was the *will*. It was the drive within him, which had only now awakened. She shivered again, and not just from the cold.

"Go," he said at length, so quietly she thought she had not heard.

"What?" she asked. "But surely you want—"

"Leave this city." He turned Frostburn, caressing her jaw with its icy length. "Go now."

She had wielded him wrong, and now she would not have what she wanted. Yet.

Keeping her eyes locked to his, she followed the angle of the sword, slipping away along its length. She slid away and around until he stood between her and the altar, with her tiny cousin left abandoned upon it. She and Davargorn both looked to the child. Then Alistra gave him a winsome smile, turned, and was gone.

She had plans to put in motion.

~

He stood over the child, Frostburn *tap-tap-tapping* at the stone.

Ovelia's child, and Garin's too. The heir to Tar Vangr and Luether both. The joining of blood from three great lines: Denerre, Ravalis, and Dracaris.

Davargorn and this child were locked together, he realized. The mother had humiliated him time and again, and he had finally had his revenge. He had killed the child's father. Why not be a bloodbreaker for true, and end it all, here and now? He held the fate of the world beneath his blade.

Instead, he slipped free Frostburn from its sheath, reveling in the cold fury that filled him. With this sword, he would carve out his own legend. His own blood myth.

He climbed out the window into the snow, which had become driving rain.

THE NAMED AND MARKED OF RUIN

Ravalis, the Blood of Summer ("Summer Lasts a Day")
Outlander Rulers of Tar Vangr, City of Winter

Cassian Ravalis (892—961): Last King of Luether (City of Summer), elder brother to Demetrus, father to Garin, perished in fall of Luether.

Demetrus Ravalis (894—981): Former King of Tar Vangr, younger brother to Cassian, father to Strevon, Paeter, Alistra, Lan and others. Slain Ruin's Night before 982 in Tar Vangr.

Ansa Ravalis nô Dorane (889—938): Wife to Demetrus Ravalis, perished birthing daughter Alistra.

Anthien Ravalis nô Vultara (916—961): Mistress and eventually second wife to Demetrus Ravalis, perished in the fall of Luether.

Toblius Ravalis (910—present): Younger half-brother to Cassian and Demetrus, husband to Alcha Varas.

Strevon Ravalis (930—961): The Hawk of Luether, first son of Demetrus, perished in the fall of Luether.

Paeter Ravalis (933—976): The Jackal of Luether, second son of Demetrus, husband to Lenalin Denerre, father to Darak and Semana, slain under mysterious circumstances.

Nameless (935—937): Third son of Demetrus, perished nameless.

Alistra (938—present): The Spider of Luether, only daughter of Demetrus, imprisoned in the tunnels for unknown crimes. Now queen of Luether.

Dorian Ravalis (940—961): The Wolf of Luether, son to Demetrus, perished in the fall of Luether.

Garin Ravalis (943—982): The Fox of Luether, former crown-prince of Luether, only son of Cassian. Slain in the liberation of Luether.

Alcarin Summer (954—present): Smallborn squire to Garin.

King Lan Ravalis (944—present): King of Tar Vangr, the Eunuch King, the Bear of Luether, son of Demetrus, husband to Laegra.

Laegra Ravalis nô Vargaen (940—present): Daughter of house Vargaen, neglected wife to Lan.

Alcha Ravalis nô Varas (930—present): Wife to Toblius, wed after Fall of Luether.

Boulis Ravalis (948—present): The Hound of Luether, son of Toblius.

Tolus Ravalis (951—present): The Falcon of Luether, son of Toblius.

Vhaerynn the Necromancer (unknown—present?): Blood sorcerer and vizier to Demetrus.

Denerre, the Blood of Winter ("Justice in the Storm")
Former Rulers of Tar Vangr, all but extinct

Aritana Denerre (885—932): Former ruler of Tar Vangr (910-932), youngest ruler of Tar Vangr in centuries, mother to Mortiun and Orbrin.

Moritun Denerre (911—936): Former ruler of Tar Vangr (932-936), elder brother to Orbrin, perished suddenly and unexpectedly in battle.

Orbrin Denerre (916—976): The Winter King, former ruler of Tar Vangr (r. 936-976), father to Althar and Lenalin and a third nameless child, perished at the hands of Ovelia the Bloodbreaker.

Matir Thorass (914—961): Wife to Moritun, political bond to Orbrin, mother to Althar and Lenalin and a third nameless child, perished in the fall of Luether.

Althar Denerre (937—955): Former Crown Prince of Denerre, perished in a duel.

Nameless (938—942): Second son of Denerre, perished in the cradle without a name.

Lenalin Denerre (940—966): Wife to Lan Ravalis, perished under mysterious circumstances.

Darak Ravalis nô Denerre (961—971): Son to Lan Ravalis and Lenalin Denerre, exiled to Ruin for treason at a young age, presumed dead.

Semana Denerre nô Ravalis (963—present): Last Heir of Winter, daughter to Paeter and Lenalin, master to Tithian. Faked death in 976 and took up the mantle of Mask.

Tithian Davargorn (963—present): Smallborn winterborn pageboy, then squire to Semana. Faked death in 976 and became loyal servant of Semana.

Dracaris, the Blood of the Dragon ("Eternal, Unyielding"):
Treacherous Sworn Shields to Denerre

Norlest Dracaris (917—961): Sworn Shield to Orbrin, father to Ovelia, perished in the fall of Luether.

Aniset Winter (922—942): Smallborn mother to Ovelia, perished in childbirth.

Ovelia Dracaris the Bloodbreaker (942—present): Sworn Shield to Lenalin, slew the Winter King in 976, mortally injured in the assault on the Summer King Demetrus in 981.

The Circle of Tears ("Ever Weep, Ever Watch"):
A consortium of Spies in Tar Vangr

———

Regel Winter the Oathbreaker (936—present): The Lord of Tears, formerly the Frostburn, Shadow of the Winter King, sworn slayer in service to Orbrin Denerre, lord of the Circle of Tears.

———

Serris (960—981): Smallborn squire to Regel, First of Tears. Slain Ruin's Night 981.

Erim (961—present): Smallborn thief, occasional lover to Serris, bastard son of a Dolvrath noble.

Vidia (946—present): Smallborn baker.

Nacacia (957—present): Smallborn warrior.

Daren (955—present): Smallborn warrior.

Krystir (955—present): Smallborn spy.

Meron (940—981): Soldier, bastard son of a Vortusk noble, slain by Ravalis soldiers.

Sarelle (979—present): Child of Serris.

Folk of Gardh

———

Phend (960—present): Protector of Gardh, a hunter.

Jeht (942—979): Former Protector of Gardh, deceased.

Tsarn (938—present): Smallborn merchant of Gardh.

Nys (936—present): Smallborn warrior of Gardh.

Hiesk (937—present): Smallborn warrior of Gardh.

Circle of High Druids

———

Erethar, the Unmoving (unknown—present): Grand druid, female.

Mayel, the Even-Handed (930—present): High druid, female.

Carr, the Axe (943—present): High druid, female.

Naor, the Raging Flame (945—present): High druid, female.

Afferath, Mistress of the Rain (950—present): High druid, female.

Fellis, the Night Wolf (948—present): High druid, female.

Saegel, the Rotting Leaves (927—present): High druid, female.

Children of Ruin

———

Dar-Karsk (961—present): Rotpriest, former squire to Afferath, male.

Kalik (950—present): Servant to Dar-Karsk, female.

Bellows in the Deep (955—present): Warrior sworn to Dar-Karsk, male.

Rending Gash (963—present): Warrior sworn to Dar-Karsk, female.

Crown of Fire (960—present): Warrior sworn to Dar-Karsk, male.

Fierce Wind (957—present): Warrior sworn to Dar-Karsk, female.

Mountain's Rage (952—present): Bodyguard to Afferath, male.

"Right" and "Left" (956—present): Bodyguards to Afferath, male brothers.

Breaker of Frost and Ice (953—present): Bodyguard to Afferath, female.

Deathless Fae

Rose (-540—-500 SA): Queen of Necthana, female after death.

Gilt (912—952): Warder, male.

Blood (952—980): Sentry of Necthana, fae.

Dawn (954—980): Sentry of Necthana, male after death.

Silver (914—946): Sentry of Necthana, fae.

Dew (897—930): Sentry of Necthana, fae.

Summit (287—340): Explorer, male after death.

Others

Shard (940—present): Skyship pirate lord, captain of the *Reaver*, self-proclaimed Emperor of the Dusk Sea. Recently revealed to be Lenalin Denerre, former princess of Tar Vangr.

Aeldad (unknown—present): Free Islander skyship pirate, first mate of Shard.

Hyldir (940—present?): Winterborn captain of the *Avenger*.

Tanak (944—present): Skyship pirate captain, in service of Lady Shard.

Chikar (950—present): Skyship pirate lieutenant to Tanak.

www.ingramcontent.com/pod-product-compliance
Lightning Source LLC
Chambersburg PA
CBHW020933020726
47495CB00002B/470